THE SORCERER'S GUIDE

TO THE

PATH OF THE PHOENIX

L. SCOTT CLARK

THE SORCERER'S GUIDE: PATH OF THE PHOENIX
Copyright © 2021 L. Scott Clark

All rights reserved

No part of this book may be reproduced or used in any manner without the written permission of the copyright owner except for the use of quotations in a book review.

This is a work of fiction. Unless otherwise stated – all names, characters, businesses, places, events, locales, and incidents in this book are the product of either the author's imagination or are used in a fictitious manner. Any resemblance to actual persons, living or dead, or actual events is purely coincidental.

ISBN: 978-1-7361598-0-4 (Paperback)
ISBN: 978-1-7361598-1-1 (Hardcover)
ISBN: 978-1-7361598-2-8 (EBook)
ISBN: 978-1-7361598-3-5 (Audiobook)
Library of Congress Control Number: 2021900218

First Edition 2021

Credits:
Book Cover and Formatting by Miblart — www.miblart.com
Editing by – Stardust Book Services, Precision Editing, and Faith Lane.

Obsidian Wolf Publishing

www.obsidianwolfpub.com

PO Box 1086

Salem, UT 84653

PART I

THE DISCOVERY

CHAPTER I

"Breathe in. Breathe out. Die."

This simple mantra burst inside Jet Black's mind like a living entity crawling about, searching for something hidden—a memory. The words were spoken with such clarity and persuasion, by one believing they had dominion, that Jet nearly obeyed.

Squeezing his eyes shut, Jet attempted to stop the assault, but the pain was unbearable, and he was stunned at the power unleashed on his consciousness. He could do nothing but slow the speed of the attack as he dangled precariously two hundred feet above a canyon floor. The malicious words echoed around the crevices of his thoughts as if searching for a hidden vault.

After what seemed like hours but was mere seconds, Jet realized the words held a deeper meaning. He felt elation by the one besieging him as the mantra closed in on its mark. A moment of déjà vu struck as the hidden memory was discovered, opened, and Jet recollected hearing the same mantra four years ago, the day his home was destroyed.

"I need more," the voice inside his head demanded.

The search became frenzied and, ultimately, a second memory was cornered. Pointed claws snatched the hidden thought, but somehow it had been safeguarded. It withstood the barrage for only a split second, then cracks appeared, and the flashback spilled out.

Jet saw himself standing at the base of his stairs, in his childhood home, on the day that everything had changed. Standing there, he'd taken his final breath, believing that he would die. It was an intimate moment, and somehow it had been erased, along with so much more. For the first time since that day, he remembered precisely what had happened. The entity attacking him was also privy to this memory.

"Yes … yes," it exclaimed.

Together they watched the house around him and Nana crumbling. The front door exploded, and shards of wood darted at Jet's chest. He couldn't survive, but then miraculously, he did.

"Wait, what?"

The entity infiltrating him did not anticipate what it was seeing, and it didn't take long for Jet to understand why. Something or someone had created a barrier in his mind, hiding all these memories and preventing him from knowing how three talents had allowed him to survive the destruction of Silverton. Jet had lived the last few years blissfully unaware of how close he'd come to his death and, more importantly, what it had taken to survive. These three abilities had let him escape as lava tore through his home.

"You're an enemy to my master," it declared.

The entity became furious at what it had opened—and released. More than that, it was a little fearful. Jet knew it would strike, and he braced for a deeper pain. But it never came. Something that could only be described as a fail-safe protected Jet and expelled the entity from his mind.

Jet hung, practically upside-down, trying to catch his breath. His thoughts swam as the memories of the darkest moment in his life flooded back to where they should have been.

"Bro. What's wrong with you?" a male voice asked from far away. "Are you too scared to move?"

Jet barely registered the question. *Who had just attacked him and why?* It took another few seconds to realize that he was still hanging above a cliff, and it was his turn to rappel down. Opening his eyes, Jet blanched as he stared into the crevasse directly below him. He knew that dozens of his classmates were watching him from far below, probably laughing. His vision blurred and his body quivered. The only thing holding him up was his climbing ropes.

As he pulled himself into the correct position, the voice of Jayco, one of his closest friends, entered his mind from less than half an hour ago. "It'll be safe. Any idiot can do it."

Well, who's the idiot now? He reached out and patted the rock wall, ensuring that this wasn't a dream.

"Are you going to sit there all day?" inquired a second male voice, different than the first. "Seriously. I'm embarrassed for you. You've been in the same spot for a full fifteen minutes."

"He's got to be afraid of heights," the first boy taunted. "I bet Jet is filled with regret. He'll fall, and bawl, and land all sprawled." The boy screamed, "Watch out below! Jet Black is going to pee himself."

"Shut it," Jet yelled but cringed as the words 'pee himself' echoed around the canyon several times.

"Or explode from both ends," this time, a girl shouted, and the last two words echoed.

Jet anchored his feet and glared up to see Vinny Estes, Jocelyn Delgado, and Jake Hurley glowering at him with such malice and hatred that Jet couldn't fully explain.

Shaking his head, he demanded, "Why are you here?"

"To wish you the best of luck," Jake said pleasantly.

Like him, they were sophomores at Chadwick's, but Jet had never spoken a single word to them. They wore matching white shirts with an insignia on the front; plus red jeans and white loafers. They were members of the Light Riders, one of several groups on campus.

Vinny hissed, "You see, Black. Unlike you, we have a reason to be on this earth. Now, do all of us a favor and slip and fall."

"That's harsh," Jet said. "I'm sure the school counselor could help you with that temper of yours."

Vinny retorted, "I'll be in line right behind you as you blab your feelings about the death of your mom and dad."

Jet ignored this. There were only a handful of people who knew about his parents, and this was not the place to have this discussion. He loosened the grip of his right hand and pushed off. "Check you guys later!"

As he plunged, his stomach dislodged from his intestines and connected with the back of his throat. Bile rose quickly. He fell fifteen feet before he tightened his right hand, stopping his descent almost instantly. He swung sharply toward the rock wall and smashed his left knee and shoulder into the wall without warning.

Even this high up, he heard the laughter and catcalls from other students at the bottom of the cliff who had evidently seen his blunder.

Vinny bellowed from above. "Who's the loser now?"

Jet managed to regain his footing, settle his nerves, and leap off for the second time. A few minutes later, he'd covered almost half the distance to the ground. He wasn't going to get the prize for the fastest descent, but he was doing well enough.

His mind shifted to another cliff, to his right, twice the size of the one he was descending. He imagined that this was where Grantham and Jayco were undoubtedly showing off. Once they learned of his blunders, they would tease him for the entire semester.

Jet prepared to push off again. But before he could, a tearing sound from the rope above him rattled his nerves. The lines were being pulled apart by an invisible force. The ropes were stretching and thinning.

Can't be my weight.

Snap!

Half of the first rope frayed and broke free; an instant later, the second rope split, and Jet abruptly dropped a few inches. He was dangling in midair, holding on by threads, and unable to reach the rock cliff. His eyes widened as the fibers began splitting one by one as if an unseen giant plucked the strings. Still a hundred feet in the air, he was about to make the biggest splash of his life.

He opened his mouth to scream, but in a flash, his life changed once again. Starting in his neck, a jolt of electricity exploded into his head. His vision changed, and time slowed around him. He could move normally while everything else was at a snail's pace. His eyesight expanded peripherally to include both sides and most of what was directly behind him. Without turning his head, he could see the landscape and dozens of students on the ground staring up at him. Lastly, his vision magnified like a microscope, and he could see the makeup lines on Mckenzey's beautiful face as she stood next to Latisha and Professor Dickerson, staring up at him. They were two of his closest friends. Neither of them had yet recognized the impending doom racing toward Jet.

His eyes focused on the rope. Using his arms and weight, he swung back and forth, inch by inch. Once his feet touched the rock, he crouched and exploded upward, just as both ropes broke completely. Reaching out, he seized the two bottom ends in his left hand and miraculously caught the upper ends with his right. His momentum carried him away from the rocks, but soon he swung back closer. He began wrapping the upper ends around his wrist and when he felt more secure, he shifted both feet, trying to roll in midair, and swing upside-down. He rapidly twisted his left leg around both upper ropes to anchor himself. A crooked smile spread across his face. What he had just done was impossible for the old Jet Black.

His smile vanished as he recognized Shane Fallon standing, not ten feet away from Mckenzey and Latisha, a hundred feet below. Shane was by far the last person Jet ever wanted to see. Equally distressing was that standing next to Shane was Ariana Flores, Jet's ex-girlfriend, and her brother Raul, Jet's ex-roommate. Jet didn't think either of them could stand Shane last year. In the last few months, so much changed for all of them. Shane's arms were pointing up at Jet as if he could see what was happening and was laughing hysterically.

"Not good," Jet hissed, and he felt his muscles tighten. He separated two of the four lines, one from above and one from below. Working upside down was challenging. The two ropes he didn't need, he pinched between his knees. Taking the bottom rope, the one with some give, he snaked it around the upper cord three times. He pulled the line through, wrapped it another three times, and created a loop. Twice, he took the frayed lower end and pulled it through the center of the loop. Pulling tightly, he made a makeshift knot. He repeated the steps with the second rope. When he finished, both lines seemed strong enough to hold his weight. He unlatched his foot and slowly returned to the conventional position.

By this time, he was breathing so hard that he started to see spots in his vision. He closed his eyes and felt his abilities fade away. Screams and shouts rang out around him, and he opened his eyes. Unsteadily, Jet pushed himself from the wall and descended fifteen feet.

Mckenzey hollered, "Are you all right? Did something just happen? You were a little blurry for a sec."

"Never better," he yelled back. "I'm starting to love this." Jet felt tense, but he couldn't tear his eyes away from the two knots he had created, willing them to hold for another few minutes.

Professor Dickerson, the Athletic Director, shouted up, "Keep moving. You're doing great."

Jet felt a small warm trickle of relief, having avoided two catastrophes, but the truth was hard to swallow.

The next few minutes were full of tension and relief. He would move down a few feet and rest only for seconds. Latisha's and Mckenzey's cheers became louder and louder. Fifteen feet from the ground, another round of tearing cut through the air. This time, Jet had no time to react. Both ropes split apart, and he fell uncontrollably toward the ground. His body rotated twice before he landed hard on his left shoulder. He felt a pop and a stabbing pain so intense that his vision pulsed and dimmed.

Footsteps approached. Hands reached out and rolled him over. Professor Dickerson stood over him. "Are you all right?"

Mckenzey Ebron and Latisha Rivera came into view. Mckenzey kneeled, took his hand, and gave a tight squeeze. Her brown hair brushed against his face. Her soft, tanned-white skin was flushed with concern. "Jet, can you hear me?" Her golden-brown eyes appeared brighter than usual as she inched closer.

Jet muttered, "Who's stabbing my shoulder?"

Professor Dickerson announced, "He needs to go to the hospital."

Other students squeezed in closer.

Mckenzey asked, "What happened?"

"Rope broke," Jet hissed.

"Completely unlikely," Professor Dickerson huffed. "This rope is of professional quality. You must have slipped or something."

Latisha said, "Uh…professor, how do you explain this?" She held two pieces of rope that were frayed and broken.

"Move aside," demanded a female voice, and Principal Jan Fletcher stooped over Jet. Two other administrators flanked her. Mckenzey was pushed aside, and she retreated next to Latisha. Principal Fletcher, bristling, said, "Tell me this isn't happening."

Jet stomped his foot as the pain suddenly flared as if someone was squeezing his shoulder with a medieval torture device.

"He's fine. He needs to go to the hospital." Searching the area, Professor Dickerson added, "We need something to transport him with."

Someone spoke, and Jet thought it was Mr. Smuin, an administrator. "There's a side by side nearby. I'll go get it."

"What happened?" Principal Fletcher asked.

Professor Dickerson said confidently, "He was coming down slowly. He ran into the wall a few times. He seemed to be a little scared and clumsy. About fifteen or twenty feet from the ground, the rope just broke."

Despite the pain, Jet felt his cheeks flush.

An ATV skidded to a stop somewhere outside Jet's view. Professor Dickerson and Mr. Smuin helped him to his feet and carried him to the ATV. He was buckled into the front seat.

"I should stay here and help the rest of the students," insisted Professor Dickerson.

"I'll take him," Mr. Smuin said.

"Can we go?" asked Mckenzey, pushing through to the front.

"No way. There's not enough room," Principal Fletcher snapped. "And students aren't allowed. Back to your dorms."

"But we're his friends," Latisha said quickly.

"We know who you are, Miss Rivera."

A slight pink glow spread across Mckenzey's tan cheeks. Latisha's dark skin didn't give away her embarrassment, but it was clear that both girls felt embarrassed. Mckenzey mouthed, "See you at the hospital," before they disappeared into the crowd.

Principal Fletcher added, "Take the school car. We'll meet you at Cottage Hospital."

"Of course." Mr. Smuin hit the accelerator, and Jet barely held onto the outer bar of the ATV as they shot toward campus.

At first, the ground was uneven, and Jet positioned his arm close to his body, which seemed to decrease the pain. However, each bump jolted his arm. It didn't take long to find the path. He rolled his eyes as he spotted Shane, Vinny, Jocelyn, and Jake standing on each side of the way ahead. Shane's hazel eyes sparkled in the daylight.

As Jet passed by, Shane shrieked, "All hail the loser, Jet Black, who can't even climb down a mountain."

Jet fumed and wondered if Shane or his friends could have found a way to sabotage the rope. He didn't have a clue how that was possible. It was more likely that Shane was using this moment to ridicule him.

Jet tried to focus on anything but the pain for the next several minutes. He pictured the insignias on the shirts of Vinny, Jocelyn, and Jake in his mind. It was an unbalanced triangle, sort of lopsided, next to an uneven star. The two objects didn't touch. They must be new members of the Light Riders. Circulating rumors hinted that this group was disbanded last year after two members were kicked out of school for cheating on a test.

Besides the Light Riders, there were a few more secret groups on campus. Each group had a leader and dressed the same, at least most of the time. Jet assumed that Vinny had been appointed bossman. But each leader, and ultimately each group, reported to one student. That person had sent Vinny and his crew to the top of Devil's Landing. None other than Shane Fallon.

Jet's mind snapped back to the first day of school last year. He had been buying schoolbooks and absorbed in meeting up with his closest friends. He hadn't seen them in years, since Silverton. A student approached and introduced himself as Shane Fallon.

This kid screamed popular. He had silky black hair, enchanting eyes, and bronze flawless skin and was handsome, tall, and athletic. They searched for their books together, and Jet thought he'd found a new friend. Several minutes later, Shane started asking personal questions. The change in his approach was subtle at first and revolved around Jet and his family. Out of nowhere, the inquires morphed into the destruction of his hometown, the earthquake that killed thousands of people, and how in the world Jet had survived. The glee and elation in Shane's eyes sent shivers down Jet's spine. Jet politely excused himself, and ever since that day,

Shane had done whatever possible to torment Jet, including sending Vinny and his crew to heckle him today.

They were still about three or four miles from campus, and the next several minutes were filled with agony. Jet stared at the landscape. Chadwick's, located in Santa Barbara, was one of the most prestigious and beautiful high schools on the western coast, and when it came into view, he was still in awe that he'd received a full-ride scholarship to this charming campus. The cobblestone paths, mature and majestic trees, and the ocean view were unreal, but then again, so was his pain. They hit a bump in the road, and Jet was forced to turn his head and vomit off to the side.

"We'll be there soon," Professor Smuin reassured him as they crested another hill.

Inhaling a deep breath full of ocean air, he felt that things might turn out all right. Then they took a sharp corner, and Jet slid in his seat, smacking his arm against the railing once again. The pain flourished, and he leaned over and puked.

Jet's capacity to focus vanished entirely. He thought he remembered being ushered out of the car and into a wheelchair. There were bright lights and voices all around him. He felt pinpricks in the opposite arm, but he couldn't focus well enough to understand what was happening. He tried to move away from the pain but had nowhere to hide. Soon, his eyes became drowsy, and all the pain floated away. It was simply the best feeling he'd had in months as he drifted into blissfulness.

* * *

A bright light burned through Jet's closed eyelids as voices murmured around him. He couldn't remember where he was or why.

A female voice hissed, "Doctor, he's awake."

Memories flooded back.

It took a few minutes for Jet's eyes to adjust to the light. They stubbornly refused to stay open longer than a few seconds.

A man in a white coat stepped into the room. "I'm Doctor Pritchard, a surgeon. Your shoulder had some damage. Do you remember what happened?"

"Unfortunately," Jet muttered, his mouth dry.

"When you landed on your shoulder, you suffered a shoulder dislocation. If that had been your only injury, surgery wouldn't have been required. But you also snapped your clavicle."

"My what?" Jet questioned.

"Your collarbone." The doctor pointed to the front of his own shoulder. "It's bad enough to require a metal plate."

"Great."

"The plate will help the collarbone heal and remain in place. You'll need to stay overnight, and if all goes well, you can return to campus tomorrow. How's your pain?"

Jet considered the question. "I don't feel any."

"That'll wear off in the next thirty minutes or so. Click the button for the nurses to get you another dose."

"Thank you," Jet mumbled.

Over the next hour, he slept. When he woke, he telephoned Nana, and they talked for a few minutes. Afterward, he focused on the flood of memories no longer hidden and tried to make sense of what he now knew. He couldn't understand how his memories had become concealed in the first place. How had he forgotten how he survived Silverton? Where had these three abilities come from and why had they disappeared, until today?

There was a knock at the door, and his friends piled into the room. First was Mckenzey, followed by Latisha, Grantham, and Jayco.

The smirk on Jayco Carter's boyish face told Jet that he would never live down what had happened today. His surfer look with soft complexion and light yellow-brown skin was intoxicating to some girls. When Jayco found his voice, the six-foot-four boy said, "How's it possible that you can't even make it down the bunny hill? You're klutzy. Remember that time, back in Silverton, when you stumbled into that ravine? Didn't you break your arm?"

Grantham Mitchell lifted two fingers. "Both arms." He was just over six feet tall and slender. He was a runner and had an athletic build. He had black skin but it wasn't as dark as Latisha. He and Jayco were best friends.

"What are the chances?" Jayco laughed. "The first campus activity, and you messed it up, big time."

"Do we have to torture him now?" Latisha asked, trying to hide her smile. Her high cheekbones and warm undertones were hidden by her hand.

"Tell us again how it looked to watch him fall." Jayco bounded to the edge of the bed, staring at Latisha expectantly.

Mckenzey shoved Jayco.

Somehow, Jet felt even worse. He wanted to slide under his covers until everyone had vanished.

"Did anyone get it on video?" pleaded Jayco.

Grantham added, "I'd pay money to see that."

Mckenzey shrieked, "Out!" She ushered Latisha, who was about her same height, and the boys from the room. She pulled up a chair next to Jet's bed. "Ignore them. They act like idiots sometimes. Do you have to stay the night?"

Pressing his head back into his pillow, he said, "Yep."

"More than a dislocated shoulder?"

"Broken collarbone as well."

"I can't believe that both ropes broke. Principal Fletcher was so upset. She's forcing Professor Dickerson to call the manufacturers."

Jayco's head reemerged in the doorway, with tears in his eyes, as he mimed someone falling. "Best day ever. We're out in two minutes."

"Give me a sec," Mckenzey replied.

Jayco feigned being scolded and retreated from the room.

"Worst campus event in five years," Mckenzey said. "People are going to talk about this forever."

"Just my luck."

"Have you talked to Nana yet?"

He nodded. "I was so tired. I'm not sure how much she understood."

"What do you need?"

"Rest. I can barely keep my eyes open."

Standing, Mckenzey asked, "What are you doing tomorrow?"

"If I'm released, I'll just sleep and avoid everyone."

"Can I stop by Sunday morning, say nine? I was wondering if we could talk. If you're up for breakfast, I'll pay."

"Can't turn that down," Jet said, mildly surprised.

"Feel better."

"I will," he whispered as he closed his eyes. Before the door closed, Jet thought he felt a soft kiss on his cheek. He slept for another hour. When he woke, he quickly summoned a nurse for pain medication. The doctor had not been wrong. Even after the medication, Jet was suddenly restless. He signaled a nurse passing by and asked, "Is it okay if I walk around?"

"Just make sure that you stay on this floor." She helped him from his bed, and he felt tightness and pain in his neck, hips, and shoulders. The nurse remained close by until he had taken a few steps down the hall. Soon, he was passing several other hospital rooms.

Turning the corner, he found Principal Fletcher at the far end of the hall, leaning against the opposite wall. She was oblivious to him, talking on her cell phone. He continued walking in her direction, intending to tell her that he was fine. After he'd covered most of the distance, she hung up the phone and disappeared into a different hospital room.

When Jet reached the door, it was slightly open. He heard voices inside.

An authoritative female spoke. "This is one of the worst sunburns I've ever seen. We've sedated her, made her comfortable, and are doing everything we can. We contacted the burn unit, but they feel she's doing well enough here. I think that with this scorching weather, they're overtaxed at the moment. Where was she found?"

"On campus, near the beach, just after lunch," Principal Fletcher explained. "One of our students found her. He immediately went to the bookstore and alerted our staff."

Jet found a female doctor with her back to him, standing next to Principal Fletcher and Mr. Smuin. He could only see a small portion of the hospital bed.

The female doctor continued, "She was in substantial pain upon arrival. Hopefully, she'll be feeling better in the next few days. Preventing an infection will be one of our top priorities."

Jet couldn't help himself as he leaned farther into the room. Redness couldn't begin to describe the skin of the girl. A sheet covered part of her body, but her neck, shoulders, arms, and face were bright red. Describing it as the worst sunburn ever was kind. She looked like she had been boiled like a lobster.

Principal Fletcher sighed, weariness in her voice. "Two students in the hospital on the same day. Almost a record. I'm going to visit Mr. Black next."

Jet headed back to his room, fearing he would be caught snooping. The name on the wall caught his attention—Trina Madden. The name sounded familiar, like he should know who she was. As he retraced his steps, the connection reoriented in his mind. She was a year older than he was *and* from Silverton. Two of her brothers and her father had died when the earthquake hit. He felt a surge of compassion for Trina Madden and everything she'd been through. The irony of the situation was not lost on him. Two survivors of Silverton were in the same hospital, at the same time, with different injuries, hundreds of miles away from where it had all started. He couldn't imagine a worse way to start the new school year.

CHAPTER 2

Jet wobbled out of the elevator, unlocked his door, and felt relieved to be back home at his dorm. After placing his things on the counter, he continued into the entertainment room attached to the foyer. He expected loud gaming sounds but was caught off guard when he spotted three people staring at each other uncomfortably. On one couch sat his two roommates, Rick Fish and Jackson Crawley. Across from them sat the floor monitor, Napoleon Bean.

Napoleon, and his curly brown hair, waved him over. "Just the man I wanted to see." The floor monitor was tall and goofy-looking. As a senior, he had a single room and a keen sense of when someone was doing something wrong. He had trouble talking with anyone about everyday things such as the weather or classes. But when it came to the dorm building, he could talk for hours and hours.

Last year, Jet and his former roommate, Raul, had been caught three times sneaking in late and twice for egging another dorm. Each time, Napoleon had gleefully caught them. They were given probation and a stern warning. His real name was Gregory Bean, but not a single soul dared to call him anything but Napoleon.

Jet quickly sat next to Rick, equally as confused as they looked. Traditionally, if Napoleon was in your dorm, you were in serious trouble. He had no idea what they had already done wrong.

Napoleon spoke in his southern accent. "Joshua. I'm glad to see that you aren't permanently disabled. But more importantly, have you noticed anyone hanging around outside your dorm?"

"What are you talking about?"

"We've had some sinister-appearing scoundrels about. I was just collecting evidence and interviewing any witnesses."

Shaking his head, Jet said, "Was this before or after I was in the hospital?"

"Don't be funny with me."

Jet shrugged. "Sorry, Napoleon. I barely had time to unpack before I almost fell to my death."

"That's no excuse. I caught a guy sneaking around outside your dorm. I've already talked to everyone else."

It took willpower and self-control for Jet not to roll his eyes. Napoleon was overreacting again. Instead, he asked, "Do you have a description?"

"Brown hair, quite spiky, plus a dog collar and bracelets with spikes. He was taller than me, dressed in all black, and had a bushy mustache."

"Doesn't sound familiar at all," Jet said quickly. "Was his hair longer than Rick's?"

Napoleon's head tilted, and he added, "When I cornered him, he said that he was just on the wrong floor."

Rick interjected, "Maybe he was telling the truth."

"I found it interesting that most of the school was away from campus, and this fella was skulking around like he owns the place."

Jackson leaned back, caught Jet's eye, and mouthed, "Skulking?"

Jet wiped his mouth to prevent himself from laughing.

"I agree," Rick said solemnly. "That's a little disturbing, but Jackson, Jet, and I have no idea who it was. Why would he be around our dorm, anyway? It sounds crazy."

Napoleon shot up. "I'm not crazy. It wasn't a ghost."

All three of them exchanged looks, and this time, Jet pinched his leg to stop from reacting. Through gritted teeth, he said, "Doubt it was a ghost. Probably someone is looking to get some action on our floor. Glad you caught him."

Jackson murmured, "If he shows up again, you'll be our first phone call."

"I'd better be."

Rick added, "Maybe you should tell the administrators."

Excitedly, Napoleon said, "Oh. I already have. They are well aware of my concerns."

"Great," Jackson said, standing.

Jet stood. "I need to go lie down. I'm not feeling great."

Napoleon strolled to the front door. "I don't need to impress upon you the seriousness of this, do I?"

"Nope," all three said in unison. They waited a few minutes after Napoleon closed the door before they burst out laughing. Jet had to use the wall to keep from falling over.

When they all recovered, Rick said, "That guy creeps me out. I thought we were getting a surprise inspection. I was livid that it was so early in the term."

"We were just playing two-player combat," Jackson added. "You can be next."

"I was telling the truth." Jet picked up his hospital bag. "It'll be a while before I'm playing again."

"Glad that you're cool. We would hate getting another set of roommates."

"Thanks," Jet said. "I'll be crushing you guys soon enough."

"Bring it," Jackson replied.

Jet's entire dorm was built to maximize space. The entertainment room held the two couches and a sixty-inch television screen donated by Rick's parents. Rick and Jackson's room was directly next to his. The foyer had the phone, a fridge, and a small pantry. The hall continued past their room, down to his. Across the way was a single bathroom with two sinks, a shower, and a bathtub.

Their dorm, Kelci Halls, was one of the many buildings on the southern part of campus. They were lucky enough to be on the eighth floor with a brilliant view out into the bay. There were four boy dorms and four girl dorms. A ninth dorm was a consequence dorm with boys on the upper two floors and girls on the bottom two floors. This was not a place you wanted to live long-term.

Tossing his items onto the second bed, he smiled at the fact that he hadn't been assigned a roommate. That could change, but he didn't think it would. Last year when he arrived, it took a few weeks to realize that Nana wasn't going to parent him, but it would be his teachers, administrators, and Napoleon. For the most part, they left him alone. He knew that would change if his grades started to slip or if he got into any sizable trouble. Napoleon came by for his weekly cleaning checks, but otherwise, things were stress-free.

He was groggy from the medications and super tired. He hadn't slept well last night and could not get the redness of Trina's face out of his mind. He undressed, removed his sling, and covered his surgical site with a large plastic bandage. He took a long, warm shower and fell asleep almost immediately after laying down. When he woke a few hours later, he grabbed a bite to eat and watched a movie with his roommates.

Just as the movie finished, the dorm phone began ringing. Jet picked it up and said, "Hello?"

"Joshua. Is that you?"

He smiled to himself. "Yea, Nana. It's me. Are you ever going to call me Jet?"

"I seriously doubt it," she insisted. "I've been so worried about you. Are you okay? When did you get home from the hospital?"

"A few hours ago. I was exhausted and took a nap. I just woke up and was watching a movie."

They talked for ten minutes, and Jet answered everything with as much excitement as possible. She was keenly interested in his accident, how it happened, and how the surgery had gone. It took a while to convince her that he was all right. He also realized that Nana missed him and wanted to talk.

Near the end of the phone call, Nana said, "Tell me about your first few days."

"Well," Jet said, "the first two days were dreary and boring. A half-day followed by a day of meeting all your teachers and signing a bunch of paperwork. Classes truly started earlier this week. I'm taking Math, French, English, PE, Geology Lab, and a few others. I've been to all of them except for my lab, which is next week."

"Are you sure you want to continue taking French?" Nana asked. "I've always wanted you to learn German."

"One day I would love to be an exchange student in Paris," Jet replied.

"That sounds fun, dear." A moment later, she added, "I pray that this year is better than last. You need to give your friends a chance. They seem to be good people. Put yourself out there and see what happens."

"I was thinking the same thing. We'll see. Mckenzey wants to hang out tomorrow. I'm sure things will be better."

"Tell your friends I said hi."

"Sure thing, Nana." He asked, "Have you had a chance to go back to the storage unit?"

There was a long pause. "No, I haven't. I know you want there to be something. It's just trash. I've been so preoccupied with you; it hasn't even crossed my mind."

"Why did Dad or Uncle Joshua have a storage unit in the first place?"

"Probably for all their junk. Why else?" Nana cleared her voice and added, "I also wanted to tell you...happy birthday! I know it's early, but I'm not sure I'll be able to call you on Thursday."

"Oh!" Jet was caught off guard. "Thank you, Nana. No worries. Today, or in a few days, it's all the same. Thanks for thinking of me."

"No problem. I love you very much."

"Love and miss you, Nana."

"By the way, it wouldn't kill you to call once in a while."

"I will."

"Well." Nana's voice became emotional. "Have a good night, and I love you. Be safe!"

"I will. Love you too, Nana."

CHAPTER 3

When the knock on the dorm's outer door came, it was far too early in the morning, and Jet's entire body ached as he stumbled to the door. Mckenzey stared back at him with enough energy and determination that Jet swung the door closed, ready to get back in bed.

Sticking out her foot, Mckenzey stopped the door and followed him inside. "That's not a good sign. Did you get any sleep last night?"

"Not enough." Jet retreated to his room. "I tossed and turned all night."

"Where are you going?" she asked.

"To change. I'm wearing my swim trunks, and you're dressed much better for breakfast."

"My swimsuit is under my clothes." She laughed energetically. "Does that mean you got dressed in your swimsuit last night before going to bed?"

"Just planning ahead." He stopped at the end of the hall, before going into his room. "Mind if I go looking like this?"

"We're in California and next to the beach. You fit in perfectly."

"Then what are we waiting for?"

"Should I carry your towel?"

"If you want," Jet replied cautiously.

"Sweet. Let's go."

Mckenzey sounded confident and happy. He couldn't remember a single time last year when she was so calm and easy-going. As they rode down the elevator, Mckenzey fidgeted with her pink skirt and cream tank top as if she wanted to ask something.

They set off toward the CeU building on foot. Jet had no idea why they named this building or what the letters meant. The campus of Chadwick's was deceiving. It had a very east coast feel with overhanging trees, cobblestone walkways, mostly brick buildings, and grass in the common areas. The school was co-ed from ninth to twelfth, with just over two thousand students living on the vast property.

The campus was divided into an east and west side by a single road, College Avenue, that traveled north and south. To the north, you would eventually find the city of Santa Barbara. The 101 scenic highway was to the south. The west side of campus held all the dorm buildings, the bookstore, three cafeterias, and most classrooms. Across the road was the CeU building, the administration buildings, staff apartments, most sports fields, and several parking lots.

As they crossed College Avenue, Mckenzey said, "It's so hot I think the asphalt is melting. I didn't even bother putting on any makeup."

"Today will be the hottest day of the year, and it's September. Isn't summer over yet?"

"Technically," Mckenzey pointed out. "Mother Nature wasn't updated. How was the hospital?"

"Weird."

"Really?"

"Yeah. I mean, I did fine." Jet ducked below a low hanging branch. "But there was a girl there, Trina something-or-other, and she fell asleep on the beach and got the worst sunburn I've ever seen."

"You saw her?"

"I snuck a look. She looked like a baked lobster."

"That's what I heard too," Mckenzey said. "You know who she is, right?"

Jet nodded. "She survived Silverton."

Mckenzey was quiet as they began up the stairs to the top of the CeU building, where two of the school's restaurants were located. This morning, they were headed to The View. "How were your first few days?"

"I love all of my classes. I have incredible teachers. You probably know that I'm sharing a dorm with Latisha again."

"I heard."

"And somehow, Grantham and Jayco found a way to be roommates. They're having a blast. What about you?"

"No roommate yet. My classes are good. All of my teachers seem reasonable."

As they walked inside the restaurant, Mckenzey said, "An interesting way to put it."

"Hey. I need good grades. Nana wasn't too happy with a few Bs last year."

They were led to a table, and it didn't take long to order drinks and be handed plates for the breakfast buffet. Soon, Jet's plate was piled with food, and Mckenzey left to get both some chocolate milk.

When she returned, she asked, "Anything cool happen this summer?"

"Not really. Though we did find an old storage unit—it was mostly filled with trash."

"A storage unit. That's random."

"Tell me about it."

Mckenzey began fidgeting with her food, and Jet recognized the gesture. He knew that she was itching to talk about the disaster they had survived a few years ago. Since they had returned to school, he had avoided this conversation too often. It was time to come clean with things he'd been hiding for the last few years.

Setting down his fork, Jet said, "Our group's friendship was terrible last year. I know that you weren't happy with me. I recognize that you made all the attempts to talk, and I pushed you away. Things are going to be different this year."

"How can you be so sure?"

"I'm ready to tell you anything you want to know. Ask any question, and I'll answer it the best I can. But don't say that I didn't warn you."

"Warn me about what?"

"The story is crazy. I doubt you're going to believe me."

"Crazy?" Her voice cracked as she glanced away, cheeks reddening.

Jet tried mightily to ignore the impulse to run and hide. He finally said, "Last year, you wanted to know about every little detail. I'm ready to tell you."

"What's changed?"

"A lot. I want us to be friends. I know that you're leaving Chadwick's, and I feel partly responsible. I don't want you to blame me."

"Who told you?" she asked. She didn't appear mad but curious.

"Latisha told me a few weeks ago. She's the only one who called me this summer besides Seyanna. She's pretty shaken up."

Mckenzey stared at her food. "I'm only going if I get accepted."

Jet countered, "Latisha told me that you're practically already in. You would've gone this semester if they could've arranged it." He took a drink of his milk and then put it down. "Interview me. Ask the questions, and I'll answer them. I'll be truthful and open."

"That would be a first," Mckenzey said as she brushed back a strand of her brown hair and concentrated. "My first question would be...what happened in Silverton?"

"A loaded question." Jet blew out a long breath. "Okay. I woke up to the house crashing down around me. Lava was everywhere. I tore from my bedroom, grabbed Nana, and we were lucky to escape. That's the story I tell everyone."

"Is it not true?"

"Oh, it is. And before a few days ago, that was all I could remember. It turns out that story is a watered-down version of what really happened. There are strange things in the world, and then there are crazy things. How I escaped falls into the crazy category. And why I couldn't remember might be even crazier. There are still things that I don't know."

"What do you mean?"

"It was like I was blocked from the real memory of what happened."

"How's that possible?"

"Your guess is as good as mine."

"What else?"

"I remember that when I woke up, I felt like something had changed within me. Looking outside, three gullies were being carved into the ground, approaching my house. Lava poured into the gullies, and soon every inch of my backyard was torn apart. Our house burned down with Nana and me still inside."

"Were you hurt?"

He nodded slowly. "My lungs were injured. I've needed an inhaler about once a month since then." He pulled up his left sleeve. "A piece of glass sliced into my arm." Pointing at his lower back, he added, "A glob of lava landed here." He lifted his leg, almost setting it on the table. "This burn happened when I stepped into a pool of lava outside my house. I still don't know how I didn't lose my leg. It was much worse than it looks now."

"Oh my gosh," Mckenzey whispered. "I didn't know."

"Truthfully, neither did I. I had these injuries, but I didn't know why. It was weird."

"What do you mean?"

"The doctor called it selective amnesia. He said it was so traumatic that I blocked out a part of my past. For years, I didn't even remember the day that it happened. There were a few months that I thought it was all fake. But I haven't even told you the real reason of how I escaped."

"Keep going."

"After I got Nana down the stairs, we were trapped. The house was on fire, and smoke was everywhere. Suddenly the front door exploded, and a dozen shards of wood were catapulted directly at me. Three abilities of enhanced vision, time slowing, and magnified vision allowed me to dodge most of the wood pieces. Nana and I were able to move through the house and find an escape. Honestly, we would've burned without those talents, right along with our house."

Mckenzey asked, "Can you still do these things?"

"Had we had this conversation a few days ago, I would've said no. But something changed when I was rock climbing. That's when my memory of this event returned, and I used these talents to avoid death again. They prevented me from falling over a hundred feet."

"But you still fell."

"I made a temporary knot that held until I was closer to the ground. It would've been much worse."

"Why do you have these talents? And where could they have come from?"

"I don't know. I have been thinking about this non-stop since it happened. I still don't have any answer."

Mckenzey sat and pondered. She muttered, "The picture is becoming slightly clearer."

"This doesn't freak you out?" Jet couldn't hide his disbelief. "How can you be so calm? I never pictured you taking this information so casually."

"Oh...I'm freaked out. I've been freaked out for years. This doesn't change anything."

Puzzled, Jet asked, "Am I missing something?"

"Do you know how lucky *I am* to have survived Silverton?" Mckenzey's voice was almost pleading.

Tears formed in her eyes. She had never appeared so vulnerable, and he understood how selfish he'd been. He never, not once, asked how she had survived or even how she had felt. Sitting straighter, he asked, "What happened to you when Silverton was destroyed? How did you escape?"

She took a deep breath and said, "I survived because of you."

"Me?"

"You forewarned me that the town was going to be destroyed."

Jet's cheeks suddenly flushed red. "Haha. I see. Now you're making fun of me. I sound crazy, so you're going to add something even crazier." He stood and placed his napkin on the table. "Are you ready to go?"

"Why won't you just listen to me?" she demanded.

"I've tried. I don't know what you want me to say."

"I'm not making fun of you," she insisted. "I need to understand why you called me ten minutes before the largest national disaster in decades and give me, my parents, and my sister a chance to live?"

"I didn't call you," Jet said honestly as he sat down.

"Yes, you did!" Her look was fierce and piercing. "I promise you did."

He thought back to that day, sure he could now remember everything that had happened. In a soft voice, he said, "I don't remember calling you."

"Trust me," she said earnestly. "You did. You were in a panic. You were irrational and screaming at me. You told me to get out of my house and out of town, or I'd be dead. You told me that something was happening outside your house and that it would spread to the entire area. I didn't believe you at first. I even laughed at you. But you sounded so serious."

"What did you do?" Jet asked, unable to help himself.

"At first, I didn't know what to do. But you kept screaming at me. I told you that I would leave. When I hung up the phone, I lied to my parents and somehow got them out of the house."

"How'd you do that?"

"The night before, we were at the elementary for that school party. Do you remember? I doubt they do that anymore. Our friends were out of town, but you and I decided to go anyway. My mom and nana were there. I think they both helped with the decorations. We were having a pretty good time. Halfway through, you got sick and had to go home."

"I remember." He'd been so excited about that party, his first-ever. There were fifty kids from his elementary school.

He was glad that Jayco and Grantham weren't there to get in his way. There'd been a few girls he wanted to talk to, but he only wanted to dance with Mckenzey. Unfortunately, he'd gotten sick. Like puke on your socks sick.

The next morning, Jet woke up with a nosebleed and pain in every joint imaginable. His memory, now perfectly intact, recalled that after they escaped his house, he had gone to the hospital and in the mirror, he noticed how his face and teeth appeared different. He'd asked Nana about it, but she'd insisted that it was just his active imagination.

Mckenzey continued, "I told them that Nana had taken you to the hospital to remove your appendix and that surgery didn't go well."

"And they bought that?" he asked, amazed.

"Sort of. My parents started driving toward the center of town. I screamed that they were going in the wrong direction, and you were at a different hospital. They almost slid off the road. The first time the ground shook, we were far enough away. When the explosion hit Silverton, my dad pulled over, and we watched the cloud of dust, smoke, or whatever it was that settled over the area." She stared at him with such force, her lower lip trembling. "We lived because you told me to leave, and we've only spoken a dozen times over the next three years. Despite both of us being at the same school, I've never had the guts to thank you. That ends today."

CHAPTER 4

Jet sighed. "Should we tell the others?"

"No. Not yet." Glancing at her watch, Mckenzey added, "I know you wanted to be alone today, but our friends want to see you. They're at the beach."

"But we're not going to tell them, right?"

"No. I think it would make things worse. Our goal should be to fix our friendships. Things have been off for so long. You've been distant from the rest of us that no one is sure how to act around you. If this works, we'll consider telling them in a couple of days."

"You're the boss."

They paid and left the restaurant. When they reached College Avenue, Latisha called and directed them to the northern section of the beach. Students lined the sand and lounged in the water. Unsurprisingly, Jayco and Grantham managed to commandeer one of the top five best spots along the coast. They'd brought a cooler, blankets, chairs, and two canvases to provide a decent amount of shade. A hole had already been dug and half-filled with ocean water to cool their feet. Latisha was relaxing in a chair, her feet dangling in the water, as Grantham and Jayco tossed a football to each other. Jayco's orange jeep was parked close by. He'd turned sixteen the day before coming back to school and was the only one able to drive legally.

Catching sight of their approach, Grantham and Jayco hurried over. Grantham said, "What a perfect day. Except for the darn heat. Glad you guys found us."

"This looks like a blast," Mckenzey said. "Why didn't we do this last year?"

Jayco said, "Jet had a stick up his—"

"We get the point," Mckenzey said hurriedly, "But this year is going to be better."

"You can't blame everything on me." Jet flipped off his shoes, found a soda, and sat in a chair facing the ocean. "Just most of it."

"You're just such an easy target," Jayco said. "Show us your surgical scar."

"There's still a bandage on it."

"How long do you have to wear the sling?" Latisha asked.

"Couple weeks, maybe more. The plate they put on my collarbone will make the healing faster. I have decent movement, but it needs to stay clean for the next few days. After that, I'll be golden."

Turning to Grantham, Latisha asked, "How was your summer?"

"It would've been a lot better if my parents had let me go with Jayco to Hawaii. But of course, they said I was only fifteen and couldn't be trusted on my own."

Jayco said, "That was the reason they gave you? Lame. Well, so that you know, it was the most fun I've ever had. I was at the beach every day with my uncle. He owns a small shop near Napili beach on Maui. We did a ton of snorkeling, and the girls were gorgeous."

"I don't want to hear this," Grantham sulked.

Mckenzey asked, "Latisha, how was your summer?"

"Oh. Pretty much like Jayco's summer. Except I went home with my mom to Florida. We spent time on our yacht.

Swimming, hanging out, golfing, and jet skiing. You know how it is."

Mckenzey smiled. "Funny. None of us except you know what that's like. I had a good summer. We went to several Colorado Rockies' baseball games, went hiking, and spent a week camping with my family. Overall, it was perfect."

Jayco asked, "How about you, Jet?"

"Same. Camping, hiking, and stuff like that. We went to the beach a few times, minus the yacht or snorkeling."

"Sounds superb," Jayco said sarcastically.

"It was good to relax around my house."

"Exactly."

"There was one odd thing that turned out to be nothing." Jet explained about the storage unit.

Grantham asked, "Why a storage unit?"

"No clue. The unit is in Eugene, two hours south of Portland. It was unopened for several years. But the person who'd registered it had the last name of Black. Legally they can't get into it until the contract expires. It looks like my dad rented it."

"Did you get a look inside?" Latisha asked.

"I was hoping for a sweet antique, but it turned out to be mostly trash and some boxes of papers. I didn't get a chance to go through everything before school started. We salvaged some books, a jacket, and a pagan mask. There were also some glass jars full of rocks, corn, rice, and other things. That was a little weird."

Jayco started clapping. "Wow. That must've been incredible."

"How was your dad involved?" Mckenzey asked.

"A copy of his driver's license from ten years ago. He'd paid in advance. When they called, the ten years were almost up. Some of the stuff might have been from my great uncle Joshua."

Latisha began fanning herself with her flip-flop. She asked, "Who's that?"

"Nana's older brother. He was downright crazy. Growing up, I was embarrassed by him. Some of the stories I've heard would blow your mind."

"I've heard of him," Jayco said dismissively. "We all have. Remember back in sixth grade, when Mrs. Beverly was talking about the history of Silverton? A naked man once went around town, spouting about some big golden creature in the hills outside of town. That was him. It gave me the idea of searching the hills around Silverton. Probably the only good thing he did."

"No way," Latisha said critically. "That guy is related to you?"

Jet felt defensive. He hated bringing up his family. Calmly, he said, "He tried convincing people that he was protecting something. He was always paranoid that people were following him. I was named after him. I changed my name when I was ten."

Mckenzey laughed, almost to herself, and added, "Nana still calls you Joshua."

"She'll never call me Jet."

Grantham started passing out cookies. He added, "I noticed Ariana and Raul at the campus event. I thought you said they weren't coming back to school this year. What's up between you guys?"

Jayco added, "It was weird that they were hanging with Shane Fallon."

"Tell me about it," Jet hissed.

"And what's up with the stupid clothing they wear?" Latisha asked. "I wouldn't be caught dead wearing the same clothes as everyone else. Lack of originality."

"You're joking, right?" Jet asked. "Haven't you seen those groups on campus?"

"I guess," Latisha said. "It's a real fashion faux pas. But he might be the cutest boy at school."

Grantham rolled his eyes.

"Thanks for the Vogue report," Mckenzey said. "Raul looked so different. Rubbing shoulders with Shane is the last thing I expected from him."

Jet said, "After Raul dropped out of school last year, I didn't hear from him again. He introduced me to Ariana, his sister, but later freaked out and demanded that I stop seeing her."

"After she dumped you, you were miserable," Grantham said.

"That's an understatement," Latisha added.

"Well...it was complicated. Something changed in Raul's behavior around Christmas. He'd miss class assignments, refuse to hang out with his friends, and was moody. He pushed Ariana to end things with me. One night, when I got home, our dorm was dark and cold. Raul was inside, and I found him unconscious. He'd tried to hurt himself, and they rushed him to the hospital."

"You're freaking kidding," Jayco said. "I didn't hear anything about this."

"Me neither," Grantham added.

"It's not like the school wanted everyone to know."

"Is he okay?" Mckenzey asked softly.

"I guess. He still hasn't talked to me. He dropped out of school after he was released from the hospital. Ariana and I stopped talking after that. I had no clue he was coming back to school."

"Who's older?" Latisha asked.

"Ariana, by a year."

Jayco said, "Things aren't good for Raul if he's next in line to become a member of the Dark Angels."

"What's the Dark Angels?" Latisha asked dismissively.

Jayco laughed. "Do you live in the Antarctic?"

"No, but Seyanna does." Jet grinned. Latisha never was good at reading sarcasm.

Jayco rolled his eyes. "The Dark Angels is a super-secret group on campus. Shane's at the top. There are other groups too, like the Light Riders and more."

"If it's so secret, how do all of you know about it?" Latisha protested.

"The secret is what they do and why they do it. But above all, Shane hates Jet with a passion."

"We met on the first day of school last year, in the bookstore," Jet said. "It started fine but got weird, fast. Since that day, he's taken every chance to get in my way."

Jayco said. "I'm pretty sure you were being interviewed on the first day?"

"Interviewed?" Mckenzey questioned. "For what?"

"To become a member of one of his groups," Jayco said flatly.

Latisha asked, perplexed, "How do you know?"

"I was interviewed just after Christmas last year."

"Really?" Jet asked. He'd never considered it an interview.

"Every member has been collected, interviewed, and placed in a ring. A leader, or a *Paramount*, directs each ring and they report directly to Shane. There are at least five or six rings at school, maybe more. I was approached by Shane too. Many of his questions were about our friend group, the Echoes, and our past lives. He knew a lot about each of you already. Someone else must've been chosen though. I wasn't told directly, but it was obvious."

"A good thing," Grantham countered. "To become a Paramount, you have to cut ties with your *old* friends."

Hearing the word Echoes was a blast from the past. Jet hadn't thought about the nickname for so long. The Echoes was a name that Jayco had picked out for the group in fifth or sixth grade. It caught on after they were hiking near Silverton and found a cave, one of many. They spent hours making echoes back and forth.

The group talked and joked on the beach for the next two hours. The day's heat forced them into the water several times. At the request of Mckenzey, Jet showed his friends the scars he'd received from surviving Silverton. He took off his shirt for the first time in years and stepped into the water. It was refreshing and liberating to allow his friends to see his injuries. They laughed and joked and laughed some more.

Something inside of Jet shifted in the late afternoon. A troubled sickness was building in Jet's stomach. A sudden icy chill generated a splash of nausea, and with it came a wave of anxiety. Something was wrong. Not with him, but with where he was standing.

"Jet, are you okay?" Mckenzey asked. "You look like you've seen a ghost."

Without thinking, he muttered, "I need to go. There's something I need to do back in my dorm."

Her eyes narrowed, her head tilted, and she stared at him, perplexed. "Is it more important than this moment?"

Trying to comprehend this overwhelming urge he felt and not wanting to ruin everything they'd accomplished today, he added, "I'm so sorry. Something feels off. I think it has to do with what we talked about at breakfast. I'll let you know, but I have to go."

Jayco and the others were at the water's edge.

Mckenzey gave a quick nod. "I've got this covered." As Jet began retrieving his clothes, she sprinted to their friends. He heard her say, "Jet has to meet with someone from the school about his injury. He'll come back if he can."

A surge of appreciation for Mckenzey affected him.

"What about a movie tonight?" Grantham shouted. "We could do it over at our place."

"Maybe," Jet shouted as he hurried away. "I'll let you know." He sprinted back to his dorm, his mind racing. The feeling was like a compulsion, as if he were in the middle of doing the wrong thing. He crashed through his dorm door and headed to his room without a second thought.

Entering his room did not appease the compulsion. He was dragged to his desk as if fate had a grip on his arm. He watched himself as if from outside his body, opening his desk's drawer. An ancient and impressive book came into view. It was dirty brown, leather, old, and the most bizarre thing Jet had ever owned. Faint golden lettering read: *The Sorcerer's Guide*.

This book was different from any other book he'd ever seen—it was authentic and ancient. You could smell the leather in the binding; a rustic and earthy scent with a splash of pine needles. But the most baffling thing about this book was that he could not open a single page. It was as if it were glued shut. He had first laid eyes on the book when his house had collapsed around him. A shadowbox on the wall, created by his dad, was knocked down. When it hit the floor, everything scattered. To his surprise, an old handcrafted wooden box splintered, and the book was hidden inside. It was the only possession to have survived that day. Over the last four years, he'd imagined it as a journal, a treasure map, or even a priceless relic that could be sold for thousands of dollars. Despite those thoughts, it had remained stubbornly closed.

As he stared down at the cover, he instinctively knew that everything had changed. This feeling of certitude was as strong as the compulsion he bore. His fingers brushed against the binding, and a jolt of electricity careened through him, and he was swept back inside his body. After picking it up, he automatically sat on his bed. Without any effort, the front cover opened, revealing an almost empty page. At the bottom were four words: Magic Has Been Reawakened.

The next page turned, and golden letters lay on the left and right pages. The writing was elegant, and at first glance it appeared to be a short story or poem. Jet was not disconcerted when the second page would not turn. Outside of the text, near the outer edges, there was an intricate set of swirls, shapes, and lines. The paper felt a hundred years old yet sturdy and thick. In astonishment, he leaned back against the wall and began reading.

The Legendary Battle

Millennia ago, Goth Airtha, the chosen land, was ruled by 10 Kings known as the Council. Peace and prosperity reigned for centuries, but a wind of change was forewarned by insight. The Grey Panther, leader of the Council, dissented and brought forth hatred and rebellion among his brethren. He desired absolute control of the Council. This was adamantly denied. In secrecy, he became bedfellows with the ancient form of magic—Runic Discipleship and was bestowed the title of Arisol, the Demon Prince. He began attacking the strongholds, and many years of combat ensued. The Council, fearing defeat, sent two of their members to distant lands to find an object of unimaginable power. Their adventure revealed a hidden bewitching—Elemental magic. Arisol was defeated near the Starving Peaks and was bound in an earthly prison.

5 of the Kings perished in battle, while 4 Kings survived to protect the land and restore order. The Black Lion, the White Snake, the Red Falcon, and the Brown Owl. Each possessed extraordinary powers of greatness, intelligence, aptitude, and skill. They ruled and protected in truth and righteousness and promised to preserve all creatures that abounded in the land. Lady Gaea, the Earth's Daughter, brought forth food, humanity, peace, and life to the earth. She bestowed gifts and treasures upon the 4 Kings. These items enhanced their powers and talents but, most unexpectedly, divided them. Peace reigned but for a short time.

2 Kings became blind to their own skills and consented to find a path to destroy Arisol. They feared his eventual escape. However, they became seduced by an ancient tale of treasure and power beyond belief along their travels. The White Snake and the Red Falcon took their gifts and secretly began searching for the Phoenix, a tablet of power. It was not long before they learned that Lady Gaea was one of the 3 gatekeepers. They summoned Lady Gaea and spoke falsely of their intentions. They were granted its location.

Intending to bless the 2 Kings, she provoked a bolt of golden lightning to strike them. Along with showing them the path, it revealed their deception. The head of the Falcon fell onto the body of the Snake, and they were amalgamated. Their minds, desires, abilities, and weapons were combined, and their true natures blackened. They became forever known as Erpofalco. They used Runic magic to shield themselves as they searched for The Phoenix. Destroying Arisol was no longer their plan; they had become corrupted.

The Black Lion and the Brown Owl vowed to stop their brethren from releasing Arisol. They also sought an audience with Lady Gaea, who reluctantly agreed to help recover the tablet of power. Her influence and blessing amassed her remaining strength, and they became the Protectors. The head of the Owl fell onto the body of the Lion, and they became known as Leotyton. They traveled with Lady Gaea to defend Arisol's prison, taking their gifts and powers. Near the Starving Peaks, they spotted Erpofalco and Arisol's allies entering a deep and majestic cave, hoping to use the Phoenix to release Arisol. Lady Gaea sealed the cave as Leotyton descended to its depths to prevent escape.

To their dismay, the power of the Phoenix nullified the prison's hold over Arisol. When Leotyton reached the bottom, Arisol was already pulled from his prison. Believing he was alone with his allies, Arisol drew a rune into the ground, and manacles of subjection formed on the wrists of Erpofalco and the other allies. The energy required to enslave Erpofalco was almost more than Arisol could bear. He drew a second rune that siphoned Erpofalco's power to him. Erpofalco hissed in displeasure as he was transformed into a slave.

Leotyton attacked, ambushing the pair in hopes of regaining control of the Phoenix. Erpofalco retaliated to protect his new master. The battle was legendary, and the ferocity was previously unmatched. Slowly the advantage shifted to Leotyton. Arisol searched for a weakness in Leotyton's defense, and when he found one, he cast a third rune intending to destroy him. Lady Gaea sacrificed herself, but in doing so, her powers vanished, and she faded into the earth, asleep and forgotten.

Leotyton seized the tablet and struck it against a rock, fragmenting it into 6 pieces, thwarting Arisol's escape. The beast was compelled back into his earthly prison. Erpofalco, now tethered to his master, was dragged into the darkness, as were Arisol's other allies.

The pieces of the tablet were placed within a casket of divine workmanship. But before Leotyton could close the casket, a final rune of unmistakable malevolence escaped Arisol's prison. It conceived of a single avenue and the Rivalry was born, which allowed Arisol a slimmer of hope to escape and survive. A countdown was initiated to a future war. Instructions vital to his escape were placed inside an ancient book for future generations.

As the first protector, Leotyton realized that he must provide balance. Arisol's imprisonment was now temporary, and it required a future battle to determine Arisol's rebirth. Leotyton willingly gave up his own lifeforce and summoned ancient powers from the 5 elements, creating a second book. A solar calendar set in motion a countdown when the two sides would one day meet again. The Rivalry would be a fight for the possession of the Kings and the tablet. Two records would serve as gatekeepers to the knowledge of the language of the ethers and the runes. Four Elemental sentinels and four Runic demons emerged from the ground as Leotyton's energy ended. Life and magic vanished from inside the cavern as the casket's lid closed.

An inscription was carved into the prison's outer edge.

Until Earth's light shines bright on Zodiac's star, the heart beats still.

CHAPTER 5

Jet slammed shut the book, feeling confused, yet a whisp of understanding itched at the back of his mind. Some of the pieces were starting to make sense. Staring at the ceiling, he tried aligning what he knew with what had just happened.

It was clear that something had attacked his mind and unlocked some missing memories. He had yet to understand what had taken place to block his memories in the first place. Something had wanted him to forget what had specifically happened in Silverton. He didn't know why this was important. Three abilities had emerged, now twice, saving him. A book that had previously been glued shut was now partly open. Was this a connection to him or his family and how did Silverton play into all of this? His last question was the most important: Why were these things happening to him?

His thoughts turned to the story he had just read. Most of it didn't make sense. Lots of names and words that he had never heard before. There was a demon, a war, and magic. He had never known anyone who could use magic and was skeptical that it had ever existed.

He slowly reopened the book and studied the words. In time, he memorized names, symbols, and the lettering, hoping that it would provide a greater understanding. Grabbing his laptop, he typed in some of the keywords. Twenty minutes later, he was exhausted, having found nothing.

He quoted aloud, "Two records would serve as gatekeepers to the knowledge of the language of the ethers and the runes."

The words "ethers" and "runes" intrigued him this time. He found a definition of ethers: "They are a class of organic compounds that contain an ether group—an oxygen atom connected to two alkyl or aryl groups." This definition was lost on Jet the moment he read the organic meaning. Chemistry was his worst class, not because it was hard, which it was, but because it was so dull. He moved on. Another definition was more about spirits, but this didn't offer any more comprehension. The final description was from ancient philosophy describing physical elements of some sort that were prevalent in the heavens.

Moving on to the next word, he found that Runes were more straightforward. They were letters set forth by something called a runic alphabet. He learned that different Runic alphabets had been discovered in various civilizations, including the Anglo-Saxons, Scandinavians, and others. Searching the first few pages, he found no hidden lettering or an alphabet by examining the book's open page.

Later that evening, he forced his mind away from the fable and begrudgingly spent two hours working on homework. He read two chapters in sociology, then worked on two math worksheets. His second week of classes would likely be more chaotic. He was downright excited for his first geology lab since he had developed an obsession with earthquakes, disasters, and rocks. Once finished, he called Grantham and excused himself from the movie.

As he was getting ready for bed, there was a knock at his door.

"Come in," Jet said as he pushed his book under his bed.

Rick peeked inside and said, "Dude, you need a cell phone."

"Tell me about it. Maybe Nana will change her mind when I turn sixteen next week."

"Let's hope—because I'm not your secretary. The phone is for you."

"Who is it?" Jet asked as he followed Rick down the hallway, trying to put his arm back in his sling.

"I don't get paid enough to ask those questions."

"Whatever." Jet picked up the landline. "Sleepy Hollow residence; this is the headless horseman."

"Jet, you're an idiot." The voice was soft and musical, and he recognized it instantly.

He said, "Ariana. Tell me something I don't already know."

"Elephants can be pregnant for up to two years."

"No way. That can't be true."

"It is." After a moment, she asked tentatively, "How are you? I mean, how's your shoulder? I heard that you had to get surgery."

"It sucks. I broke my collarbone and dislocated my shoulder. I needed a metal plate, but it'll heal just fine."

"It looked terrible."

Jet changed the subject and said, "How was your summer?"

"Oh," she replied. "Not too bad."

"And your classes?"

Ariana spoke calmly. "My classes look pretty sweet—I got all the teachers I wanted. This summer went by too quickly; my parents had to drag us back to school. How about you?"

"Not bad, sort of boring."

She said quickly, "Look. I've wanted to talk to you for a while now. I owe you an explanation of how last year ended."

"You really don't," he insisted. "That was last year. I understand. No big deal. It was a stressful time."

"But Jet, I can't. Things were going so well for us, especially before Christmas. Then Raul—"

"—said we couldn't see each other anymore," Jet finished. "I remember."

"I'm sorry. I know that you haven't seen my brother since he was pulled from school."

"I saw him at the rock-climbing event. Standing next to you and Shane Fallon. I'm so glad that both of you made it back to school this year."

"I can explain."

"It's fine."

When Ariana spoke, it was monotone. "There are some things that you need to understand. Shane's parents and my parents go way back. Both our dads went to San Mateo boarding school in Texas when they were younger. With everything that had happened with my brother, my parents blamed the school. Shane's parents helped calm our family. The principal came to our house over the summer and spoke with us, and things got smoothed out. Shane's parents are board members. I should've told you this last year, but you always had something negative to say about him. Shane stopped by a few times during the summer, and he and Raul hung out. But if it weren't for you...I mean, I'm so thankful that you found him. You're the one that saved his life."

"It was a scary moment," Jet agreed, his mind reeling.

Ariana continued, "But you and I are no longer together, and you guys aren't roommates or best friends."

"I haven't spoken to either of you in months. It's cool that Shane and his family helped you guys. Don't worry about me."

Ariana sighed. "Are we ever going to get over this?"

"Of course," Jet said. He changed the subject once again. "What else did you do this summer?"

Ariana calmed down and dove into talking about the summer. She spoke about visiting her family in Mexico. Raul went to therapy and started doing better around July. Her parents wouldn't let either of them out of sight for the first two months.

Jet recalled that last year, Ariana claimed that her parents didn't 'get' her, and she told stories of how controlling they were. Jet had heard this from most of his friends. When Raul decided he didn't want Ariana hanging out with Jet any longer, he threatened to tell her parents. That had just about done the trick.

Ariana continued, "I saw some of the pictures you posted online. Your summer wasn't that boring. One picture looked weird; it was the one with a metal door."

"You saw that?" he asked, genuinely surprised.

"I did. I mean, I wasn't stalking you or anything."

"Right," he said playfully.

"No. What was it?"

"Nana got a weird phone call about a storage unit they thought was ours. We went and checked it out."

"A storage unit?"

"It hadn't been opened in years."

"How odd."

"The owner said it wasn't that uncommon. When we got inside, it turned out to be mostly trash. There wasn't anything of value."

"Did you go through everything?"

"Pretty much."

"Whose was it?"

"My dad and my great uncle Joshua's. He was a hoarder."

"Who's he?"

"Nana's misguided brother. He was downright crazy."

Ariana laughed for the first time, and it was nice to hear. He couldn't help but smile.

"Our family has a few crazies too. I'm pretty sure that all families do."

"Uncle Joshua died years before I was born. Unfortunately, I was named after him. He was always the brunt of so many jokes growing up."

"Was he that weird?"

"He was an outcast and drunk most days. Some townspeople spotted him in the hills chanting and calling to the skies. He told them he was a sorcerer, searching for lost treasure."

"What if I told you I'm a sorcerer?" she joked.

Jet shivered unexpectedly, and the covering of his book formed in his mind. Recovering quickly, he said, "That would be highly unlikely. Sorcerers dress in dark clothes and have these large wooden walking sticks with an orb on the end. When I was in your dorm, I failed to find a single orb. It's a safe bet that you aren't."

"Oh, you searched my dorm, did you?" Ariana said warmly.

"And on top of that, great uncle Joshua wasn't a sorcerer either. He could barely tie his shoes. He did this ritual thing every time he left the house; he'd walk around the block three times in the same direction. Same thing when he came home. The town's infamous story was of him insisting he found a large door dug deep into the side of a cave. He described a huge bird carved into it. He swore to it for weeks. A dozen people were stupid enough to start looking for it themselves, even me and my friends. No one ever found a thing."

"Sounds like he'd be fun at parties. I bet Raul and Shane would've liked him too."

The air in Jet's lungs spilled out like water from a broken vase. There was a deep pause on the other end. The comfort he'd felt for the last few minutes evaporated instantly. Then the questions that had been burning in his mind slipped out. "How well do you know Shane? Are you guys together?"

"That's not fair," she said quickly.

"I'm just asking."

"I didn't call to talk about Shane."

"I see." Gripping the phone, a wave of anger rolled over him. "Why did you call then?"

Defensively, she answered, "To see how you were doing. I was worried. Especially after that fall."

"No need to worry. I'm fine. Please tell Raul I said hi. I'll catch you later, Ariana." He slammed the phone down before she could respond.

* * *

By Tuesday afternoon, the entire campus was swamped with homework. It was as if the school was trying to set a Guinness world record for the amount of work given. Jet was just excited that he was finally going to his geology lab. The science building was, by far, the oldest building on campus. It sat northeast of the girls' dorm, five minutes from the bookstore. Sweat dripped down his back, arms, and legs by the time the building came into view. There was no way this building would be found anywhere on the brochure for prospective students.

"Are you coming inside, or are you just going to annoy me for the rest of your life?"

It took a moment for the question to register. Scanning around, Jet wondered if someone was talking to him.

"Over here." The voice was high-pitched and amused.

Jet spotted a girl standing near the building, holding open the door. His stomach lurched. It was Autumn Bells, the most attractive girl on campus, whom he had never spoken to before. Was she talking to him?

She seemed to guess what was going on inside his head. "I don't bite."

She smiled sweetly, almost expectantly, and Jet forced himself forward. Her blond hair was long, full, and slightly wavy. Her makeup was perfect, and she wore a tight-fitting yellow sundress that complimented her figure. She was a few inches shorter than he was. Most boys had a crush on her, as did a few of the girls. Rumors circled that she'd kissed Shane, some of the teachers on campus, and even the father of another student. Jet wasn't sure he believed half of what he heard about her. For Jet, the most compelling reason to stay far away was that Autumn and Ariana had been best friends up until two years ago. Their friendship had ended in disaster.

"Thanks," Jet mumbled, and he walked toward the door.

"Glad to see your fall didn't cause any permanent damage."

Jet's face flushed. "You saw that?"

"Honey, the entire school did. How did your surgery go?"

Jet, trying to sound casual, said, "Broken clavicle and dislocation. Surgery to place a plate."

"Ouch. That sounds painful."

Jet had stopped on the threshold of going inside. He asked, "Are you taking a class here?"

"Not really." She continued holding the door.

"Just finished a class?" he asked.

"Nope." She grinned at him. "See you around."

"Thanks," he muttered as he strolled inside, unsure of what had just happened. Stepping inside his lab room, he found three rows of black counters, each with three sinks. A few pieces of lab equipment were arranged in the center of each counter. Semi-bright lights illuminated the classroom. Students surrounded most of the counter spaces, but Jet found an empty chair between two students he didn't know. He eased his backpack onto the floor, resting his arm carefully on the counter. A dry-erase board stood at the front of the room with the words "Geology Lab."

For the next few minutes, a few students shuffled into the classroom. A hush fell over the class when a large man sauntered into the room from a door at the front wall and deposited his briefcase on the floor. The man cleared his voice and said in a lofty professorial tone, "Welcome to the lab for historical geology. I am Professor Gerald Blum, and this is my fourteenth year teaching here at Chadwick's."

Clapping erupted spontaneously from a few students as several others rolled their eyes.

"Thank you," he said, waving cheerfully. "This class is the practical application of your geology class, though it doesn't require that you're taking it concurrently. It is doubtful that your studies will completely cover the material necessary to accomplish some of my assignments. Therefore, we will cover some material in class for the first few minutes. I have a syllabus that I would like to pass around, but I forgot it back in my office."

At that precise moment, the doorknob turned.

Professor Blum said quickly, "My teaching assistant went to get it. This is probably her. I'd like to introduce Autumn Bells as my TA."

Jet heard a groan escape from his own mouth. A few students close to him, almost all boys, glared at him as if he had done something horrific. Autumn stepped into the room and held the stacked papers in her hands.

Professor Blum said, "Autumn will pass out the syllabi."

She began at the far end of the room. Her eyes found his a few moments later, and she smiled mischievously. Jet's cheeks flushed.

Professor Blum continued, "Don't forget to look at the class schedule and the expected lab write-ups. The biggest concern for many of my students is the change in the status quo when it comes to lab write-ups. I don't mind chemistry, but I never want to retake another chem lab, and I won't make you do their silly requirements for my class."

This time, the clapping included more students, along with a few cheers, and included Jet.

"Not everything in this class will be exciting, but in the end, it has been my experience that you'll enjoy this class immensely. Today, however, it will be quite basic. Next week, things will fall better into place."

Autumn finished passing out the syllabi, walked to the front of the room, and pulled down a screen. The lights dimmed, and she clicked on a projector. The screen brightened to illustrate a black object, circular and large. It took a moment for Jet's concentration to focus on the item shown. When it did, he almost fell out of his chair. A feeling overwhelmed him: a sense of regret.

The circular object was a black rock, and he'd seen one just like it before. He'd held it several times. He and Mckenzey had found a similar rock while hiking in the hills outside of Silverton a few days before it was destroyed. On the way home, they played a game, and he'd won the right to bring the rock home. He'd planned on giving it back to Mckenzey the same day the disaster destroyed the town. The rock, which had been on his table, was buried beneath the rubble of his home.

"We will study a lot of rocks this semester," Professor Blum said, his voice resonating throughout the room. "Rock types, locations, and structures. So today, I thought it would be nice to show you a rock that isn't native to our planet. What you are looking at is a chondritic meteorite. These are stony meteorites that have become trapped in Earth's gravity and are pulled to Earth's surface. These are progenitors for the early solar system, primitive asteroids. Note that there are chondrules in this type of asteroid."

Autumn pointed to small craters in the rock.

Professor Blum continued, "Chondrules are small granules formed as molten droplets in space. They display textures of extreme cooling, fibrous crystals, porphyritic textures, or other pyroxene fibers. Most meteorites found on earth are chondrites. Throughout the world's collection, there are more than twenty-seven thousand chondrites. Take a look at this next slide; it shows the largest stone ever found, weighing in at over seventeen hundred kilograms. It was found during the Jilin meteorite shower of 1976."

The next slide clicked over, and a gigantic rock filled the screen.

A student next to Jet gasped, then said, "That thing is enormous."

"Another type of meteorite is called an iron meteorite," Professor Blum explained. "It's hypothesized that these meteorites may be part of a former planetary core. Autumn will pass around two chondritic meteorites. Don't take long to identify the chondrules. Feel the texture, draw a quick picture, and pass it to the next student."

Jet felt like his heart was racing.

Autumn walked briskly to the far side of the classroom and set a meteorite on the counter. The entire class watched her like a hawk, Jet included. She placed the second meteorite a half-dozen students away from him. Almost everyone's eyes lingered on Autumn, but Jet was fixated on the meteors. Excitement bubbled within him, and he felt a connection to the rock. He heard Professor Blum talking but couldn't concentrate on anything but the meteorite.

Finally, it was his turn. The small, half-dollar-sized rock felt more substantial than he expected. The cold metallic surface was familiar, and it sparkled with each tiny movement. Closing his eyes, he sensed a spark of warmth in the palm of his hand. Soon his entire arm felt like it was on fire.

"What's happening?" he hissed to himself, and his eyes flashed open.

But the light around him had disappeared entirely, and Jet was plunged into absolute darkness.

CHAPTER 6

Jet couldn't fathom what was happening. He was confident he was no longer in a classroom at Chadwick's, but that didn't explain where he had gone. He couldn't feel his limbs or suck in a deep breath. A small light blinked into existence, strong enough to affect his eyes and he squinted. It was so far away, and he couldn't make out where it was coming from. The brightness slowly became more distinct, and it started contending with the darkness around it. As if alighted on the wings of the wind, Jet flew forward for what felt like miles. When he stopped, he found himself inside a damp stone cavern. A figure lay on a rocky surface in the center of the space, surrounded by a small pool of water. Jet noticed that the glow illuminating the room came unevenly from a clenched fist.

The figure began to stir, shaking its head, and trying to stand. When it finally found its footing, it began exploring the room. Jet followed them with his eyes, taking in everything they did.

Three cylindrical rocks hung from the stone ceiling like decorations. The room had stone walls, a damp ceiling, stalagmites, and a stone floor. A magnitude of unusual colors dotted the walls. Closer to the ground, the walls were filled with majestic red and yellow hues, but farther up, blues and purples became more extensive. The ceiling, twelve feet up, was forest green. Somehow, the colors transitioned perfectly. Jet had never seen anything so beautiful.

In places, some of the cave walls were crumbling. On one of the walls held an interesting pattern. It was more like artwork than random erosion from rainwater. A thickened line of rock ran perfectly straight down the wall for five or six feet, starting from the ceiling. It split into two diagonal lines when it reached the halfway spot. Several inches later, the lines changed directions again, reconnecting to create a diamond before continuing to the floor.

The figure reached out and touched a dark, circular object in the center of the diamond. It had been positioned in the wall and could be turned with ease. Six shapes were carved into the dial—a square, a triangle, a diamond, a circle, a single line, and a double line. Another six shapes were carved into the wall outside the dial—six hieroglyphic animals. The first three images depicted different types of birds: a raven, a hawk, and an owl. The following three animals were a snake, a panther, and a lion.

The figure gripped the dial and began twisting it back and forth. With lightning speed, the dial moved. It did not take long for a pattern to emerge. It recurred five times in a row, and Jet tried to memorize the arrangement.

Almost muffled, a sound caught Jet's attention, and the figure stopped playing with the dial immediately. Their eyes searched a corner of the room that had previously escaped Jet's awareness. Obscurity prevented the light from their hand from penetrating this section of the room effectively. The figure's hand trembled as it held it above its head, attempting to get a better look. There was movement, and two rats scurried across the back wall. The figure relaxed slightly, but then a light blue fog started seeping into the room. There was a sound like fingers on a rock wall and more movement. This time, the shadow of a tall silhouette became emphasized. This creature, taller than any human, had razor-sharp teeth and a long snout.

The human figure spoke for the first time, but it was Jet's voice who asked, "Who's there? Why have you summoned me here?"

Powerful, rich, deep, and ancient, a second voice spoke. "I am Faunal. The end is near, the beginning has passed, and you are not worthy to carry this burden."

"Who are you?"

"I am the designer of this dream, the legend of this lair."

"Stop speaking in riddles," the figure demanded.

A throaty laugh clamored around the room. "You know nothing and would not command me if you did."

"What do you want from me?"

"Failure and death."

The light in the figure's hand pulsated, blasting outward, cutting through the fog and the blackness. Jet's eyes widened as he beheld the creature, somehow trapped within the cavern wall. He'd never imagined such a beast. Black fur covered its entire body. Pointed ears jutted from the top of its head, and a long snarling snout revealed sharp glinting teeth. Standing on its hind legs emphasized its tall, muscular, and formidable frame. It resembled a wolf in all but speech.

"That's a powerful emblem in our hand," hissed the creature.

"The principle of light."

A howl cut through the air as if the creature wanted to attack but was unable. Breathing heavily, Faunal managed to say, "This is your one free pass to my domain. If you come here again, it will be for a greater purpose. Depart now."

The creature's hands moved in a blur. A gust of wind, like a veiled attack, shot forward against the more petite figure. The figure's hand reflexively opened ,as if shielding from the attack, and a rock clattered to the floor. The light in the room vanished, as though it had never been there.

CHAPTER 7

Loud laughter berated Jet's ears, and the brightness of the lights was staggering. It took several long moments before he realized he was sprawled on the floor of the science building. Around him, several students were openly laughing at him and a few pointed fingers. Luckily, he was lying on his uninjured arm. Suddenly, hands were helping him into a seated position.

Autumn's voice said, "Let's try to get you to your seat without hurting your good shoulder."

He pushed himself up and mumbled with some effort, "My bad. That's one slippery stool."

A few students clapped in jest as he returned to his seat.

"Do you want to hold the meteorite again?" Autumn was staring at him, trying hard to hold back a fit of laughter.

"No." He sighed, placing his head back onto the counter. "I had my turn."

"Feeling a little jumpy?" she snickered. "Or a little clumsy."

Before he answered, Professor Blum materialized at her side. "Is everything all right, Autumn?"

"Yes, professor. Mr. Black just asked me a question."

"Oh, good." The professor stared intently at Jet. His head tilted to the side, and he asked, "Are you sure you're all right, young man? You're pale."

"I'm fine." Jet sat up quickly. He wanted to melt into the cement and disappear.

"Good!" Professor Blum exclaimed. "Did you say you were Mr. Black?"

"Yes, sir."

"Can you please follow me for a minute?"

Jet glanced at Autumn. She gave another one of her dazzling smiles and handed the meteorite to the next student. "I guess," he replied.

Together, the three of them walked to the front of the classroom. As Jet stepped through the door, he found a back room, like a spacious storage room with several shelves full of Bunsen burners, microscopes, beakers, and other pieces of equipment. Against the back wall, he also noticed some water baths, a centrifuge machine, and a large autoclave for cleaning instruments. Turning left, he followed Professor Blum into another room, almost like a single office, with only a small desk, a shelf, and two chairs.

Professor Blum opened his briefcase and said, "Joshua, please have a seat."

Jet fidgeted with his hands. Glancing at Autumn, he felt helpless, but her face revealed nothing. He sat in the closest chair.

A laptop computer, books, and several papers were situated on the table. Two insulated boxes lay open—each one was rectangular and half the size of a shoebox. A circular portion in the center of each box was missing as if an item could be stored there.

Temporarily forgetting his trepidation, Jet asked, "Is this where you keep the meteorites?"

"It is," Professor Blum said distractedly. "These cases are more for travel purposes than anything else."

"The meteorites are pretty sweet."

Moving the cases to the floor, Professor Blum asked, "Have you ever seen one before?"

"No," Jet said quickly. "But I'm impressed."

"That's the spirit, young man," Professor Blum said. "I'm looking for another assistant in the lab, and I've heard that you might be the perfect person. As you may have seen, many items are used during the different labs taught in this building. Autumn is my primary assistant, but she'll be busy with many of the classes in this building. She's already taken this class. Every year I pick a current student to be involved with."

He snuck a glance at Autumn. She'd known this entire time. Her eyes sparkled mischievously. He mouthed, "Thanks."

She winked back.

Professor Blum seemed not to notice. He continued, "You seem excited about this class, and I think you'll find yourself learning immensely. It's a great opportunity."

"Is this something I could think about?"

"I'd prefer to have this settled today. As a teaching assistant, you'll have some free access to the supplies and extra time to work on the projects. Additionally, you'll learn about other classes, and you may be asked to help them from time to time."

This was a double-edged sword. He wanted access but working with Autumn would be interesting. Finally, he said, "I'll do it."

"Fantastic! It shouldn't take much of your time, though some weeks will be busier than others." After a moment, he added, "And it pays, just not very well. But for high school, that's pretty good."

"Even better."

Professor Blum reached out his hand and shook Jet's. The next instant, he and Autumn were being ushered back into the already emptying classroom. As Jet made his way to his seat, he noticed that the palm of his hand was beginning to itch. There was a sizeable blister and two cuts at the center where the meteorite had touched his skin. His fingers rubbed the area, but it was painless.

Jet picked up his backpack and headed to the door. Autumn was gone, but Professor Blum was exiting the front room. Jet hurried forward and held the door open. He asked, "Professor, where did you get those meteorites?"

"Truthfully, I bought them from a scientist." In a boastful voice, he added, "And can you imagine where he got them?"

"No clue."

"Silverton, Oregon. Have you heard of it?"

Jet's heartbeat quickened. He managed to say, "Who hasn't. Are you sure?"

"Without a doubt, my boy."

"That's incredible."

"Meteorites discovered in Silverton are one of many scientific oddities in that region. Other types of rocks found there have also been remarkable. There are four high-threat volcanoes in Oregon, but Silverton isn't close to one of them. It wasn't on anyone's radar. The gashes in the ground have been studied from the air, and they frankly don't make any sense. There will be so much more to study; they're just scratching the surface." Professor Blum continued through the open door. He added, "We will explore Silverton more during the year."

"I'm intrigued," Jet said.

"At the end of the week, stop by my office to sign some paperwork."

Rising pressure at his temples caused Jet to close his eyes. It was the same external force that had tried entering his head when he was rock climbing. He quickly added, "No problem," but feared another attack.

Professor Blum asked, "Are you sure you're feeling okay?"

"Oh, yes. I just forgot something at my desk. I'll talk to you later." Jet retraced his steps but had only gone a few feet when he felt another mental attack pressing on his mind. As the classroom door shut behind him, he closed his eyes and clenched his fists.

Into this mind came another vision of sorts; it was the silhouetted creature he'd seen inside that cavern. This time, he saw a protective chest plate and silver greaves on its thighs and lower legs. A dagger with a black handle hung across its chest.

A raspy voice, ancient but clear, entered his mind. "Bravo, apprentice, for making it this far. But you're several steps behind. You're quick to judge and quick to dismiss. Your gifts are decaying, and your future is bleak. You may have survived my first attack, but I am waiting for the day I can openly attack the Elementals. Torment looms on a wave of darkness that will punish the Sorcerers, the Mystics, the searchers, and the protectors. Your worth is still being measured."

CHAPTER 8

Following the end of class on Thursday, Jet waited with little patience inside his dorm. His friends were already late. When the door eventually flew open, Jet found Jayco and Grantham standing on the precipice, shaking their heads at him.

"Where have you been?" Jet demanded, hurrying from his dorm.

"Chill, bro," Grantham replied.

"I was just excited to see you guys," Jet replied, trying to calm his nerves as he pushed the button to open the elevator.

"Are you ready to have some fun?" Jayco asked.

"Of course."

As the elevator descended, Grantham said, "It's too bad you missed my cross country meet last night."

"I wanted to go," Jet said. "How did you do?"

"Several high schools were there—it was an invitational. They had some speedy runners, but we did well. Our school's top runner was Cory Jenkins. He's a beast. I ran a personal best of sixteen minutes and twenty seconds. I was just outside the top fifteen. It was a great race."

"I didn't know you could run that fast."

"Neither did he," Jayco said.

Jet asked, "Have you been training?"

"Almost every night. It's way too hot during the day. They held the meet at ten at night because of the heat. Five people went to the hospital for heatstroke-like symptoms."

"That's scary."

"Tell me about it."

The elevator door opened, and Jet followed his friends to a side room on the first floor, large enough for the twenty or so people waiting for them. He saw Ariana, Raul, Mckenzey, and Latisha up front and center. There was a giant birthday cake, several presents, loud music, and a disco ball.

As he stepped into the room, everyone shouted, "HAPPY BIRTHDAY!"

Jet stopped walking, shocked. He had no idea that his friends had gone to all this trouble to surprise him. He had thought they were just going for dinner. He turned to Jayco and Grantham to say thanks, and the smile on Jet's face must've told the story.

Grantham said, "Looks like we fooled you."

"You can say that again."

Jayco added, "Can the fun start yet, officially?"

Jet was swarmed by people he knew and didn't. He was pulled into several different conversations, enjoying every moment. He scarfed down three pieces of cake and thoroughly enjoyed himself.

Jet made his way toward Raul and his sister, wanting to clear the air with them. As he approached, he said, "The Flores siblings."

Ariana asked, "Did you know about the party?"

"I didn't."

"Leave it to Grantham and Jayco to keep this good of a surprise."

Jet eyed Raul. "Thank you guys so much for coming."

Raul touched the collar of his shirt and said, "No problem. It's been a while, and I wanted to see you."

"You look great. Classes treating you well?"

"It's good to be back. I feel better, calmer. Not too stressed. I think I've turned a corner." Raul was two inches taller than Jet but skinnier. He had brown hair and brown eyes. Those eyes had been full of excitement last year, especially when he and Jet talked about the future, girls, and exploring campus. Now Raul's eyes appeared slightly duller. He had been through a difficult time; Jet knew that.

Turning to Ariana, Jet said, "Glad you *both* made it. I miss you guys."

"We miss you too," Ariana said, her smile genuine and happy. Glancing around, she said, "A great turnout." Ariana was several inches shorter than her brother. She was so charismatic. He'd always connected with her easily. What set Ariana apart from others was that she made you feel like the center of the world. Jet missed that.

Jayco bellowed to the group, "Time for the piñata! Then we have karaoke. Jet, you're up first."

Ariana's cell phone rang, and her face flushed slightly. She mouthed, "We can't stay. Just wanted to stop by and see you. Let's meet up for lunch or something."

"Sounds great."

Raul half hugged Jet, adding, "Happy birthday, bro."

"Thanks, man. It means a lot."

Jet was suddenly dragged to the center of the room. He watched Ariana and Raul disappear, more confused than ever. It was great to see them, but so much had changed. A part of him wished he could go back to last year. Jayco had brought the biggest piñata he'd ever seen. It was a large donkey consisting of several bright colors and plenty of sparkles.

Jayco announced loudly, "There are the coolest prizes inside. Gift cards for food, drinks, movies, and more. There are some candy, headphones, and other toys. All of which was Jet's idea."

Jet was suddenly blindfolded, handed a broomstick, and spun around three times. He couldn't see anything. He started swinging, but it was a pathetic attempt with only one good arm. He swung three times, and his only connection was a glancing blow. Fifteen students later, the piñata finally broke. Jayco pummeled the neck of the donkey, and it crashed to the ground. A frenzy broke loose as everyone dove for all the treats.

Karaoke turned out to be the funniest thing ever. The first five contestants used their usual voices, but to spice things up, Latisha had created a spin wheel. You were given a character by spinning the wheel, and you had to mimic their voice while singing. The voices included: Roger Rabbit, Darth Vader, Gollum, and a bunch more. The ensuing songs were hysterical. Grantham's attempt at singing in a Yogi Bear voice to a rap song caused Jet to laugh so hard he cried.

The party started to thin out an hour later, and Jet was hopeful to finish a paper before tomorrow's classes. Latisha and Mckenzey had already said their goodbyes and left. As the lights were turned out and the door closed, he turned to Jayco and Grantham and said, "Thanks, guys. This has seriously been one of the best days I've had in my life."

"No problem," Grantham said. "It was a blast."

Jayco added, "It's not every year you turn sixteen. Now we just need to work on getting your license."

"Very soon." Jet added, "That piñata was as big as me. Thanks for supplying all those gifts. I owe you big."

"No worries," Jayco said. "Just glad you liked it."

Grantham slapped his shoulder and added, "Have a good night. We'll catch you later."

Jet smiled to himself and headed for the stairs. Suddenly, Mckenzey stepped into view and asked, "Can we go for a walk?"

Without hesitation, he said, "Let's go."

As they stepped outside, Mckenzey said, "I can't understand how there's a chance that the temperatures next week will be even worse."

"This heat is making everyone angry. I shower a few times a day just to cool down. My air conditioner can't hold on much longer."

He was about to tell her about his geology lab when she handed him a package and said, "Happy birthday."

"What's this?"

"Open and see."

He tore open the package and stared at it. It was a very detailed and accurate painting of his house back in Silverton. It was from the vantage point of his backyard. He could see part of the barn and the small pond, but most of the painting was the back of his house and the wraparound porch. It affected him more than he thought possible. He longed to be back home, felt the happiness of living there, and regretted that it had been destroyed. He asked, "Did you paint this?"

"I did. I hope you like it. It took me the last two weeks of summer. This house has always been so special to me. I was debating on still giving it to you. I wasn't sure you'd want such a reminder."

"It's perfect. Amazing! I love it."

She grinned, a clear sense of relief spreading across her face.

They stored their items at the beach, including Jet's backpack and the painting, and walked toward the water.

Mckenzey asked, "Can you tell me again about escaping Silverton?"

"Like what?"

"You said a gully hit your house. What did you mean?"

"There were three. I didn't see them at first because there was so much blue fog around my house. I heard a crashing sound—dozens of breaking trees. The first gully hit the pond, the second the barn, and the third crashed into my house."

"I don't remember you talking about blue fog before?" She had stopped at the water's edge, staring at him with disbelief.

"Sorry. There is always fog around Silverton. It was just weird that it was blue. It made the entire landscape look ghostly."

Mckenzey eased farther into the water. "What else?"

"Inside my room, when the house was crashing down, the shadow box on the wall fell and broke. I had to step over it to escape my bedroom."

"Wasn't it on the wall?"

"Yes. Everything inside was scattered, and the only thing I could reach was the wooden box. I picked it up, but it wasn't empty. There was an old book hidden inside. I grabbed it, sprinted upstairs, and found Nana. She was already halfway down the hall with this big duffle bag. When I came down the stairs, things started to get worse. Somehow, we got out through the back door and crossed a river of lava. You know the rest."

"And what part did you forget?"

"How I escaped from the house. I remembered the blue fog, an old book, and gullies the entire time."

"That's crazy."

"One of many things, I guess."

A moment later, she said, "I've something I need to tell you."

Jet felt his insides squirm, and he held his breath. Was he about to hear his worst fear? If she was leaving, should he tell her how he felt? *No*, he thought. That would only cause more problems. He hesitantly asked, "What kind of something?"

"For the last week, I've had the same dream over and over." Her hand touched his arm, and she said excitedly, "In my dream, there's this crazy thick blue fog. It's eerie."

Jet wasn't sure he heard correctly. "You dreamt about fog?"

"For the last week. But..." —she moved closer — "I also dreamt about blue fog the night before Silverton was destroyed. The two dreams are different from each other."

"I don't think I understand."

"In my first dream, I pictured fog descending like a waterfall onto Silverton, and it was somehow alive. It was searching for something. I raced outside of town, maybe as far as your house." She paused to brush a strand of hair from her face and behind her ear. "The fog was rolling over itself, like worms in a bucket. It was so cool. In the dream, my vantage point was from above, like from the eyes of a bird. I never saw it reach your house because my phone started ringing. You were calling. It was the most vivid dream I'd ever had. I didn't even put the pieces together until you mentioned the blue fog."

Jet said, "I don't think it's that unusual to dream about fog."

"That's what I thought." She glanced at him, her eyes sparkling. "I've had the same dream for the last five or six nights."

"The same dream as before."

"A different one. Again, my perspective is from above, and I see this fog, and it's everywhere—an ocean of fog. Later in the dream, I realize that below the fog is some water, and an object is just below the surface. It seems like there's a light shining from under the water. A feeling of impending doom overwhelms me, and I wake up."

"That's intense. Why blue fog?"

"Not sure," she admitted. "At first, I thought something bad would happen last week, like before. Last night, I was allowed to see a little more of the dream. I think that under the water is a boat or something."

Jet considered her words. In his mind, he thought a puzzle piece had fallen into place. Indeed, he didn't understand most of what he wanted to know, but he was reasonably sure that the beginning of whatever story he was allowed to see must be with the book he found. Then the wolf creature's image entered his mind, and there had been blue fog at the end of the vision. Something strange was undoubtedly taking shape.

Jet said, "Everything doesn't fit perfectly, especially not about the fog, but I think I'm beginning to see a connection with some of the bizarre things happening around us."

"Glad it does for you, but I'm completely lost."

"I think I have a few more pieces than you do."

"What do you mean?"

"It's the book I was telling you about."

"The one you found inside the shadow box?"

"The very same." Noticing her confusion, he added, "It is different than any other book I've ever seen. It's old but in good shape. I know how crazy this sounds, but I think it had a spell that prevented me from opening it. That was, until a few days ago."

"A spell?" she asked skeptically. "And you couldn't open it?"

"For the last three years, it's remained stubbornly closed. Not a single page would open. I can show you."

"I guess," she said doubtfully.

He ran from the water to his backpack and returned with the book in hand a moment later. He opened it to the first page and tried turning the second page without success.

"What the …?" Mckenzey took the book and tried unsuccessfully to turn the page. She closed the book and studied both the front and back covers. She ran her hand along the spine. "I wonder if there's a button or lever of sorts." Finding nothing, she said, "*The Sorcerer's Guide*. It does look old."

"Read what it says."

She tried to open the book, but it remained closed. Tilting her head, she asked, "A joke?"

"Not at all."

Taking back the book, and with minimal effort, he opened the first page and handed it back to her.

Glancing down to read, she suddenly thrust the book back at Jet and asked, "What are you trying to prove?"

"What do you mean?"

"The page is blank."

"No, it's not." Pointing to the first few lines, he read, "Millennia ago, Goth Airtha, the chosen land, was ruled by 10 Kings known as the Council. Peace and prosperity reigned for centuries, but a wind of change was forewarned by insight. The Grey Panther, leader of the Council, dissented and brought forth hatred and rebellion among his brethren."

"I don't see that," she interrupted. "It's just blank."

"Can you read it if I'm holding it?" He turned the book toward her.

"Nope."

"I promise. This book has a story in it. I wouldn't prank you about something like this."

"Read it to me," she said calmly.

He did. She had him stop and restart every few lines, as if trying to catch him in a lie. But soon, he could see her mouthing the names Arisol, Leotyton, Lady Gaea, and Erpofalco.

CHAPTER 9

After Jet read the fable another few times, Mckenzey asked, "Do we know the name of the tablet?"

"Maybe the Phoenix," he said, but he wasn't sure this was accurate.

"Maybe," her voice hesitated for a moment. "What kind of gifts are they talking about? What's the importance of a lion, snake, falcon, and owl? What's a Rune? How did Arisol draw a Rune into the ground? What kind of power is that?"

The questions surprised Jet and made him feel a sense of relief. She was taking this better than he'd hoped. When they began talking about a solar calendar countdown, and two books, a chill emerged on the base of his neck, as if someone were watching them. He quickly turned, his eyes raking up and down the shoreline. He saw no one, but it was starting to get dark. He was surprised to find how much time had passed.

"I need to tell you something else," he whispered.

"Like what?"

"I warn you, more weirdness." He gently guided her toward their belongings. "You see, I had a vision or something that I can't even understand. It happened a few days ago in my geology lab. Do you remember that rock we found in the hills outside of Silverton?"

"The one that we found together, but you took home first. Then you promptly lost it."

"Yeah, that one."

"How could I forget?"

"Turns out, it wasn't a rock after all. It was a meteorite."

"A meteorite? Are you sure?"

"I saw two more of them in my geology lab. They were the same, and I touched one of them. When I asked the professor where he'd gotten them, he said Silverton. I mean, what are the chances?"

"Could one of them be the one you lost?"

"I doubt it," Jet said. "Anyway, I had the vision when I first touched the meteorite." He described everything inside the cave, including the creature and the blue fog. After finishing, he held out the palm of his hand. "Take a look at this."

"What is it?"

"When I touched the meteorite, it must've burned my skin."

Her fingers explored his wound carefully. "Could that thing you saw be one of the creatures in the story you read me?"

"I never thought of that."

"And again, we have blue fog." Her smile was contagious, and his heart skipped a beat.

Jet managed to recover. "Exactly. There's a connection with the fog, your dreams, Silverton, the meteorites, and the opening of my book. I'm pretty sure the fable is the central piece."

"It's time to tell the others," Mckenzey said.

Jet asked, "Do you think they'll believe us?"

"I doubt it. But this book, our stories, and that emblem on your palm are hard to overlook. I say we find them tonight. Let's head to my dorm and we'll call over Grantham and Jayco."

"Okay," Jet said hesitantly. "If you say so."

"This is the first time in four years that I have answers. It's the first time I feel that my life is starting to make sense."

They quickly found their possessions and stopped at a washing station. They cleaned off their feet and hurried along the boardwalk. Hundreds of students were still playing volleyball, football, or splashing in the water. The sun had dropped below the horizon, and twilight had settled in, but the heat was unwavering.

As they neared the center of campus, the path became crowded with other students. Mckenzey tugged at Jet's arm and said, "Let's cross here."

They stepped into the street along with two dozen other students. Halfway across, someone slammed into him from behind, sending him sprawling face-first onto the ground. He instinctively rolled to protect his shoulder and ended up on his side. The person who'd crashed into him landed a few feet away. Pain flared, but it could've been worse. He rose to his knees and frantically made sure his backpack was firmly attached. After standing, he made his way over to the guy who had crashed into him and reached out his uninjured arm. "Sorry about that."

There was no response.

Jet's head tilted slightly, and he asked, "Are you injured?"

The boy stared unblinking at the ground, and Jet thought he looked familiar. Two similarly dressed male students with white jeans and brown shirts lifted the boy from the ground. In an instant, the figure was recognizable. He was a picture-perfect description of the person Napoleon had characterized outside his dorm in the first week of classes. The boy had brown spikey hair, a dog collar around his neck, and two bracelets on his wrists.

The boy unleashed a wicked grin and winked. A chill ran down Jet's spine. A hand gripped his wrist, and he was pulled by Mckenzey to the opposite side of the road.

She asked, "You okay?"

"No permanent damage. But I think that kid ran into me on purpose."

"Why would he do that?"

"Not sure. But the first few days of classes, Napoleon stopped by and told us that someone had been lurking outside our dorm floor. That was him."

"Are you sure?"

"One hundred and ten percent."

"Do you think it means something?"

"Without a doubt. He's also friends with Shane." Jet's fingers felt the smooth leather binding of his book, safe in his sack. "Let's hurry to your dorm."

Ahead of them, several of the streetlamps blinked as they stepped out from an alley and into one of the largest open spaces on campus. There were a dozen study tables throughout this area, several trees, two volleyball courts, and three different walkways. They hurried forward on the far-left path when there was a flicker of movement ahead of them. Mckenzey must've seen it too, as they stopped moving at the same time. Four figures spilled out of the same alley.

"We're being surrounded," he hissed.

Mckenzey said, "This is not what I was hoping for tonight."

They moved forward cautiously. A figure stepped out from behind a tree and onto the path; it was Shane Fallon. More figures emerged, and soon in front of them was a boy named Rocky, two more boys, and a girl. Jet sighed as he realized none of them were Raul or Ariana. Shane was the leader of the Dark Angels, and these four must be in the inner circle. Besides Shane, Jet only knew Rocky.

"Well, if it isn't Black and his new girlfriend," Shane sneered.

Nodding to the girl standing near Shane, Jet said, "Looks better than what you've got."

The girl stalked forward like a predator. She was quick, intense, and her vibe screamed cruelty.

"Stop!" Shane shouted. The girl paused but continued to glare. Shane's voice was musical when he said, "Funny, Black. Where do you come up with these jokes?"

Jet remained silent. He didn't like how this was going.

"Let me introduce you to my friends. This lovely lady is Jessiva, next to her is Clyde, and then Nash. They're transfers from Dillon Lake, another boarding school. You probably remember Rocky."

Mckenzey's head tilted up.

"Can't say that I do," Jet lied. "But thanks for the introductions."

Clyde was stocky and appeared shrewd next to Jessiva. Nash was slightly smaller than a giant, and Rocky could bench press a submarine. He had two arm sleeves of tattoos, bulging biceps, and resembled a college student with his beard.

It was Jet's turn to take Mckenzey by the arm. He led her onto the grass. Nash and Clyde quickly stepped in front of them.

Jet asked, "What do you want?"

"We just want to talk," Shane scoffed.

"Tempting, but no thanks. We've got somewhere to be. If you could let us pass, we could meet up tomorrow and chat."

Inching closer, Shane said, "I don't think so. This will only take a sec." Clearing his voice, he asked, "Question number one: Are you dating Ariana Flores?"

"Why don't you ask her? I'm sure you've seen her more this summer than I have."

"I guess that's a no." Shane snorted. "And this girl," he added, nodding to Mckenzey, "is a few steps down."

Jet felt Mckenzey tense as Shane's inner circle snickered.

"Question number two: Do you own a car?"

"An even dumber question," Jet said, wanting to get this over as quickly as possible.

"I guess that's a no too. I knew that one before I asked. I mean, check out your clothes. You couldn't wear those and own a car. Mommy and Daddy probably can't afford one." More laughter. Holding up three fingers, Shane asked, "Oh, wait, question number three: Did your parents die when you were younger?"

Jet tensed, and his right hand squeezed into a fist that he kept low and out of view. He remained silent as Mckenzey gripped his sling.

Shane inched closer, a look of triumph on his face. "Well, that was a free question because I already know that answer. I want to know if they died here in the US or in another country like Germany or Egypt? Were they tourists or just plain idiots?"

Jet lunged at Shane, his fist swinging wildly. Shane sidestepped him easily. Nash, despite his size, shot out like a cannon and crashed into Jet's side. A blast of pain ripped through his shoulder and ribs. An instant later, Clyde hit from the opposite side; this time, Jet was lifted off his feet and thrown to the ground. His backpack remained firmly attached, but Mckenzey's picture flew several feet away. Jet willed his vision to slow or for time to stop, but neither happened. Nash smacked the back of Jet's head, and his vision blurred.

Clyde grabbed a fistful of Jet's brown hair and breathed into his ear. "Let's see if your girlfriend is a better fighter than you are."

Reacting without thinking, Jet jerked his right elbow back, and it collided with the side of Clyde's mouth. Blood gushed from a deep gash on his lip. Jet sprang to his feet; his next fist connected with the side of Clyde's head, who wobbled slightly, and Jet followed this with a punch to the stomach. Clyde leaned forward, gasping for air. The last strike was a knee to Clyde's face, and he toppled to the ground, unconscious.

Rocky reacted much slower. He kicked, but Jet responded by lifting his leg to block. The pain in his shin was intense, but he stayed on his feet and was pushed back a few feet. To his surprise, Rocky had received the brunt of the pain and was bent over, holding his leg. Nash bull-rushed Jet and slammed into his uninjured shoulder, spinning him around. Before he could react, two quick jabs smacked his face, and blood started to flow from his nose.

From what seemed like far away, Jet heard Shane's voice declare, "You're not special at all, neither of you is. What a waste! I couldn't have been more disappointed. Just like your parents."

Jet lunged again at Shane, rage almost entirely blinding him. Nash quickly knocked Jet to the ground. Jet's chest heaved up and down. The fight was over, and Jessiva stepped into view. The cruelty on her face was unsurprising as she aimed a kick at the side of his head. Then, suddenly, hair flew, and Jessiva went feet-over-face as Mckenzey crashed into her. Somehow Mckenzey landed on top and started raining down blows. A wave of primeval anger washed over him, and he rolled onto his knees to stand. Nash was momentarily distracted by Jessiva's fall from grace, so Jet kicked the side of his knee as hard as possible. The impact sound was unnatural, like a hollow piece of wood slamming against a rock. Nash screamed as he fell to the ground.

Jet turned to Shane, who stood there confidently, with a smirk on his face. Shane raised his hand into the air. Unsure what was about to happen, Jet lifted both hands protectively and retreated to where Mckenzey was. He picked up the painting, pulled her to her feet, and they both sprinted down the path, running all the way to Mckenzey's dorm.

As they reached the front doors, Jet bent over, trying to catch his breath.

Mckenzey asked, "Are you okay?"

Unable to answer, Jet tried to slow his breathing. Using his shirt, he wiped the blood from his face. Half his head felt swollen. His left arm throbbed and wasn't working very well—he hoped he hadn't reinjured it. But despite all his pains, he felt dangerously enraged.

Mckenzey guided him into the lobby and onto a couch. A few students stared at them.

Jet asked, "How are your hands feeling?"

"Good. Real good."

Jet burst out laughing.

Mckenzey left and returned a moment later with a wet paper towel. She fussed over him for the next few minutes. Once finished, Jet said, "After getting the crap beat out of me, I'm fine."

"I think you held your own."

"Me?" He laughed again. "You knocked over that girl and pounded her."

"I went to a fighting gym this summer."

"I didn't know that."

"Putting that stuff into practice felt pretty sweet."

"You flattened her. That was awesome."

Seeing Mckenzey smile, Jet's anger began to fade.

"Should we report them?"

"I don't know. I shouldn't have fought like that."

"They were baiting you. Those were horrible questions for Shane to ask, especially about your parents. It made me angry. I can only imagine how you were feeling." She added, "Want to come up and talk to Latisha? Those wounds need to be cleaned better."

"No. Not tonight. I just want to go home."

"Come on, Jet, please come up."

He stood, adding, "Thanks for saving my bacon. I'm going home and taking a shower. I'm okay, Mckenzey."

"Let's hang out tomorrow after school."

"Maybe. I'll let you know."

CHAPTER 10

The revelation that Shane potentially knew more about Jet's parents' death than he did was not sitting well with him. He kept replaying the exchange with Shane from four days ago. As far as he knew, Jet's parents had died in a bus accident six years ago. The entire bus had rolled down an embankment. His dad had started drinking again, which led to several arguments with his mom. Jet's dad had promised to do better and took his mom on a getaway for their anniversary. Had what he been told by Nana been the complete truth?

After his parents' deaths, Jet went to live with Nana. He had no siblings, and with his grandpa dying several years earlier, it was a perfect fit.

Jet had skipped classes the day after the fight, a Friday, and emailed his teachers. He also missed the school's paintball outing later that night. Afterward, Jayco and Grantham had gushed about their team winning all their matches.

To get his classes excused, he had to explain to the school nurse that he was in a bike accident and had to meet with her in the admin building. She was easy to convince with all his face, shoulder, and leg injuries. She had commented that she'd seen a similar injury a few days before, and also that riding a bike was a stupid thing to do so soon after surgery. He was admonished to 'be more careful.' All his

86

teachers sent over notes and his homework, and he spent the weekend inside his room, feeling sorry for himself.

Mckenzey had called four times. His friends tried to convince him to go to Jayco's first football game of the season on Saturday. The Chadwick's Dolphins had won all but one game last season and lost in the championship game. The hype was steep, but they already had a preseason ranking of number three. Jet declined but passed along his hopes that they trounced their rivals. Sunday afternoon, Jayco called back, giving him a play-by-play on their 40-14 win.

Jet rolled out of bed; his pillow and shirt were drenched with sweat, and salt crusted his face. His head pounded like he'd been hit by a train as he dragged himself into the shower. It was a new week and a new day. He was ready to return to classes. After showering, he left his dorm with plenty of time to make his first class. The thermostat on the ground floor read one-hundred and two.

"Chalk this up to global warming," insisted a short, brown-haired girl with beige skin standing near the front door of the building. Several heads nodded at her words. One girl did not, and she shook her head decisively. Jet had seen this girl on campus, and thought her name was Keesha. She had rich black hair and dark brown skin with a soft rose undertone.

The girl argued, "Ideas about global warming are rubbish; all they want is to tell others how to live."

The first girl appeared to grow agitated at this. "Either way, Keesha, the temperature is scorching. It has never been this hot this late in the year. How do you explain that?"

"Never is a little dramatic, Rebecca. But I'll agree on one thing; it's hotter than an angry devil." Keesha turned and smiled at Jet as he tried to slip out the front door. Her face contorted as her eyes settled on his face. "Honey, that looks like it hurts."

He wasn't surprised by the comment. His face could double as a punching bag; in fact, it had. Forcing a smile, he said, "Flipped over the handlebars while biking. But I have a test this morning, and I have no choice but to go to class."

She nodded. "Next time, choose a softer landing."

"Good advice."

"And by the way, you should get your head checked for a concussion. It's Monday and a holiday, so there's no school."

"Best news of the day." Jet sighed. "And fantastic advice."

"You're not going out in this heat, are you?"

"Just for a short walk."

"It's already hotter than my momma's BBQ ribs. And that's saying something."

"Those sound delicious. I've been cooped up in my dorm for a few days. I'll find some air conditioning. Anywhere except inside my dorm."

"Go have yourself a blast."

"You too." He stepped into the scorching sunshine and immediately regretted leaving the comforts of the building. He would've gone right back inside if he hadn't just talked with Keesha.

He strolled aimlessly across campus. There were only a few students near the beach or anywhere in sight. After ten minutes, he found himself turning the corner of the science building. This would give him a chance to look around. Using the key he'd been given, he let himself inside. He placed his backpack on the front table and began to explore. He started making his way toward the back room when a man emerged from there, startling Jet. The man, well over six feet tall and broad-shouldered, barely reacted.

"Excuse me," the man said suspiciously as Jet tried to regain his footing. "Sorry to have surprised you."

Jet answered quickly, "I didn't realize anyone else was here."

The man wore thick black glasses and a white lab coat. He held a beaker of white liquid with some brownish gas escaping from the opening. "Me neither." The man scrutinized Jet.

"Ah. Yes." Jet smiled. "This is my classroom for a geology lab with Professor Blum. He asked me to help him as a TA. He wanted me to drop by and become familiar with the classroom and the lab room in the back."

"I don't think that he's here today. After all, it is a holiday."

"I know. I wanted to look around."

"Right. You must be…Mr. Black." The man held out his hand. "I'm Professor Rysen. I teach basic chemistry."

"Lucky you," Jet said hastily.

"A lover of chemistry, I see."

Shaking his head, Jet said, "Not really. How did you know who I was?"

"Professor Blum told me that he'd asked three students to assist our other two TAs. If my memory serves me, I think you'll be working with Autumn, who will be the TA for three of the classes in this building. I've already met the other two—Rachael Donaldson and Gregory French." Leaning against the desk, Professor Rysen asked, "Are you from around here?"

"No. I'm not from California, though sometimes I wish that I were. I'm from Portland."

"Well, welcome."

"I don't remember you teaching chem last year."

"This is my first year. I transferred, lucky for me. California is amazing! Well, Mr. Black, I'll let you continue looking around. I'm across the hall if you have any questions."

"Thank you, Professor Rysen."

After the door closed, Jet walked into the back room. It was impressive for the sheer volume and variety of items it held; it could rival most medium-sized colleges. Bunsen Burners, beakers, and pipettes were strung along the right side of the room. On the back wall were shelves of rocks, crystals, and microscopes. Several signs identified the rocks: obsidian, pumice, basalt, tuff, granite, rhyolite, diorite, andesite, quartz, mica, and fluorite.

To his right sat a shelf full of flat rocks with designs. As he approached, he was surprised to find a collection of fossils, including fishes, trilobites, plants, shells, and other things he didn't recognize. The largest fossil was a square rock with several circular shells like snail shells. It was as big as a door. Some shells were embedded within the rock, while others stuck out. It was remarkable.

Over the last few years, he had developed an obsession with volcanoes, earthquakes, and lava. He desired nothing more than to learn everything about why Silverton had been destroyed. Dozens of scientists had descended on his hometown and stayed for years trying to do the same thing. They barely understood what had happened; maybe he could find a breakthrough if he was lucky enough.

Twenty minutes later, he stepped back into the classroom and groaned. Professor Rysen was back, but he wasn't alone. Autumn sat at one of the workstations talking with him. Looking up when he stepped into the room, she waved him over.

As Jet approached, Rysen said, "It was destiny that both of you came here today. Autumn and I were going over some of the requirements of the TAs. I guess you guys haven't had a chance to talk yet. This is perfect timing."

Autumn said quickly, "Thank you, Professor Rysen. This has been very helpful. I didn't expect Josh to be here, so this works out well." Did he imagine it, or did Autumn look as uncomfortable as he felt?

In that instant, Jet realized that his torture was officially beginning. His mouth went dry, and his legs were thick and immovable. He sat quickly as Professor Rysen left the room.

"Looks like you took a beating," Autumn exclaimed as the door closed.

"Oh, me? That's nothing. Just riding a bike and crashing. It seems like everything hurts."

"A bike accident?" she asked questioningly. "So soon after your last fall. Those bruises look like they hurt." Reaching out, her fingers brushed up against his left cheek. He instinctively jerked back. She rolled her eyes playfully. "Settle down there, tiger."

"Uh—"

"So, only your face was injured."

"I've got a few scrapes on my knees and elbows."

"Looks like you did a number on yourself." She frowned at him for several seconds. "You've had a chance to look around?"

"Yeah." His eyes settled on her face, and just as quickly, he glanced away. She was adorable, and he hated how easily his hormones kicked into gear. He felt his cheeks blush. This was downright embarrassing.

"Josh, did you hear me?"

Clearing his throat, he said, "Sorry, I didn't."

"I was asking if you had any questions."

"You can call me Jet."

"Like an airplane?"

"Yeppers."

"We'll see," she teased. "Questions?

Leaning back in his chair, he asked, "Why choose me? Was it punishment?"

"What do you mean?" Autumn asked innocently. "You were the only one for me."

"So, it wasn't a coincidence that you chose me?"

"It wasn't anything more than picking a name from a list."

He wasn't convinced.

She continued, "A few teachers use these classrooms, not just Professor Blum. You and two other students will help the five teachers in this building, not including Professor Rysen. He just told me that he doesn't get one."

"Fabulous."

"It'll take a few weeks to get more comfortable. Luckily, though, your assignment will be helping with just your class unless there's an emergency. The single best part is that this is a paying gig."

"That's why I'm here. That, and I love self-torture."

Autumn laughed. She added, "I spoke with Professor Blum, and he wants you to pick a day to come in and help set up."

"How about tomorrow afternoon?" Jet asked, running his hand through his thick hair. He had a distinct feeling that she was watching him closely.

"Perfect. This week is different, and your lab has been moved to Wednesday. I think the best day for you to come in is Monday. Will that work?"

"No problem."

"I'll pass along your schedule. Professor Blum said he'll bring the paperwork you needed to sign on Wednesday."

"It's settled."

There was a sense of finality in Autumn's last statement, and after a long pause, Jet stood.

Before leaving his seat, Autumn said, "Can I ask you something personal?"

He wanted to scream no, but he hesitantly replied, "Depends."

"Did you know that Ariana and I were friends a few years ago? I know that you guys were an item last year."

"I knew I wasn't a random choice," Jet said. Autumn remained quiet. He continued, "Ariana told me you *were* friends."

For the first time, Autumn appeared unsure of herself. "I saw the two of you together for part of last year. Ariana refuses to talk with me, even to this day. Raul will say something now and then. It's regrettable what happened to him. I was shocked."

"What do you mean?" He doubted that she could know.

"You know exactly what I mean. I heard about it and was very surprised."

"Heard about what exactly?"

"When you watch things and ask the right people the right questions, you usually get the right answers." Her stare was severe and unflinching.

His heart sped up. His entire perception of her was evolving.

"You seem surprised," she said.

"I am. Some of my closest friends didn't even know. I wanted to keep it quiet."

"So does the school." She leaned closer. "Has Ariana said anything about me?"

He lifted both hands in front of him. "If Ariana finds out that I even talked to you, she'll kick my butt, literally."

"I bet she would," Autumn conceded. "You could lie."

"You don't know me very well. I'm a terrible liar."

"Well, how about this: I'll just tell my side, and you don't have to say anything." Without waiting for a response, she began, "We met back in ninth grade. Two of my older brothers went to Chadwick's. One was a senior when I started. He and I aren't close. Ariana and I became friends instantly—best friends. Our personalities are different, but it worked. She's quiet, keeps to herself, and holds grudges. She rarely opens up, especially when she's upset. I talk to everyone about everything. I'm a habitual flirt!"

Jet clamped his mouth shut; he didn't trust himself to speak.

"Initially, though, Ariana didn't seem to mind my flirting. She was my first real friend who wasn't consumed with my behavior. She started hanging out with this boy, who was a junior, and my brother's friend. He was easily as much of a flirt as I am." Her voice squeaked. It took a moment for her to regain some calm. "He hid being a flirt when Ariana was around initially. One night he started coming on to me, and I with him—like my stupid self. We hooked up. He broke up with Ariana the next day, and she blames me."

Jet said noncommittally, "Well—"

"I doubt you'll believe me, but I asked him if they were together before anything happened. He told me no. Ariana doesn't believe me."

"Even if that were true, what about the off-limits rule between friends?"

"If there's such a rule. I didn't know about it. I should have, though." Autumn peeked down, taking a long breath. Jet felt tiny wisps of empathy for her. She added, almost absentmindedly, "I was so stupid."

"You're a cute flirt." His hand flew to his mouth, and he closed his eyes. He could've kicked himself. When he dared to look at her, she was staring at him, amused. "What I mean is—"

"I know what you mean," she said. "You think that Ariana should have expected as much."

"I'm pretty confused as to why I opened my mouth in the first place. You must have a trick that controls my mind. When's the last time you talked to her?"

"The beginning of last year. It's over and done now. I just wanted you to know."

"Why?"

"Because you're friends with her. Maybe you can say something."

"No promises. She's likely to drown me in the lagoon before listening to anything about you."

"Your problem, not mine." She winked. "Do you have a cell phone number I could give to Professor Blum?"

"Not yet. I'm hoping to get one this week."

She wrote down her number and handed it to him. "Text me your number when you get it." She walked to the door. Before leaving, she turned back and said, "But seriously, you should have someone look at your face to ensure there isn't any permanent damage to *your* cuteness." With that, Autumn left the classroom. It took several moments for Jet to regain the use of his legs.

CHAPTER 11

Stepping back inside his dorm after crossing campus, Jet had no desire to do anything but munch some food and melt into the couch. He was pleased that his roommates were nowhere to be found. He was king of the dorm, if only for the next few hours. He microwaved a hot pocket, turned on the TV, and mindlessly began clicking through channels. A heading caught his attention. On the screen was an anchorman who appeared solemn and anxious. The red letters across the top read, NATIONAL HEATWAVE: A PRODUCT OF GLOBAL WARMING?

The weather, especially the surging heat, was a hot topic in every conversation around campus and on every local news station. Onscreen, the prominent anchorman sat at his desk, and there were three screens near the bottom filled with different faces.

The man on the far right spoke, and Jet was interested to realize he spoke in a British accent. "A point of focus of this unseasonably high temperature is that no other countries are experiencing this same climate change. Our BBC headquarters here in London has been tracking a high-pressure system across the entire lower forty-eight states. It's difficult to assess how long this system will remain."

The anchorman asked, "Mr. Wiggins, in your opinion, what is causing this high-pressure system?"

"We only have speculations. Occasionally, high-pressure systems can last for several days, but this is extreme. It is important to note that two low-pressure systems are hovering above and below the U.S. One is northeast of Mexico City, and the other is near Montreal."

The anchorman smiled serenely into the camera. "I'm here with Lark Sampson from the National Weather Institute, Mr. Sam Wiggins from the BBC newsroom, and reporter Vanessa Scott in Phoenix, Arizona. In Arizona, we see some of the highest temperatures in our nation."

The screen changed, the two men disappeared, and the focus became on the female reporter. The anchorman said, "Miss Scott, how has the heatwave affected the people of Phoenix?"

Vanessa Scott's forehead glistened, but her smile was from ear to ear. "Hot temperatures are nothing new to this sunny state, but a national emergency has just been put into place because of the spiking temperatures. Our average temperature in September hovers around ninety-nine degrees. We are currently sitting at one hundred and thirty-one. This shatters our previous high-temperature record of one hundred twenty-two as the hottest day on record. It also shatters the hottest September day of one hundred-eighteen. Around the city, dozens of shelters, churches, and even the Arizona Cardinals' football stadium have opened their doors."

"Have there been any deaths directly related to the heat?"

Nodding, Mrs. Scott continued, "Every year, Phoenix and the surrounding cities experience a handful of deaths due to the heat. But in the last two days alone, we've seen six hundred hospitalizations and one hundred and five deaths attributed to the heat."

Jet shifted in his chair, trying to wrap his mind around the details.

"This matches the number of deaths over the last three years combined. Donations for water, ice, and other provisions have been sent out. Equally alarming is that the temperatures don't drop below one hundred and ten degrees at night. There's no reprieve."

"What is currently going on in the background, Mrs. Scott?" the anchor asked curiously.

"Well, Matt, I'm near the capitol building in downtown Phoenix. Behind me is the Coalition for Global Warming, a group protesting for funding and research into global warming. They're wearing bathing suits, shorts, and umbrellas. It is quite a sight to see. Recently, Governor Hernandez spoke and informed the public that he instituted a curfew, placed the state on high alert, and called in the National Guard. Interestingly, he is limiting the blame on global warming. He reasoned that the heatwave was primarily restricted to the lower forty-eight states."

The anchor-man continued, "Thank you, Vanessa. One thing is for sure: we are experiencing unprecedented temperatures. Almost ninety percent of the lower forty-eight states are seeing triple-digit temperatures. Alaska and Hawaii are experiencing normal temperatures."

Using the remote, Jet turned off the television. He couldn't stand any more coverage of the weather. His eyelids had become heavy, and soon he was asleep.

A few hours later, he was jolted awake by the ringing of the dorm phone. Jet groggily stood and answered it. "Hello."

Grantham said, "Bro, you've got to get a cell phone."

"Tell me about it," Jet said. "What's up?"

"After school tomorrow, we're thinking of going down to the beach. You in? Jayco has a place he wants to show us, and he wants all of us to chat together. Meet us at Latisha's dorm around six."

"I'm in."

CHAPTER 12

Tuesday was typically Jet's easiest day of the week, and the day passed quickly. After his regular classes, he stopped by the science building and spent ninety minutes preparing the lab for tomorrow. Autumn left a detailed to-do list. Once finished, his next stop was the cafeteria for a quick bite to eat before heading back to his dorm. He still had an hour to kill before meeting up with his friends and returned to his dorm to change and grab a towel.

Jackson and Rick were busy inside the entertainment room, but they weren't playing a single video game.

Jet asked, mildly surprised, "Has the world ended? You're doing homework."

"Ha. Ha." Rick said. "Don't rub it in. We'll lose the Xbox and the TV if we don't get our assignments in. Jackson's mom isn't too thrilled with how this semester has started."

"She's lame," Jackson protested. "No one cares about grades until the end of the term. Can't she see that?"

Rick countered, "I guess that missing classes for three straight days will do that for you."

Jackson replied, "Lame."

"Just think, though," Jet said. "If you have fabulous grades, she'll reward you with additional games. This could be a win, win."

Jackson groaned and rolled his eyes. "You sound exactly like my mom. Did I already mention how lame this is?"

A sensation of urgency, like the guilt of forgetting something important, entered his mind. He barely managed to say, "Like three times," before sprinting to his room. He quickly reached inside his backpack and pulled out *The Sorcerer's Guide*. Just below the fable, a sketch of a small black-and-white rock appeared. As if animated, it began rolling from the left side of the page to the right, then disappeared. As if in slow motion, the page started rolling upon itself, finally tumbling over.

Jet's eyes were drawn to the top left corner of the page as words began to appear:

The Path is First Cut From Stone.

Below these words, another message surfaced. It was as if the letters were being pressed into the paper this time. The handwriting was noticeably different from the fable.

This tome was taken from a cave near the Starving Peaks and hidden. It's a sister to a darker and more nefarious counterpart, but only one will prevail. Learn your part. The Rivalry has begun. Be wary of the Occultists—they feed off deception. You must learn the required rituals to compete for the Phoenix. The champion will control the tablet and the prison that holds the demon. Nature binds it sealed, but the hold is only temporary.

The day approaches that he will no longer be restrained. He will search for the tablet, and it will replenish his powers if found. We are protectors of this book and the ancient tablet. The tablet was found and broken into pieces and rehidden. We do not know when or how. The Brotherhood has searched for many years. Do not forget that the powers and endowment of each of the tablet pieces are immense.

Those pieces will be used one day to destroy the world or eradicate Arisol. You must find them and protect them from whatever may come.

Signed, Marval Liken,
The Sixth Preparer and Protector of the Tablet.

It was unnerving for Jet to think that the fable might mean something more than just a fable. Over the last few days, he'd gone back and forth from a real story to more of an allegory with a deeper meaning. However, this letter indicated that the fable was likely a legitimate story. He focused his attention on the surprising amount of information within this short letter. Two books, the tablet's importance, learning the rituals, protectors, the tablet pieces rehidden. He had no idea what an Occultist or the Brotherhood was. Somehow, everything felt more substantial and riskier. What if they failed?

Jet flinched as below the letter, another sentence appeared.
Say these words aloud –Fireton, Secula, Riversiden.

Pausing, Jet felt a sense of uncertainty. Did he want to follow this book blindly? What was the worst that could happen? He hesitated, his voice unwilling to obey his mind. Three more sentences materialized at the bottom of the page, swaying back and forth, each at a different speed.

If you fail to produce a symbol, you are a Preparer.
You must hide this tome until the one with blackened air can unlock this guidebook.
Guard it with your life.

A burst of confidence overcame him, and he forcefully whispered each of the words: "Fireton. Secula. Riversiden."

Fearing that this might be the dumbest thing he'd ever done, he put his head in his hands. His own voice of uncertainty whispered inside his head. "Just a Preparer."

The room went quiet, more than naturally possible, and he was gripped by invisible tentacles wrapping around his torso, arms, and neck until it was impossible to move. The pressure in his chest tightened, and his air was slowly pushed out. Every pore ignited as if a blazing fire sat on the desk next to him. A sudden dousing of arctic water followed this. A gust of wind originating from the top of Everest swirled around him. But nothing could prepare him for the next thing, the pressure on his entire skin as if he was being buried alive. He tasted the dirt in his mouth and for an instant couldn't move.

After some time, he found himself sitting in the same chair in his dorm as if nothing had happened. Next to him, on his desk, the book lay open. The words were still visible, but they no longer moved. A bright and fantastic new image sat on the right side of the page. Four elements, almost like emblems, were perfectly captured on the page, strongly interconnected. There was a campfire with smoke, a glacier lake, an immense and ancient tree growing from a hill, and the last picture was a trace of a descending sun behind a masterpiece of a mountain encircled with rolling and spectacular clouds. Jet shivered at the images on the page. Because of the coloring, the lighting, and the precision, it was the most beautiful picture he'd ever seen.

Reaching out, he touched the image, and when his fingers brushed the page, he heard an audible clicking sound, as if something had been unlocked. Before he could react, the picture transformed from a solid image to something similar to a reflection on the water. The bright colors disappeared, and it became a silver liquid that bubbled and oozed and splashed onto his finger, migrating up his hand. When the entire silver liquid had leached off the paper, it was absorbed into Jet's skin, disappearing.

Pain sprung up in the middle of his back, like a stabbing knife assaulting his skin. Once the pain had decreased, he tore off his shirt and checked in the mirror. He found a perfect replica of the image that had been in his book, now in the middle of his back just like a tattoo.

After a moment, he sat down and turned to the next page of his book. The four images were now separated and perfectly replicated. Below the pictures were two sentences:

Learn to manipulate each of Earth's elements.

Concentrate and adjust; advance and attack.

CHAPTER 13

Jet hoped he was only a few minutes late when he closed and locked the door to his dorm and sprinted down the stairs. He turned south and, using his longboard, made quick time, all-the-while thinking about the tattoo on his back. When at last he passed the most southern building, a storage building, he could see his friends waiting for him at the curb. As he approached, they glared at him.

When he skidded to a stop, Jayco shouted, "Glad you could join us."

"Only fifteen minutes late," Latisha pointed out.

Trying to act calm, he said, "Did you know that a concussion can cause an inability to remember things?"

"Shove it," Jayco said. "Are we ready yet?"

Latisha asked, "Does any part of your face not have a bruise?"

"Maybe the back of my neck."

"Nope." Mckenzey's hand brushed his skin. "There's one back here too."

Jayco lightly pushed Jet forward. "Are we done inspecting Jet's adorable neckline? We've got places to go."

Grantham said, "Lead the way."

"Where are we headed?" Mckenzey asked.

Jayco smiled. "I found this sweet place on the beach. There's a cove, and I doubt anyone else knows about it. I brought down some food and drinks earlier today."

Getting to the cove was quite the adventure. They first longboarded on Ocean Avenue south of campus for another ten minutes before finding a huge group of trees. They hid their boards in a ditch and hiked down a ravine, through a thicket of trees, and down two dozen rocks. When they stepped onto the beach, Jet felt that it was worth it. Despite being drenched with sweat and slightly frustrated, it was the best ocean view for a hundred miles.

"Last one in the water buys breakfast this weekend!" Jayco yelled as he tore down the beach with Grantham and Latisha only a few steps behind.

Jet removed his sling and found the perfect spot to hide his backpack before sprinting to the water. He was the last one to arrive. Mckenzey splashed him, soaking his back. Jet returned the favor but was soon drenched by the cumulative effort of all his friends.

"What do you think?" Jayco asked as he wiped the water out of his eyes.

"Best spot ever," Grantham roared. "How in the world did you find this place?"

"Determination and a bit of luck."

They stood in a large cove separated by a gigantic rock wall on the right side. The left wall was slightly smaller and far less steep. It appeared to have several ledges and crumbling rocks. The rocks continued into the water for over a hundred feet and narrowed to a small opening. A fair number of boulders in the water at the opening prevented any boat or watercraft from entering the cove. The yellow sandy beach was fifty or a hundred feet wide, and the water was sparkling and beautifully clear. Behind them, the immense trees and full bushes blocked their view of the path to the road. This place was as secluded as if they were on their own tiny island.

Grantham and Jayco dove into the water and began swimming toward a ledge on the left side. They pulled themselves out and started climbing.

Jet, Latisha, and Mckenzey just watched as they continued upward for thirty or forty feet. They stopped at another landing and yelled, "Bottoms up," before diving into the water below.

Mckenzey leaned in, asking, "Are you thinking what I'm thinking?"

"If you mean that Jayco and Grantham are specimens of great manly awesomeness, then yes."

"Seriously?" she asked.

"Just throwing that out there."

Mckenzey rolled her eyes.

"Or," Jet added, "this might be a good time to tell our friends what's going on."

"Now we're talking."

Jayco and Grantham swam back to the group and caught their breath. When Jayco could speak, he said, "Jet, when your shoulder is healed, we are coming back here to try that again. That was exhilarating."

"No promises," Jet said. "I really can't swim."

"What better way to learn?" Grantham joked.

"Not on your life."

They chatted, explored, and cliff jumped for the next hour, and even Latisha dropped once, but only from about five feet in the air. Jet searched some of the rocks for shells and other sea creatures. They talked and laughed. It was the most fun he'd had with the Echoes in years.

Finally, Jayco said, "Let's get some food."

They headed back up to where they'd come into the cove. Next to the trees, they found several rocks in a circle, like a fire pit.

Jayco explained, "It took me two days to arrange all of these. This is going to be the coolest place on campus."

With Grantham's help, Jayco dragged out a large cooler from behind a tree. They started a fire and soon were cooking some hot dogs and brats. Twenty minutes later, the sun began to drop, and Jet reached over and pulled out his backpack.

After they finished eating, Jayco suggested, "Let's share some campfire stories. The scarier, the better. Who wants to go first?"

Jet cleared his throat. "I've got a pretty incredible story."

"This better be good," Jayco said.

"Can you give us a hint?" Grantham asked.

"Silverton, blue fog, and an antique book."

Jayco groaned. "Lame. Last year, Mckenzey tried to get everyone to talk about their feelings. We need to let the past go."

Latisha added, "Look. Silverton is a sore subject for all of us. We all lost friends. Don't you remember how upset you got last time we talked about this? Let's not ruin the night."

"Things have changed. I'm going to do most of the talking. I'm just asking you to listen."

Mckenzey interjected, "And keep an open mind."

"What's that supposed to mean?" Jayco asked.

"Jet and I—"

"Are you guys dating?" Grantham asked.

Jet scoffed. "That's the first thing that comes to your mind?"

"If you are."—Jayco fished out another drink out of the cooler— "there's no way that I want to hear about it."

Mckenzey said, "Guys, will you just shut up and listen."

"What's going on?" Latisha asked.

Jet thought for a moment. "I'll buy breakfast and dinner if, after listening for five minutes, you ask me to stop. I will tell you things that you'll have a hard time believing."

"What kind of things?" Grantham asked.

"Wizards and bewitchment."

Jayco mumbled, "This is the stupidest conversation I've ever had."

Latisha stood. "I'm going back into the water."

Jet held up his book. "I'll give you fifty dollars if you can open this. You can't throw it into the water, crush it with a rock, or use a chainsaw."

"I knew I was missing something." Jayco smiled. "I'm game."

As Jayco pulled, shoved, and screamed for the book to open, Grantham and Latisha watched with interest. Grantham was next, followed by Latisha. Ten minutes later, the three of them peered at Jet skeptically.

"Give it to me." Jet pushed open the front cover with a single finger like it was nothing.

"This isn't magic," Jayco scoffed. "What game are you playing?"

Jet asked, "Which of us is most likely to get a tattoo?"

"I have three," Grantham boasted.

Latisha asked, "Three?"

Jayco said, "My parents won't let me. Once I turn eighteen, or if I can escape to Mexico, I'm getting one."

"Who's the most unlikely."

They all laughed. Grantham said, "You."

"But I have one."

"Get out of here," Jayco said.

"I'll show you if you listen to what we have to say."

"Is this a joke?" Grantham asked. "I'm already curious about the book thing."

Latisha added, "There's no way you have a tattoo."

"We have a lot to explain."

Reluctantly, Jayco said, "Bring it on."

He recounted the same story that he'd told Mckenzey. He talked about his memory block, the rock-climbing adventure, how he escaped his house, and the opening of *The Sorcerer's Guide*. Over time, Jayco and Grantham became less skeptical, while Latisha seemed more. She huffed, puffed, and glared. A few times, he thought she was going to hit him. He described his powers, the meteorite encounter, and almost everything that had happened thus far. Near the end, Jayco and Grantham appeared boyishly enthusiastic.

There was complete silence once he was finished. Jet caught sight of Grantham and Jayco sharing a look and shrugging. He wasn't surprised when Latisha stood, placing her arms on her hips, and hissed, "Are you trying to be funny? A real friend wouldn't stand here and flat-out lie like this. This is the last straw for me. We've tried and tried. Jet, I don't want to be friends with you anymore. You're making fun of me."

Mckenzey stood quickly and asked, "What about me? Can you be friends with me?"

"Of course! You're not spinning this implausible story. You're not a pathological liar." Latisha glared stubbornly at Jet.

"Actually, I am."

"What do you mean?" Latisha asked, her voice shaking.

"Jet saved my life. I've never told this to anyone, but he called me and told me to leave Silverton minutes before it was destroyed. He doesn't remember. I've also had some unexplainable things happen." She recounted both her dreams about the fog.

"Fog is one thing," Latisha huffed. "But this book, vision changes, and seeing a creature in a cave. How can you prove it?"

"How can you prove it didn't happen?" Jet said hotly.

"That's a dumb question," Latisha said dismissively. "I mean, do you have one shred of evidence?"

"Of course I do."

"Really?" Grantham asked, excited.

"That's what this book is." He held it up.

Jayco said, "Let me see you open it again."

Jet did and turned a few pages, but when he went to turn the next page, he couldn't.

"Can I read it?" Grantham asked.

Jet handed the book to Grantham. "Be my guest."

"It's blank."

"Not for me."

"You're lying again," Latisha said crossly.

"I'm not. There's a fable in here. I'll read it to you later. But I have more proof," Jet said, catching Latisha's eyes. Opening his hand, he said, "This is where I held the meteorite." The wound was healed, but a blackened replica was cut into the skin. In this instant, he realized that it also looked like a tattoo.

Grantham asked in disbelief, "That's from the meteorite you were holding?"

"Yep."

Latisha tentatively touched the palm of his hand. "That's barely a piece of evidence." But her tone was far calmer, and she was leaning toward the group.

"That's nothing. I've got something even more impressive."

"What do you mean?" Mckenzey asked.

"The real reason I was late meeting up with you guys wasn't a concussion or that I forgot. Something weird happened back in my dorm. Can I have the book back?" Jayco handed it to him. He opened the first page and then the second. He said, pointing to the page, "There's a letter on this page. But just an hour ago, three words appeared at the bottom of this page. I was supposed to speak them out loud."

"And did you?" Latisha whispered, as if afraid of the answer. "Because that would be stupid."

"I did. There were also three sentences." He explained how they moved back and forth. "When I said the three words, something happened."

"This happened today?" Mckenzey asked.

"Yes," Jet said. "Hey, Jayco and Grantham. Do you remember playing volleyball last week?"

"We destroyed you and Mckenzey," Grantham replied.

"Like always," Jayco added.

Jet asked, "Did I have any tattoos?"

"Are we going over this again?" Jayco answered.

Jet pointed to the book. "Back in my dorm, I touched this picture, and it formed a tattoo on my back."

"Impossible," Latisha hissed.

Pulling off his shirt, Jet turned around and waited for a response.

"No way!" shouted Grantham

Jayco's voice held amazement when he said, "That's the coolest thing I've ever seen."

Latisha added, "Oh my."

He felt fingers prodding his back, and Grantham said, "Four elements: earth, water, fire, and—"

"—Wind," Latisha finished.

Grantham continued, "The redness of the flames is amazing, as are all the colors. Does it seem like the tattoo is moving?"

"I just felt a gust of frozen air," Mckenzey said. "How's that possible?"

Jayco added, "There's not a single scab or redness of a recent tattoo."

Latisha cleared her voice, "Is this all for real?"

"A hundred percent." Jet pulled back on his shirt.

"I'm not saying I believe you, and I hate the idea of what you're saying, but this is some pretty compelling evidence. But what does it all mean?"

"Now, that's the real question."

CHAPTER 14

Jet was not prepared for how comfortable it was to open up to his friends. It felt almost surreal. Together, they connected on a few ideas and speculated about other possibilities. They laughed and joked for over an hour. Latisha remained reserved but still added a thought or two. By the time they left the beach, the world had realigned itself with how things should've been.

The mood was tested when Latisha asked Mckenzey, "How does it feel to know that you finally got accepted to Dillon Lake? What does Eric think?"

Jayco asked, "Who's Eric?"

"Mckenzey's boyfriend," Latisha said. "He's so handsome and from Colorado."

"Is Dillon Lake a different boarding school?" Grantham asked.

Mckenzey said, her voice shaking, "Yes. It's in upstate New York."

Jet knew about Dillon Lake, but he had no clue about Eric. He remembered that Shane had said something about his friends attending Dillon Lake last year.

The group fell silent as they maneuvered their way up the ravine. As they retrieved their longboards, Grantham asked, "When are you starting at the new school?"

"I haven't decided yet, but it looks like January right now. Eric is thrilled, but I'm hesitant. I need more time to think things through."

"Ditching us," Jayco said abruptly.

The group stopped and stared at Mckenzey.

She muttered, "That wasn't my intent when I applied. It was partway through school last year when none of us were talking. I—"

Grantham placed an arm on her shoulder. "Don't mind Jayco. He hates goodbyes. We'll all support you no matter what you choose."

They started longboarding slowly back toward campus, Jet's mind racing the entire time.

Latisha, grasping for another topic, asked, "Mckenzey, were any of your pieces accepted for the art competition? Did they invite you to Washington, D.C.?"

"What competition?" Jayco asked.

With significant effort, Jet pulled his mind back to the conversation.

"It's this art competition in Washington, D.C.," Mckenzey said. "I was on the shortlist of students to participate in a competition held every year. Typically, the top four students from several schools get invited. There are ten categories. I came up a little short. I was number five, and Chadwick's is only sending four. Over in the CeU building, a glass case exhibited all the artwork. They left a few days ago. It sounds like they are going to have a blast. They get to fly on a private jet and stay in some posh hotel."

Latisha said quickly, "Next year, I bet you'll do great."

"Maybe," Mckenzey said quietly.

The Star Wars theme song chimed from Mckenzey's pocket, cutting through the awkward silence. Pulling out her phone, she answered. A moment later, she stopped her board and turned to Jet. He watched as the look on her face turned from curious to murderous. She held out her phone and hissed, "It's for you."

"For me?"

She shoved it into his hands.

He took it, held it to his ear, and said, "Hello?"

"Hi, Jet. It's Ariana. Sorry to call. But your hall monitor, Napoleon, contacted me. It looks like someone broke into your dorm."

"What?" he said, his heart racing. "My dorm?"

"That's what he said," Ariana insisted, her voice distant.

"I'm on my way," Jet said. After hanging up, he explained what Ariana had said.

Fifteen minutes later, when Jet and his friends stepped out of the elevator, the foyer outside his dorm was almost entirely full. It was just after nine-thirty. He handed his backpack to Grantham and headed toward his door.

"There you are," Napoleon said, face flushed as he stomped toward Jet. "Took your sweet, pretty time, didn't you?"

"Relax. I got here as fast as I could."

"Campus security has been here for thirty minutes. Your roommates are nowhere to be found."

"Sorry," Jet muttered, without feeling particularly sorry.

Ariana walked up behind Napoleon but kept her distance.

"How bad is the damage?" Jet asked.

But before either of them could answer, a man with a crisp white shirt, black hair, and a solid build approached. "Mr. Black, I'm Officer Reynolds. Can I take a moment of your time?"

"I guess." Jet shook the man's hand and glanced helplessly at Ariana. She began walking toward his friends but quickly veered away. Napoleon followed her with a strange look on his face. Three students caught his attention near the elevator. He recognized them but also noticed that they were lurking. Vinny, Jake, and Jocelyn—the same kids he'd seen when rock climbing—were huddled together, likely gossiping.

Officer Reynolds guided him toward his door. Jet could see that someone had pried it open even from here. Officer Reynolds said, "Thank you for coming so quickly."

"How bad is it?" Jet asked.

"Well, the deadbolt is broken, and the door's handle is missing. Inside, there are plenty of broken items. "Where have *you* been?"

Jet recounted his movements for the last few hours. He pointed to his friends and said, "They're over there if you want to talk to them."

"I just might do that."

"Am I in trouble?"

"Nothing to indicate that. Why do you ask?"

For an instant, Jet felt that he was being scrutinized. "No reason. But why would someone break into our dorm? We've nothing of value."

Officer Reynolds waved to another officer, who approached quickly. The gruff man pulled out a large notebook. Officer Reynolds took it and pointed to a sketched image. "We spoke to a few of your neighbors. One girl saw this guy hanging outside your dorm. Do you recognize him?"

Jet stared in disbelief at the pencil sketch, trying to remain calm. His hand went to his chin, and he said slowly, "Can't say that I do. Is he a student? I doubt he was visiting us."

"Why don't you take a closer look?" Officer Reynolds insisted. "Maybe that black eye and swelling on your face make it hard to get a good look."

Jet swallowed slowly. Taking the sketch in both hands, he acknowledged that it was a good depiction of the guy he'd run into last week, before the fight with Shane. There was a patch of hair under his chin. Jet cringed. He remembered that Napoleon might recognize this guy as well. Maybe Napoleon had already told Officer Reynolds, and this was a test. He had no choice but to continue down the same path. Jet replied, "Sorry, I've never seen him before."

"We have someone coming over from the administration. They'll have personnel files. If he's a student here, we'll know. Thank you for your time."

"When can I go inside my dorm?"

"Not for another hour or so. You'll be able to return once we've gone through everything. We'll call and let you know. Leave your number with one of my guys." Officer Reynolds hurried away as if Jet had become the least important thing in the world.

"How did that go?" Ariana asked as he approached.

"I guess my dorm is toast," he said.

Napoleon inched closer, and his friends hurried over. Jet waited for Napoleon to say something about the guy, but he remained quiet.

"Who did it?" Jayco asked.

"Not a clue."

The group chatted for a few minutes. Napoleon gave weird scenarios like aliens, the mob, and even ghosts. The onlookers mainly had vanished, including Jake and the others.

Ariana lingered around. Finally, she grabbed his arm and said, "Can we go somewhere and talk?"

"I guess." Jet shrugged.

"Somewhere besides here."

"Sure." He fetched his backpack and waved goodbye to his friends. They headed into the elevator, and he asked, "Where do you want to go?"

"Porter's is open for another hour. Want some ice cream?"

"Perfect."

Ten minutes later, Jet and Ariana stepped into the other restaurant on campus. It was also located on top of the CeU building, but it was for burgers and ice cream and was open most days. They fell into line behind another dozen students.

When it was their turn, Jet ordered two scoops of cookie dough, and Ariana ordered rainbow sherbet and two glasses of water. They sat down and began eating in silence.

"What are you thinking?" Ariana asked after a few minutes.

"Funny. I was going to ask you the same thing."

"Who would want to break into your dorm?"

"No guesses here. I've got nothing of value."

"What about a computer?"

"Maybe." He leaned back in his chair. "But why our dorm? Every student on campus has one." His thoughts turned to Shane, and now Ariana was sitting across from him. "But they have a sketch of someone hanging around outside our dorm. Did you get a look?"

"I didn't recognize the guy." She appeared confident; her eyes didn't look away. "Let's hope nothing was taken."

"Does this happen a lot?" Jet asked. "I know you've been a student worker in the admin building before."

"More than you think. Things like this, and more, happen all the time. Kids and adults sneak onto campus almost weekly. There've been some weird things. The vice-principal suggested a fence and a gate on the two main roads for next year."

"The campus is huge, hundreds of acres."

"I know. Hence why nothing has happened yet; they're just looking at options. In recent months, there has been an uptick in complaints. And when a rich parent complains, things change. Some of the wealthiest families on the West Coast have children that go here."

He noticed that her eyes lingered on his face. She pushed forward, "There have also been some attacks."

"Like what?"

"Did you hear about that girl at the beginning of the year? Trina Madden."

"I remember her."

"She was released from the hospital. She told her parents she was attacked on the beach."

"By what, the sun?"

"I'm just telling you what I heard." Ariana smiled hesitantly and gave a long sigh. "What happened to you?"

"You don't know?" he asked.

"Why would I?"

"Shane and his friends cornered me."

"Are you sure?"

"I was there."

She shook her head. "We all do stupid things sometimes. Even you."

Jet sat back, confused. "What's that supposed to mean?"

It took a moment for Ariana to contemplate her answer. When she did, it was monotone and soft. "I heard that you met Autumn."

Jet's mouth felt dry, and he tried swallowing. A minute later, he gasped out, "Yes. I did."

Ariana waited for him to continue.

After taking a drink of water, Jet explained, "I'm taking a geology lab, and Professor Blum asked me to help out.

Autumn is the primary TA for the class. It's not like I had a choice. We've met once in the lab room." He hoped that it sounded like Professor Blum had been there as well.

"Is that the only time that you've met?"

The question surprised him. "Pretty much."

"Really?" He heard the pain in her voice, mixed with a splash of anger.

Giving up the pretenses, he asked, "What do you want me to say?"

"Admit that you went out with her on a date just a few days ago?"

Jet was shocked. "No, I didn't."

"A few of Shane's friends said they saw you two together."

"What?" he seethed. "How would Shane's friends know what I'm doing? Are they watching me?"

Ariana's voice held a trace of irritation. "That's not the point."

"Then what is?"

She glared at him. "Well, you know!"

Jet said, "She's flirty and talkative. What else do you want me to say?"

Ariana's teeth ground together. "So, you did go out with her."

Jet remained silent, his arms folded, as he studied Ariana. He was having trouble wrapping his head around what he was hearing. But why would she lie?

"Did I come up in your conversation with Autumn? What did you tell her about me?"

Somehow, he imagined this conversation going much differently.

Talking more calmly than he felt, he said, "I was hesitant to talk with her about you."

"What do you mean?"

"I knew that you'd be angry, and I realized that it's none of my business. I told her that I wasn't going to betray my friend. She said that I only needed to listen. She talked, and I didn't say a word. But this happened in the classroom, and we certainly never went on a date."

Her face contorted. "I don't believe you."

"Why?"

"Because you were with her last night too."

"That's not true."

"That's not what Raul said."

Jet's anger peaked, and he hissed, "I've never hung out with Autumn, and I certainly wasn't with her last night or any night."

"I don't believe you."

He stood, spilling his ice cream. "Tell Raul that he needs to get his eyes checked. I was in my dorm all night. Maybe next time, you should get your information straight before making accusations. Tell Shane and his friends to stop following me. And if they break into my dorm again, next time, I'll—"

"What are you talking about?"

"Never mind." He turned to leave.

Ariana pleaded, "Stay for a moment. Explain this to me. This is crazy."

"You said it. I guess I'll be seeing you around. Or not." His hands shook as he exited Porters. His anger was only partially directed at her. Naturally, she would want to know what he and Autumn had talked about. He certainly couldn't blame her for that. But more importantly, it was obvious that he was standing directly in Shane Fallon's crosshairs, and he had no idea why. They were following him, had attacked him, and now they'd broken into his dorm. He needed more information, and he needed it fast.

CHAPTER 15

"We're almost finished," Officer Reynolds said as Jet stepped out of the elevator. "Someone from the Housing and Residential Services stopped by, and they'll be bringing some replacement furniture in the next half hour."

A second officer escorted Jet to the front door. A man was already working to replace the entire door. Stepping across the threshold, he felt that he was looking at the aftereffects of a hurricane. Food, papers, and shattered glass were everywhere. The television had been used as a piñata, and the couches had been reduced to tinder. He staggered past another two workers on the way to his room.

As he passed his roommates' room, he understood why he'd been the target of the officer's questions. Things were tipped over, but everything was still intact. His room, however, was officially a disaster area. The carpet lay hidden underneath all the broken items, torn papers, mangled books, and shredded clothing. Ceiling tiles were torn, the walls were gashed, and everything was overturned or broken. Jet bent down and picked up wood from a broken picture frame. Mckenzey's picture of Silverton lay fragmented on the floor. His stomach dropped. It had survived Shane's attack, only to get destroyed today.

Footsteps approached from behind. Officer Reynolds said, "By the way, no one was helpful enough in identifying the man from the sketch. It doesn't appear that he's a student here. Are you sure you want to stick to your story? They could come back."

"For what? Almost everything I own is gone. I don't know who broke in."

Jet's eyes focused on the sidewall above his bed, where the drywall appeared to have been attacked with a jackhammer.

Officer Reynolds continued, "I'm not sure what they were looking for. But they went to a great deal to find it."

Jet was saved from responding by a loud knock at the front door. He stepped past Officer Reynolds and found a middle-aged man standing just inside the newly placed door with a tan-striped suit. His white shirt was wrinkled, and only half tucked in. He was disheveled. He waved at Officer Reynolds and Jet.

The man spoke rapidly. "Hello, son. My name is Mr. Beeker, and I am with janitorial services."

Officer Reynolds said, "I'll be leaving. Contact me if you can think of anything else." The officer placed a card on the counter.

"No problem," Jet said. Turning to Mr. Beeker, he said, "That's a huge trash bin."

"I heard there was a lot of trash." The man eyed the room knowingly.

"You heard right."

"We'll replace the couches and some of the smaller items tonight. Can I help with anything?"

"Got any trash bags?"

"No problem." Mr. Beeker reached into the bin and pulled out a large box of black plastic bags. Jet grabbed a handful. "I'll have a few boys here in a few minutes to start repairing anything we can."

"Good luck."

Jet returned to his room and attacked the catastrophe for the next few hours. He tossed his damaged mattress, desk, and wall pieces into the hallway. Things piled up quickly. Three workers arrived and started cleaning the carpets, removing trash, and fixing holes. Rick and Jackson appeared just after eleven-thirty, and it took twenty minutes to explain what had happened.

"I think they were after you," Jackson said after Jet showed them the differences between the two rooms. "But what were they looking for?"

"I've no idea. Everything I own is destroyed besides my school books, and I mean everything."

Jet was downright giddy to walk out of his empty room around twelve thirty to find that the front area and hall were slightly better than a warzone. A new mattress, bed, and desk arrived forty-five minutes later. Soon, another crew was bringing in a bookshelf, a small television, a new computer, and a throw rug.

Rick, sweating profusely, said, "My parents will flip about our television being smashed."

"Hopefully the school will get you a better one," Jackson said confidently.

Rick smiled. "I can handle that."

Jackson and Rick received their own computers as well. Just before two in the morning, Jet was informed that repairing the hallway and the bathroom would require too much work for tonight. The crew began preparing to leave.

As they sat on the sofa for a quick snack break, Rick jokingly said, "We made out better than before. Everything of Jet's is a total loss."

Jackson jumped up from the sofa and hurried to his backpack. "Actually, that reminds me." He unzipped his bag's outer pocket and pulled out a green piece of paper and an envelope. "I forgot to give these to you a few days ago. They're from the mailroom."

"Me?" Jet asked, confused. "I rarely get mail." Reaching out, he accepted the items. The first was a letter from Seyanna Motick. He hadn't heard from her in weeks. It was weird because she usually emailed him. The other piece of paper was a notice to pick up a package. "It's from Nana. I guess I forgot a few things at the beginning of the year."

"Look on the bright side," Rick said. "Not everything of yours was destroyed. Forgetting things has its advantages."

From the doorway, a voice called, "Is there a Mr. Joshua Black here?" A tall, heavyset man in his late forties stepped into the dorm. Jet wasn't sure if he'd ever seen a more nervous man.

"I'm Mr. Black." He heard a chortle from either Jackson or Rick as they retreated to their room.

"Thank goodness. Can … I … um … come in?"

"Have a seat on my new couch."

"Oh, yes. Um … I see." A flash of panic crossed the man's face, which appeared downright pale.

Jet sat across from him. "How can I help you?"

"My name is Mr. Shepherd, and, um, I am the manager … of the housing services. And I … I wanted to … apologize to you, that is, um, about this incident." The man's eyes shifted around the room. "You see, we pride ourselves on…security. It's just, is um—so surprising that this happened." He stood quickly and muttered, "I've got to go. Here's my card; please call if anything else … um … needs to be done."

Jet watched, bewildered, as Mr. Shepherd retreated from the room as if staying another moment would cost him his job. But just seconds later, Mr. Shepherd poked his head back through the open door.

"Sorry, I ... I forgot to give you this." And he passed over a white envelope. "I ... was told that your room and all your clothes were ... um ... destroyed. This should help." And he was gone again.

Jet opened the envelope, and inside was a check for five hundred dollars from the school. This would undoubtedly help replace some of his items, but it couldn't settle his nerves.

Mr. Beeker and his workers piled out of the dorm ten minutes later. Before leaving, Mr. Beeker, said, "I'll send someone later in the week to patch up the holes and fix the bathroom."

Returning to his room, Jet tore off his clothes and stared unblinkingly at his new tattoo. The day had been a complete shock. He was exhausted, and he didn't want to move for a week. He already planned on missing his morning classes. Before turning out his lights, he opened the letter from Seyanna.

Hey Jet, what's up? Miss you guys tons. The coolest thing happened here. We flew a helicopter to a huge glacier and landed on it. We found some crevices, and I got to climb into a few of them. It was probably the most remarkable thing I've gotten to do in a long time.

The temperature here is freezing compared to you guys. Well, everywhere is cold compared to you. Mom and Dad are thinking of heading back to the States in the next month or two. We could leave any time, but this recent glacier visit was exciting and a little weird.

Maybe we'll have time to stop by and see everyone in Cali if we do leave. I'm not sure, so don't say anything to the rest of the gang. Latisha and Mckenzey emailed me and told me that they finally told everyone that Mckenzey might be going to a different school. That sounds totally crazy to me. Jet, you've got to do whatever it takes to convince her to stay! If she leaves, I think the whole group will fall apart. They also told me about Raul, both last year and seeing him again this year. That's gotta be crazy, seeing him again. Do you know what made him freak out?

I'd better be going. Hope to see you in a month or two. Tell everyone I said hi.

Seyanna

CHAPTER 16

The following day, Jet felt horrible, both physically and mentally. He'd wanted to sleep in but was too anxious to stay in bed. Ten minutes after arriving at his first class, he realized that this was something more than fatigue after getting only five hours of sleep. He didn't want to get sick. Things went from bad to worse in his second class when his vision blurred and the worst headache in years sprung up. Instead of getting any food for lunch, he went home to sleep.

He barely registered that his bathroom had been repaired as he sunk next to the toilet and vomited. Sweat dripped from every part of his body, and soon he resembled a river monster, so he removed his clothes and slipped into bed. He was asleep mere seconds later.

A nightmare of swirling blue fog, red eyes, and a distant howling plagued him. Sometime later, a hand gripped his shoulder and shook him.

He lashed out, subconsciously fearing an attack. Fog clouded his mind, and it was a struggle to pry open his eyes. As he stared at the ceiling, he wasn't sure where he was. Tilting his head, he thought someone was standing over him, trying to speak. It sounded like incoherent mumbling.

Someone or something clasped onto his arms and legs. He tried kicking but didn't have the energy. The world began to sway as if he were on a boat. After a few seconds, the pressure on his legs lessened. Something cold splashed onto his face and shoulders, and the wet spray soon engulfed his entire body. The flowing water switched from ice cold to warm. The haze of the dream vaporized, and the fluorescent lights blinded his eyes.

Glancing out of the shower, Jet saw the faces of Jackson, Rick, and Mckenzey peering back at him. Mckenzey was horrified while his two roommates grinned from ear to ear.

Jackson spoke first. "I enjoyed that way too much. Do you know where you are?"

"In my dorm, in the shower, with my freaking underwear soaked, you idiot."

"Back to normal." Rick smirked. Staring at Mckenzey, he said, "Thanks for the shout. That was awful fun."

Mckenzey didn't seem to hear him; she kept staring at Jet.

"Do I look that bad?" Jet asked.

Mckenzey took a tentative step forward. Her voice wavered as she said, "I tried waking you for ten minutes. You were not yourself. You were burning up and mumbling."

Turning off the shower, Jet reached for a towel. "I got sick before lunch. I had a headache, and I was exhausted. I just laid down a few minutes ago."

"Lunch was more than six hours ago."

"You're joking."

"It's completely dark outside. A lot has happened. I'm going to get you some clothes."

Before she reached the door, he asked, "While I was asleep, did you say something to me?"

"Screamed your name, tried to force you awake. Your face might hurt a bit. I slapped you a few times."

"Figures."

Two minutes later, she returned with a change of clothes and retreated out of the bathroom. After dressing, Jet stepped back into his room and found Mckenzey gathering his backpack, book, and laptop. She was ready to leave a moment later. She wore jean shorts, a white T-shirt, a light jacket, and flip-flops. Her brown hair was tangled and disheveled.

"Are we going somewhere?"

"My dorm. We need to go now."

"But why?" he asked, confused.

Refusing to answer, she pulled his arm until he followed. As they crossed campus, he tried asking a few questions but wasn't even sure Mckenzey heard them.

As they ascended the stairs of Mckenzey's dorm, something clicked in his head. "It's cool outside. Is the heatwave over?"

Mckenzey answered dully, "Tell me about it. You won't believe what's happened."

Jet suddenly stopped. "What do you mean?" A chill ran down his spine. "Was it an earthquake?"

"Keep coming." Mckenzey unlocked her door and took a deep breath. She exclaimed, "There was no volcano or earthquake that I can see, but a huge storm has hit the eastern United States. There is a ton of confusion."

Mckenzey's dorm was bigger than his, but it only housed two people. It was much more like an apartment. Latisha had connections that allowed them to have one of the best girls' dorms on campus. The front door opened immediately into the kitchen. They stepped around the large dining table and walked past the fridge, sink, counter, and some cabinets along the far wall.

Jet followed her to the entertainment room. There was a small desk in the far-left corner. Between the two rooms, a short hallway continued to each girl's bedroom. Latisha was the first door on the left and Mckenzey on the right. They each had their own bathroom.

"Where's Latisha?" he asked, trying to catch his breath as he walked to the couch.

"Hanging out with Jayco and Grantham. They tried inviting us. I didn't want to go. You need a cellphone. They left for the movies a while ago."

"Tell me about this storm."

"Not much to tell. A warning flashed on the screen two hours ago. Initially, there was some information, and then a blue screen emerged on every channel. That's when I came to find you. The internet, radio, and television are all out-of-whack."

Jet sunk onto the couch, having used all his energy crossing campus. "That's impossible."

She tossed him her cell phone. It read 'No Service.'

They talked casually for the next twenty minutes, then Jet's stomach began to rumble. "Are you hungry?" Mckenzey asked.

"I haven't eaten anything all day."

"I've got some leftovers."

After all the food was arranged, Mckenzey asked, "Do you think this could be related to the fable? I mean, I know we all talked. I just don't see how the weather is involved."

"Me neither. We still don't know if there is a connection between earthquakes, volcanos, fog, and the fable. It doesn't make sense." Jet took a large bite of pizza. After chewing for a few seconds, he asked, "Have you had any more dreams?"

"It's still the same one over and over again." Mckenzey passed over some delicious-looking pasta and shrimp.

Jet continued, "The last time I read the fable, I was intrigued by a future war and a solar calendar."

"What's a solar calendar?"

"I researched it on the internet. A solar calendar is why we have three hundred and sixty-five days in a year and why there's a leap year. It's all about the Earth's position as it rotates around the sun."

"Why would the fable mention a solar calendar?"

He took a long drink of milk. "If we could understand what a solar calendar means to the fable and how it affects Arisol's release, and if there is a relation to the weather or natural disasters, I think we might find a way to prevent them."

"Prevent them? So, you do think that natural disasters are somehow involved?"

"Maybe. I'm grasping at any possibilities."

"It could be global warming."

"That's true," Jet conceded. "We might need to go back to Silverton and try to learn what happened."

"Like go for a visit?" Mckenzey asked. "I don't know if I can ever go back."

"It's just something to think about. We could go up there on the weekend, just drive up and look around."

"That makes me feel anxious," she admitted.

Beep ... beep ... beep. The sounds came from the television. A few seconds later, the screen was no longer blue.

Jet felt anticipation as the screen changed. Mckenzey jumped next to him, burrowing into his side. The first image on the screen was an older man with a tweed jacket, sitting at a news desk. He let out a low whistle and said, "Here we go."

The man glanced off-screen, nodded, and stared back at the camera. Smiling, he started speaking. "For many of you, this is the first opportunity to listen to our broadcast here on the BBC. We'd like to welcome you. We've recently and temporarily joined forces with CNN and Fox News in the

States. We are currently sitting at the Broadcasting House in Portland Place, London. My name is Mark Davie, and this is the BBC."

Jet and Mckenzey shared a look.

"A natural disaster has struck the Eastern Coast of the United States, and the damages are potentially serious. We come to you this early morning because the destruction has been so widespread that it was determined that a united programming would be both practical and beneficial. The brunt of the destruction began a few hours ago as two powerful storms collided along the eastern United States. They produced a record amount of rainfall, flooding, and other natural disasters. The epicenter of this disaster stems from Washington D.C. to Kentucky."

"Oh my gosh," Mckenzey said softly. She unfolded a blanket from the end of the couch and pulled it over her legs, leaning into Jet.

"The two storms invaded from Canada and Mexico. The lower forty-eight states had been experiencing an unprecedented heatwave, which came to a dramatic end. In the affected areas, temperatures dropped by more than forty degrees in a matter of minutes. The two systems met and fused, generating one of the largest storm systems ever seen. We hear reports of tornados from Florida to Maine. Flooding and loss of electricity are the most pressing concerns. Significant amounts of rain have already fallen and will continue. Nearly twelve inches have fallen in places like Dover, Delaware; Washington, D.C.; Charleston, South Carolina; and Richmond, Virginia. Air Traffic Control has halted all air travel across the United States. All international flights coming into the U.S. have been routed elsewhere, and all future flights have been grounded."

Jet's gaze fluttered to the window, expecting to see threatening clouds and a plane crashing into the ocean. Instead, he could barely make out a few stars.

"Let's bring in Ken Faukland for further information."

A portly man walked onto the screen. A large coffee stain covered half his shirt. He had two days of stubble on his face, and his hands were full of papers. He shuffled more than walked, and when he sat, the chair buckled under his weight. After a moment of laying out his papers, he started. "Thank you, Mark, ladies and gentlemen. I recently was on the phone with air traffic control, and the unthinkable has happened. As of fifteen minutes ago, we are aware of fifteen plane crashes. Those planes were flying over the eastern portion of the United States when the storms hit. Their crash sites will need to be confirmed, and it is inadvisable to release which planes have been affected. I know that might sound callous, but we have a lot of missing information. Please be patient with those involved; we understand your anxiety."

"Is this happening?" Mckenzey whispered. "How can they be so calm? I can't believe this." She began shaking uncontrollably.

Jet wrapped an arm around her, pulling her tight, trying his best to reassure her.

Mr. Faukland continued, "There are possibly another twenty flights unaccounted for. Remember that flights have been rerouted to several cities, including those in Mexico and Canada."

"Thank you, Mr. Faukland, a consultant with the Air Traffic Control," Mr. Davie said as he shook the man's hand. Turning back to the camera, he continued, "We will bring in Amelia Knightly, a forecaster at MeteoGroup U.K., with more information. Good morning, Amelia."

The screen changed, and a woman in her fifties, dressed in a brown full-length dress came into view. She stood near a map of the United States. Several of the larger cities of the Eastern Coast were plotted behind her. She said, "Good morning, Mark and Ken. We are indeed looking at a record-breaking storm system in the United States."

Jet watched as a computer animation showed two large high-pressure systems over Canada and Mexico.

Amelia explained, "The impact region of the two storms occurred over Kentucky, West Virginia, Virginia, and Washington D.C."

Jet watched as the storm systems moved together and collided on screen. The storm's size tripled to cover more than half of the United States.

"As you can see," Amelia Knightly continued, "this storm's sheer size is unprecedented. Several colored areas on the map coincide with the impact area, amount of rainfall, and damage. Red is depicted for the primary area." Pointing to a line from Washington D.C. to Kentucky, she added, "This area has received the largest damage, wind, and rainfall. Orange is the next color out from that central line, then yellow, and finally white."

Amelia added, "These four colors illustrate substantial changes in the storm's severity from one location to another. The red area has seen over twelve inches of rain in an hour and a half. Orange has seen above eight inches, yellow has seen four, and white two."

Mark Davie's voice could be heard off-screen. "These are just averages, aren't they?"

"No, Mark. That's one of the many particulars of this storm. There is a precise boundary that divides the precipitation amounts. Rainfall has stopped in and around

Washington D.C., New York, and most cities on the Eastern Coast. Normally, the storm would push off into the Atlantic. But this storm is now moving in the opposite direction, toward the West Coast. Several states are being placed on high weather alerts, from Missouri to Colorado. This storm is heading directly toward California."

CHAPTER 17

The news began repeating an hour later, and fortunately the local cell service became usable again. Using Mckenzey's cell phone, Jet called Nana, and he found her surprisingly calm and unworried. They chatted for a few minutes about the West Coast's potential risks and the fallout from this storm. Nana was far more concerned that he hadn't picked up the package she'd sent. His ears perked when he learned there was a birthday present inside. After assuring her that he would retrieve the package at the earliest possible moment, they hung up.

His feelings of relief were mirrored on Mckenzey's face as she hung up the phone after her call with her parents. She said, "I don't know how I forgot, but my parents are in Costa Rica. My dad had a business trip, and my mom and all three sisters went. They're on alert, but they haven't had any questionable weather. They were shocked to hear about the storm. How's Nana?"

"She's fine. She's more worried about this box she sent me for my birthday. She doesn't think that Portland is in any danger."

"Same."

"How's Eric?" he asked.

"He's fine. His entire school was up in Canada on a field trip. Can you imagine? When they get back, their school might be underwater, if it's still standing at all."

"Yikes. What are the chances?"

Mckenzey fell back onto the couch, exhausted. "Will you stay awhile? I don't think I can stand being alone."

"You bet." He wasn't sure he wanted to be alone either. He shuddered to think that maybe all of this could have been prevented, if only he had more information.

Over the next few hours, they moved or talked very little. It was calming being with Mckenzey, and he thought she felt it as well. It soon became clear that California was going to get some rain, but otherwise, they'd dodged any significant damage.

Mckenzey fell asleep next to him a few hours later. He tried to untangle himself from her, but she pulled his arm and refused to let him go. Around two in the morning, he paused the television and closed his eyes, falling asleep immediately.

* * *

Jet was nudged awake from a hand on his shoulder. His eyes fluttered open, and he found four people hovering over him. His eyes landed on someone he hadn't seen in years. *Not possible*, he thought. "Seyanna, is that you?"

"The one and only." Seyanna Motick was taller than both Latisha and Mckenzey. She was athletic, intelligent, and quick-witted. Her smile was dazzling, and she seemed genuinely happy to see him.

Jumping to his feet, Jet hugged her for a long time. "What are you doing here?"

"In the neighborhood for some coffee." She ruffled his hair. "We flew in this morning after hearing about the disaster. My parents were selected and tasked with analyzing the data from this storm. Our options were Florida or California. It wasn't a hard choice."

Glancing at her wrinkled clothes, he added. "Looks like you slept on the plane. Did you guys just get here?

"An hour ago. The parents dropped me off before heading to our hotel."

"How bad is it out there?"

Jayco answered, "We got almost four inches of rain. There are ponds between buildings. I doubt we'll have classes for a few days."

Mckenzey stirred on the couch. She asked, "Why's the television screen so blue?"

Jet turned to find the television picture paused, but the blueness was noticeable. He suddenly felt uneasy.

"Not sure," Grantham said. "Anyone know where the remote is?"

"Over here," Latisha said. Picking up the remote, she hit play.

The picture, very grainy when paused, improved the moment the video started playing. There was a low buzzing sound from the wind, and the image appeared to be from a video camera several feet above the water and moving fast. There was a mixture of blue and green covering the screen.

A choppy voice spoke. "Dawson … hear you? What … on? … do you see?" The crackling increased, but no voices could be heard. It was several moments before the conversation improved. The voice spoke again. "Dawson … Daw … Can you hear us?"

"Is that you, Phillip?"

"Yes. Yes. We hear you. This is Phillip Andrews, in studio, at Fox Five News. Our helicopter is reporting to you from Washington, D.C. Our crew is over the Potomac River.

This picture is coming to you live near the Ronald Reagan Airport. They are ten minutes from downtown Alexandria. Our helicopter has been circling the water for the last twenty minutes. They received several reports of lights escaping from the middle of the river. Dawson Riley is on location."

A harsh voice vibrated as Dawson Riley asked, "Can you hear me in the studio?"

"Yes, we can. Tell us what you see."

Dawson continued, almost yelling, "We're over the Potomac, half a mile south of the airport. Air traffic has been completely shut down. Only the Coast Guard, military, and emergency helicopters have taken off. On our approach, we noticed a deep fog that was difficult to maneuver through. Light escapes from the cold dark waters below if you look north and midway into the Potomac. Because of the wind, we had to drop back. We're making a second approach now."

The blueness of the fog increased Jet's unease. He wasn't sure what he was going to see, but it was going to be bad.

The helicopter inched closer to the diffused light. Rain fell hard, but they could make out a white beam of light exiting the water skyward. A second light came into view, different than the first and likely a spotlight from the helicopter. During certain moments, the blue fog blinded the camera. It took another thirty seconds for the image to improve.

When the helicopter was almost directly above the light, a gasp escaped from Mckenzey. "Holly hells. That is the exact picture from my dream."

Seyanna asked, "What's she talking about?"

"We'll explain in a minute," Jayco said abruptly.

"There's something just below the surface." Grantham pointed at the screen.

The helicopter inched closer, and the picture became more evident.

"What is it?" Seyanna asked.

Latisha answered, "Maybe it's a boat."

"There!" Jayco yelled. "Are those letters?"

As if on cue, a voice said, "It looks like something is in the water. Can you move closer? There may be some writing on the far side."

In a muffled voice, Dawson yelled, "Davie, get us closer!" In response, the helicopter moved cautiously forward.

Mckenzey said, her voice restricted, "It isn't a boat. It's an airplane!"

Seyanna asked, "How can you tell?"

Jet was stunned by the sight. He could just make out the fuselage of the plane. At least one of the wings appeared to have snapped off and was missing. It was white and lying on its side. The helicopter finally got close enough to read the side of the aircraft: THE PRINCESS.

Mckenzey's sharp voice caught everyone by surprise. "Oh no …! How can this be? Holly hells!"

"What's wrong?" Seyanna shouted.

Mckenzey's body started shaking. Somehow, she managed to whisper, "I know that plane."

Jayco asked, "How could you know *that* plane?"

"Because I was promised that I would be on it, flying to D.C."

"Are you saying what I think you're saying?" Latisha asked, shocked.

Mckenzey tried wiping the tears running down her face. In a soft voice, she said, "That plane, The Princess, came from our school. It was the plane that took our students to D.C. for the art competition."

"Oh freak," Jayco hissed.

"A parent of a senior student owns that plane. On special occasions, they let the school use it. The school has an appearance to uphold."

Seyanna asked, "Are you telling me you dreamt about this happening?" A look of disbelief and confusion spread across her face. "What's going on here?"

Jayco stepped in. "I'll tell you everything I know. Jet, do you have the book?"

Without glancing up, he said, "In my backpack."

"I'll get it." Grantham hustled to the hallway.

Jayco guided Seyanna into the kitchen. "Let's talk about things in here."

Latisha sat next to Mckenzey and wrapped her arm around her. Jet sat back down next to Mckenzey.

"I can't believe this is happening," Mckenzey sobbed.

Jet wanted to find the right thing to say to Mckenzey, the perfect something. Instead, he struggled to find the words. Finally, he mumbled, "We're going to figure this out."

Mckenzey jumped to her feet. "I can't just sit here. I'm going to shower."

"I'll head home," Jet said, feeling slightly bewildered. "Meet back here in thirty minutes?"

Mckenzey was already gone. Latisha shrugged and walked Jet to the door.

"Where are you going?" asked Seyanna.

"Just to shower. I'll be back soon."

Jayco said, "Will try to explain things the best we can."

Jet hurried back to his dorm, showered, and changed. It was like one punch to his stomach after another. He couldn't wrap his mind around the damages in D.C. Mckenzey was acting like a yoyo—she wanted him close then pushed him away. He chatted with his roommates for twenty minutes to clear his mind before returning to the girls' dorm.

Walking in, he found his friends seated at the table talking much more animatedly than when he left. Even better, there was a ton of food set out. He found a seat and started shoveling food onto his plate. He grabbed a slice of pizza, a burrito, a hand full of chips, and two sodas. But the best part was that he could smell homemade chocolate chip cookies in the oven.

Seyanna sat across from him with Latisha and Mckenzey flanking her. She had a determined look on her face. Grantham and Jayco sat next to Jet. "I want to see you open this book, and I want to see this tattoo on your back."

The Sorcerer's Guide lay on the table, and Jet pulled it closer. Like before, he used a single finger and flipped open the book.

"Close it again, and let me try." Seyanna tried prying open the book. Next, she said, "The tattoo?"

Jet removed his shirt and sat on the top of the table, facing away from the girls. He felt several fingers tracing the image. "This is beyond remarkable."

Throwing his shirt back on, he sat down.

Jayco and the others explained most everything. Seyanna pulled the open book toward her and said, "It really is blank."

"Told you," Jayco whispered.

Latisha said, "You're handling this much better than I did."

"Only on the outside," Seyanna admitted. She lifted her shorts to reveal a fist-sized purple butterfly on her upper thigh. "I got this six months ago on a trip to Norway. I lied and said I was eighteen, but I'm not sure they really cared. It's a reminder that life is still beautiful. It's one of the best I've ever seen. But it doesn't even compare to yours."

Seyanna had a dozen more questions, and Jet answered each of them. Partway through, Grantham and Latisha started searching the internet for stories related to the storm. Jet read the Marval Liken's letter, then the fable twice over, and explained the other things he'd seen. Seyanna was thoughtful and evaluated each piece she heard carefully. Jet couldn't tell if she believed him. After he was finished, Mckenzey explained her experiences.

At some point, Grantham shouted, "Come take a look at this." The group turned their attention to him. "The school blog reported it thirty minutes ago. All eleven people on board the private plane—The Princess—were killed. Five were students from the school, two pilots, two teachers, and two parents. The names have yet to be released so that the families can be contacted."

Grantham added, "Principal Fletcher gave a statement. 'This natural disaster has had far-reaching effects. We are saddened to have learned of the tragic deaths five students, two faculty, two parents, and two pilots. Our hearts go out to the families of those aboard the private airplane that went down near Washington D.C. yesterday. We join a long list of those who've felt the aftermath of this enormous catastrophe gripping our nation. All sporting activities, campus activities, and classes are suspended. Further information will be sent out accordingly.'"

"This whole thing is mind-blowing," Latisha said. "Do we need to tell someone what we know?"

"Like who?" Jayco said. "We don't even know what's going on. No one is going to listen to us."

"We must figure this out for ourselves," Mckenzey agreed.

"But how?" Seyanna asked. "I don't hear a lot of substantial information. Most of what you have is guesses. Stopping all of this, as good as it sounds, would be impossible. You have little information and no plans."

Jet said, "We need a break for a few minutes. Pass over some milk and cookies. Let's give ourselves ten minutes to relax."

During the break, Jet heard Jayco ask, "Seyanna, I thought all planes were grounded. How did you get to Cali?"

"My parents aren't your typical civilians. The military is flying around, and we caught a ride with them. We left during the storm, stopped in Japan, then Hawaii, and landed in California. Most of the grounded planes are on the East Coast."

"So," Jayco asked casually, "are you going to be here for a while?"

"Depends on what my parents find."

As his friends talked, he felt that he was overlooking critical information. While eating his cookies, he tried to go through what he knew. The feeling continued to grow even after they started making plans. Jet was assigned to reread everything in the book, scrutinize every word or meaning, and report back in one week. Jayco was going to follow Shane while Mckenzey and Latisha would start keeping track of some of the secret groups on campus.

When it was time to leave, Seyanna put on her coat and stood next to Jet. She asked, "Can I walk you back to your dorm?"

"I guess," he said.

Jayco overheard the question and flashed Jet a tight smile. He shrugged, opened the door, and Seyanna followed him outside. They stayed silent during the first half of the walk. Jet realized that she was still on the fence about what they'd just talked about in those few minutes. This information went against everything Seyanna had been learning in the last few years. According to Seyanna, science and nature had an answer for everything, even if we couldn't unravel the truth at this precise moment.

Seeing Seyanna also sparked several memories. Seyanna's family had moved to town during their second grade. They had met on the first day of school that year. Later in the year, he was introduced to Grantham and Jayco. It wasn't until third grade that they started hanging out in the cafeteria during lunch. Latisha joined the gang in fourth grade. That year, the name Echoes was suggested by Seyanna after they spent hours yelling in a cave just outside of town. Mckenzey had been the last to join as her family moved in during the summer before their fifth grade.

Seyanna cleared her voice and said, "Just so that we're getting a good look at all angles, this storm was a once-in-a-million experience. It might be something that's never happened before."

"What do you mean?" Jet asked.

"My parents called it El Niño!"

"What's that?"

"It's a weather pattern seen every five years in the Pacific. It's called El Niño-Southern Oscillation. It could even be called the La Niña-Southern Oscillation."

"Like that's not confusing."

"But it's so simple! El Niño causes weather disturbances every time it's around, from tornados to hailstorms, flooding, lightning, and extreme wind. And it occurs when two environmental factors collide. Temperature is central to this, along with temperature of the water's surface. La Niña happens when the pattern has a cooling temperature and El Niño when it has a warm temperature."

"Oh," Jet said, trying to sound confident.

"The second factor is an atmosphere change—hence, the Southern Oscillation.

"Is a normal person supposed to understand what you're saying?"

Seyanna laughed. "That was the easy part."

"Brilliant," Jet said. "I hope you're joking."

"You need to understand that El Niño or La Niña can combine with the Southern Oscillation."

"I thought that the Southern whatever-you-call-it was the atmospheric pressure."

"Exactly."

His dorm came into sight. "I'm officially lost! Why is this important?"

"I just want you to look at all the possibilities. My parents think that this recent event could've been a weather pattern. We're going to be here for a while. In the next few days, they're looking for a place to rent. UC Santa Barbara has the 3DVAR weather evaluation data that my parents can use."

"A weather pattern can't explain the tattoo and the book?"

"Not exactly," Seyanna said after a minute of silence. "What if two different things are happening?"

"What do you mean?"

"What if this tattoo thing and the book have nothing to do with what happened in Silverton or D.C. What if you are just connecting them?"

"I've thought about that. It's the blue fog that makes me believe they are connected. Silverton had the fog, my vision did, Mckenzey's dreams, and what we just saw on the television with the airplane crash. No. After today, I'm positive that they're connected. I just need to find out how."

Thoughtfully, Seyanna said, "I just want you to decide how far down this path you want to go. The real concern, if my parents are right, is this could happen again. Global warming is being accused of igniting this pattern, and my parents are trying to find out if this could be the beginning of something worse."

"Something worse is happening, but, in this case, I don't think it has anything to do with global warming," Jet said confidently.

Seyanna laughed awkwardly as if she was keeping something from him. "I hope you're wrong."

CHAPTER 18

Jet watched Seyanna leave and was more than grateful to see her again. He had telephoned her a few times a year and sent letters and emails. He had missed her a great deal and couldn't believe how much she had grown. She was beautiful and independent. Time, distance, and life had pulled them apart, but he still felt a connection with her. Instead of heading inside, he wanted some time to process everything that had happened.

The smell of rain and a fine mist touching his forehead pleased him, if only for a second, like a memory of home. He wiped away the moisture and for the first time, noticed his surroundings. Water had pooled between buildings and covered several of the paths. Dark clouds hung above him with fast moving clouds rushing out to the ocean as if they had somewhere else to be. A gust of wind nipped at the back of his neck, and he jerked his head. The boardwalk was almost entirely underwater, and the ocean waves were as murky as his thoughts.

The sensation of being in the wrong place itched at the back of his mind, but this time, it wasn't coming from his book. Back in Mckenzey's dorm, he felt that he was missing something and that feeling intensified in the damp air. He marched forward, letting his feet carry him away.

Twenty minutes later, he stepped around a large sycamore tree and found himself gazing at the alley leading to the science building's back door. He unlocked the door and stepped inside using a key that Autumn had given him. While heading in the direction of the classroom, he came across a staircase he hadn't seen before. It led to a lower level or basement. He didn't think he was completely underground as he reached the bottom. There was a large hall with several doors, some of which were locked. A few of the rooms beyond the open doors were empty, unused. On the far side of the building, he found two rooms full of random items—several old and outdated glass jars, broken tables, chalkboards, amongst other things.

Farther down the hallway, another room was full of old and broken furniture. He stepped inside to get a better look, but the door swung closed behind him. The room fell into darkness. Except the darkness wasn't as complete as he expected. Inching toward the back, he found a faint light piercing through a pile of crates. He placed his backpack on a broken desk then began pushing a few crates out of the way. The outline of a door producing a sliver of light appeared when he finished. He found no handle but rather a circular recess cut into the door. He felt around, hit a button, and heard a click. The door unhitched and swung inward.

A second room, considerably larger than the first, emerged. The only light source came from a row of three frosted glass windows near the wall's ceiling to his right. He couldn't make out anything specific from the outside. Each window was about six inches tall and two feet in length, all set into the red brick wall. The back wall was also brick, while the inner walls were concrete.

A small table sat in the center of the room and a closet and shelf against the back wall. The ceiling was a foot taller than he was. He ran his finger across a one inch layer of dust on the table. No one had been in this room for years. He returned to one of the other storage rooms and retrieved four glass jars, some chairs, and other items.

Once finished, he ran back upstairs, and ten minutes later, he was back in the room with the necessary supplies ready to work. It took him the better part of two hours to vacuum, dust, and clean. It was blissful to do something that didn't require any thinking. Once finished, he took the trash bags upstairs and dumped them in one of the alley trash bins. His stomach grumbled, but he ignored it. It was around 8 p.m., but he decided to continue working.

Finding some water and dirt and placing them in separate jars wasn't hard. He put some newspaper clippings that he'd torn apart in the third jar, prime for burning.

Once situated, he pulled out *The Sorcerer's Guide*. The words he'd read a few days ago were still visible:

Learn to manipulate each of Earth's elements.

Concentrate and adjust; advance and attack.

Did this tell him anything of use? No, it didn't. How was he supposed to manipulate the elements? He had some knowledge of fire, wind, water, and earth. But how did someone manipulate them?

He sat and considered what he'd already experienced with the book. The simple act of opening the book could not be explained independently. He hadn't done anything, to his knowledge, to trigger it. The same went for the turning of the pages. The tattoo on his back had appeared after he'd said a few words and touched the page. Maybe that was it. Aloud he repeated, "Learn to manipulate each of Earth's elements. Concentrate and adjust; advance and attack."

Nothing.

Taking his finger, he reached out and retraced each letter as if writing them for the first time. Again nothing. He struggled to brainstorm other options. The memory of when he'd spoken words after they appeared came into his mind. "What were they?"

It took a moment to remember. "Fireton. Secula. Riversiden."

This time, a thick haze rose from the floor. He watched as a page turned on its own accord without any prompting. This was the fourth page. A shadow appeared far in the distance of the page, moving directly at him like a runaway train. It started small, but it enlarged quickly. A nondescript image formed, and Jet felt that it might be a face. He couldn't identify a distinct mouth or eyes, but he clutched at the idea that someone or something was staring at him.

His suspicions were confirmed when the picture spoke. "Hello, Sorcerer." The voice was musical, deep, entrancing, and ancient yet Earthly. It oozed power.

The image in the book spoke again. "I am Wier of the Hearthstone plains—one of thirteen brethren and a trapped soul. I entered this servitude to mentor those on Elemental magic and manipulation. I am here to counter the Balakcursen tribe and their accursed phantom assassins. Most of my brethren have long since perished. Arisol enticed one of his assassins into *The Mage's Letters*. Leotyton, my master, requested that I give myself to *The Sorcerer's Guide*. I am your tutor."

Jet sat back, astonished. When he could speak, he asked, "Can you hear me?"

The image continued, "My overt power is minimal, as I am but an apparition. Doubt not my intention, skill, and qualifications. I can shift the balance of power through my words and guidance. Your understanding of magic is primitive. This tome, and so it should be called, is designed much like you entering a dark, vast, and expansive castle for the first time. It is unknown to you; the landscape and treasures are hidden within. The first step is the front door or the opening of this book. Then you must travel the long hallway of the castle. Every door and passage is locked, just like every page. At the end of the hall, there is another passage. Behind each door is a new room, letter, artifact, or another piece of information. I can sense your accomplishments or lack thereof and can help.

"However, if you refuse to move or are led down the wrong path, the next door will always be locked. So far, you have opened all the right doors, therefore I will give you the next manifestation."

A word bellowed into the room. "Geoagroterra."

In an instant, the room's light was sucked out, just like the vision before. Again, Jet was propelled forward, but this time, into the book. He landed hard on a sandy beach. The ocean breeze wafted over him. It was nighttime, and it took a moment for his eyes to adjust. He was crouched in a tree-covered area overlooking the ocean. A full moon reflected off the water, and the stars of the night were as bright as a million fireflies dancing in the sky. Peering between the trunks of palm trees, he could make out a dozen hooded figures facing the same direction. They stamped their feet rhythmically on the sand. A melancholic beat began, and Jet's heart matched each thump, a shot of adrenaline invigorating his mind. He counted the figures—thirteen in all, standing in a half-circle.

Boom, dah dah, boom, dah dah, boom…boom, dah dah, boom, dah dah, boom.

In the center of the twelve hooded figures, one man, the thirteenth, fell to his knees as if worshiping. He chanted in a language unlike anything Jet had ever heard. The pure white sand of the beach swayed back and forth in accordance with his words. The figure's pitch and cadence changed, and the sand reacted by flattening, as if bowing. Seven rows of raised sand formed in front of the fallen figure, reaching upwards a foot in the air. The first three rows turned gold while the back three rows became black, like sand from Iceland. The center row remained pristine and white.

Boom, dah, boom, dah, boom...boom, dah, boom, dah, boom.

The kneeling figure ceased his chanting, stood quickly, and stepped away from the rows of sand. The white sand, like a snake, slid out from the center, and it promptly encircled both colored rows of sand.

Boom, boom, boom, dah...boom, boom, boom, dah.

From somewhere unseen, a Chinese dizi flute began an up-tempo, reedy melody that matched the beating of the drum. From where this music came from, Jet did not know. He shivered as the musical cavatina unfolded. All thirteen hooded figures began a deep, ritualistic chant. He sensed more than anything that an ancient kindred spirit was being summoned.

All six rows of colored sand began interlacing, forming a creature from the sand. The legs and torso were built first. Soon the head, chest, and arms followed. The creature was made of earth and taller than any man. It stood nearly ten feet in height.

Suddenly, the drumbeats, flute, and chanting fell silent. The silence was breathtaking.

From this distance, Jet could see the creature's mouth open. It bellowed a single word. "Terranaeth."

The power of this word was deep and piercing. A heap of sand, mud, and rocks exploded into the air and encircled the entire group. The storm dissipated, and the debris fell harmlessly to the ground, covering the hooded figures.

The creature's hand waved back and forth in the direction of the ocean. A circular object, cobalt blue, rose from the depths of the water. It might've been the strangest object Jet had ever seen. It was not solid but fluid in its movement, and it glowed. The outer edges danced back and forth, not constrained to any one shape, though it primarily stayed in roundish form. Its movement reminded Jet of a droplet as it ebbed and flowed.

A second deep and archaic word echoed from the earth being. "Aquaenaeth."

The creature tossed the circular object above the heads of the thirteen hooded figures. It levitated several feet into the air and flattened out then popped like a bubble, and the liquid inside dispersed and fell onto the hooded figures.

The earth creature took several steps back, placing distance between itself and the group. It waved at the ground, but this time, a piece of driftwood emerged from the sand and sat at its feet. Whispering, a fire erupted onto the dried wood, and even from this distance Jet could feel the heat. It lifted its arms toward the sky and bellowed, "Ignisnaeth."

The fire propelled skyward, turning the night as bright as day for many seconds. Thirteen fragments of fire broke apart and descended onto the hoods of each figure. The instant the embers contacted the hoods, it was absorbed.

The creature stood to its full height and roared, "Ventusnaeth!" A wind as mighty as a hurricane formed not far from shore. It advanced toward the group at an astonishing speed. A wall of wind crashed into them from the side. Each coat was tossed, and the figures braced themselves against the power.

Jet could also feel the powerful blast even from this distance. A moment later, the wind disappeared entirely.

The creature's head perched skyward as the figures adjusted their clothing. To Jet's astonishment, a high-pitched sound and a flash of light rose from above them. Not long afterward, a glowing object came into view. There were red and orange flames surrounding it as if it fell from the sky. It was a stunning sight to behold. The item circled the beach as it descended.

The object crashed into the beach, spraying sand into the air. After hitting the ground, it slid forward with purpose. The object came to rest at the feet of the creature. Bending down, it picked up the item. Jet recognized the item as the biggest meteorite he'd ever seen. The creature easily crushed the meteor, and two dozen smaller pieces emerged. Three rocks were thrown to each of the hooded figures who gripped them in their cupped hands.

Instantly the drumbeats, chanting, and flute began anew.

Boom, dah dah, boom, dah dah, boom...boom, dah dah, boom, dah dah, boom.

The rocks began to glow.

Jet's view of the beach began to diminish. It did not take long for the image in his vision to become blurry. Soon it was entirely black.

Once he'd returned to the basement room, he found himself in the exact spot as before. The voice of Wier entered his mind. "You've beheld the melding of the Elemental Alliance. It was arranged by the father of mother earth, who helped birth this planet. Life became complete as the five elements combined, and Elemental magic was tamed. Go forth and learn how to control the elements. You must be diligent and precise. If you fail to do so, all may be lost."

CHAPTER 19

The next several days passed in a haze. Classes had been canceled from Thursday, the second week in September, to the following Wednesday. The destruction from the storm boggled the mind. Thousands and thousands of homes were destroyed beyond repair. Flooding continued in dramatic form. The nation's president called for immediate international relief and funding for those affected. Cholera and other infections, waste, inadequate sewage storage, and lack of food and water, were among some of the most challenging sufferings in the days that followed.

It was the most substantial single weather destruction in the nation's history. Jet couldn't imagine how the country would react. He was convinced that every looter would be out taking advantage of the situation. And plenty of that did happen, but surprisingly far less than he expected. Instead, the nation and the world found a way to work together. Millions of dollars, supplies, and relief workers deluged the affected areas and brought about unimaginable miracles.

On Saturday, Jet, Grantham, and Jayco escaped the campus for several hours as they piled into Jayco's yellow jeep. After receiving the go-ahead, they slipped into Santa Barbara for some much-needed shopping. Jet bought new clothes, books, a cellphone, and a dozen other items.

Jayco insisted that Jet pick out every clothing item two sizes too small.

"Better to see your biceps and abs," he'd explained.

After five shirts with hideous colors that almost cut off his windpipe, Jayco was relegated to the bench. Grantham's help was much more helpful. His style wasn't the same as Jet's, but it worked. He purchased new bedding and a pillow. The instant his cell phone came out of its box, he sent a dozen messages to everyone he could think of.

The next few days were full of guilt and melancholy. Jet repeatedly wondered if he could have prevented the disaster, realized he couldn't, but felt guilty nonetheless. Jet learned that twelve students had left school with no intention of returning. Everywhere you turned, someone talked about the plane crash, family deaths on the east coast, or the country's general state. No amount of miracles could overcome the fear that had begun to infest the nation.

To the joy of everyone, classes restarted Thursday morning, just over a week after the disaster. Both the students and teachers alike had difficulty getting back into the mindset of school, but they appreciated the distraction that classes provided. They were lucky if they received ten minutes of effective teaching for the first few days. Each evening, Jet returned to the science building for more practice using the elements. There had been small movements in everything but fire. He'd even managed to knock the lid off one of the jars using *Ventusnaeth*. He had yet to share his very basic magical talents with his friends. In fact, he barely saw any of them.

After Friday's classes, Jet returned home and found a pink piece of paper on his door. It read: "Mr. Black: Your parcel has yet to be claimed. Unless it is picked up soon, it will be sent back to the sender."

Jet groaned, sprinted back downstairs, stepped outside, and crossed an open courtyard in the direction of the La Jolla dorm building. This was the largest boy's dorm on campus and was the central location for all the mail in the entire school. Most days, several student workers separated mail and smaller parcels into slots assigned to each building. At a designated time, they would be transported to each building. Jet was fortunate that he didn't have to go across campus to get his package.

The outer door into the mailroom was open, and several students were finishing up the day's last-minute arrangements. Jet crossed the room and found a smaller room with the door open. A short brunette, with her back to him, was still working. She glanced up as he stepped into the doorway.

"Can I help you?" she asked. Her brown bangs nearly covered her eyes. Reaching up, she brushed them aside.

Pulling out his campus ID and the pink notice, he said, "I guess I have a package that needs to be claimed."

Eyeing the pink notice, she said, "That particular color tells me you haven't picked up what you were supposed to."

"It's been a busy few weeks," he said, feeling defensive.

"Your package has been here so long we thought the world would end before you picked it up."

"Really?"

The girl blushed, and her green eyes quickly looked away. Somewhat apologetically, she said, "I guess it just about did." She smiled awkwardly, and Jet wondered if he'd ever seen her on campus. She was likely the same year or older. He doubted a first-year student would get this good of a job. She added quickly, "We took bets on when this would be picked up. I guessed that we'd have to send it back. I almost won ten bucks!"

"Nice," he said as he glanced around to see if anyone could overhear their conversation.

"Any chance your roommates are here with you?"

"Afraid not."

"It's way too heavy for one person."

"Really?" Jet asked. He didn't think he'd forgotten that many items.

Before he responded, she said, "I could let you borrow a dolly, but it's in the basement, so you'll need to give me a minute." Without waiting for an answer, she nudged him out of the doorway and closed the door.

"It can't be that heavy, can it?" he asked.

"It is." She walked toward a hall he hadn't seen before. At the end of the hall, she opened an elevator and stepped inside. As the door closed, a look of triumph spread across her face. She said, "Catch you on the flip side."

Shaking his head, he smiled. Five minutes later, the elevator opened, and the brunette was back with a dolly.

"I appreciate this. While you were gone, I noticed this door in the back. Does it lead outside?"

"It's an emergency exit." She leaned in and whispered, "But nothing alarms when you leave. Sometimes, I need a little break, and I'll sneak out back."

"I bet," he said covertly. "Where does it go?"

"An alley. No one can see you." She winked. "But don't tell anyone."

"No way." He smiled reassuringly at her. "I'm Jet."

"Brenda." She bounced to the mailroom door and reopened it. "Your package is doubling as my table."

"Really?"

"Without a doubt."

The package was more like a trunk, and it indeed was cumbersome. There were several books, a drink, some flowers, and a lamp on top. Brenda quickly moved the items, and together they tied a cord around it and transferred it onto the dolly.

"What do you have in there?" Brenda asked after they finished. "It felt like a secret weapon."

"I wish," he said, unsure if he should trust her or not about this package from Nana. Instead, he said, "I'm a TA for a science class, and we needed some equipment. I ordered a ton of things. I must've accidentally given them my dorm address rather than the schools. Though honestly, this will probably end up working better. And with this dolly, I can get it to where it needs to go."

Brenda interrupted his thoughts. "Just bring back the dolly."

"No problem."

"I'll be gone by the time you come back, but you can leave it in the corner." She pointed to the far side of the room. "This is kind of exciting. I bet there is treasure inside."

"Definitely."

Brenda shot him a look, and he was confident that this was the most exciting thing to happen to her for a while. Anything entertaining was probably better than her typical day.

He played along. "I'll go as quietly as possible. Make sure no one sees me."

"Will do."

"Close the door behind me."

She nodded excitedly.

Pushing open the door, it moved soundlessly. Jet was relieved to find that the alley was empty. There was no way in the world that he was going to keep anything of value at his dorm. He knew the perfect spot. Brenda's eyes blazed with triumph as she watched him go. The end of the alley merged onto a campus walkway. Guiding the dolly to the science building and down the elevator was painless. It took a few minutes to clear a big enough path to get the crate inside the second room, and then a bit of ingenuity and sweat to get the crate onto the table. However, opening it was another story. No matter what he did, it remained closed. He wondered if there might be a tire iron in the building that could help.

His cell phone rang, and he hesitated in answering. He glanced down and was surprised to see Grantham's name on the caller ID. He answered, "Hello."

"Get over to Latisha's dorm right now."

"Why?" he asked.

"Someone just tried to break into their dorm."

"What?"

"The girls got home tonight, and their door was wide open. When they entered, two people rushed past them. One of them knocked Mckenzey to the ground."

"I'm on my way."

He hurriedly rearranged the closet, then exited the room. He guided the dolly upstairs and ran for the front door. He passed his classroom when he realized that he had intended to leave through the back door. The dolly slipped from his hands and crashed to the floor.

"I don't have time for this," he muttered, bending over to retrieve the dolly.

"Can I help you?" The voice was tense and caused Jet to pause.

Jet turned and stood.

"Is that you, Mr. Black?" Professor Rysen asked.

"Yes." A sense of relief flooded over Jet.

"What in the world are you doing here on a Friday night? I haven't seen any other students in hours."

"I know. I tried taking advantage of the empty building and trying to create a distraction with everything going on. The last place I wanted to be was in my dorm tonight. I was cleaning and moving a few items around. I brought this dolly over and just finished. It slipped through my hands as I was leaving."

"I hear you're doing a great job. Autumn and Professor Blum talk very highly of you. But on a Friday night, I strongly advise you to hang out with your friends rather than work."

"Good advice. I just needed a few hours alone."

"Need any help?"

"I'm all finished. Just bringing this dolly back to my dorm. I couldn't find one here."

"I don't think we have one upstairs, but have you checked the basement?"

A feeling of anxiety seized him. Had Professor Rysen been in the building when he arrived?" Jet managed to say, "I didn't know there was a basement."

"Not many students do, even the ones that work here. I just came to drop off a couple of things. Can I give you a ride back to your dorm?"

"No, I don't want to be a bother."

"I insist. Just give me a moment." Professor Rysen disappeared across the hall, and less than a minute later, he reappeared. "My truck is in the alley; we can throw that into the back."

Relief washed over Jet. There hadn't been a truck in the alley when he'd arrived.

Professor Rysen placed the dolly into the back with ease while Jet climbed into the passenger seat. As the truck started, Professor Rysen asked, "Now, what dorm are you in?"

"Kelci Halls."

"I'm getting used to most things here, but you'll have to show me which one."

"No problem."

Professor Rysen continued, "If I remember correctly, you're a sophomore."

"Yes, sir."

"But not from California. Where did you say you were from?"

"Portland."

"And you like it here?"

"I do. I love living near the coast. That's the main reason I chose to come here."

"I was teaching on the East Coast. California is very different from there. I'm glad for the change though."

Jet nodded.

"Terrible what happened on the East Coast. I just can't believe it. And to think, a plane with some of our students. I can hardly believe it."

"I know," Jet said. "Things always seem worse when you know someone involved."

"I agree," Professor Rysen said. "I love science and struggle to imagine how something like this could've happened."

"My friend says her parents think it could be something from El Niño. But I'm not sure."

"A very reasonable concept."

Pointing down the street, Jet said, "Second building on the right."

When the truck stopped, they both got out. Professor Rysen removed the dolly and handed it to Jet. "Have a good weekend, Joshua."

"You too, Professor. And thanks for the ride."

"No problem."

As Jet stepped toward his dorm, Professor Rysen asked, "Are you going to the memorial tomorrow? It seems like the entire school is invited."

Jet said, "Yes, we are. One of my friends was in a class with some of those who died. I think it's important that we go to remember their lives."

"I guess I might see you tomorrow."

"Goodnight."

Jet felt the professor's eyes on him to the building. He waved as he stepped inside. He quickly found a place where he could watch Professor Rysen leave. A moment later, the truck disappeared down the road. Jet waited two minutes before exiting the front door and crossing the courtyard back to La Jolla. Letting himself in from the alley, he placed the dolly against the wall. Soon he was sprinting up the beach toward Latisha's dorm.

CHAPTER 20

Mckenzey and Latisha wore looks of venom as Jet stepped into their dorm. For some reason, they were both glaring at him.

Grantham rolled his eyes and said, "Took long enough." Seyanna arrived like thirty minutes ago.

"Sorry. I came as fast as I could." He searched the dorm, expecting the worst, but was surprised to see that there didn't seem to be any damage. "Is anything missing?"

Latisha hissed, "We got back from shopping just in time. They couldn't have been in our dorm for more than a minute. No damage and nothing missing."

"What were they after?" Jet asked.

Latisha answered, "No clue. But on Monday, I'm going across the street, and I'm going to make a stink."

Mckenzey finally spoke. "But this time, we *know* exactly who broke into our dorm."

"We do?" Jet asked. "Did you see their faces? Was it that same kid who broke into mine?"

"No. It was that Jocelyn girl and … Ariana."

"Are you sure?"

"Don't you believe me?" Mckenzey stared at him intently. "I'm one hundred percent positive."

Jet was overwhelmed by the idea. "I didn't ask her to do it, Mckenzey. Why are you mad at me?"

"She was at your dorm, pretending not to know anything. They didn't find what they were looking for, so they came to break into my dorm."

Seyanna asked, "What were they looking for?"

"I bet they're after the book," Jayco said.

Grantham stepped closer. "I agree. Where's it now?"

"With me. I always keep it close."

"Good," he said. "If they're looking for the book, we're all at risk. We need to be more careful."

"Any ideas?" Latisha asked. "What do you mean, 'be more careful.'"

"Watch what you say and where you say it. You never know who could be listening."

"But that's a defensive position," Jayco insisted. "We need to be attacking somehow."

Seyanna said, "I can help with that. They have no idea who I am. I'll try to find some information."

"How?"

"As a prospective student. I received a scholarship here as well. Let's see what my parents and I can find."

"Don't tell them too much," Jet insisted.

Seyanna rolled her eyes. "No kidding."

An hour later, Jet left the dorm. The idea of Ariana breaking into Mckenzey's dorm made him angry. The last thing he wanted to do was go home and sulk. He was half tempted to stomp over to Ariana's and demand answers. But he had no idea where she was living right now. Even if he did, he realized that he wanted to look inside the crate more than anything else. As he stepped away from Mckenzey's dorm, another thought overwhelmed him. They were likely being watched. Ariana had hinted at this before. He began an elaborate series of direction changes, circling buildings and running through water up to his knees. Along the way, he willed his vision to change, and for the first time, it obeyed his directive. After ten minutes of maneuvering, he was confident he was alone. When he finally reached the science building, he realized that the stories about his great uncle were much less farfetched than he had grown up believing. He had also likely assumed that he was being followed.

Once he slipped inside the science building, he allowed his vision to normalize. He quickly ran down the stairs and into the hidden room. The crate was still in the center of the room. He tugged, pulled, and kicked at the chest with similar results as before. Searching the room, he found a metal hanger and straightened one side. Using this, he tried to pick the lock. It turned out that this was far easier than he imagined. He heard a click, and the lid opened.

The box was six or eight inches wide and four feet long. There were several layers of sheets, followed by crushed newspaper. When he removed the last protective layer, Jet was astonished at what he was looking at. There were dozens of bizarre objects placed throughout the crate.

"How's this possible?" he muttered. Where in the world did Nana get a golden pyramid?

The pyramid was not the only shocking discovery. He began stacking the items on the floor around him. Christmas had never been this good. He placed several books, small glass jars, and clothing to his left. Closer to the door, he put some elegant jewelry and an old picture with markings closely resembling Egyptian hieroglyphics. Reaching inside, his hand brushed a soft cloth, and a connection, as thin as a wisp of smoke, developed in his mind. An instant later, the link was gone.

He recognized a few glass jars from their family's storage unit, but he couldn't remember seeing such an assortment of ancient and impressive items. Most of what he'd seen this past summer was junk. But not a single item before him could be described as junk, except the moth-eaten coat shoved between a few items preventing them from crashing together.

Under the cloth was a small envelope. Jet recognized Nana's writing on the outside. He bent over, picked it up, and tore it open.

Dear Joshua,

I'm unsure if anything I write will satisfy your curiosity or adequately explain what you're looking at. I know very little about the meaning of most of these items, but for you, their importance will likely become apparent over time. This is your true heritage. Please forgive me for the delay. You see, I've kept a few of these items hidden to pass them down to you at the right time. Some of the other things were found in the storage locker of your great uncle Joshua Taley.

Uncle Taley was much more than a bumbling drunk. Your parents learned this the hard way, as did I. It was too late for me to do anything productive to help him. Your parents tried following in his footsteps, but they most likely failed as well. Now it's your turn. Uncle Taley was a protector of something magical and of great importance. He never told me what. He did say that something of incalculable value needed to be found. I believe you are a protector of it as well. These items helped him, and they may help you. Keep them safe and secure, and let only those you trust know of their existence.

Joshua, please forgive an old lady for her follies. I should've talked to you about this obligation a long time ago. The Taley, now Black, family heritage is a rich history of intrigue, danger, and regret. Much of that history has been withheld from you, for better or worse. The surname Taley was chosen by our family when we came to this country many years ago. After Uncle Joshua died, you know that we changed our family name to Black. With mixed emotions, I inform you that we are not descended from Irish and English settlers as you were told growing up. We are a family with German ancestry and are proud of it. Our German surname was Traugott, which means 'trust in God.'

Two weeks before he died, my brother came to me and told me that he was a protector of the lost truth of Egyptian civilization. The understanding of our family's quest and purpose has changed over time. I don't know if you remember that your parents spoke to you in German when you were younger. It wasn't until after my brother died that your parents began searching for an item that was important to them. I do not know if they found it.

You may ask why I've kept these things hidden from you. I don't have an adequate answer. Maybe I was hoping that the dangers would pass you by. My suspicions that you were more than a typical child arose the day we lived through the destruction of our home. But then you forgot most of what happened, and I hoped to believe. But when someone came looking for the storage locker, everything fell into place. I sincerely believe they were searching for some of the items I am sending you. I've always known about the storage unit. I'm sorry that I lied, but it was to protect you.

If you are a protector, you may be the first to have such a collection of items. Uncle Joshua and your parents found and passed these items to you. You need to understand the dangers that will come in the days ahead. As a protector, you'll need to guard these items and be prepared for an attack. The person who came to look for the storage unit might eventually connect you to them. More importantly, I fear that you can't accomplish this task without help. Find those who are worthy to stand with you.

Mag Gott ihr licht sein—May God be your light

Nana Black

PS: Don't send correspondence back, and if we talk, only do so in generalities, unless in person.

Jet sank into his chair, both crushed and astonished by what he read. He was part German, and he felt validated for what he and his friends had learned so far. Reading Nana's words unlocked memories of when his dad spoke a few words to him in German. Another time, he'd overheard his parents talking but couldn't understand what they were saying. Nana had hidden many things from him, and so had his parents. He suddenly remembered the questions Shane had asked. *I want to know if they died here in the US or in another country like Germany or Egypt? Were they tourists or just plain idiots?*

Jet felt a pang of regret and anger. He needed to find out how and where his parents had died.

"It's for your protection." His voice mimicked Nana's.

Jet placed the letter back in the envelope and tossed it onto the table. He needed to mentally compartmentalize his thoughts and feelings about Nana and his parents. This was not the time to focus on his hurt feelings toward them. This crate might explain why his dorm, and even Mckenzey's, had been broken into. Maybe they weren't looking for *The Sorcerer's Guide* after all.

He settled down and began cataloging the items inside the crate. The first was a jar half-filled with black powder. Other jars held a variety of objects, including two dozen multicolored stones, dried corn, feathers, dark red dirt, eagle talons, shark teeth, and one with a hundred or more arrowheads. The jewelry entailed at least ten rings, three necklaces, and two bracelets. He touched each of them—most were warm, but two of the rings were icy cold. Next, he flipped through four ancient books, followed by four black-and-white photos, one of a small room and three others of Egyptian paintings.

He found a metal vase with several long sticks with a coating on one end. A few hieroglyphics were etched on the vase's smooth, pristine outer edge. There was a faint aroma of burning sticks. The smell was mesmerizing. It prompted a forgotten memory, a story his father had once told him about an ancient box. He remembered thinking that this box was one of his father's most prized possessions as a child. The way his dad had talked about it, and if Jet listened well enough, he'd believed that the box would be his someday.

An image burst into his mind of an ancient box of black stone covered with concentric circles, animals, and hieroglyphics. His dad had drawn it once, shown it to him, and threw the drawing in the fire. He tore through the rest of the items, hoping the box was one of the items, but he came up empty-handed.

Something caught his eye. This item he recognized and had even played with it when he was younger. It glimmered black like snake scales. It was smaller than he remembered. The amulet had a small loop at the top that didn't entirely close. It was designed in the shape of a cursive, elegant, lower-case L. When Jet was younger, he would place the circle around his finger and twirl it repeatedly.

He placed the amulet on the table then returned to the collection. There was a circular stone with several hieroglyphic markings on both sides. He turned it over and found that a portion of the backside was crumbling away. He gently placed it on the table before it broke completely. Scattered on the bottom of the crate were a dozen small silver coins with an engraved wolf-like beast on their backsides. The last item was tucked into the far bottom corner. It was a gaudy, greenish-gold necklace that was circular and flat. An animal medallion hung at the apex of the chain—a bird, probably a falcon. Jet lightly placed it next to the other jewelry and surveyed everything he'd been given.

Despite everything he saw, he was still most intrigued by the pyramid. It was heavy, and he thought there was a good chance it was made of gold. Each side of the base was eight inches in length. It had to be more than twenty pounds. His fingers traced a set of grooves facing the same direction on two of the four sides. He fumbled with it, and the pyramid slipped from between his fingers and fell end over end toward the ground. To his amazement, it moved against gravity, rotated itself, and slowed. The bottom end hit the ground first, entirely noiselessly.

CHAPTER 21

Early the following day, Jet dressed hastily and dashed from his dorm to meet his friends. He wore shorts and a Pink Floyd tee-shirt. He no longer required his sling. He was feeling better than he had in the last few weeks. He wasn't the only one running late, and he passed several other students, teachers, and parents.

As he walked, there was a buzz in his pocket. Checking his phone, he found that he had a voicemail. He hadn't heard the phone ring at all. He expected the message to be from Mckenzey or Latisha, telling him how late he was. It wasn't. Jet hadn't yet programmed in the number, but he recognized it immediately as Ariana.

After clicking a few numbers, Ariana's voice echoed, "Hey Jet. I got your number from Napoleon. Glad to hear you have a cell phone now and that you've joined the twenty-first century." There was a short pause. "You know why I'm calling. Here's the truth. Jocie and I were tasked to approach Mckenzey and Latisha and warn them. We arrived with a plan to talk to them. But their door was wide open, and it was my choice to go inside and make sure they were all right. It looks bad, I admit. I'm telling you that we didn't break inside. Staying and explaining things wasn't exactly the best idea either. Please pass it along."

Jet hung up the phone as he crossed the street. He was angry, and the story Ariana told him made no sense. He doubted any of his friends would believe it either. When he reached the pavilion, catching up with his friends didn't take long.

"About time," Latisha hissed. "They're starting in less than five minutes."

"I made it, didn't I?"

The day couldn't have been more perfect with blue skies and a pleasant cool breeze rising from the bay. A makeshift memorial had been organized just hours after learning of the crash, not far from where they stood. Three of the five students were from California while another was from Japan, and the last one was from Arizona. Funerals were scheduled over the next few days for each student in their home cities.

Principal Jan Fletcher stood on the platform and directed parents and other visitors to their seats. She shook hands with the governor of California and Santa Barbara's mayor. The area in front of the platform had been roped off. Onlookers stood to the side of this area and farther back. A massive memorial with an almost life-sized picture of each student or teacher was arranged on the grass. There were hundreds of flowers, presents, personal items, and much more strewn across the lawn.

Grantham eyed the onlookers. "More people than I thought."

"This is a big deal," Mckenzey said.

Scanning the crowd, Jet quickly located Ariana standing on the opposite side of the memorial. Just seeing her made him upset.

Jayco stepped close and whispered, "I guess you see her then."

"Did Mckenzey?"

"Not yet, but World War III might erupt if she does."

Jet whispered, "She called me this morning trying to explain. She said they were told to follow Mckenzey and Latisha and talk with them. When she arrived, the door was already open."

"Do you believe her?"

"Not really. Should I tell Mckenzey?"

Jayco whistled. "Not today."

"My thoughts exactly."

Jet continued to scan the crowd. It didn't take long for him to spot Shane. He stood apart from his friends. Raul was a dozen people away from his sister. Jessiva and Clyde were closer to Jet on this side of the memorial. He'd heard that Nash had taken medical leave for surgery on his knee. Vinny, Jake, and Jocelyn were also spread out at the back of the open area staring at the pavilion. Suddenly, Jet realized that none of their clothing matched.

Jet pulled at Jayco's shoulder just as Jan Fletcher tapped the microphone and spoke. "Good morning all—students, families, and visitors, we come together at this difficult time in part to celebrate the lives of those lost—"

"Jayco."

"Yeah?"

"Shane and all his friends are spread out in the crowd."

"That doesn't mean anything."

"They're all wearing different clothing. None of them match."

Jayco's head snapped toward Jet. "They're up to something."

"My thoughts exactly."

"Be ready," Jayco hissed. "I'll tell Grantham."

Jet stared at Jan Fletcher as she spoke, but he heard nothing. Time passed. The governor began speaking.

A voice spoke into his ear. "Are you ignoring me?"

Jet jumped. He hadn't heard anyone approaching. "Not really," he muttered when he realized it was Mckenzey. "I just thought you were still upset at me."

"I was never furious at you. I just can't stop thinking about what they were searching for."

Jet leaned closer. "I have an idea. I'll show you after the memorial if you're up to it."

"Did you find something?"

As Jet turned toward Mckenzey, movement caught his eye. At that precise moment, Shane nodded at someone closer to the pavilion.

Mckenzey's voice sounded annoyed. "Is there something else going on?"

Jet said quickly, "Shane's up to something. Be on guard."

"What do you mean?"

"He and his friends are all spread out. Just be ready … for anything."

An eruption of clapping caused Jet to glance up at the stage. The mayor of Santa Barbara had just finished. A dozen people walked onto the scene with an impressive display of flowers.

Jet hadn't heard what had just been said, but soon the flowers lined the front edge of the stage, becoming increasingly crowded. A glass gallery was pushed onto the stage, and it wasn't hard to realize that it held some or all the students' artwork. The clapping around him was thunderous.

Mckenzey wrapped an arm around him and asked, "What is going on?"

"I don't know. They aren't dressed the same, and they are spread out."

"They better not do anything stupid here."

The next speaker introduced each student and their families. The words spoken were energetic yet appropriate. He mixed in humor, stories, and sadness. The entire crowd seemed to be engaged, laughing and crying simultaneously. His words and voice were mesmerizing. The crowd clapped loudly when he finished.

The next speaker spoke similarly for the teachers. She was equally effective, though in a different way. Love, honor, and sacrifice for their students were expressed repeatedly.

The last speaker, Principal Fletcher, began her final remarks with, "Let us remember, not just today, nor tomorrow, but forever those who—"

A loud crack vibrated in the air like a firework prematurely set off. The crowd gasped.

Three black sparks flew into the air. Jet was transfixed as the flares traveled upward, peaked, and exploded. Light shimmered throughout the field. There was a mass of 'oohs' and 'aahs' from those on the stand and in the crowd. Over the noise, Jet could hear Principal Fletcher thanking everyone for coming. Three more fireworks exploded overhead, this time closer to the stage. He watched as some debris fell around them. He felt tiny sand-like crystals washing over his face and arms. Suddenly his skin felt like it was on fire.

A moment later, Grantham rushed at him from several feet away, almost shoving him face-first into the ground. "Get down!"

"What are you doing?"

"The color of your skin is changing!"

"To what?"

"Red. Very red!"

Jet was shocked to see how bright red his arms were. It had taken only seconds. He had a flashback of lava, and suddenly he smelled burnt skin. Someone stepped on his ankle, and he howled in agony. His vision blurred, and the burning intensified.

There was a distant scream, and he also registered someone pulling at his arm. He thought he heard Mckenzey asking, "Jet, is that you?"

As hard as Jet tried, he couldn't speak. What was happening to him? More screams erupted around him. It sounded like panic was running wild. He fell to his knees and vomited. A picture of a girl with burned skin came into his mind. She'd been attacked, and so had he.

"Get out of here!" Jayco's voice pierced the air. "I need to find out what's going on. Mckenzey and Seyanna, get Jet out of here. Latisha and Grantham, come with me."

Hands tugged, and a coat with a hood was pulled over him. Two arms, one on each side, pulled him to his feet and steadied him as they began to move. He lost track of what direction they were headed. They walked for an eternity. Jet's legs gave out; the pain was so intense. He was dragged back to his feet for another several steps. He finally stopped moving, and he wasn't sure he could take another step.

"You're going to be all right," someone whispered. He heard a car door open a moment later, and he was shoved into the back seat.

Seyanna asked, "Where do we go?"

"My dorm," Jet answered.

The car shot forward.

Seyanna said, "Mckenzey, your skin is turning too. Not as bad as Jet, but it's obvious.

"How's this possible?" Mckenzey asked.

A minute later, Seyanna hissed, "Nuts."

"What is it?" Jet asked.

"There's a ton of people at your dorm. We can't sneak you inside without being seen."

"I'm having trouble breathing." Jet wheezed, wishing he had his inhaler with him.

A phone began ringing. Mckenzey answered. "Jayco. What's going on?" A short pause. She roared, "Shane or his friends shot something into the air. There were another three students affected who also lived in Silverton during the disaster. Two of the three ran from the memorial as quickly as they could. Shane and his friends cornered Kevin McCormick."

Jet tried to concentrate on what was being said. It was as if a vice had been set over his lungs. Without warning, a set of images flashed into his mind. Jet wheezed, "Where's Jayco?"

Mckenzey said, "Still at the memorial. They wanted to show Shane that they weren't affected."

"Tell him to meet us at the science building."

"What?"

"The science building. Trust me. The alley in the back."

"Okay," Mckenzey said.

Sometime later, Jet was jolted awake. His mind felt fuzzy, and he couldn't open his eyes.

"We're here," Seyanna said. "Now what?"

Reaching his hand in his pocket, Jet pulled out his keys. "The back door. Basement."

"We're here too," Jayco said.

"You need to carry Jet. Mckenzey is affected too. She is starting to feel the burn."

Grantham asked, "Where are we going?"

Jet hissed, "Inside, turn left. Down the stairs, turn right, and walk for a while. Find a room with three broken tables and two chairs just inside the door." Jet was lifted and carried into the building. They quickly moved downstairs and through the corridor.

Grantham yelled, "I think it's down here."

Jet whispered, barely able to speak, "There's a second door in the back. Open the door and get inside."

He heard someone say, "Why did we come here?"

Jet's pain was overwhelming. "There's a second door farther inside the room."

"Found it," someone shouted. "What the—"

"Next to the crate on the floor."

"What now?" Mckenzey asked.

Jet mustered all his remaining strength. The pain was beyond anything he'd ever experienced. He croaked, "The crate ... glass jar ... black powder."

He slumped to the floor, unconscious.

CHAPTER 22

A light, a hundred miles away, blinked into existence. Jet felt as if he was being pulled through the mind of an ancient intelligence. Many of his insecurities were exposed for all to see. A cacophony of voices, both praising and accusatory, could be heard all around him. He was being examined in such a personal way; he loathed it.

Suddenly the lights turned back on, and he was an outsider watching as six white-tailed deer roamed through the underbrush of a forest floor. What he saw felt as real as anything he'd ever experienced. The wind brushed against his face, and there was the sweet scent of the forest. Dawn hadn't yet arrived.

The dead leaves and debris rustled as the deer continued moving forward, searching for food. Suddenly all six deer stopped as if sensing something alarming. An implausible figure drifted into view. It was dark, yet transparent, and it hovered several feet off the ground, much the same as a spirit would. The deer scampered away promptly.

As the deer escaped, the spirit hissed, "I would kill you if he could. But my orders include only two deaths today. Count your blessings, little ones. You survived Kardsten the Assassin."

Jet felt tied to this creature, and without a conscious decision, he followed the figure. Kardsten wove between several trees for the next few minutes. A sense of déjà vu overcame Jet. As the building skirted into view between the trees, Jet knew precisely where he was, and he felt destined to be there.

As Nana's house came into view, Jet felt his mind unite with Kardsten. He could hear the thoughts of this spirit and understand its intentions. "Two important tasks to accomplish tonight. One of far greater importance than the other, but I am uniquely capable of accomplishing both."

In the distance, Kardsten could see the yellow farmhouse, and he shivered with glee at the opportunity he'd been given. His fiendish brothers could only loathe his fortune. He was virtually untraceable, unseeable, and powerful. He was a *Rogue*—a minor demon that still retained some of its magical abilities.

Otherwise, magic had been forgotten on the Earth by humans for the last few centuries. That would change tonight, for better or worse.

Frost covered some of the branches, the rocks, and the ground. Kardsten was now at the back border of the land surrounding the farmhouse. From his viewpoint, it was two stories high with an attached garage. The backyard was large, and the barn and small pond were a nice touch. The wraparound porch, a dozen windows, and French-style construction were authentic, picturesque, and striking.

A single road led to its front door, and Kardsten understood that he had to get closer before his attack. His essence lightened as he prepared to approach the house. As he wafted forward, he unexpectedly crashed into an unseen barrier, and his progression halted. He'd been warned that this might occur; he just didn't believe it could happen to him.

His fury rose. He was a dark assassin. In the beginning, he was one of thirteen. His brethren had been used in this war for hundreds of years. They were the Balakcursen. But now, only four of them remain. Yet, he was the only one the master had entrusted to complete this mission. His Runic magic was powerful but limited. He had the power to kill the boy but required his brethren's help to pass through the barrier. But their involvement was minimal compared to his.

Interlacing his fingers together, he sent a signal and waited for his brethren to react. He would be free to enter the yard if they did their part. He waited. Like thunder, a sound erupted in the pristine cloudless morning above a hill north of Silverton. A torrent of wind exploded outward in the direction of the farmhouse. A blue fog formed from nothing, and the wind gathered steam as it rolled forward. The fog slithered over every rock, bush, and between every tree until it reached his perch. The mist surrounded the border of the farmhouse. It pushed and gnawed, and finally it seeped inside the boundaries. The instant the fog spilled into the yard, a shot of electricity escaped into the air. The barrier had fallen.

"Free to strike, free to kill," Kardsten said with excitement.

He drifted across the lawn to a back window. Peering inside, he found a room that was empty of life but detected two people somewhere inside the dwelling. Farther, along the back of the house, he found a second window with a young boy with brown hair, no more than twelve, asleep at the far end of the room. To Kardsten delight, the rock sat on a table next to the boy's bed. He couldn't have arranged things better. The other human was old and frail; she was no threat to him.

He lifted a dark, translucent limb derived from murk and began to draw in the air. A triangle, then two wavy lines, one above the other and both within the bounds of the triangle. He added two dots between the lines, *Adormiere,* the rune for sleep. A cloud of green vapor whirled out from the triangle and encased the entire house. The smoky substance penetrated the window's seals and consumed the home entirely. Both humans slipped into a profound trance, just a breath away from death.

"Far too simple," the creature hissed.

But an instant later, he realized his words were premature. As if sensing an assault, a red flare erupted from within the house, lashing back at the darkness and igniting the night's air. Even the fog was compelled to retreat.

"A defense system," Kardsten hissed. "And a fight after all! It'll be my pleasure."

He traced the air once again, drawing two non-touching circles, one above the other with a single line connecting them and a single dot in the middle of each circle. He reinforced the center by throwing a gray powder from a collection of his stock—*Destrexitium.*

The center of each circle began rotating, and two obsidian blades emerged from within. Once the blades were fully formed, they flew end over end, faster than a human eye could see, and slammed into the window. The sound echoed in the surrounding forest, but somehow the window held steady. Again, a flash of red light pulsated from inside the room. It was less powerful than before but just as effective. The blades splintered and fell to dust.

Peering inside, Kardsten grew incensed at what he saw. The red glow was coming from the rock itself.

"How's that possible?" he questioned.

But the rock was doing more. It began vibrating back and forth, and power emanated from it. A growl tore from

Kardsten's tormented lips. He was not going to get beat this easily. He drew a large circle this time, followed by a square within the circle. Inside the square, he drew two diamonds, the bottom points touching each other, creating an hourglass appearance. Then he placed a five-sided star inside each. Lastly, he drew three slashes across each star to complete the rune—*Ventus*.

An icy gust of air from an unseen dimension blew through the six slits and easily penetrated the house's barrier, flowing into the room and surrounding the boy and the rock. An angry scarlet glow pulsated from the outer crust of the rock. Heat pierced the air, splashing chasms of fiery light on every wall. The second wave of heat shattered the frozen wind's hold. It was clear that the power of the rock was fading.

Kardsten was prepared. He was already halfway through depicting his most powerful rune—*Spiritus*. He created an octagon with a set of triangles attached to every outer side. A second smaller octagon was placed inside the first, and it was pierced through the center with three puncture marks. A silver-blue dragon's head erupted from the smaller octagon as if stepping through a porthole. As it congealed into a Runic montage, the barometric pressure inside the room plunged, and the air was entirely sucked away.

The boy's skin flattened against his cheekbones, and his lips curled impossibly. His back arched past its breaking point. A sob of agony escaped the boy's lips, but he remained unconsciously transfixed. Kardsten's dragon entered the room and stalked over to the boy. It opened its mouth and devoured the boy and the rock.

The rock ceased its reverberations, and the red glow vanished completely. Its power had been overwhelmed and conquered. It lay still on the table, ready to be plundered.

The boy's breathing slowed, and before long, it stopped altogether. His eyes suddenly flew open, unseeing, as if he were being tortured endlessly. Froth settled at the corners of his tightened mouth as his body convulsed forcefully.

There was a snapping sound and Kardsten beheld, with pleasure, as the boy's face became disfigured. His teeth, nose, and facial bones sunk inward from the force of the rune. From the corners of his mouth, streaks of blood slipped down onto the bed. This would be Kardsten's most celebrated kill ever.

The dragon circled the room, guarding the boy and the rock. Kardsten turned his attention to the next phase of his plan. As he did so, the fog instantly parted and brought into view the hill just north of town. This was where the war was to begin. His master had instructed him well. His sacrifice would be the final step in his journey.

A movement from back inside the house caught his attention. The rock was sliding toward the boy's body. When it was a few inches away, it exploded with the force of a hurricane. The windows rattled, and the dragon disintegrated. Kardsten felt the concussive energy and was forced to take shelter below the window. When he had gathered enough courage, he glanced back inside. A cloud of superfine dust sat afloat at the ceiling, gathering all of its particles. The mist propelled itself forward like a snake, and without hesitation, a tendril of dust sprang into the unconscious boy's nose.

It did not take long for all the particles to disappear. Kardsten watched in horror as the boy's mouth wrenched open, and it closed again as if unsticking from the glue. His body stiffened, his back and chest arched toward the ceiling, and his arms and legs bent unnaturally. His eyes fluttered back and forth, while his nose cracked, somehow realigning itself. The boy's bottom jaw opened as if unhinging, and bumps arose along the gum line. A set of new pristine teeth cut through the gums and fell perfectly into place. Oxygen gushed back into his lungs like a tornado, and a rosy color emerged on his cheeks. As quickly as it started, the boy's body fell limply back onto the bed, somehow healed from the attack.

He had failed miserably. Kardsten shrieked his displeasure. The boy and the rock had been within his grasp. His master would know the truth soon enough. Should he run and hide? He had more to accomplish tonight, and failure was not an option.

Turning his attention toward town, Kardsten bellowed, "Soon enough, my master will be free. He will rise again."

Kardsten knew that his sacrifice could bring about the escape of his master. Pushing himself from the window, he lifted his arms and sketched six circles into the air, each ring formed within the preceding one. Once finished, he tossed in a dash of black powder. His last act would be a sacrifice. He plunged his entire arm into the center—*Bullseye*.

A javelin formed at the far end while a rope fastened to Kardsten's entire arm. The weapon launched forward, directly at the hill. When the rope tightened, he was plucked from his spot. His sacrifice would initiate the countdown, and nothing, not even the boy, could stop his master's release if he lived long enough. As the javelin picked up speed, he felt his shadowed form gradually becoming more corporeal. An incredible burning sensation befell him, and he wanted it all to end. He bellowed in agony one last time as the javelin impaled the side of the hill. All sounds ceased instantly.

The dead silence lasted but for a moment. The mountain began to rumble, and a spray of lava exploded upward just as dawn cut through the sky. A wave of heat blasted outward just as three trenches hunted for a home on the outskirts of town. The war had begun, and those who stood in the way would be the first to die. The master's release was now unstoppable.

CHAPTER 23

Jet tentatively opened his eyes, tasting dried blood in his mouth. His body was sore, and his mind was acutely aware of the torment he'd gone through. The nasty coat from the closet was tucked under his head. It smelled like mothballs and reminded him of Nana. He was surprised to see that the items from the trunk had been arranged on the floor. His friends were whispering and pointing to different objects.

Jet's voice sounded odd when he said thickly, "That was an adventure."

The group hurried over to where he lay.

Grantham chuckled. "Bro, you gave us one helluva scare."

"Am I still a lobster?"

"Only half baked," Seyanna said, her face concerned.

"I'm fine. How's Mckenzey and the others?"

"I'm better now," Mckenzey said.

"Aaron Flemming and Hunter Smith got away, but they caught Kevin McCormick." Jayco kneeled and helped Jet to a seated position. "It was Shane and his friends. He had spotters all around the pavilion. Somehow, whatever they shot into the air was intended to mark certain people."

Mckenzey added, "Just like Trina Madden, at the beginning of the year."

"Not just mark, but attack."

"What do you mean?" Latisha asked.

"Not entirely sure. A feeling more than anything."

Mckenzey said, "From what I heard, you were even worse than Trina."

"I've never felt that much pain." He recoiled slightly at his memory. "I feel so much better now." On wobbly legs, Jet stood and sat in a chair. "What happened after I passed out?"

Latisha said, "Seyanna brought that jar over. When she opened it, the powder swirled around both you and Mckenzey. It purged away whatever was making you sick."

Jayco continued, "I'm surprised that whatever Shane did, it didn't affect me, Grantham, Latisha, or Seyanna. We've been talking, and we were out of town when the disaster hit. You and Mckenzey were both there. And I'd bet that Trina, Aaron, Hunter, and Kevin were there as well."

Grantham added, "I bet he was marking them, trying to find out who has the book."

"Maybe," Jet said. He glanced at all the items laid out on the floor.

Seyanna said quickly, "Oh, sorry. We couldn't help ourselves. This is some pretty impressive stuff."

Jet wheezed out a laugh. "Things are getting weird."

Mckenzey brought over a glass of water and handed it to him. She said, "Turns out there's a fridge upstairs and a small kitchen."

Jet drank greedily. Once he could speak, he asked, "How much have you searched through?"

Grantham answered, "Well, bro, you've been out for three hours. We've seen everything."

"Good. There were a few things I wanted to talk to you about." Jet recounted his memory of the black box and described it, at least what he could remember. He finished by saying, "That box is the key to everything. I think it's the same box discussed in the fable."

Seyanna asked, "Have you ever actually seen it?"

"No. But I will sketch out everything I can remember. If we can find that box, that will help us a great deal."

Grantham said, "That's going to be a hard find."

"What else can we do?" Seyanna asked.

Jet said, "A few of us need to continue watching Shane. We can't be surprised again. Mckenzey and I need to be seen by Shane as soon as possible. Others can catalog these items and see if they can figure out what they are. The rest can start looking for the crate."

"Sounds like a long shot," Jayco said.

Mckenzey asked, "What else are we going to do with Shane? They are attacking people now." Passionately she added, "We need to fight back."

Grantham picked up the pyramid. "I want to see what this is."

They spent the next hour checking out each item carefully. Jet felt excitement as his friends gawked at each item. They would lift an object, inspect it, and put it down, only to pick it up again later. But he couldn't stop thinking about the dream. He now knew what had happened to the meteorite. He'd been attacked, and something had tried to kill him. He also remembered *The Sorcerer's Guide* talking about someone with blackened air who could open the guidebook. That explained why he could. He was starting to understand more about Runic magic. But seeing himself attacked and transformed was sobering. After consideration, he decided to keep this information private. His friends didn't need to know everything.

Seyanna interrupted his thoughts. "I've got to meet with my parents for dinner. Let's catch up later next week."

As they prepared to leave, Jayco asked, "Who wants to be in charge of what?"

Seyanna said, "I'm going to watch Shane. But I could use some help now and then."

Jayco added, "Grantham and I will search for the crate. Jet, get us that description as soon as possible."

Latisha thundered, "I've kept my mouth shut long enough. What you guys are talking about is impossible. Shane is attacking the school. Let's bring this information to Principal Fletcher. We don't have to tell her everything."

"Bad idea," Jayco said.

"But why?"

"If we had a video of Shane shooting off whatever he did, then maybe. But there's no way the principal will believe us. But more importantly, Shane will know that we know something. Finding this box will be nearly impossible, especially with Shane breathing down our necks."

Latisha said, "Don't fool yourself—a box from Jet's memory. It's already impossible."

Jayco said, "Grantham's got a guy who is a genius with searching online for hidden or lost items. If it's out there and Jet gives a good enough description, he'll find it."

"Are we sure we want to involve someone else?" Seyanna asked.

"We'll give him a few items to look for. This will be one of a half dozen."

"Latisha and I," Mckenzey said, "will catalog all the items here."

Latisha huffed. "I'm not putting myself at risk over this. I'll help in the background."

Turning to Jet, Jayco asked, "What about you? How are you going to help?"

"I'll help everyone out." Jet knew that he also needed to spend time training with the elements. He was also going to keep his magic abilities a secret for the time being.

As if assuming leadership, Jayco said, "Let's meet back here in two weeks and see what we've found."

* * *

Over the next several days, Jet spent most of his time alone and trying better to understand magic. It took less than a day to sketch a picture of what he remembered about the box. He met up almost daily with his friends, but he snuck away to practice late in the evenings. A few times, he had a distinct feeling of displeasure from Jayco, like he wasn't doing enough.

The group enjoyed two of Grantham's cross country meets and one of Jayco's football games. Each of them was a star player in their respective sports. Jet had never given high school sports a second thought.

During this time, Jet learned a few things about Shane. He had several girlfriends, none of whom seemed to be Ariana. He loved paintballing and hiking. A typical afternoon found Shane and his friends disappearing off the trail just south of the CeU building. They would reappear an hour later, all colored up with paint. They would be laughing and didn't appear to have a care in the world. Shane never missed class, and none of his friends did either. Shane's teachers and most of the other students seemed to get along with him great, and he was a model student.

Seyanna brought some new information to the group. One day, she noticed that none of the secret groups were dressing the same. This included the Dark Angles, the Light

Riders, and the other groups. Over the next few days, they spotted the paramounts, but something had caused them to stop dressing alike.

Practicing with the elements was far less successful. Wier of the Hearthstone Plains' hadn't given him any new advice, and no additional pages had turned. Mckenzey and Latisha spent their time in the science building basement, scourging over the items and cataloging them, mainly after hours and on the weekends. This gave Jet far less opportunity to practice with the elements. But when he did, he soon wondered if his progress was worsening. He lashed out at the table, a chair, and even the wall. His real problem was lack of sleep. He struggled to get more than two or three hours a night. But every night, he dreamed. Sometimes it was about his parents, other times a howling wolf, and now even Kardsten attacking him.

* * *

Jet found himself crouched in a now-familiar spot, on top of the CeU building, near the back, ruminating on everything he hadn't accomplished in the last two weeks. He was to meet his friends in an hour and had nothing to share. A low hanging cloud had been pushed to shore and visibility on campus was hit and miss. Even with a long-sleeved shirt, he felt a chill travel up his spine.

This portion of the roof was far enough from any foot traffic and hidden by several air conditioners. He managed to place his back between two large pieces of equipment. With minimal movement, he could glance over the side of the building. Several shapes came into view along the pathway toward the rappelling cliffs as if on cue. The clouds broke apart momentarily and Jet could make out Shane, Jessiva, Clyde, Vinny, Jake, and Jocelyn. There were three other students that Jet recognized but didn't know their names.

They walked directly toward the CeU building. But this time, they weren't wearing any paintballing gear. They stopped a hundred feet away under the shadow of a gigantic tree and grouped around Shane. They were too far away for Jet to hear anything. Shane spoke animatedly and waved his hands around. He noticed that one of the kids wasn't listening to Shane. This kid stood in the general direction but didn't seem as involved as the others. Shane quickly noticed and flared his hands in a twirling movement, and suddenly the kid's arms shot to his side, his feet snapped together, and he fell backward like a dead tree, landing hard against the ground. The group erupted in laughter. This had not been an accident. There'd been purpose in Shane's gestations, but what exactly had he done?

Shane maneuvered his hands, and a second student fell. This time he landed face first. Vinny and Jake ran forward and helped the kid to his feet. The boy didn't look to be injured at all. Instead, he had a broad smile on his face. Clyde, Vinny, and Jake all began clapping. Shane took a half bow. Soon, they stepped from the path onto the asphalt and passed out of view. Jet remained hidden for several more minutes. He recognized that Shane was using Runic magic, but more alarming was the proficiency that Shane demonstrated. It was far beyond Jet's skill.

He stopped by Porter's for some ice cream before heading to meet up with his friends. When he stepped inside the secret room, there was a buzz in the air. Grantham was pacing around the room, and Latisha and Seyanna tried to calm him down.

Seeing Jet, Grantham screamed and ran toward him. "'Bout time, bro. I'm glad you finally arrived. I can barely control myself."

"What are you talking about?"

Jayco said, "Apparently, Grantham has found something he wants to share but didn't want to start without you."

"That's promising." Jet quickly passed out the ice cream as Grantham gathered a few items.

Barely maintaining control, Grantham shrieked, "I think I found something mind-blowing. About thirty minutes before I came, I received an email from my friend. He has a bot that can search for things."

"How does it search?" Latisha asked.

"Not important," Grantham countered. "Suffice to say, you input some basic information, and it starts searching."

"Doesn't make sense, but okay," Latisha said.

Grantham snatched two sheets of paper from the floor. "At first, we searched for anything resembling a casket or box, like the one Jet described. Nada. Then, I remembered Nana's letter and thought there may be a connection with Germany?"

"And…" Seyanna encouraged, not yet understanding.

"I found a document that mentioned a beast. It was written in German, which caught my attention, but fortunately, we found a translated piece. It's an abstract with some information. It appears to be around the period of World War II. Items such as photos, paintings, artifacts, dressers, desks, china, and many other things were taken after 1945, when the Allies, and possibly the United Nations, refused to return certain items to the Germany people after the war. Over the next three decades, dozens of documents have been in the restoration process. I found something that may have relevance to our search. It's believed to have been written around 1942 or 1943. It's a little farfetched, so don't jump to any conclusions too fast."

Grantham began reading aloud. "During an excavation, several documents were found within two tin boxes, buried beneath a home in Berlin, Germany. Three of the four documents in the first tin were severely damaged by water. The primary text appears to be in good shape. It is entitled *The Hero's Request*. It was only partially affected by water. Of importance, this document is believed to have been written by Adolf Hitler to one of his officers, Hermann von Brandt. Von Brandt is relatively unknown, and his life is being investigated.

The two tin boxes were found inside von Brandt's wife's house. He lived there until his untimely death, but she remained in the house for years, as did their children. Records suggest that Hitler banished von Brandt sometime in early 1943. It's believed that he later killed himself following Operation Valkyrie in 1944. von Brandt was pictured as a traitor to the Third Reich for years. But the text of this letter leads to a more pressing question: What was Officer Brandt doing in 1943? The letter reads:

> *Dear Herr Von Brandt,*
>
> *With great respect, I implore you to take advantage of the good fortune we have been given. The box of truth is the key. We've discussed it openly before, and I know your stance on this topic that this story is nothing but a child's bedtime story.*
>
> *Notwithstanding, it has been shared with me that whoever possesses the box will inherit the power within. I do not share the belief that there is a beast that has control over the item in question. I do adamantly believe that this artifact cannot be overlooked. We must do our utmost to find this item.*

The road will be burdensome, but I trust that you will find success. I have attached the map and coordinates to where you should begin your search. As a member of our team, you will procure the means by which the Third Reich will reign forever. I command you to do your duty in service to the Fatherland and do so in secret. You have the power to save the German people and preserve our way of life.

Take two dozen soldiers and begin your search. There is a connection between Egypt and this box, though I cannot be sure what it is. When you arrive in the region, acquire workers to accompany you on your journey. They will help you read and understand the signs given. Once the artifact has been found, you know what to do with it. Be strong and diligent in the face of uncertainty. This is a Hero's request.

Sincerely and with Respect, A. Hitler

Pausing for a moment, Grantham allowed everyone a moment to process what he'd just read. Jet felt overwhelmed. Was this a hoax? Glancing around at the others, his confusion and skepticism were mirrored in their expressions. Grantham added, "There's a summary below the letter written that has also been translated into English. Do you want me to continue?"

"Clearly," Jayco said.

"The handwriting analysis confirms that Hitler himself wrote this document. Unfortunately, the meaning behind the letter remains a mystery to this day. Several theories have been put forth, but little is indeed known. Von Brandt had been loyal to Hitler for many years before his fall from grace. This letter was discovered in 2005, and it is now believed that Von Brandt may have taken part in a tactical search team under one of Hitler's many research programs. Some believe this research department oversaw many unimaginable experiments intended to find answers to the Fuhrer's questions.

It is also surmised that Von Brandt may have been partially successful in his mission. Known movements of German soldiers in Egypt around this time lend credence to this letter's contents. It is unknown if the box mentioned in the letter was ever found. It was certainly not part of the objects taken from the home of Hermann von Brandt years later.

Time has distorted much of our understanding of Hitler and his ambitions. World domination was his goal. It could be argued that this letter shows Hitler's intent for an unconventional pathway to world domination. He was, as history shows, unsuccessful.

Summary and translation from German to English by Peter Gooden."

"So, this item was searched for by Hitler and the German army? Does anyone find this as crazy as it sounds?" Mckenzey asked. "There's no way we're talking about the same box."

"I don't even know what to think," Jet said. "The box, a beast, and a power. Each of these coincides with what we are looking for. How is it possible that Hitler could be involved?"

Grantham added, "There's more. Once a connection between Egypt and Germany materialized, I started looking into Hitler's possessions."

"Wouldn't that mean Hitler had the tablet?" Jayco pointed out.

Latisha said quickly, "Maybe he found something but died before he could use it."

"Are you telling us you found something in Germany?" Seyanna challenged, her voice forceful.

"My friend initially searched for museums displaying items from the Nazi regime in Germany, France, Switzerland, Italy, and the United States. Most of the places he checked out didn't have any items resembling what we were looking for. But there's a museum in Bern, Switzerland, that houses hundreds of old artifacts from countries involved in both world wars. Some of the items include tanks that landed on D-Day, Japanese planes, and many other collectibles. It's an entire historical collection."

Mckenzey grinned. "I'm dying here. Did you find anything Egyptian?"

"I did." Grantham's smile widened. "There were a few weapons, a few books, and that's it."

"Oh, man, you're killing me," Seyanna said.

Jet felt his heart drop.

"Oh, yeah. My friend found this mysterious box that's been on and off display for the last ten years. I tried to get a good look at the box, but I only got a single picture." Grantham pulled out the second piece of paper, a small photo, and passed it to Jet.

"Is this a real picture?" he asked as the others swarmed around.

"No way," Mckenzey said excitedly.

Jet could barely control his emotions. The photo depicted was a black object, like a box, sitting on a display stand, with several hieroglyphics adorning the edge of the box. He beheld a carving of a falcon with a snake's head and another of a lion with an owl's head.

"I think," Jayco said respectfully, "that this changes everything. That looks exactly like what Jet described. This must be it."

Jet fell back on the couch, more overwhelmed than he had ever felt before. He gasped. "This is bigger and better than anything I could've imagined! Do you understand how amazing this is?"

"Grantham is a rock star, pure and simple!" Seyanna shouted. "We're golden!"

Grantham continued, "The box was found in Poland about twenty years after the fall of Nazi Germany. But the owner absolutely insisted that it had been smuggled out of Germany. He was convinced it was a prized possession of Hitler himself. Though beautiful and amazing, this relic is not at all important in the eyes of World War II historians. I'm not even sure if it's on display anymore."

Latisha said, "A forgotten treasure."

"More like an asinine decision," Jayco said.

"How are we going to get close enough to see this box?" Mckenzey wondered.

Jayco shook his head. "My gut says that our only choice is to see this box in person. All the photos in the world won't help us."

"Are you suggesting that we go to Switzerland to look at the box?" Latisha asked, doubtful.

"We may not have a choice," Jayco said. Turning to Jet, he asked, "What do you think?"

"I completely agree." Jet smiled broadly.

Grantham hugged Latisha. "We're going on a vacation to Europe."

CHAPTER 24

The idea of traveling to Switzerland fizzled after only two days. The reality of taking time off from school, flying to Europe, and hiding the fact from their parents and the school, was incredibly daunting. Sure, Latisha's bank account had enough money to get them there, but what would happen when they arrived? Cameras, security, and more just to get a peek at a box. Jayco and Grantham were both worried about missing any games or practices. One by one, each concern was solved, and the trip was back on the table.

The weather had improved dramatically after D.C. and flights overseas had ramped up again as soon as possible. It took four days before flights across the U.S. restarted. The East Coast, however, was the hardest hit, and it would take years for them to recover. The airports of New York, Washington, and several other cities would take another several weeks to reopen. Heading that direction was impossible.

The most challenging thing for Jet to come to terms with was understanding that viewing the box alone would not be enough. He needed to get his hands on it by any means necessary. Latisha was appalled and threatened to quit the friend group when the topic was discussed. It took Mckenzey another three days to convince her to remain part of the Echoes. Miraculously, when they met a week later, Latisha was on board, but she refused to be personally involved in stealing the box.

To her credit, Latisha began searching for hotels and flights and the best route to get to Bern. Grantham started to scope out the museum, but they ran into the same problem repeatedly. There was no way for them to get ahold of the box. Depression sunk in as they went their separate ways after the meeting. Latisha and Grantham left together, as did Seyanna and Jayco. Each couple was spending more and more time together. Mckenzey was always the first to go.

* * *

Monday afternoon, after his classes, Jet walked into the science building to prepare the lab. He'd spent so much time in the building that it was slightly awkward to go into the classroom instead of the basement. Autumn had been absent for the past two weeks, and Jet had done everything on his own. The classroom was empty, and he quickly found the instruction sheet Autumn had left.

It was impossible to keep the counters and floors clean no matter what he did. It was as if a horde of toddlers had created a trash volcano throughout the entire classroom. He swept and washed off the counters then began placing five specific kits on each table. This week, they were scheduled to use tools to identify minerals. Jet pulled out hand lenses, glass plates, and a few microscopes. As he walked toward the supply room to collect the rocks, he heard movement from behind the door.

Jet crept forward, trying to listen intently. There it was again as if a chair was being moved. He slowly pushed open the door and leaned in to see a figure frantically searching through a box of trash items next to the autoclave. Silently, Jet stepped into the supply room. To his surprise, he recognized Professor Blum searching the shelves.

Jet cleared his throat and asked, "Professor Blum, can I help you?"

Professor Blum spun around, caught off guard, nearly falling off the chair. He recovered quickly. "I didn't think anyone was here."

"Just getting things ready for this week."

"Oh. I see."

Jet added, "Can I help you look for something?"

Absentmindedly, Professor Blum said, "Don't bother. It's not here."

"Professor, are you okay?"

"Do you remember the meteorites sent around the first day of class?"

"Of course."

"I can't seem to find them," Professor Blum hissed. "They're missing."

"Are you sure?"

"I had them yesterday. I normally lock them inside my office or bring them home. I'm certain that I didn't do the latter. There've been so many people interested in seeing them; it's nearly impossible to take them off-campus. This morning, I had an appointment to evaluate the meteorites' worth. When I opened the box, it was empty."

"Maybe you misplaced them."

"I've looked everywhere I can," he said as he stepped off the chair.

"Who in the last few days had a close look at them?"

"Mostly students and teachers. No one specific." Professor Blum leaned against the wall. "There was someone from the school newspaper, but he didn't seem interested in the meteorites themselves, especially where I got them."

"I thought you said that you've had them for years?"

"True indeed. I've had them for four years, and this is the first year anyone has shown interest. More people have been asking about them in the last week than in the last four years combined. I bought them from another scientist who was willing to part with them. He'd found them near a rockslide and was desperate for funding for his next project. I was more than happy to take them off his hands. Sadly, a few months after he sold them to me, he was crossing a fixed rope in Argentina, and the rope broke, and he fell to his death."

"That's terrible," Jet said.

Professor Blum continued, "These meteorites are far different than any others I've ever seen. I learned so much from them."

"Learned from them? What do you mean?"

Professor Blum shook his head and walked away. "Oh, nothing. You wouldn't believe me."

Jet followed. "Professor Blum, what did they teach you?"

Making his way toward the door, he laughed. "I have no desire for you to think of me as crazy. I admit it is a little far-fetched."

"Try me. I want to know."

Professor Blum stopped abruptly and turned to face him. "All right, I'll take a chance." After a long pause, he said calmly, "I think the meteorites are more than they appear. One person who touched them had an increase in their strength. Another time, I knew instinctively when an unexpected blizzard would hit my hometown. One time, I had a friend do something unexpected—I won't go into details—but it wasn't a good outcome. There's a power in them. I've got to find them."

"That does sound a little far-fetched," Jet lied. "Could that be why they're missing?"

"I don't know."

"You should tell someone across the street."

"Who would listen?"

"Enough people saw that you had them; it shouldn't be too hard. The administration itself should be made aware."

"It'll be impossible, I promise. Chadwick's have their backs to cover. There isn't much to do but look for them myself." Peering around the storage room, he added, "They certainly weren't misplaced here. I'd better be going."

"Good luck, Professor."

Without another word, Professor Blum hurried from the classroom.

Jet spent another hour getting the lab prepared, but it was impossible to get the meteorites out of his mind. He'd wanted to see them for weeks. If they had been stolen, only one name came into his mind: Shane Fallon.

As he crossed campus, Jet's cell phone rang. "Hey, Seyanna, what's up?"

"I've got some bad news."

"What do you mean?"

"I'm packing for a trip. I'm heading to Argentina with my parents for the next few weeks."

"What?" he asked, surprised. "Argentina? What about Switzerland!"

"We're still waiting for your passport to arrive. I've never been, and it sounds like a blast. My parents wouldn't take no for an answer."

"But why?"

"Argentina had a weather disaster a few years ago, and things were parallel to what happened in D.C. We will be gone for a few weeks."

"Let me know how it goes." It was not lost on Jet that the country of Argentina had come up twice in conversation in the last few hours.

Seyanna said quickly, "There's something else."

Jet was deep in thought. He finally said, "Like what?"

"It's Mckenzey. She's been different since what happened in D.C. Latisha and I have been talking about it. She's always alone, and if you've noticed, she leaves the meetings right away. I think you need to talk with her."

"All right. I'll try talking to her."

"Thanks, Jet. You're awesome."

"Have a good trip."

Ten minutes later, he stepped into Mckenzey's dorm and knocked on her door. There was no answer. He retreated to the elevator. Stepping inside, he collided with someone just as they were exiting. He caught his balance, but the same couldn't be said for the brown-haired girl who crashed to the ground.

"Jet. Did you do that on purpose?"

"No way," he insisted. Bending down, he helped Mckenzey to her feet.

"You scared the heck out of me. And you just about ran me over." They spent a few minutes gathering papers.

Jet said, "I've been looking for you. Do you have a few minutes to talk?"

"Sure. I was just getting back from class. It was boring, so I slipped out early to do some reading on von Brandt."

"Really?"

"I was curious why he went from a Nazi leader to being pushed out of the inner circle. Just the idea of Hitler searching for this item has made me a skeptic. But the picture of that box is compelling."

Jet added, "It seems like something else is bothering you. We've barely talked."

"Want to grab something to eat?"

"Sure," Jet said. "Any suggestions?"

"Right now, I can only afford the cafeteria."

They descended the stairs and entered the cafeteria. After getting their food, they found a table near a window. They talked about the school, the group, and the box for over an hour. The conversation was surprisingly comfortable and relaxing.

Mckenzey asked, "Any crazier things happening?"

"A few." He thought about the meteorites and his control of the elements. He told her about Professor Blum and the lost meteorites. He was about to say something about Elemental magic when he noticed that she wanted to voice something.

"I've been officially accepted to Dillon Lake. I haven't told anyone. Not even Latisha or Seyanna. I wanted to tell you first."

Jet practically choked on a spoonful of soup. He hadn't expected this. "When do you start?"

"January fourth. They received my transcripts, and I have my schedule mostly in place."

"In two and a half months? That seems so soon. I thought it might be next summer or something."

"Nope. Eric says that next summer is too far away."

"Wow. So, it's final then. After Christmas break, you're out of here." Feeling slightly panicked, he asked, "Are you still coming to Switzerland?"

"Wouldn't miss it for the world. One last adventure with the Echoes."

CHAPTER 25

Jet was far from enthusiastic as he descended the stairs of the science building. How had things gone from good to bad so quickly? It had been two weeks since Mckenzey had stunned Jet with the date of when she was transferring to Dillon Lake. Just when the group was meshing well, the carpet was about to be pulled from under their feet. He hated the idea of losing one of his best friends. Just as frustrating, he hadn't come up with a single idea of how they would steal the box. His brainstorming, and brain function for that matter, had gone from bad to worse. The group had to settle on a final plan tonight. Jayco had suggested an after-hours break-in as their only real option. Jet was leaning toward this as well.

The reality of Mckenzey leaving for Dillon Lake was far more personal than he ever wanted to believe. She had chosen Eric over him and their friends. Nothing romantic was going on between him and Mckenzey, but he was jealous of Eric. He was caught between doing something irrational with the hopes of keeping her here or trying to appear supportive. Both options had risks.

Seyanna had texted everyone two nights ago that she had returned from Argentina. She was going to be there for tonight's meeting. She described her trip as the best and worst trip of her life. The only hints she'd give about it was that the devastation was different than D.C., and she wasn't sure if it was connected to what they were working on. She was sleep-deprived and needed rest before tonight's meeting.

Arriving fifteen minutes early, Jet wanted to tell his friends about his magical abilities. It would distract them from his lack of imagination and give him a few more days to develop a better idea on how to steal the box. He opened the first door; it was dark and quiet. As he stepped farther into the room, he heard a scraping sound against the wall. He froze and listened again. He thought he could hear movement in the next room. Could someone have found their secret spot?

He carefully pushed the door inward; the room was completely dark. He reached out to turn on the light, but a rough hand gripped his arm before he did, and he was forcefully pulled into the room. Another set of hands clasped onto his other arm. Something was shoved onto his shoulders. It was as if he was wrestling with several unseen people.

Laughter erupted from the darkness, and this confused him. Was Shane attacking him again? Both arms became immobile as a sleeve was thrust on both arms. More laughter resonated in the room. Adrenaline pumped through his body, and his eyes automatically magnified, and the room, although dark, came into better focus. Dark shadows huddled around him. Jet bellowed, "Ventusnaeth!" and a powerful push of wind shot outward, knocking the figures down.

"Stop," someone screamed. "It's us."

Jet thought he recognized Jayco's voice.

The light flickered on before he could say anything, and he found that Jayco, Latisha, Grantham, and Mckenzey were all lying on their backs. Jayco and Mckenzey were rubbing at the back of their heads. Seyanna was bent over at the wall, laughing hysterically. He realized that he was wearing the horrible old, tattered coat from Nana. It was moth-eaten with several gaping holes. It had to be at least a hundred years old. He tried pulling his arms from the sleeves, but they had twisted around him.

"Whose brilliant idea was this?"

Latisha lifted her hand and stood. "Mine."

"And it was brilliant," Grantham gushed. "I bet you didn't know that Latisha is the biggest prankster of the group."

Jet hissed. "No way, she's a fashionista. She knew that this horrible smelling thing would look terrible on me. Someone help me out. This thing is going in the trash."

Mckenzey asked, "What did you just do?"

"Controlled the elements."

"Like magic?" Grantham asked as he dusted off his shirt and stood.

"Exactly."

"That's pretty cool." Grantham hummed.

Latisha screamed. Pointing at Jet's chest, she asked, "What's happening?"

Stunned, he was speechless, as he watched the material begin to shrink. Dozens of liquid bubbles formed on the outer edge of the coat's sleeves as if it were a science experiment. The coat's color was changing—first red, then purple, then black, then blue, and on and on, like a slot machine with rainbow colors spinning out of control. After ten seconds, the colors slowed, but the sleeves tightened.

Jet had a fleeting thought of a medieval torturing device, being attacked by one's own clothes. As quickly as it started, the shrinking and bubbling instantly stopped, but the material kept changing colors. Several inches of material dropped to the ground and covered his feet. Heat, like a furnace, radiated from the coat and into his arms, shoulders, chest, and back.

"Please end on pink," Jayco pleaded. "It would match Jet's eyes."

"I'd prefer indigo-yellow," Grantham added.

"Should we help him?" Mckenzey asked, moving forward. She leaped back when her hand touched the fabric, as if she had been shocked.

"What's happening to me?" Jet demanded.

When the color spinning wheel finally stopped, it landed on a dark gray, and the moth-eaten, nasty coat had transformed into a perfectly fitting cloak. Lifting his arms, the material flawlessly moved without tightness or catching.

Mckenzey whistled. "That's breathtaking."

Jayco stepped forward. "Let me try."

Jet effortlessly slid out of the cloak and passed it to Jayco. He expected another firework of changes as Jayco pulled it over his shoulders, but nothing happened. Jayco slipped his arms in the sleeves, screamed something unrecognizable, and began tearing at the material, trying to pull it off. A black smoke exited the sleeves, and when Jayco finally extricated his arms, he had two flesh burns dotting his arms.

"I guess this cloak is only for you." Jayco winced as he passed it back over.

"Anyone else want to try?"

Grantham said, "We're good, bro. We're definitely good."

Jet shrugged and put the cloak back on.

"It looks good. I mean, fantastic," Mckenzey said, her voice carrying a tinge of astonishment. "It fits you perfectly."

"What kind of material is that?" Latisha asked, suddenly interested. She ran over and felt the sleeves. "I've never seen something so smooth. It's as durable as leather but softer than cotton."

The front of the coat opened like a trench coat, and it tapered at the waist. The sleeves were long, and the bottom extended to his ankles. When he thought of a cloak, his mind went to a plump, dull piece of clothing that lay awkwardly on the shoulders. This was trendy enough to wear anywhere he wanted.

"Is that a hood on the back?" Seyanna asked.

Jet reached his hands over his head and found the hood. He flipped it onto his head, and the room's colors brightened significantly. He could detect things about the room that he'd never known before.

There were screams, and Jet spun around, expecting the worst. No one stood behind him. Taking a few steps, he glanced at the others.

Jayco was shouting and pointing at where Jet had been. "What the ..."

Latisha seemed to be losing her balance as if fainting. Jet glanced at Mckenzey, and she held her arms out in front of her, searching the air for something. It was the exact spot where he had been standing. Her head swiveled back and forth, looking for something out of sight. He noticed that each of their hair was being whipped around in a frenzy, as if they were in a windstorm. He lifted his arm to reassure them, and that was when he noticed that every inch of his body had disappeared. Reaching up, he tore the hood from his head and instantly reappeared.

Seyanna's head jerked in his direction. "How did that happen?"

"Where did you go?" Mckenzey demanded.

"No clue," he mumbled, his eyes wide and his heart racing. "Did I vanish completely?"

Latisha fell back onto the couch, mumbling, "That's not freaking possible."

"That couldn't have been any freaking cooler!" Grantham howled in delight. "Why can't something like this happen to me?"

Mckenzey reached an arm out and touched Jet ensuring he was standing next to her. "Try it again. But don't move."

Flipping on his hood, he disappeared. Mckenzey's hand passed directly through where he should've been. It was creepy to watch. When he reappeared, she slapped him across the back.

"Oh," she said. "You're back."

Latisha started hyperventilating. "I don't know how much more of this I can take. Every time I turn around, there's something else to deal with."

"Deal with?" Jayco questioned. "This is incredible. And more importantly, we now have a solution to how we're going to get that box from the museum."

The chatter of excitement was constant as the final piece of the plan fell into place. It was an unanimous vote to steal the box, which meant they needed a replica. Jayco and Grantham had suggested this idea and had already started to work on the facsimile.

Seyanna added, "We'll need a distraction at the museum. I have some ideas. Turning to Jet, she said, "Any idea when your passport will arrive?"

"Hopefully, in the next week."

"I have a hotel in mind. They will get us rooms without questions."

Grantham added, "I've made copies of the museum's layout. Everyone needs to study them for the next few days. We also need to ensure we have a few options to get back to the hotel and a direct route to the airport. Never can be too careful."

"We've got this," Jayco said assuredly.

Mckenzey said, "Now the planning is out of the way, I would love to see what kind of magic Jet can do."

CHAPTER 26

There was almost nothing better than the idea of a campus party, and Jet, Rick, and Jackson were excited as they walked across College Avenue toward the CeU building. It was nearing 11 p.m., and most of the school was lit up beautifully. There was music, costumes, and an early morning curfew. Candy was freely passed out, and there were dozens of small booths at several of the school buildings and some of the dorms. Most of the teachers were dressed up, attempting to shock or impress their students.

Jackson said, "Don't you think that the best prof' costume was Professor Darwin, who teaches Spanish. Her outfit is perfect. A Spanish dancer and all."

Rick said, "Yeah, yeah. We know. It's designed after the most famous Spanish dance—the Flamenco. It's authentic. Bright red and all." To Jet, Rick said, "But Jackson thinks she's charming. That's *why* he thinks she has the best costume."

"The hots for a professor?" Jet asked. "Is that even possible?"

Jackson said, "The only reason you wouldn't agree is that you haven't taken a Spanish class. She is so hot."

Rick countered, "The best costume goes to the teacher from woodworking, Mr. Hawthorn. His werewolf costume is out of this world."

"You've got a point there," Jackson conceded.

Up ahead, several students sprinted across the street, heading in the direction of the science building.

Jet said, "The coolest thing we've done so far was with Professor Rysen. Freeze drying a pumpkin and dropping it from the roof was epic."

"I agree," Rick said. "But it was closely followed by the obstacle course Professor Dickerson created. I bet even your friends Grantham and Jayco loved that one."

"I crashed into the water when the alligator came out of the shed. I wasn't expecting that. I couldn't stay on the rocks while crossing the pond." Jackson added.

Jet nodded. "Yeah. That was pretty sweet."

"What I wouldn't do for another cup of that homemade root beer float." Rick added, "That was delicious."

"So tasty," Jackson said.

The CeU building came into view. It held the night's culminating event, a masquerade party, and Jet and his roommates were dressed to impress. Rick wore a red and silver phantom mask, and Jackson wore a black and white Venetian mask. Five red ribbons with a ball on each tip dangled from the top. It reminded Jet of a Jester's costume. Jet wore a navy-blue beak mask with the beak extending six inches. Including their clothing, it was almost impossible to identify who they were.

As they approached the CeU building, they were awestruck by the two hundred or more carved pumpkins arranged on the lower level. There were also skeletons, flying witches, zombies, orange streetlights, and more, transforming this area of campus. Just like last year, there were three main entrances. Near Porter's was the entrance for the games and food. The second floor was for the pictures and dancing, while the bottom floor, near the pumpkins, was for the haunted house.

"The line to the Black Hole isn't very long," Jackson said. "Perfect timing."

Jet had always loved the idea of a haunted house but never dared to try one out. That was before tonight. Stepping around the building's corner and into view was Napoleon Bean arm in arm with a girl, a senior, who was tall and awkward with frizzy hair.

Rick mumbled, "I'm so glad that we talked him out of coming with us. It would've been hard to have fun with him around."

"I can't believe you told him that Darla wanted to spend some time with him. How did you know?" Jackson asked.

Napoleon and Darla hurried up the stairs and into line on the second floor.

"I didn't," Rick confessed. "But she's his perfect match. Awkward, tall, and eccentric. They look good together." As Rick pulled open the door, he said, "Let's get our danger on!"

After they paid and waited for their turn, the big gate finally opened, and they were let in. Darkness was sudden, and the floor tilted. It spun, and suddenly they had no idea what direction they were moving. The floor stopped, and Jet and his roommates were forced into a hallway that was well-decorated. It was dim and gloomy, and linens draped the walls from floor to ceiling. A breeze pushed the fabric back and forth ominously. The floor glittered as if they were spacewalking, and stars dotted the floor. A purple and red glow emanated from around them just as a low hypnotic tune pulsated in their ears. From ahead, a fluorescent liquid flowed down the walls.

Exchanging glances with each other, they tiptoed forward. A whitish fog began cascading down the corridor as if on cue. A high-pitched screeching sound berated Jet's ears, and he flinched and leaped into the air. Five steps later, a burst of liquid misted their faces in the same instant as a blade, near the ceiling, cut through a skeleton hanging upside down. Half of the corpse fell to the ground, still moving.

Jackson laughed hysterically as he stepped over the skeleton. He shouted, "Not bad. This is the least scary—"

Crash.

A seven-foot figure with a bloody mask shrieked at Jackson and attacked through an opening in the wall. Lifting both arms, it struck. It held an ax in one arm, and the second had been partially amputated, but it held a pirate's hook at the end. Jackson released a shrill scream and cowered away, shouting, "Leave me alone!"

A second figure attacked from the opposite wall, diving and sliding across the floor, catching Rick around the left leg. Jet didn't see him until the last second and couldn't shout a warning.

Rick bellowed, "Help me," as he was dragged to the floor.

Jet reached down to pull up his friend, but he didn't react in time. Two other figures crashed into Rick from behind, and soon a small dog pile ensued.

Jet dodged the twitching body and hurried to help his friends. He never saw the two figures as they stepped into the hall. Suddenly, from behind, he was lifted into the air as arms grasped him tightly in both armpits. He was dragged forward, kicking and screaming. Nothing he did released their grip. When they reached the end of the passage, they turned left. As they rounded the corner, Jet glanced back to see water balloons and other projectiles thrown at each other. Rick and Jackson had regrouped and were now on the offensive.

His hijackers scurried several more feet, stopped, and tossed him forcefully directly at the wall. Jet landed hard and pushed out both arms, hoping to prevent himself from smacking the wall. But instead of crashing into it, he slid several feet into a room just off the main corridor.

This room was almost entirely dark. He listened intently but heard nothing. Spinning around, he noticed that linen covered the door. Some light was streaming in. He wasn't sure exactly where he was. He strode toward the door, hoping to rejoin the fray.

A shadow blocked his way, and he stopped abruptly. He was wary and alert, but he didn't feel threatened. He would use magic if he had to. Focusing on the outline, he noticed plenty of curves, and the figure was taller than he was. It was definitely a girl.

A soft and soothing voice purred, "How do I look?"

His eyes adjusted. She wore an elegant masquerade mask. It was partially made of satin with several jewels. The mask covered her nose and eyes and continued to her forehead. There was a grouping of feathers on the left side. Her hair was tucked behind her. She wore black pants and a black shirt. It was impossible to tell who she was. He tried to concentrate on her voice but was drawing a blank.

"You look pretty terrific," he said hesitantly.

She blew him a kiss.

From here, he couldn't tell the color of her skin, eyes, or hair. Not a single distinguishable feature, except her lips. He wasn't sure how tall she could be either. Whoever this was had gone through the work to ensure the deception.

The girl said, "I've been waiting for you."

"Really?"

"Of course." She strode in his direction.

"I think you've mistaken me for someone else."

"Oh, Jet. You're so adorable when you're trying to be modest."

Again, the voice told him nothing. She sauntered with purpose, like a model on the runway. Every step accentuated her figure. She stopped directly in front of him and giggled. "Relax," she soothed. "You're so tense."

"Trying," he said. A nervous shudder ran through him. Nothing like this had ever happened to him before. Truthfully, he didn't know what was unfolding.

Both of her hands shot out and grabbed him near the shoulders. She pushed him backward, farther into the shadows. Her laugh echoed in the darkness; it was intoxicating. Her steps matched his as he stared directly at her eyes, never wavering. Her teeth glistened as she smiled.

"Trick or treat?" she asked.

"I don't want this to be a trick," he said. His back collided with the wall, and her body pressed against his. Her hands gently swept from his shoulders, to across his arms, and stopped on his chest. With one hand, she reached up and pulled up his mask so that it sat on his head. Her mask was soft and far different than his. She leaned forward, her soft lips brushing against his neck. Jet sighed in surprise and shivered.

"Hold still," she purred.

Her lips were soft and tender as she kissed him. Another shiver shot down his back, and he jerked slightly. This seemed to amuse her. Using his thumb, he traced her lips as if trying to discern who she was. He leaned forward, intending to kiss her back. Her other hand extended, pushing him back against the wall. She whispered, "Not yet."

She smelled like lavender, and it was surprisingly calming. She began kissing the other side of his neck as if this was a game, and he had to stay completely still. She nibbled his ear, and he shivered again. This time, he moved quickly and slipped past her guard. He kissed her neck, her ear, and it was her turn to shiver. Her mouth moved to his, and they kissed heatedly.

Sometime later, she pushed Jet back against the wall with remarkable strength. He was breathing hard. She took a small step back and glanced at him appraisingly. She sighed reluctantly. "Even better than I imagined."

"Seems like you know me, but I can't say the same."

"Don't you?" she rebuked playfully. "That's the whole point of a masquerade. That's what makes it so fun."

"I'll second that."

"No guesses?"

"Your voice is faintly familiar," he said. "Your height is throwing me off."

"Then, it's been a success." She giggled and added, "This has been the most fun I've had in months. Such a gentleman. See ya around."

She twirled athletically and sprinted out of the room, into the hall, turning left. Jet took a moment to react. He quickly followed her, lowering his mask, but she was gone when he stepped out of the room. The hall was empty, but it was still dark. Music assaulted his ears. He turned and ran toward the gym. He slid to a stop as he entered the spacious room. There were hundreds of students milling around, dancing, talking, walking, and sitting next to each other. No one in black was sprinting away from the corridor.

Jet released a huff of air. The decorations and ambiance were perfect. His mind was jumbled with what had happened. He began weaving in and out of groups, keeping to the outskirts of the room. After fifteen minutes, he gave up and began searching for his roommates. It took another five minutes to find Jackson and Rick.

Rick saw him first and said, "This place is so awesome. But where've you been for the last thirty minutes?"

"Looking for you guys."

"After we came in here, we didn't see you. So, we headed upstairs for a while." Rick handed Jet and Jackson a drink.

"What's up there?"

Jackson said, "Games, poker, and more things to do. We didn't see all the rooms. This is by far the best it's ever been. They're trying to build up the school spirit."

"What's next?" Jet asked.

"Let's dance," Rick said. "What time did you say that Grantham and Jayco would arrive?"

"They should be here," Jet said.

As they began walking, Rick pointed to the center of the room. "Sure enough, there they are."

Grantham, Latisha, and Jayco were dancing near the DJ sound desk in the center. His friends were out of control. He wasn't surprised to see that Mckenzey was nowhere to be seen. He hadn't seen her in a week, and when he'd stopped by their dorm a few days ago, Latisha had explained that she was at the administration building frustrated about something. She had been super busy getting everything into place for a smooth transition to Dillon Lake. Latisha explained that Mckenzey had been told that Dillon Lake would accommodate her scholarship from Chadwick's. After getting accepted, they denied the request. Mckenzey was a frantic mess.

Yesterday, Latisha texted that Mckenzey's boyfriend, Eric, and his parents had gone to the dean at Dillon Lake and convinced them to uphold her scholarship. It would take another few weeks to get all the paperwork filled out. He guessed that she was too tired to hang out tonight. To him, it appeared that she had one foot in the group and one foot in her new school.

Grantham said, "Finally, you guys showed up. What took so long?"

Jet said, "It took a little while to get through the Black Hole."

"How was it?"

Jet smiled. "Better than I could've imagined."

"Sweet."

Jackson grabbed Rick's arm and said, "Hey. There's Tammy and Becca. Let's see if they'll join us." They disappeared into the crowd. Turning to Jayco, Jet said, "Did you finish the replicate?"

Jayco glanced around. "Almost. We'll be good to go soon."

"Sweet."

Grantham and Jayco had spent several days working in the machine shop, trying to replicate the box. Jet stopped by every few days to try to give his input and check out their progress. Initially, it took a few days to get all the supplies and convince Mr. Hawthorn to let them use the building after hours. Three days ago, Jayco refused to let Jet inside and view any more of their work. He wanted the final project to be a surprise.

Jet asked, "Where's Seyanna?"

"She went to get drinks for us. I bet she'll be back any minute."

Jackson returned with Becca and Tammy just as Seyanna returned to the group. She carried four drinks. When she saw Jet, she said, "I didn't know you were here, or I would've grabbed you one."

Holding up his drink, he said, "No worries."

They all danced to the music for another twenty minutes. Then, the song changed to a slow one. The picture of the situation cleared instantly. Jackson and Becca, Rick and Tammy, Jayco and Samantha, and Grantham and Latisha. Jet was the odd one out, again. He quickly weaved his way out of the congestion of people. A blond-haired girl hurried toward him. The mask she wore was sparkling silver and as simple as possible, covering just her eyes. She wore a very form-fitting black dress that stopped mid-thigh. Her smile was as bright as ever, and it was impossible to miss who she was. Autumn curtsied and said, "Hello, Joshua. Let's dance."

Jet protested, "I—"

"It's fine. I promise. This dance is to say thank you." She moved in without an answer, wrapping both arms around him and pulling him as close as possible.

Jet's hands went to her hips instinctively. Several people glanced at him with jealousy, even several already dancing with someone else. They began dancing slowly. He said, "What do you mean, a thank you?"

"Ariana and I talked for the first time a few weeks ago. We even hung out last week."

Jet chuckled. "She was so upset at me. She thought you and I had been out a few times."

"I can only wish," Autumn said flirtatiously. "Ariana told me. She admitted that she wasn't nice to you."

"I told you that this would happen."

"Forget about it. It's no big deal. She also told me that she was caught inside Latisha's dorm. Totally embarrassed."

Jet just nodded. He wasn't sure what else to say. "How do you know all of this?" She rested her head against his neck, and he smelled an expensive and well-known perfume. It smelled amazing, but it was nothing close to lavender.

She said, "I'm a great listener." After a minute of silence, just dancing, Autumn leaned back and stared at him intently. "She also mentioned that you don't like Shane Fallon."

Shaking his head, Jet said, "We're not the biggest fans of each other."

"I see that. Ariana told me why she was following Latisha and Mckenzey. She also left you a message." Autumn smiled disarmingly. "Look, I'm not taking sides. I'm just relaying information. Shane asked Ariana to watch Mckenzey, and Raul to watch you. I know it sounds terrible, but before your dorm was broken into, so was Shane's. They got this guy on video. That same guy was seen walking outside of Mckenzey's dorm. That's why Ariana was sent to watch the building. That is what Shane does. He has several friends in different groups, and they help him."

"I don't know what to think," Jet said.

Autumn added, "I don't trust Shane, that's for sure. He's a problem. I don't know him that well. My understanding is that he changed a lot right before coming to Chadwick's."

The slow song ended, and Jet stopped dancing. A second slow song began to play.

Autumn said, "You're not getting off that easy." She pulled him, if possible, even closer.

After a moment, she said, "This is the last thing I'll say about Shane. He was at a different boarding school before coming here. He hated it there and transferred here. That's when he changed. A friend of his died. I don't know the details."

"What are you talking about?"

"It happened at another boarding school. It's one of the reasons why he transferred here."

"What other school did he go to?"

"I'm not sure if you've heard of it. It's called Dillon Lake."

Jet said, trying to sound anything but shocked, "I have. Are you sure about him going to Dillon Lake? I met him at Chadwick's at the beginning of last year."

"Dillon Lake is designed like our school, except it starts in seventh grade. He transferred here for ninth."

Trying to remain calm, Jet added, "Why did he come here?"

"He chose Chadwick's over the other four schools."

"Four schools?" Jet asked.

"Two generations ago, this family called the Middlesex family began creating several boarding schools. They had a boat full of money. Anyway, there are five schools connected to this family: Dillon Lake, Chadwick's, one in Florida, another in Texas, and one in Connecticut. At least, I think. Collectively, these five schools are the premiere five. I think Shane wanted to be closer to home, and California was the best option."

"I get that."

"Enough of Shane." Autumn leaned in closer and placed the side of her head on his chest. They finished the rest of the song in silence, and she refused to let him go when a third slow song began. As the last song ended, Autumn hugged him for a long time. She said, "Thanks again for talking to Ariana; it means so much to me." She leaned in and kissed him on the cheek and whispered, "Maybe we could hang out as Ariana suggested."

"Yeah. I'd like that."

He thought his night couldn't turn out any more confusing until he ran into Ariana forty minutes later as he was refilling his drink. His friends and roommates were all getting along great. The night had been a perfect success.

A hand touched his shoulder, and he turned around. Before he could react, Ariana reached in and hugged him. "I know you're mad at me. I also know that Autumn talked with you and hopefully explained everything. Please understand that I was trying to do a good thing."

"I do," Jet said as she released him. "I'll try to explain it to everyone. Don't worry."

Ariana wore a bright red flowing dress that perfectly matched her mask. The mask's facial part was silver with intricate markings, and she had two horns shooting straight into the air several inches. There were no feathers.

Jet asked, "Was it weird talking with her after so long?"

"Yes, and no. Weirder for me, I'm sure. She's the same as ever."

"How are things otherwise?"

"You know. It's our sophomore year. I tried out for the volleyball team. I made it. I'm playing mostly JV and get to suit up for some of the varsity games. It's fun. You should come to watch a game; only a few are left this season."

"I might do that."

An awkward silence fell between them.

Ariana said, "I thought you should hear it from me first. I'm hanging out or whatever with Shawn Stevens from the basketball team. He says he knows of you from your geology lab class. Autumn set us up. I know there has been drama between us, but no hard feelings, okay?"

"I agree," Jet said quickly. "Uh. Thanks for letting me know. No worries from my side."

"Have a good night, Jet."

"You too, Ariana. See you around." She disappeared toward the stairs.

Pulling out his phone, Jet texted his friends and his roommates. It was far too much to process, from the kissing girl, to Autumn, to Shane, and finally Ariana. He was calling it a night.

PART 2

THE RECOVERY

CHAPTER 27

Jet anxiously pushed through a set of screaming two-year-old twins to find his seat before the plane took off. This was his first time on an airplane, but emotions were on high alert as the realization kicked in that they were traveling halfway across the world for a hunch. He knew that it was well planned, but anything could go wrong. The rest of the gang was spread throughout the plane. He dreaded the first leg of their flight, knowing how much he needed to sleep. He had two different over-the-counter sleep medications in his pocket, just in case. The LAX airport was a madhouse with travelers, and they'd barely made it to their gate in time.

Over the last week, Jet had worked hard to turn in his assignments. He seriously doubted there would be any time to study during his first trip out of the United States. Jayco had a brilliant idea of staying up all night to prepare for the time change. That meant Jet hadn't slept in the last twenty-four hours. Switzerland was nine hours ahead of California, and it was already in the afternoon, and their flight would take more than twelve hours. Barring any unforeseen delays, they would arrive early the following day. If Jet didn't find a way to get some sleep, he would be useless the entire time in Europe.

Opening his newly purchased German dictionary, he studied simple words and phrases for the next fifteen or twenty minutes while the plane taxied to the runway. As the plane took off, he closed his dictionary and held on for dear life. He panicked slightly at the thought of all the plane crashes that had happened weeks ago. He became convinced they were about to fall from the sky. When they were airborne, he relaxed only slightly and resumed studying. He was either going to learn a few sentences or fall asleep fast. Switzerland was a melting pot of languages, but Swiss German was their primary language. An hour and a half later, he closed the book and his eyes. To his dismay, he couldn't remember a single word that he'd tried memorizing.

As sleep escaped him, he opened his eyes and tried to find his friends. He quickly spotted everyone but Jayco and Seyanna. He growled as he found all of them fast asleep. The knot in his stomach grew, just as it had every day for the past week.

Jet worried that none of them were ready to take on what was coming, especially him. Adding to his worries, Jayco had made it clear that he thought Jet wasn't doing enough, and if Jayco had been given these talents, they would be much further along. But what concerned Jet the most was an unexplainable feeling that a figurative door was closing. Their chances of seeing this box were becoming dangerously tenuous.

Jet must've fallen asleep at some point. But when he awoke as the plane touched down, he felt worse off than before. He gathered his belongings and zombie walked to the next gate, following the others. He remained silent and shook his head when food was suggested. His friends didn't seem to have a care in the world. They laughed and joked and sprinted around the Orlando airport. Two hours later, they boarded their plane for Munich.

His seat was around midplane, alone again, as Jayco and Grantham sat next to each other across the aisle and two rows back. Mckenzey was one row behind the boys, while Seyanna and Latisha were at the back of the plane. Jayco yawned and downed a large gulp of his coffee. It seemed as if Mckenzey was hunkered down listening to music.

The instant the plane left the ground, the most surprising thing happened. Jet's anxiety melted away like ice in warm water. It didn't take him long to realize that something in his lap was warming his entire body. His first thought was that he'd spilled his coffee, but only his backpack lay in his lap. Reaching inside, he pulled out the tome of *The Sorcerer's Guide*. Jet instinctively knew that the sixth page would turn without difficulty as he opened it. There was a message, and the name at the bottom of the page sent a chill down his neck.

Dear Sorcerer,

Evidently, I did not get the chance to meet you, but it is the farthest that anyone has read in this book in the last two hundred years. You deserve congratulation. But there is plenty of work ahead of you, and you must do so alone. As you have been made aware, this tome will act as a guide. There are a few pearls of wisdom that I want to share with you. First, this is really happening, and you've been chosen for his work. Second, and you may already know this, but there are two tomes. I came close to getting the second tome in Sydney, Australia, but I failed, and it was moved. The second tome shares the secrets of Arisol's deception, and it teaches how to use Runic magic. The last and most important advice I can give you is, don't get used. Some may see you as a tool in this imminent war. They may try to play you. People have been fighting this war for years. They have often forgotten the goal. Remember, you are the only one who can read the Sorcerer's Guide. Therefore, your services will always be crucial. Constantly ask yourself: who has the control, and who is the pawn? If you need a bigger hint: you're not a pawn. I wish you all the success with your travels, discoveries, and especially your chances of keeping the tablet from those who conspire with Arisol.

Joshua Elbert Taley

After finishing, a new paragraph appeared on the opposite page.

Copied by Joshua Taley from a letter that I received:
Dear Brother J,

Much has changed since our last correspondence. I am almost sure that this will be our last. As you can see, I have finally sent you the cloak for you or your apprentice. Also, there is a golden pyramid, some jewelry, and a few more sacred items. Keep these hidden at all costs. If you have not received these items, then I fear all is already lost. You are the best hope for my people and those who support us. It is also time to reconnect with a hidden ally. Speak the words Pyramis of Aurum around the pyramid, and it will obey its master. Time is a virtue, and when the new century unfolds, the clock will begin to count down to the release of the beast. Whoever controls the tablet will ultimately control Arisol. We have become convinced of this. Understandably, you have had some difficulty accepting your role as protector of the tablet. I hope that I have passed enough of my knowledge on to you. Sometimes, though, I despair that it still won't be enough.

Last week I began noticing suspicious characters around my town, as recently as two days ago, I have since learned that they have been asking questions about an old fable. Since I am the historical leader of this town, I knew they would arrive on my doorstep eventually. That day came today. They have skilled British accents, but they are unmistakably German and follow leads from their homeland. I do not know how they have tricked some of the others in the village into helping them. New information was uncovered about our town of Asyut. I was commanded to comply, and I have for as long as possible. I was forced to give away some valuable information that I have shared with you and the Brotherhood.

I am confident that they know I've held some information back. They will return soon. My days are now numbered. Their looks of defiance and determination were enough to put my final act into motion. I have sent you the tome we have spoken about and the items mentioned above. I pray that I have sufficient respect in this town that they will not attack tonight. But only the gods know. We have yet to uncover the locations of the tablet pieces. I now believe that they were scattered throughout the world. Your description of the cavern door in the mountain leads me to this conclusion. You have found one of the caverns of the tablet—of that much, I am satisfied. The Brotherhood has uncovered proof that the pieces were taken to remote places and hidden. It seems the dark one still has a level of command over those who were in possession of the tablet pieces.

I charge you to continue as the protector, but you may be the mentor for the apprentice one day. They must have the ability to open the book's pages without the keyword. The keyword will only allow minimal entrance into the book. We've studied it for decades and cannot get it to open without it. The magic that binds it closed is powerful and resists our many attempts. With the use of the keyword, we could add the fable and some additional markings. Our most prominent mage has added Wier to the tome as a last resort and a measure of protection.

The Brotherhood will continue to work on your behalf if possible, but I cannot guarantee that they will have any contact with you, as their knowledge of you is already minimal at best. If I survive or escape, I will contact you again. Do not respond to this letter until I have contacted you, and do not accept anyone unless the watchword and crest are presented.

Take care, and good luck, my friend and brother.

Gamal.

Jet's heart raced as he realized he had just read a letter from his great uncle. Every one of Jet's suspicions and concerns with him were misplaced and naive. More importantly, Uncle Joshua had been searching and doing much of what he was doing now.

He spent the next hour reflecting on Silverton, the cave in the mountain, the hike with Mckenzey where they'd first found the meteorite, and his great uncle. Back in Silverton, on the day they found the meteorite, they had been on the backside of a hill near Silverton. He recalled the moment when the sun had just touched the horizon. Something had scared him. There had been two eyes in the darkness as he navigated through his memories. Those eyes had been in a deep and mysterious cave. After that, he didn't want to go any farther. If this letter was correct, a piece of the tablet might have been hidden in that same mountain.

His mind focused on the second tome. He was sure that Shane owned it, and that he was proficient in Runic magic. He came from Dillon Lake, and now Mckenzey was transferring to the same school. It was impossible to know how long Shane had studied the second tome. Ariana's explanation on Halloween of Shane's behavior only made partial sense. There was a much more of the story still unexplained on why Shane was at Chadwick's and why he had left Dillon Lake.

Twenty minutes later, an intense fatigue settled over Jet. He had just enough energy to put away his tome before dozing off. He dreamt about water flowing from a river. At first, it was gentle, but it quickly became suffocating, icy, and deadly. The water was familiar yet uninviting. When he awoke, he was dry but bone cold. Checking his watch, he realized that he'd been asleep for a full eight hours.

With a thick accent, a voice rasped over the intercom, "We're entering our final approach." The same voice repeated the information in German and French.

Mckenzey caught up with him as he stepped out of the plane. Rolling her eyes, she said, "You slept the entire time, didn't you?"

Jet shrugged. "I was tired."

"I hate you."

This time, Jet was the one with an abundance of energy. His friends barely dragged themselves to their next gate. Once they found a small area, they piled onto the floor to get some rest.

Since they had another two-hour layover, Jet began to people watch. They were miles from Munich, as the airport sat on the outskirts of town. He concluded that stepping into the airport didn't count as visiting Germany. Watching the people pass by was exciting. Somehow, everyone looked different. It was hard to explain; maybe it was their clothes or walk, but they were definitely not in America anymore.

A delicious aroma of freshly baked bread and minted coffee assailed him. He began salivating on the spot. His stomach growled, and he could barely contain himself. Glancing at the others, he decided to take a chance. Jayco and Mckenzey were drooling on their shirts, and Grantham's head nodded to an imaginary tune. Seyanna appeared the most comfortable, but that wasn't saying much.

Jet found a queue and exchanged some cash. He was able to get both Euros and Swiss Francs. Once finished, he took his new riches and searched for the source of the phenomenal smell. He passed a brewery with a sign reading: Airbräu. Several patrons were waiting to be seated. A man caught Jet's eye as he passed by. He was a business type, with brown dress slacks, an orange sweater, and silky-smooth black dress shoes. Along with his dark complexion, he was sophisticated and well-dressed. The man intently watched Jet walk by.

A dozen more steps brought him to the front doors of the Aran Bakery. Once inside, his olfactory sensors were introduced to heaven whiffs of brewing coffee, teas, pastries, cinnamon, oats, and honey filled the air. A white decorative canopy spread above his head. To his right and left were several wooden tables and benches. To his liking, everything on the menu was written in German and English, and when he reached the counter, he ordered the first item he recognized—warm bread with butter, a pastry with cinnamon and raisins, and some black tea. Ten minutes later, his food arrived. He sighed in relief—a small victory.

Jet decided to take a short walk around the terminal as he left the bakery. When he returned to his luggage, his friends were still passed out on the floor. He was perfectly relaxed watching those around him for the next forty minutes.

A scream echoed through the airport terminal, and Jet's head swiveled to find a man rushing in his direction. The man wore jeans and a button-down blue shirt. Jet instinctively took a step backward. Before the man reached Jet, he changed course and sprinted down an adjacent path.

Seemingly out of nowhere, two police officers crashed into the man with such force that Jet winced with sympathy.

The pinned man started shouting quickly in French. Jet closed his eyes and concentrated. He was speaking fast. *"Vous avez volé ma pochette et mon sac. Je sais que c'était vous. Vous payerez ceci."* The loose English translation was that something had been stolen, and someone would pay for it.

"What's going on?" Mckenzey asked in a hushed voice, stepping up next to him and rubbing her eyes.

Jet turned to answer, but he spotted the man with the orange sweater at a table nearby. Was he trying to hide from view? Jet said distractedly, "A man just got tackled by the police."

"Seriously! Did you see what happened?"

"The man was screaming about somebody stealing his bag. He was running across the terminal when he was tackled." Looking back, he found the man was being handcuffed.

Where did you get that?" she asked, pointing to his cup.

"There's a bakery down that hall. The food is to die for."

"Can I come with you?" Latisha asked. "I'm starving."

"Here," Jet said, and he handed them some Euros.

"Thanks," Mckenzey said, squeezing his arm as they disappeared.

"Who's that guy being taken away in handcuffs?" Jayco asked, five minutes later.

Jet explained what had happened.

"Where are the girls?" Grantham asked groggily.

"Latisha and Mckenzey just went down to the bakery for some food."

"Thank goodness. I'm starving," Jayco said.

"We're boarding soon," Jet said, passing them a few Euros. "Hurry back."

Jayco and Grantham woke Seyanna, and they made their way toward the bakery.

The man was now handcuffed and standing. The police were trying politely to talk with him, but he became more agitated. The man nodded to the left of Jet. He followed their gaze, but no one was there. The officers refused to release him, and soon they'd hauled away their prisoner.

Five minutes later, the man with the orange sweater stepped into the gate line next to theirs, also about to board. His plane was going to Cairo, Egypt.

That would be an awesome place to visit, Jet thought.

His friends returned with their hands full of new foods. On the plane, they were all seated close to each other. The flight to Bern only took sixty minutes, and they chatted the entire time. Stepping off the plane, they retrieved their luggage, including the faux box, and made their way toward the bus station.

Grantham said, "Flughafen Bern. We've done the impossible."

Jayco complained, "I never realized that a trip to Europe would be so uncomfortable. Those seats are not made for anyone over four feet tall."

Seyanna joked, "Latisha should've bought you two seats."

"Actually," Jayco said, "that's a great idea." Turning to Latisha, he said, "Can you make that happen on the way back?"

"No way," Latisha muttered. "You didn't even have to pay for your ticket."

"I know, and I'm grateful. But I also want to be comfortable."

Twenty minutes later, they piled onto a small shuttle heading in the direction of the center of town. An older man and woman were the only other passengers. When they reached the train station, Jet bought six tickets into Bern. The train into town was the pure enjoyment of new sights. The countryside, small towns, and the buildings were remarkable. Jet had never seen anything as historic and extraordinary.

Mckenzey, sitting next to him, said, "This place is magical. Can you believe we made it this far?"

"Truthfully, I'm in shock on both accounts."

"Look." Mckenzey pointed out the side window. Bern itself came into view. A light dusting of snow had covered the trees and some of the roofs. The buildings were white, and those roofs not covered with snow were orangish-brown. The train crossed over a bridge, and the buildings were directly pressed against the aqua-blue water.

Latisha began reciting, "Bern is located near the center of Switzerland. It's the capital, though not the largest or most industrialized city in the country. It's built on both sides of the river Aare and is home to over a hundred thousand people."

Five stops later, they exited the train at the station. It was gigantic and full of people. They found a bus that took them close to their hotel. The bus ride was quick and easy.

As the bus drove away, Grantham pointed down a street. "Our hotel is close by."

Taking their baggage, they made their way to the street.

There were several cars, buses, streetcars, and even bicycles despite the snow. The temperature was warm enough, and most of the snow would likely melt by tomorrow. Swiss flags were plentiful as they crossed the cobblestone streets.

Jayco asked, "Are we there yet?"

"Relax," Grantham said. "The hotel is up here."

The front of their hotel had two pillars sitting as sentinels, several feet off from the main street. This caused the front of the hotel to sit back in a nook. A small cobblestone path where guests could be dropped off was situated in front. Walking through the front doors, the scene again changed. The hotel lobby was, without doubt, the most beautiful room Jet had ever seen. Marble structured columns were positioned throughout the main floor. Inspiring chandeliers hung from the ceiling with actual candles. The room spoke of luxury, taste, and romance. And a sizeable decorative glass window was the final fragment of the masterpiece.

Latisha shuffled to the front desk and returned a few minutes later with two keys. "Boys in one room and girls in the other. We're on the third floor."

Jayco asked, "How did you get the rooms so quickly?"

Latisha glanced nervously at Jet. "Don't get upset, but I had to tell my aunt that we were coming. I didn't say much, but it was the only way to reserve rooms. It was all paid for in advance. And my aunt couldn't care less."

"Now, this is living in *style*," Grantham said as they handed their luggage off to two bellmen.

The dark hardwood staircase up to their rooms was impressive. Once on the third floor, the group separated to get a better look at their living quarters. The boys' room was spacious with two beds and two leather chairs. The dark hardwood stretched into the room. White and red decorations marked the walls, picture frames, candles, and curtains. The view was spectacular, and they could easily see the Aare river and a perfect view of the part of town they were so desperate to see. Jet also spotted an outdoor café on the main level. Almost like a house, a second building sat another level below the cafe and closer to the water's edge.

"Can you believe the view?" Jayco said in awe.

Grantham added with bravado, "My bros, this is one Romeo room. I could get my mood in here."

"But don't," Jayco added with a laugh.

There was a knock at the door.

"We'll see," Grantham replied. "No promises."

Jet opened the door, and Latisha stepped in, looking around. "Our room is so much better."

"Doubt it," Grantham said.

"Follow me."

The girls' room was impressive. They had roses on each of the three beds. They also had a bowl full of strawberries and a bottle of wine sitting in a bowl of ice. Their television was twice as big, and that was all before the full-sized jacuzzi bathtub.

"I take that back," Grantham said. "Your room is twice the size of ours."

"I know," Latisha gushed.

Jayco, stepping to the table, asked, "Is the wine free?"

Latisha smiled. "Not in your life. It's like three thousand dollars."

Jayco quickly returned the bottle to the silver bucket. "I knew that."

Mckenzey said, "We've got a perfect view of the museum district. Should we start there tonight or tomorrow?

Jet said, "Let's get unpacked and take a nap. We're going down tonight. We need to be completely ready by tomorrow."

CHAPTER 28

Late in the afternoon, and on a bench across the street, Jet focused on the steps leading into the Museum. They were within the city district of Helvetiaplatz and had crossed the river Aare via the Kirchenfeldbrücke bridge.

Jayco and Grantham stood in line to enter the museum while Mckenzey and Seyanna were already inside. The plan was for Jet to enter last. Latisha remained stubbornly defiant about having any significant role to play. Jet guessed that she wasn't entirely on board with stealing the box. Yesterday, Grantham had found the museum's electrical box, but it was too complicated to hack into the system or plant a decoy video projector. It hadn't taken long for Jet to come up with Plan B. The real difficulty would still be switching the boxes.

A chime sounded on his watch; the museum closed in sixty minutes. It was time. Standing, he strolled to where Latisha sat alone on a different bench. As he approached, he could see that she was well past panicking and was venturing into breakdown mode. He said, "Please try to calm down. You'll be fine out here. You're not going to be at any risk."

"Easy for you to say." Latisha's eyes glinted with terror.

"It's fine. Check out everyone who goes in and out. That's all."

"I look pathetic."

"You're supposed to."

"How much did we pay for these clothes?"

"It was well worth it."

"They stink!"

Jet stifled a laugh. Latisha exceeded her part. She appeared homeless, haggard, and drunk.

"Where's the box?" he asked as he spotted Jayco and Grantham separately stepping into the museum.

She sighed. "Under my blanket."

Taking the faux box, it didn't take long to attach it to his chest and reattach his cloak. The box was less than eighteen inches in length, six inches in width, and four inches in height. Jet had finally seen its design just this morning. Jayco loved to keep the surprise. Jayco was impressed with the faux box.

The rest of his friends had also extensively changed their appearance. Each girl had either cut or colored their hair. Latisha had chopped off more than six inches. It was far frizzier and more afro than Jet had ever seen from her. She was almost unrecognizable. Mckenzey had colored her hair dark black, and Seyanna had found a red wig. They had purchased some clothing, with some smelling better than others. Jayco, the size of a small brick building, wore a hat and hadn't shaved in two weeks. It didn't alter his appearance too much. Grantham had found some circular glasses and a top hat and colored his hair a slight gray.

Jet had also made some changes. He'd colored his hair black, spiked it, and matched it with entirely black clothing. The only exception was his cloak.

Ten minutes after the guys walked through the doors, Jet stood and made his approach. Only fifty minutes left until closing. His arms were free with the box strapped to his chest by two pairs of suspenders. Three doors sat at the top of the concrete stairs ahead of him. The museum was older, built of red brick, and several stories high. It was fascinating to stare at the outer structure with its integrated carvings and markings. He could get lost in Switzerland, just looking at the buildings.

Jet was surprised at the large volume of people trying to enter this late at night. And most of those standing in line were very well dressed.

The first obstacle ahead of him was the two metal detectors stationed inside the front doors. As planned, Mckenzey stood inside the doors waiting for him. She bent low and dumped a handful of metal balls onto the floor.

Jet willed his vision to slow, and he watched the two dozen metal balls bounce and ricochet through the detector, simultaneously and in slow motion. To his surprise, the alarm did not sound. He wondered if the metal balls were large enough to set off the alarm. Several patrons shrieked before the answer presented itself as they began tripping over the rolling objects. Feet flew everywhere.

Jet's vision remained overactive, and ahead of him, an older couple fell on each other. A giant of a man bent down to pick up a fallen purse, only to be crashed into from behind. Using the commotion to his advantage, Jet slid through the open doors and quickly caught up with Mckenzey.

"Why didn't the alarm go off?" she asked.

"No clue. They're probably just for a show." Jet moved quickly forward. The first floor was tile and expansive with some decoration but mostly bare of any museum items. The walls were colorful and appeared like marble. The vaulted ceiling was incredible. Ahead of them was the staircase upwards to the museum portion of the building. They were on the main floor, and a banner hung down above several decorated tables. It read in English: *In Honor of Those Who Haven't Been Forgotten.*

Jet barely sidestepped a waiter carrying a tray of baked bread with cheese. For his troubles, Jet received a dirty look from the man. The waiter shot forward toward an elevator. Farther away from them, there were several tables decorated with white tablecloths, flowers, and a centerpiece. There were two dozen elegantly dressed individuals socialized and mingled around. He thought he heard multiple languages being spoken.

Jet said, "Let's start upstairs."

"Grantham, Jayco, and Seyanna are on the second floor."

"The third it is."

"I thought Grantham said the box has to be on second?" she questioned.

"Better safe than sorry."

They started up the steps. Halfway up the first floor, there was a loud chirping sound from the front door.

"Is that the warning sign?" Mckenzey asked as she spun around.

Jet followed her gaze, partially upset. "I think so. But why in the world would Latisha sound the alarm this soon? If she's jumped the gun because she has cold feet, I will throw something at her."

Latisha's voice bellowed above the commotion at the front door. "Es ist kalt. Es ist kalt. Sehr kalt". She told the front staff that it was cold outside. This signaled that danger was approaching.

"What is happening?" Mckenzey asked. "Do we abort?"

Jet tapped his forehead for a few seconds, thinking. "Keep moving." Reaching out, he took Mckenzey's hand, and they ascended the stairs two at a time. They didn't stop until they were on the top floor. They slid behind a pillar and poked their heads out on each side to look better. A chill ran down Jet's back as three figures stepped onto the tile floor far below.

"Is that who I think it is?" Mckenzey asked.

"Yep. Shane Fallon."

"Is he here for the same reason we are?"

"I think that's a pretty sure bet. And look, he brought some friends."

Mckenzey frantically looked around. "How do we warn the others?"

"Let's pray they heard it, but we need to keep moving." Turning, he found that this floor opened to a large and beautiful room with several statues to their left and mismatched artifacts on the right. Hundreds of objects were separated throughout this vast room. More than a dozen people were studying different items. In the center, Jet saw several epic machines, including dismantled bombs, a tank, and a portion of a field gun. There were mannequins dressed in all types of combat clothes.

"Let's separate," Jet hissed. "I'll go right. You go left."

Mckenzey nodded and set off quickly.

Jet sprinted forward, passing a few patrons and several items. He felt dismayed as he spotted thousands of items. How were they going to find a box? Jet twisted through several aisles and reached the sidewall. Nothing. He decided to head toward the back of the museum. A plan started to form in his mind of waiting until Shane found the box and stealing it from him. It would be a long shot.

Up ahead, Jet noticed a break in the back wall as if leading to another room. He hurried forward.

"Pssst." A sound echoed, and Jet turned. Mckenzey was sprinting toward him with Grantham and Jayco.

"What are we going to do now?" Jayco asked.

Grantham said, "Are we going to abandon the search for the box?"

"And let Shane get it? No way."

Seyanna sprinted to meet them from another direction. As she spoke, she was filled with terror. "Shane knows where the box is. It's here on this floor. We need to leave now and escape."

Grantham added, "The museum is going to close early. I guess they have a celebration downstairs. Maybe that will deter Shane."

"I doubt it," Jet said. They stood on the edge of a hallway that exited the main room. Jet continued, "Grantham and Seyanna, get close to Shane and see what they're planning. You guys look unrecognizable. If Jayco's spotted, they'll know him in an instant. Sneak downstairs and create a distraction."

"What about me?" Mckenzey asked.

"I think the box is in there." He pointed to the back wall. "You and I are going to go find it." As the others sprinted off, Jet walked briskly, with Mckenzey a step behind. It looked like there were possibly five rooms, each connected by the same corridor. The first room held vases, pottery, and other precious items. They searched the walls, and several things were in glass cases in the center of the room.

"Nothing," Mckenzey said.

They moved to the second room. It was lined with statues situated on the room's outer edges—no place for the box. Twenty people or so were roaming around this room, appreciating the artwork. He was instantly drawn to a glass display in the third room, one of four, in the far corner.

"There it is," Jet said, pulling Mckenzey forward.

"We found it," she said excitedly. They reached the item and surveyed the area. A pedestal was underneath, and the black casket was inside a clear display case. The walls of the case were easily two inches thick. The casket was identical to the picture he'd seen and the description his father had given him. It practically shimmered in the light. There were hieroglyphics, a giant beetle on one side, and other beautiful carvings. He saw a falcon with a snake's head and a lion with an owl's head.

"We are staring at a tangential item that connects our weirdness to the fable. This is monumental." He spotted four keyholes on the display case, one at each corner. He groaned. "This will be harder than we thought."

"Someone's coming," Mckenzey hissed.

Jet found brown-hair striding down the corridor, less than twenty feet away. He shoved Mckenzey into the corner and against the wall. They wrapped their arms around each other, and Mckenzey's lips rested against his neck as she watched the display case. A shiver ran down Jet's back.

Into his ear, Mckenzey said, "He didn't even glance at us. He's staring at the case."

Brown-hair squawked into a two-way radio. "Third floor ... toward the back is a corridor. It's on display. I'm there now."

The radio chirped. "On my way." Brown-hair turned back to stare out of the opening.

Jet whispered, "Join that group at the far corner. I'm going to disappear." Flipping on his hood caused a slight breeze to shoot through the room. Ten heads searched for the source of the commotion.

Shane Fallon, flanked by a large burly boy in his early twenties, stepped into the room less than thirty seconds later. The muscular guy was roughly the same height as Jayco but substantially thicker in the shoulders. A fourth guy was also present—tall but thin and wirily. He appeared to be older, maybe around twenty one, and wore a security officer's outfit that matched others Jet had seen. Everyone, including Mckenzey, had been ushered out of the room in an instant.

Shane demanded, "Let's take it now."

The security guard answered, "Not possible. You can't." Nodding his head up to the camera above them, he added, "Someone is in there now, watching the entire place. If something goes missing, they'll lock this place down."

Unperturbed, Shane said, "Then I want a closer look."

"As a guest of the museum, you can do that. Certainly." The man stepped forward, pulling keys from his pocket and selecting a long black key. The security guard unlocked each of the display's four corner locks. The case was opened, and Shane lifted the casket from the display. The moment all ten of his fingers touched the box, it seemed that a surge of energy shot into Shane. He stiffened his back as a dazed look crossed his face.

The muscular boy stepped forward. "What was that?"

Shane smiled. "A gift, I think."

"Of what?" the guy asked.

"Imagine your energy level is like a gas tank in the car. It can only get so full. Well, my energy level just increased tenfold." Shane glanced around and found the camera in the upper ceiling and said, "Watch."

His fingers moved in a blur, and to Jet, it seemed like he was drawing a picture in the air like he'd done back at school. He pointed his hand at the camera. Even off to the side, Jet felt something unseen whirl toward the camera. It slowly changed directions to point at an adjacent display, as if someone was pushing it. Turning to the others, Shane added, "That normally would've cost me half of my energy. Now, it barely even touched it."

Before putting the casket back in the display, Shane pulled a small black circular object, the size of a quarter, from his coat and placed it on the underside of the box.

"What's that?" the man asked.

"Don't you worry, Lawrence." Shane lowered the box into the display and closed the lid. As Shane stepped from the room, it was again confirmed that he knew far more about magic than Jet did.

CHAPTER 29

Mckenzey and several other patrons waited two minutes after the group left to return to the room. So many people had been staring into the space that Jet could not remove his hood from his cloak until it was more crowded. A soft breeze swept through the area. Mckenzey ran to the corner and said, "Jet. Are you here?" Her voice was high-pitched and anxious.

When the coast was clear, he reappeared a few feet away, and the draft vanished.

Mckenzey asked, "What just happened?"

"Shane used magic to move the camera. He also got a boost of energy when he touched the box. They placed a small black item on the bottom; I think it's a tracking device."

Mckenzey, her face turning pale, whispered, "This is not good. We can't do this with them watching. We're going to get caught."

"No," Jet said. "We can't stop now. The camera is no longer pointed at the box. Right now is a perfect time, our only time." Jet moved toward the display when a loud commotion erupted from the large room. Jet peered around the wall and into the corridor. Shane was shouting, and it looked like he was lying on the ground. Brown-hair and muscular guy were hovering over him, trying to help him to his feet.

Jet's jaw dropped when he saw who was standing next to them. A dark-skinned man with an orange sweater was apologizing profusely for having knocked over Shane. Suddenly two security guards came into view. Jet sprinted to the display, putting his back to the corridor.

Even from here, he could hear Shane bellowing, "Someone, help me up."

Jet whispered, "Mckenzey, the display is unlocked. I need you to open it and remove the box while I make the switch."

"Not a good idea." She hesitantly flipped the corners, reached in, and quickly removed the box while Jet unfastened the faux box from his chest.

Once that was done, Jet said, "Let's switch the boxes, and you put the faux box into the display."

Mckenzey nodded, and they made the switch.

"The box is glowing turquoise," Mckenzey muttered. "Look at the scarab."

Jet almost dropped the original box as he felt the infusion of power released into his body. For him, it wasn't energy, but more like something was unlocking in his mind. The color of the box returned to normal. Jet was about to strap the actual box onto his chest when he said, "No, wait."

Mckenzey had already placed the faux box back into the display.

Shane's voice echoed, "I'm fine. We're leaving. I just need to take a photo of this piece of art in the back. It'll take a few seconds."

The voice of a security guard said, "The museum is closing. Please come back tomorrow."

Lawrence, the security guard, said, "Raynaud. It's fine. I got this. This man is a guest, and I can accompany him."

"Thank you," Shane said hotly. "I'm seriously considering having my father pull his donation to this museum."

Raynaud responded quickly, "No, sir. Lawrence will show you any artwork you want. We have a few more minutes."

With a thick accent, a third voice said, "My apologies, sir. I'm so sorry that I ran into you. Let me buy you a cup of coffee."

Jet removed the black device from the real box, handed it to Mckenzey and whispered, "Bottom left corner."

Shane's voice, noticeably closer, screamed, "I'm fine. Leave me alone. I don't want your damn coffee."

Jet asked, "How close is Shane?"

Mckenzey stole a glance over his shoulder. "A few feet from the entrance. But there's a man in an orange sweater standing in front of him. Wait. Shane just pushed the man to the side."

Mckenzey closed the display, and without another thought, Jet yanked her toward the back of the building. They hurried through the hallway and into the next room. He knew this was probably the wrong move, as they were now cornered, but they had no other choice.

Shane, brown-hair, and Lawrence sprinted into the room and encircled the box. Shane demanded, "Was anyone standing near this?"

Brown-hair said, "I didn't see anyone."

Jet and Mckenzey moved through the fourth room and into the fifth.

Shane's voice was loud enough that it echoed for them to hear. "It feels like something is going on here. That man was insistent that we didn't come back in this direction. I mean, who crashes into someone that hard."

"No one has been back here."

"Go, take a look."

Scuffling feet approached and sweat ran down Jet's back. He pinned both of them into the corner. He stared at Mckenzey's face and saw the fear in her eyes.

"Just a heads up, if he comes into this room, I'm going to kiss you."

A faint smile crept onto her face. "I dare you to do it."

As the footsteps approached, he leaned forward, mere millimeters away.

A voice came over the intercom above them, and he jumped. The voice said, "The museum is closing early tonight. If you bring today's ticket tomorrow, you get half price off."

Mckenzey teased, "Someone is entering the room."

Jet licked his lips and leaned in closer.

Shane shouted, "We're fine. Everything is in place. False alarm."

The figure turned and ran from the room.

Jet stepped away.

Mckenzey said, "Aren't you the shy type."

"Let me explain," Jet said.

Mckenzey shot past him and peeked around the corner. Jet joined her. Three figures were walking away, the faux box still in the display. As they began walking toward the stairs, Mckenzey's hand latched on to his. Her face revealed nothing. They fell into step with five other patrons leaving the third floor and descending the stairs.

"That's him," a voice shouted from halfway down the stairs. The voice was unmistakably Shane.

Jet tensed as everyone stopped moving.

Shane Fallon was several steps ahead of them, pointing down the stairs to the bottom floor. Brown-hair and Lawrence stood next to him. Shane yelled, "That big guy down near the entrance, is that Jayco Carter from high school?"

Brown-hair said, "I can't tell."

Shane gripped Lawrence's shoulders and said, "You stand next to that display and make sure no one gets near it. I'll be back up there in five minutes. This is turning into an absolute disaster. If we don't get this item, you will pay the price. Get up there now."

The guard sprinted up to the third floor, passing Jet and the others just as Shane and brown-hair ran ahead.

Mckenzey whispered, "Did they really see Jayco? If so, we're screwed."

Breathing quickly, he said, "No clue."

"They're going to be watching the front doors."

"I know."

"How are we going to get out of here?"

Jet considered their options. When he spoke, he said quickly, "On the first floor, I saw a waiter bringing food through a side door. I'm going to go invisible, but I'll follow you. I'm not sure I can hold onto you. Together we'll find an exit through those doors."

"Really?" she questioned. "I'll be exposed."

"I'm here. I'll protect you. If someone comes too close, they'll never know what hit them."

"You better be right."

"We've got this." Jet pulled on his hood and disappeared. A gust of wind followed, knocking three people ahead of them aside. Mckenzey sprinted between them; Jet was a step behind.

When they reached the bottom step, three lines had developed at the front door with about ten people in each line. Shane, the muscular guy, and brown-hair were scanning everyone.

Mckenzey whispered, "Let's hope Jayco escaped."

"No kidding."

Together, they kept far away from everyone else. Using the back wall, they inched toward a door ahead of them. It was slow going. They stopped just next to the open door several minutes later and scanned the room.

Jet whispered, "Let's go."

Mckenzey turned and had to leap back to avoid the door as it suddenly swung outward. She narrowly avoided crashing into the waiter exiting the door. The girl began loudly berating Mckenzey in German, then walked off. Mckenzey, ignoring the rebuke, caught the door before it closed and stepped into the hallway with Jet closely behind.

A red carpet covered the hallway, which was empty. Together, they sprinted forward, passing three or four doors, before the door behind them crashed open.

A voice echoed from behind. "Who are you?" It was Shane.

"Keep going," Jet hissed.

A force slammed into him from behind, and Jet was lifted into the air and propelled forward. While in the air, he was turned sideways, and his back slammed into the wall. It felt like he slid into a heap on the floor. He tried catching his breath as he felt the box still attached to his chest. It didn't appear to be damaged.

The attack didn't seem to connect with Mckenzey quite as hard. She was thrown to the ground and rolled twice. Jet could see her against the opposite wall, unmoving.

Shane shouted, "Whatever is protecting you, I can still see you. There are two of you, and you're not as hidden as you might think. This is going to be fun."

A hidden fierceness snapped inside Jet's entire body, from head to toe, as if an outer crust succumbed to the pressure of an inner force. He stood, extending his right arm, and bellowed, "Ignisnaeth." A fireball burst from his hand, igniting the carpet as it sped toward Shane. Shane barely had time to react, and he waved his hand and slightly deflected the fire as it crashed into the floor, wall, and the door behind him. A crimson red inferno barrier emerged.

Shane had no option but to retreat. He covered his head and ran. Before he disappeared, he yelled, "If you were here for the casket, it's mine. Now I know you're out there, I'll do everything I can to find out who you are." He vanished through the doorway.

Jet felt dizzy and his head pounded as he trudged over to Mckenzey. They had no time to waste. Shane might be searching for another entrance. Mckenzey was unconscious. Removing his hood, he placed her over his shoulder and carried her down the hall. If someone saw her floating, they would be far more likely to take notice. He wound through the building and found an exit on the far side. Smoke was filling up the halls. He kicked out and the door swung open and they burst from the building. Jet sucked in a mouthful of air and lay Mckenzey on the ground behind some bushes.

He whispered, "Aquaenaeth," and a controlled spurt of water rinsed her face.

Mckenzey sputtered awake, coughing. Her head swayed back and forth as she tried to focus on him. When she was able to speak, she asked, "What happened?"

"Shane attacked, knocking both of us to the ground. We barely escaped."

"Where is he?"

"I hope back in the building. The museum is sort of on fire."

"How did that happen?"

"Magic. It was enough of a diversion. But we need to go."

"Where?"

"Far from here. We need to leave town tonight."

"What do you mean?"

Pulling her to her feet, Jet said, "It wasn't a clean escape. Shane knows why we were here." He asked, "Can you walk?"

Mckenzey nodded.

As soon as they put some distance between them and the museum, Jet called Jayco using a prepaid phone they'd purchased that morning.

It rang twice, and Jayco answered. "What's up? Where are you guys?"

"Shane saw you," Jet said as they crossed the street behind the museum.

"No way."

"We were ten feet away from him. He said your name specifically."

"I don't think it was me. Are you guys near the museum? There is smoke pouring out of it."

"We made it out. But we have to leave town."

"What now?"

"Get back to the hotel, pack everything, and head straight for the train station."

"Seriously?"

"I'll explain everything later."

After a pause, Jayco asked, "Did you get it?"

"Somehow, we did."

"Catch you later."

Jet heard the excitement in Jayco's voice. After hanging up, they jogged for two blocks. Stepping onto a sidewalk, they tried to blend in with other shoppers and strolled casually. The sun shone off the buildings, but it was setting fast. As they went another two blocks, a feeling of lethargy and fatigue overcame him. He said, "We need to get some new clothes."

"Everything I have is back in the hotel."

"I know."

"Let's find a store, and quickly."

"The street to our right looks like it might have something."

"I've got a problem."

Mckenzey asked, "What's up?"

"I'm toast. My energy is gone." He added, "We're close to the water. I have this urge that I can't explain."

"Why not rest in that shop across the street? That seems like a better choice."

"Trust me. There's something I need to do. Find us both something good to wear."

"Split up? Bad idea."

He limped off the sidewalk between two buildings without saying another word and down a slope toward the water's edge. There was some trash scattered under some bushes, and without thinking, he reached down and picked up an empty plastic water bottle. He plunged his hands into the mud and stuffed enough dirt to fill half of the bottle upon reaching the water's edge. Next, he filled the rest with water and mixed the solution. Without a second thought, he gulped down the sludge and water.

Mckenzey caught up to him as he finished the entire mixture. He downed two more sludge concoctions. He'd never tasted something so blissful and replenishing, and there was a noticeable surge in his energy.

"That looked nauseating. This was your brilliant idea?"

Licking his lips, he said, "Best thing I've ever had."

"You're joking, right?"

"The idea slipped into my head. I've been craving it for the last ten minutes. I think magic does something weird to my body."

"Nope," Mckenzey said. "You're just weird."

"True that," Jet said. Before standing, he filled the bottle once again. "Just in case," he replied as Mckenzey shook her head.

"Can we go shopping now?" she asked.

"After you."

Retracing their steps, a small shop came into view. Jet began wiping off the mud from his knees. Mckenzey linked her arm under his and pulled him into the street. They hadn't yet reached the opposite side when glass windows around them shook from an explosion that ripped through the air. There was a plume of dark smoke back in the direction from where they'd come.

Mckenzey gripped his arm and asked, "Was that the museum?"

"I think so."

"What happened?"

"No clue."

They sprinted into the closest clothing store. Fifteen minutes later, Jet and Mckenzey exited the shop dressed far differently than when they'd entered. Jet wore a brown flannel shirt, blue tapered sweatpants, and a wool hat, with the box securely fastened to his chest. Mckenzey wore a black sweater hoodie and cream cargo pants. On top of everything, they'd also both purchased two skateboards.

Mckenzey said, "While you were changing, I studied the map."

"I didn't take that long," Jet interrupted.

Her expression told him otherwise. "We're the farthest away from the train station as possible. If only we could've exited on the opposite side of the museum, we would've already been there. The best plan is to go north from here, cross the Nydeggbrücke bridge, and into Old Town again. It's a straight shot to the train station."

"I'll follow you."

It took thirty minutes to cross the bridge and go another twenty blocks to the train station. It was dark, and they had to walk the last few blocks to avoid getting hit by any cars or buses. They ditched the skateboards in an alley but had saved an hour of walking. A block away, Jet's prepaid phone rang.

"Hello," he said.

Jayco said quickly, "The train leaves in five minutes. Where are you?"

"Almost at the entrance."

"Better be. This is the last train that leaves tonight."

"Why?" Jet asked.

"I think they're about to shut down the city. There was an explosion thirty minutes ago. It looks like Shane blew up the museum to escape. People were still inside."

CHAPTER 30

Jet and Mckenzey fell into their seats, trying to catch their breath, and were nearly exhausted as the train picked up speed and left the station. Jayco and Seyanna sat opposite Jet and Mckenzey, while Grantham and Latisha were across the aisle facing each other. The train car was empty of any other passengers.

Jet gasped, "Did you get all of the luggage?"

"I think I forgot your bathroom stuff," Jayco said, shrugging his shoulders.

"Doesn't matter. I stole it from Grantham's house before we left for the airport," Jet said.

"Wait?" Grantham glanced up from his backpack. He was just about to pull out several bottles of water.

Jet continued, "I completely forgot my toothbrush and toothpaste. That was all I borrowed."

Mckenzey let out a laugh.

Grantham responded quickly. "You know how my mom is. She's going to notice that some of that stuff went missing."

"I didn't know dentists could bring home that many supplies."

"Shut it," Grantham barked as Latisha opened two pizza boxes and set the cheesy bliss on the table as Seyanna passed around the plates. The smell was delightful.

Jet snatched his first slice and said, "Just don't tell her it was me."

"Oh, I bet she already knows."

The group attacked the food furiously without much talking.

After finishing his second slice, Jet said, "Not as gourmet as mud water, but it'll do."

"What are you talking about?" Latisha asked.

Jet smiled. "You'll see." He finally unlatched the crate and placed it on the table. Everyone stopped chewing, and the silence was breathtaking, as was the box.

Seyanna's hand tentatively reached out and touched the item on the table. Jet watched with interest, but nothing happened. "So, this is it. I hope it was worth the risk."

"Things got crazy back there," Jet agreed. "What happened?"

Jayco reached over and grabbed another slice. "It was a total screw-up."

"How did Shane know we were there?" Latisha asked.

Mckenzey answered, "I'm not sure he did. It might have been a coincidence that we showed up at the same time."

Jet said flatly, "Not a coincidence on what he was searching for. We barely made it out."

Grantham said emphatically, "One thing is sure: Latisha saved our bacon. Without her warning, we were toast."

"I second that," Jet said, his voice dry and rough.

Everyone clapped softly.

Jet said, "Shane knew exactly where the casket was." He explained the magic Shane used, the tracking device, the distraction by the man wearing the orange sweater, the swap, and the escape. He also explained about seeing the same guy back in the airport in Munich.

After hearing the end of the story, Jayco insisted, "I was outside of the museum, trying to find a distraction. Two blocks away, I found a food cart. It was small. I stole it and was running back when I ran into Latisha."

Seyanna added, "I saw the big bloke they thought was Jayco. Easy to mistake the two, but the man was twenty years older and not from America."

Latisha said, "Let's hope it was just Shane's paranoia and not something more."

As Jayco reached for his fourth slice of pizza, he asked, "Why did that guy help you out?"

"I've been thinking about it since we escaped the museum. The answer might be complex and simple at the same time."

"What do you mean?" Latisha asked.

"On the flight over from Orlando, the tome opened again. I didn't get a chance to tell you what was inside." He fished out the tome and read his friends both passages from his uncle. "I think this Brotherhood has been searching for the tablet pieces and the two tomes. I bet this guy in the orange sweater is associated with the Brotherhood."

"That doesn't answer much," Jayco said. "Can we trust him?"

"Without him," Mckenzey insisted, "there is no way we had enough time to switch the boxes. Shane was overly suspicious and heading back."

Grantham asked, "How did Shane see you under the cloak?"

Jet stretched his legs, trying to avoid Seyanna. "My guess. It's either part of his magic or something we don't yet understand."

Latisha said, "There's too much of that going on already."

Jet's eyes locked on Latisha, and he said, "Grantham is right. Without you, this all fails. Without you, Shane would be holding this box now and not us."

A smile played on her lips. She said, "Then let's look at the prize."

The crate was passed around, and each carving was inspected. The lid opened effortlessly, but it was empty. As his friends examined the box, there was no release of energy or an inkling of a color change.

"Tell us more about the explosion at the museum?" Mckenzey asked, burrowing into her seat.

Grantham explained, "We met up on the bridge back to our hotel. We hoped that you had escaped and made it back to the hotel first. We were almost back to the hotel by the time you called Jayco. We hurried up to our rooms and started packing. I had finished early and was looking for you guys. I was staring out of the window when it happened."

"How bad was it?" Mckenzey asked.

"Truthfully, I couldn't see much from our window of the actual explosion, but I could feel it. After getting to the train station, we learned a ton more." Grantham continued, "On the television, they showed a video captured outside the museum. Four people, completely dressed in black and wearing masks, exited the building opposite where I think you guys did. Four officers cornered the four masked men. One of the masked men held up this gun-like device, but it was like an electric charge shot out and hit each of the four officers instead of bullets."

Jayco continued the story. "One of the guys held a black bag in his hand. Probably the duplicate box. The four guys sprinted away from the building."

Seyanna added, "Another camera, from a distance, picked up the four as they ducked between buildings. Before they disappeared, one of the figures stopped, turned around, and clicked something in his hand, and the rest is history." She added, "Right now, the best guess is that half the building was destroyed, and over a hundred people died."

Blowing out her breath, Mckenzey said, "Is this our fault?"

"Shane would've done it anyway," Jet tried to reassure her, "regardless of if we were there or not. They had this plan long before they came across us."

"It won't take Shane long to realize the other box is a fake," Grantham pointed out.

Mckenzey added, "And then because he saw Jet and me, he'll realize that we had the box."

"If he didn't know that you had the box at the time," Jayco said, "it makes me think he might not be able to see details when you're under the cloak. Maybe that's why he didn't recognize you."

The group nodded.

Jet sat back and thought about an idea that had also come up while making their way to the train station. He didn't want to say it out loud because he didn't know the answer. He'd assumed, like Grantham, that it wouldn't take long for Shane to realize the box was a fake. But really, how would he know one way or another? If he had access to some carbon dating, then maybe. Jet would have to be on the lookout for any changes with Shane.

Twenty minutes later, Latisha announced proudly, "Our flight back home has been changed to tomorrow afternoon. This will be a long train ride through the night, with us arriving in Munich around five in the morning. It was the earliest flight I could find."

CHAPTER 31

Leaning back and resting his eyes, Jet replayed today's events over in his mind. His breathing and heart rate were just starting to settle. He came to the same conclusion each time. They'd barely been good enough to escape the museum and Shane with the casket. It was the luckiest thing they'd ever done. He had used some magic, but Shane had easily deflected it. The burning carpet saved them. Latisha had saved them. But he also had to admit that something in him had changed. He could almost feel the magic within him, as if he had been shown a glimpse of his power. This was the only redeemable aspect of the entire trip, outside the casket.

Shane was powerful, skillful, and knowledgeable. Jet needed to be much better prepared if they ran into him again. He felt like a hamster on a treadmill, unable to catch the prize as he fell asleep. He slept for three or four hours, but the rest of the gang was still sleeping when he awoke. Compulsion had once again pushed him awake. Reaching behind his back, to where he'd hidden the tome, he pulled out the book. He was unsurprised as the next page turned freely.

Writing began to take shape at the top of the left page. It was slow, as if someone was actively writing, and the letters were small.

Welcome, Sorcerer. It is I, Wier. And it's time for you to discover the nature of magic. As you already know, there are two types of magic: Runic and Elemental Divination. These magical abilities are simple and complex, just like me. You've been taught about the origins of Elemental magic through the vision on the beach. Elemental magic grants you the use of the elements around you—seen and unseen.

Furthermore, it requires compensation and pulls from you a measure of energy. You are the complete Sorcerer or the Mikado, and you have access to all the elements. You read from the tome The Sorcerer's Guide. Your progress with Elemental magic will be limited only by your need, strength, and proficiency.

Your counterpart in Runic Magic is the Czaric, and he can use the entire spectrum of runes. The Czaric reads from —The Mage's Letters. Both tomes are similar yet significantly different.

Except for the Mikado, who uses elements, a Sorcerer is an Occultist, and a Mage other than the Czaric, who uses runes, is a Conjurer.

A chosen Occultist can only use a single element in their magic. Don't be misguided into thinking that you will be the strongest in a specific discipline, but your ability to intertwine the elements will make you challenging to overcome. Your manipulations will be through words, thoughts, determination, and necessity. Words are but a gateway to power. You might have ten people capable of voicing the same word, but significantly different things will happen, yet they will all resemble the element and the purpose.

For example, a fireball. Each of the ten will say the same word, and ten different fireballs will occur. The fire will be the constant in one, but the ball, color, shape, or size may be different. One time, I saw a fire rope instead of a ball. The language is the backbone and gatekeeper of its use. Without the correct word, even the most powerful would fail. Once the name is known, then skill, determination, and ability take over.

Five recognizable words appeared on the opposite page. They were spread out as if broken up into tables or columns.

Ignisnaeth   **Ventusnaeth**   **Aquaenaeth**   **Terranaeth**   **Ethernaeth**

Jet was drawn to the word in the fifth column; it was new to him. The writing continued, and a new grouping of words emerged into view below each of the main columns.

Ignisnaeth	*Ventusnaeth*	*Aquaenaeth*	*Terranaeth*	*Ethernaeth*
Fire	*Wind*	*Water*	*Earth*	*Spirit*

More writing appeared, this time at the far bottom of the page.

I will teach you three basic spells for each element. You will work on them, and you will not share them for the moment. Master their usage, their limitations, and most of all their effect on your energy. If you spend too much energy, a greater price will be taken.

Under each column, three words appeared:

Ignisnaeth	*Ventusnaeth*	*Aquaenaeth*	*Terranaeth*	*Ethernaeth*
Fire	*Wind*	*Water*	*Earth*	*Spirit*
Angi	*Aer*	*Ogen*	*Pan*	*Ea*
Chango	*Enlil*	*Yemoja*	*Artemis*	*Maia*
Kali	*Urania*	*Abzu*	*Pachamama*	*Vesta*

The next page turned with ease, and additional writing materialized on the left side.

These three spells in each Elemental category make up the basic level. Unseen is the intermediary level, which includes three additional spells. Two spells make up the expert level, and one spell will make up the master level. It may take years to learn anything beyond the simplest spells. Nine total spells for each element are three, three, two, and one.

You are the fifth and likely last person to have the talent to use all five elements. Remember that most Occultists will use a single element, and there have only been a handful suitable to utilizing two elements.

Runic Divination also has five categories. I cannot share a single depiction or description with you. It is unlikely that you could see the Runic Symbols on the page. The five categories include: Motion, Life, Darkness, Matter, and Mixture. There are more runic drawings for each category for unknown reasons. There are twelve: Four, Four, Three, and One in their respective levels.

I personally have access to all the spells and Runic drawings but can only grasp a few. When I was mortal, a close friend had mastered all the water spells, even the master level. But he was killed by a basic Mixture rune. Your proficiency level in each individual spell will be the difference-maker.

Don't use a spell, unless forced, that you haven't become skilled at. To sum things up, there are five categories, and currently, you have access to three spells of each element. They each will do something different for the person who uses the spell.

It is essential to understand that you will have a proficiency level. Imagine that you have an Occultist using the Ogen spell, and she, for example, might pull water to drink from the ground with low proficiency and can only pull water for herself. A second Occultist's use of Ogen might be to control the movement of existing water through space. His proficiency could be much higher, and he could learn to control an entire river. They both have magical powers, but their use might be significantly different. In the desert, dying of thirst, the first occultist may be more potent than the second based on need. In short: find your ability and proficiency as quickly as you can.

Sitting back, Jet felt overwhelmed. This would've been far more helpful several weeks ago. But seeing his magic in use today solidified what he'd just read. There was a slight warmth of excitement. *This is what I'm talking about.* He finally felt that he was making progress. Turning back, he reread everything twice and began memorizing the spells. Once finished, he closed the tome and became lost in his thoughts. For the first time since the tome opened, he might be fighting to get back on a level playing ground.

CHAPTER 32

The München Hauptbahnhof train station in Munich was impressive, even more so than the station in Bern. The main hall was enormous. They'd heard the large clock had been taken down until construction had been finished. The landscape along their travels was breathtaking. Jet had slept fitfully on and off, and when he dragged his suitcase from the train, he felt like a zombie again. It was cattle-ranch early, and he was starving.

Jayco said, bleary-eyed, "I need food."

"Same," Grantham said.

The city of Munich was night-and-day different from Bern. First and foremost, it was significantly more extensive, modern, and innovative. In Jet's mind, this truth didn't take anything away from Bern. It was just a different experience. Glancing up at a window in the train station, he noticed a large Coca-Cola sign over an entrance. Not far from there was a small coffee shop.

"Oh, blessed. That's the best sight I've seen all morning," Latisha said.

Without a word, Jet and his friends strolled in that direction. After getting some much-needed caffeine, they waited another thirty minutes until a food vendor opened. Rubenbauer was well-rated, and the food came quickly. The bacon, eggs, and potatoes were some of the best food Jet had ever eaten. Jayco and Seyanna inhaled the omelets. Everyone was pleased.

"What now?" Seyanna asked as she yawned. "Sleep or adventure?"

Jayco stood quickly. "We can sleep on the plane."

"I'm not dragging my luggage around," Mckenzey insisted.

Pointing across the hall, Grantham said, "There are luggage lockers. We can store our stuff in there. We'll need to come back this way to get to the airport."

"Perfect," Jayco said. "Let's get out of here."

They stepped from the train station ten minutes later, eager to explore. Jet had the casket, his tome, and a few other items in his backpack. As they set off, and Jet heard those around him speaking German, he found that he loved listening to them. Their accents were different than those in Switzerland, and he understood next to nothing.

"Where to?" Latisha asked.

Grantham pulled out a map. It appeared that there were several areas already circled. "I was reading the last hour or so before we got here. There are a bunch of churches here and a few castles. The town center is supposed to be rocking, and there are some cool museums."

"Not happening," Mckenzey said. "I'm not stepping foot into another museum for the foreseeable future."

"Suit yourself." Grantham grinned. "You'll be missing out."

"I'm totally with Mckenzey on this," Latisha added.

"Whatever." Grantham began walking. He closed his eyes and picked a random place on the map, and mumbled, "Where to start?"

He led them to the Englischer Garten, a large public garden. It was green and very open, with a few rivers and tons of statues. The most surprising thing in the park was a Japanese Teahouse on a small island in the middle of a lake. They tried crossing a small bridge during their exploration, but it was closed. There was also a Chinese tower that had been rebuilt after it burned down. The entire garden was incredibly peaceful.

Their second attraction was the Munich Residenz, the largest city palace in Germany, which turned out to be part museum. It sat a few blocks south of the garden. It was where previous dukes, emperors, princes, and even kings had come to visit and where some of them had lived. Despite it being a museum, it was impressive and unique. There were ten courtyards divided into three main sections. They were mesmerized as they walked through the Antiquarium, with checkered flooring, paintings on the walls and ceilings, and several statues lining the walls. Overhead, there were a dozen pillars incorporated into the ceiling architect.

Jet had never seen anything like it. There was almost no place on the walls or ceiling that didn't have a painting. At one point, he sat on a marble bench that continued the entire length of the hall and appreciated the magnificent room.

They finished off by visiting the Neues Rathaus, the New Town Hall. They'd passed the opera house along the way, but the vote was five-to-one against going inside. The Neues Rathaus was where the public servants worked. They could see a few conference rooms, some staircases, and hallways. Even these normally mundane places were intricate and picturesque. The building was made of brick and shell limestone with six courtyards. It had a massive tower on the south side with a spectacular view.

After spending three remarkable hours exploring parts of Munich, they found a small café near the center of town for lunch. The café was near Marienplatz, a large central square not far from Neues Rathaus. The food was delicious, and they spent over an hour just watching the people walk by. As they stepped out of the café after finishing, they all had smiles on their faces.

Latisha asked, "What's next?"

Mckenzey suggested, "Let's split up and meet back at the train station in a few hours. I just want to walk around and window shop. I don't think my brain can stand another museum or place to visit. As amazing as this city is, I just want to relax."

Jayco said, "Sounds lovely."

Jet took a step in the guys' direction when Mckenzey said, "Jet and I will head this way." She pointed to the far side of the square to several stores.

Jayco said, "Seyanna and I will head this way." Pointing over his back.

"That leaves this side," Grantham said. "Have fun, but not too much fun."

Jet's heart raced as Mckenzey gave him a big smile. "Are you okay with this?" she asked, looking vulnerable as her eyes darted to the ground.

"Better than okay. Exactly what I wanted."

She glanced up quickly and somehow, her smile brightened as if he'd said the perfect thing. Her arm intertwined with his, and they crossed the center square.

Mckenzey said, "Europe is totally romantic."

"It's unbelievable."

"You've surprised me these last few weeks," she said after the silence. Ahead of them was a large white building with a tower and clock.

"What do you mean?"

"Look where we are. Look at what we've accomplished. At the beginning of the school year, I would've never imagined that we would all be this close. On top of that, we've come together and solved some huge puzzle pieces. But for me, the craziest thing is that I no longer feel alone. Most of the things that have haunted me over the last four years now make sense. I'm telling you, I felt like I was so different from everyone else. I had these weird dreams and bizarre things that had happened. And when you're weird and all alone, it's terrifying. But being weird *with* you is exhilarating."

They explored the stores and shopping and lost track of time. Jet found some gourmet chocolate, and Mckenzey bought a bag full of candy, some postcards, and souvenirs. They strolled hand in hand toward a fountain with a fish statue while exiting the last store. It was chilly, but the sunlight and the ambiance were unbeatable. As they walked, Jet's heart raced.

When they reached the fountain, Mckenzey said, "There's no one I'd rather be with, and nowhere I'd rather be, than here with you."

Jet replied honestly, "Same."

Mckenzey's eyes sparkled, and she leaned into his chest. Her hand clasped his at the same moment that Jet cupped her chin. His thumb brushed her skin, which was soft and warm. She held his gaze. The first kiss was soft and exploring. As they broke away, her smile was broad and inviting. Her lips were silky smooth. The next kiss held more urgency and passion. She pulled him onto a bench near the fountain. His backpack clattered to the ground between his feet. Time passed blissfully. Jet noticed that Mckenzey couldn't stop smiling as they walked back to the train station. And neither could he. He wished this day would never end.

CHAPTER 33

The train ride from the Munich station to the airport took forty-five minutes, and the moment they stepped onto the train, the S-Bahn, it started raining again. Fog encroached their view, and it made what they saw all the more majestic. By the looks of the others, they'd also had an enjoyable few hours before heading to the airport. Jet held Mckenzey's hand the entire train ride. He felt exhausted and confused. Mckenzey explained on the walk back to the train station that she and Eric had put things on hold for now. She wasn't even sure if she was still planning on transferring to Dillon Lake.

They each bought steaming cups of coffee at the airport. After the check-in process for their boarding pass and luggage, Jet followed the others to the entrance to the terminals. Instead of getting in line with his friends, he continued forward and found a nearby bathroom. The airport was busy, and Jet had to wait his turn to find an open stall. His eyes remained fixated on the floor, and he was too nervous to glance around.

When it was his turn, he hurried into the stall and changed his clothes. He had been wearing the same clothes from the day they went into the museum, all black. He would switch into something more his style and trash the other garments. He didn't think going through the TSA line with a hidden artifact was the best idea. He attached the casket to his chest and flipped on his hood. A gust of wind whirled around the bathroom, and the doors to half of the stalls sprang open. Before his door closed, he managed to sneak out of his stall and out of the bathroom.

Ten minutes later, bypassing the TSA line, he walked carefully to the terminal. He found a bathroom and reappeared. He met up with his friends, and they found seats until their flight began to board. This time, their layover was in Atlanta.

Their seats were relatively close together. Mckenzey, Jet, and Seyanna sat in a row in front of Latisha, Jayco, and Grantham. Within minutes of taking off, everyone fell asleep. After their layover in Atlanta, they boarded their plane home. When they finally landed at LAX, it was four in the morning, and classes started in a few hours. An SUV with a driver waited for them—a gift from Latisha's aunt.

An hour into their ride back to Santa Barbara, Jet said, "I know we just barely returned from Switzerland, but we need to turn our attention to the next step."

Latisha asked skeptically, "What does that even mean?"

"Shane will be a problem. I realize that we've already been watching him, but we need to know the moment he figures out the box he has is fake."

"I can make a schedule," Seyanna said.

"Perfect." Jet cleared his voice and added, "We also need to make a plan to visit Silverton."

Hoots and hollers erupted from almost everyone.

"I can't go back," Latisha screamed. "That gives me too much anxiety."

"I'm with Latisha," Jayco said.

"Remember back to the letter I was telling you about. My uncle was protecting or looking for something in the mountains. Mckenzey and I found a meteorite. Silverton is where we need to go."

Mckenzey sucked in a deep breath, and Jet feared that she would disagree with him. Instead, she said, "Jet's right. I don't want to go back there. But we should."

"What exactly is the plan?" Jayco asked.

"The hill outside of town is where Mckenzey and I were hiking. That's where we need to go."

"I think I remember where we were," Mckenzey added.

"But why?" Latisha asked.

Jet said, "I think there is a tablet piece hiding in the hills outside of Silverton. It's the only thing that makes sense. Shane has been very interested in Silverton all along. He must have suspected something. I'm not sure he'll know where to look, but I'm certain that is where he will be going next. We need to get there first."

"He could be going there now," Latisha said.

"Maybe," Jet conceded. "But I think he will need to prepare. He will want to look at the box first."

Jayco said, "We can't let Shane win. When should we go? This weekend?"

"No," Jet said. "We're not ready. I'm not ready either. Maybe in a few weeks."

Grantham said, "But Shane could beat us there."

"That's why we need to watch him closely."

"Makes sense." Grantham nodded.

"So, when?" Mckenzey asked.

"Let's plan on Thanksgiving weekend."

Latisha sighed. "I never thought I would return to Silverton. Ever."

They spent the next forty-five minutes planning. They were all wide awake now. Jet sprinted to his dorm when they arrived on campus, showered, grabbed some breakfast, and was only thirty seconds late to his English class. His next class that morning was math, and he turned in two of his assignments. Later that afternoon, after the remainder of his classes, had finished, he placed the casket in his backpack and set off to the science building, intending to prepare the geology lab for this week's classes.

When he stepped into the lab room, it was empty. He threw his backpack by the front door and found a note from Autumn about how to prepare. At the bottom, she added:

I hope you're feeling better. I stopped by this weekend, but your roommates told me that you weren't feeling well. I better not find that Halloween was too exciting for you to handle.

He busied himself as he thought about her words. *Could Autumn have been the girl he kissed?* He saw her later that evening, and her costume was entirely different.

The lab prep this week was more time-consuming than usual. He had a lot of small items to get ready. As he started removing several microscopes from the back wall, he noticed Professor Rysen step into the room.

"Mr. Black. How was your weekend?"

"Friday and Saturday morning, I was feeling a little sick," he said, and it took all his willpower to avoid sneaking a look at his backpack. "But yesterday, I felt much better. A friend from Portland came into town and surprised me. I haven't seen her in months. We went to the movies. Today I feel great."

"A lady friend?" Professor Rysen winked optimistically. "Why doesn't she go to school here?"

"She's just a friend. She's not the private school type. I didn't think that I was before coming here. The only way I came here was through a scholarship."

"You and so many others."

"What are you working on, Professor?"

"We're doing something called the Old Nassau. I realize that Halloween was last week, but this reaction is remarkable. It's a clock reaction that changes the chemical solution from orange to black. It takes a little preparation, but it's well worth it."

"That sounds amazing. I don't see how it could be as fun as your Halloween experiment of freeze-drying a pumpkin and launching it from the roof."

"That was entertaining," Professor Rysen agreed.

"I'm jealous. I wish my chemistry teacher had shown me all these cool experiments."

"Open invitation for tomorrow. Well, I better get going. Have a nice rest of the afternoon."

Professor Rysen exited the classroom with a bucket in his hands. For the first time, Jet wondered why Professor Rysen kept walking through his class. He remembered seeing a door in the back room. It had always been locked. Grabbing his backpack, he decided to take a look. He turned right and hustled past several shelves. The door was ahead of him. As he turned the knob, it opened with ease. Jet stared at what he saw with disbelief.

This room was nothing more than a closet with a mop, a dolly, a bucket, and a single shelf of cleaning supplies. Jet closed the door quickly and tried his keys. He only had three. One for the door from the alley, one for the classroom door, and one for the professor's small office. None of his keys worked to lock this door.

A sinking feeling overcame Jet. He wondered if Professor Blum had asked Professor Rysen to watch him, ensuring he did his job correctly. At least two separate times, Professor

Rysen had been waiting for Jet to come to the lab room. He'd always assumed there was a way to pass through from Professor Rysen's chemistry office to this lab and back into his classroom. That was simply not the case.

Jet returned to the classroom and worked extra hard to make sure he perfectly prepared all the instruments. Not ten minutes later, Professor Rysen entered again, his face flushed. He mumbled, "I forgot to lock the closet. I'm losing my mind today."

Jet said evenly, "I didn't even know we had a closet back there."

"Oh, yes. It's not very big or useful on most days." Holding up a bucket of cleaning supplies, he added, "But when the toilets get clogged, there's almost no one to take care of it. There isn't much space on this floor, and it's located in the worst location."

Jet felt the tightness in his chest release. He remembered Professor Rysen holding a bucket when he left earlier. "Good to know."

Professor Rysen disappeared momentarily and reappeared with a smile on his face. "Glad that's out of the way. Are you almost finished?"

Glancing at his checklist, he said, "I have a dozen more rocks that I need to pull out."

"Need some help? I just finished up."

"No, thanks. You're busy, and I like the quiet time to think."

"If you say so. I'll see you around."

"Sounds good." Jet pulled out dozens of different types of rocks. There were two parts to the next lab. First, they were going to look at the velocity of seismic waves after earthquakes through different materials. For this, each group would need a metal slinky that was moveable. In the second part of the lab, they would examine a dozen rocks found close by to either an earthquake or a volcano. Many were geodes, fossils, agate, quartz, opal, and other materials that would require microscopes. Jet was thrilled.

After finishing the lab preparations, he searched the entire building to ensure he was alone. When satisfied, he snuck into their hidden room and placed the new box from Switzerland with the other ancient items. He was relieved to find that no one had been in the storage room. He'd set up a string on the inner door. It wouldn't stop the door from opening, just let him know that someone had entered the room.

* * *

Over the next several days, Jet spent his time studying and attempting to understand Elemental magic better. His friends felt it was best to stay in contact through text messages for the first few days. He was tempted to sneak over and see Mckenzey, but that was out of the question because she had asked they keep what happened in Switzerland between just them.

Shane returned to school Wednesday afternoon, a few days after they had. He appeared precisely the same and not the slightest upset. Jet caught himself staring at Shane a few different times, trying to guess what he knew and what his next step was likely to be. He often found himself contemplating how much Shane knew about Silverton.

The explosion of a museum in Switzerland was front-page news around the world. Grainy pictures could be seen of the four people escaping the museum and causing the explosion. The faces were impossible to identify. Rumors and theories abound about possible motives to destroy the museum. He learned about other museum attacks that had happened. The common consensus was that, like the others, the Switzerland attack was believed to be a terrorist attack.

Friday evening, he left the central part of campus and returned to the hidden beach south of the school. Jet climbed through the trees and down the hill, and when he stepped out onto the beach, he was alone. He started by picking one spell from each of the elements. He chose Chango from Fire, Enlil from Wind, Ogen from Water, Pan from Earth, and Vesta from Spirit.

He learned a lot and a little from each of these spells. Each time he spoke one of the spells, it cost him an amount of his energy, even if it didn't work. He was utterly void of energy after an hour. He drank some sand water, and a portion of his energy returned. The first three spells had limited use. Chango warmed the air of a large area around him. Ogen spontaneously caused rain to fall, also in a limited space. Pan shook the ground in one direction, about three square feet in front of him.

Standing next to the ocean was one of his favorite spots, especially with breeze and moon cascading off the water. He took several deep breaths, listening to the wave slapping against the beach. After taking a twenty-minute break, he tried Enlil and Vesta but there were no noticeable effects. He wanted to test more of the spells, but at this point, no amount of mud replenished his stamina.

Jet was exhausted as he made his way back to campus. His mind wandered to Silverton, and he wasn't sure what to expect. He remembered the painting that Mckenzey had given him, destroyed when his dorm was broken into. It had been the only picture he'd seen of his house and Silverton in years. He guessed that the town had changed immensely. He wondered if it would be recognizable at all.

Over the next several days, the Echoes met a few different times. Twice they met on their secret beach, once at a volleyball game, and once in the science building. Jayco, again, became convinced that they were all being followed. They went through elaborate efforts to make sure they were alone. Twice, meetings were canceled after Mckenzey and Jayco felt it wasn't safe. When they finally did get together, they fell into discussions about Shane's movements and their plans for Silverton.

Today, they were walking west of school toward the rock-climbing canyon. Jayco was walking backward as he said, "He threw a huge temper tantrum today."

Mckenzey asked, "Are we talking about Shane here?"

"Yes. His whole attitude changed yesterday. He's certainly upset about something."

Jet could only think of one reason that he was so upset. "Shane must've just learned that the box was useless."

"I wish I could've seen it," Grantham added.

"Does he know it was us?" Latisha asked.

Seyanna added, "I overheard him talking about the tracker. I didn't hear everything, but he's confused."

Jet asked, "Any chance you heard what his next step is?"

"Nothing. I mean, I barely caught anything in the first place. They happened to be eating near me. They didn't even know I was there."

So. How are we going to make this work?" Jayco asked.

"We'll go to Silverton the day after Thanksgiving," Jet insisted. "We can all go to Nana's for the holiday.

"That's a fourteen-hour drive," Jayco said.

Grantham joked, "More time for you to make out with Seyanna in the back."

"You mean more time for you and Latisha," Jayco shot back. "Now that Jet has his license, he and Mckenzey can take turns driving. Eric isn't around, and Jet has trouble keeping a girlfriend."

Jet was surprised that none of his friends had caught on yet. He and Mckenzey had held hands a few times over the last few days. They certainly didn't parade their affection like the others.

Mckenzey said, "Eric and I broke up." She grabbed Jet, pulled him close, and kissed him hard on the lips.

"No way," Jayco said.

Seyanna appeared downright shocked.

CHAPTER 34

The maneuvering for celebrating Thanksgiving together required Jet's friends to convince their parents that the Echoes should spend the time in Portland rather than at home. This turned out to be almost as tricky as retrieving the crate. Mckenzey's parents were the most upset, but each parent wanted their child home for the holiday. In the end, they'd found a way to make it work. The same SUV that picked them up from the airport was waiting at 3 p.m. on the Tuesday before Thanksgiving. They'd been given a half-day and were eager to get started. Latisha had the keys and rounded up everyone to go.

Geology lab had been canceled due to the short week, which gave Jet an extra hour to pack. He stopped to see Brenda again and convinced her that he was hiding treasured secrets. She allowed the use of the dolly and he packed everything from the science building. Brenda had been so excited and had offered to tag along and help. It was nearly impossible to convince her that two people would look too suspicious.

Latisha pulled up, picking up Jet last, and it took ten minutes to load all the items from the alley near the science building. Jet returned the dolly to Brenda and gave her one of the rings from their collection. It was the least shiny, and it felt almost breakable and old. The smile on her face was as bright as Jet had ever seen.

"Keep it hidden," he'd advised as he silently closed the back door.

With Jayco driving, the SUV drove off-campus at three-thirty in the afternoon, and they were some of the last students to leave. The first few hours heading up the 101 were occupied with the standard catch-up conversation while ripping some of their classmates and professors. Jayco gave a play-by-play of their most recent football game. They'd won an abbreviated playoff game, the last of the season. He explained that they'd won a championship, but because there were several games canceled in the first few weeks, five other teams also won their respective games.

Jayco bragged, "A championship is a championship," when Grantham teased him relentlessly. Jayco added, "Who runs slower when it gets colder?"

"Shove it," Grantham replied. He explained to the rest of the group, "My record this year was sixteen minutes five seconds. However, the colder it got, the slower I got. Most other people's time improved. In my last race, last week, I was back at my sixteen minutes forty seconds pace; good enough for thirty-fifth place."

"Still way fast," Latisha assured him.

"I know." With tremendous exaggeration, Grantham rolled his eyes at Jayco.

"Much better than the volleyball team," Latisha said. "They lost their last six matches. I think they only won two games all year."

Five hours into their drive, they stopped and ate a quick dinner in San Jose. It was Jet's turn to drive. When they reached San Francisco, it took a few turns before they ended up on Interstate 5. Hours later, when they crossed into Oregon, Seyanna took over the SUV controls. The rest of the group happily sat back, slept, and relaxed.

Around seven in the morning, they entered the outskirts of Portland. With all the bathroom stops, filling up on gas, and food requirements, it had taken longer than expected. Seyanna was still driving while Jet navigated the directions from the front seat. The roads were again under construction, a constant in this city. Portland was the perfect place for him and Nana after Silverton. They had awesome neighbors, including Ruth Sanders, who lived only a mile away and had quickly become Nana's best friend.

"Can't wait to see Nana," Mckenzey said from the seat directly behind Jet.

"Me too," Seyanna added as she yawned. "It's been years."

Two minutes later, they were swallowed by a forest of trees. Mckenzey sighed in amazement at the breathtaking views. A drizzle fell in typical fashion.

"I love the smell of it here," Seyanna said. "It reminds me of Alaska. That seems like such a long time ago."

"Why did you choose Alaska after Silverton?" Mckenzey asked.

"My parents wanted a real-life adventure and experience. They both were stationed in Alaska for the summer, and then we went to Svalbard Island. Homeschooling just worked for me. I don't feel like I missed a beat. Technically, I could be a senior next year and graduate early."

Grantham joined the conversation. "Is that the plan?"

Seyanna smiled. "I'm enrolling in Chadwick's and will start after Christmas."

The houses on this street were several feet off the road and nearly impossible to see. A driveway on the right approached. Jet pointed and said, "Turn here. This is home."

Seyanna turned up a long driveway, and after twenty feet, Jet's home came into view. It was a beautiful two-story house from the fifties. Seyanna parked the SUV, and the gang piled out. They stretched and walked around for a moment.

Soon, Jet opened the front door, and Nana hurried from the kitchen and threw her arms around his shoulders. "Joshua. So glad you made it." She separated from him, glancing at him from head to toe. "Have you gained some weight?" She gave a reproving look.

He flushed. "No, Nana. I'm not getting fat."

"Uh-huh." Her hands reached up and pinched both of his cheeks.

"You remember everyone?" Jet pointed to his friends.

Nana said smugly, "I'm old, not senile." She began to hug everyone in turn.

The aroma insisted that the Thanksgiving preparations were well underway.

"That smells so good," Grantham said. "I didn't realize I was this hungry, but I'm pretty sure I could eat everything inside your house."

"Dream on," Jayco said. "I'm going to eat you under the table."

"Come get comfortable," Nana ushered. "Bring in your stuff. Boys upstairs. Girls downstairs. Jet, you get your room—the perks of coming home." Her eyes beamed as she took everyone in.

It didn't take long to haul the entire stash from the back of the SUV into both rooms upstairs. Jet began unpacking and arranging his things. When he finally went back downstairs, he found Mckenzey and Nana talking like old friends in the kitchen.

Jet cleared his throat. "Where's everyone else?"

"Taking naps," Nana said. "Which is where you should be."

"I have superhuman abilities and no longer need to sleep."

"I doubt that," she scoffed. "You'd sleep until noon if I let you."

Moving closer and placing an arm around Nana, Jet asked, "How are things?"

"Fine ... fine, dear. Everything's the same."

"Somehow, I doubt that," he mumbled.

Nana smiled. "You're feisty this morning."

"That's sleep deprivation talking."

"I thought you were superhuman?" Gazing at his face and arms, Nana said, "Now, Joshy, you're so tan. Have you been spending all your time at the beach? I bet all the girls are talking about you."

In the corner, Mckenzey suppressed a laugh by pinching her lips closed. Her face reddened.

Shrugging innocently, he dared not looking at Mckenzey. "It's a school in California. We spend a lot of time at the beach."

Nana continued, "I told you to be careful of the girls in California. They might just run you over."

"Tell me about it," he said.

Nana added, "Joshy, did you notice anything different?"

"I thought you said everything was the same."

"Yes, dear." She patted his back. "Take a turn and tell me what's different."

Starting in the kitchen, he moved throughout the house and finally retraced his steps, "You've got a new couch."

"I did." Nana laughed. "But that isn't the only thing."

"I give up."

Nana beamed excitedly. "I got a new car!"

"A brand new one, or new to you?"

"Brand new."

"I didn't see that one coming," Jet said. He knew that Nana had owned the same car for the last twenty years. She didn't drive much, so it wasn't an issue. But a new car was something she'd never done before. This was like the moon falling to the earth; life-shattering.

"Go take a look." She dangled the keys in front of him.

When he returned from the garage, he was smiling. "You didn't get rid of the old one."

"No, I didn't," she smirked.

"Do I dare need to ask?"

"Not at all. My old car is now your new car."

As he moved closer for a hug, Jet thought he saw regret on her face. That passed quickly. Soon she was bubbling over with a bright smile. "It isn't a BMW, and it's a little old. But it'll work perfectly for you."

"I agree," Jet said. "Good thing I passed my driver's license test a month ago. Thank you so much, Nana."

Mckenzey said, "That is so nice of you, Mrs. Taley."

"Call me Nana. You know the rules."

Mckenzey gave a dazzling smile.

Taking a seat at the kitchen table, Nana said, "Mckenzey, you come over and tell me everything. Joshua, you unload the dishwasher and set the table."

"Are we eating today?"

"Of course."

He unloaded the dishwasher as Mckenzey caught Nana up on her family and school life. Unloading the dishwasher was an everyday chore for Jet, and he didn't mind. When he finished setting the table, Nana ushered them upstairs for a nap. Jet was feeling the effects of the long drive. Closing his curtains tightly, he threw a towel or two on the window ledge to prevent the remaining light from entering his room. He was delighted to be here but nervous. He worried about Mckenzey, Silverton, and the rest of his friends.

Jet slept until four in the afternoon. Nana shook him awake. "The Thanksgiving feast is ready."

He asked, "Why are we celebrating tonight?"

Nana sat on the edge of the bed. "You didn't come all this way just for Thanksgiving dinner. I know that you're up to something."

"How could you know? We've barely talked the last few weeks."

Nana appeared to be considering her next set of words carefully. Finally, she said, "I learned in the last few months that my brother was working with a group called the Brotherhood."

"I've heard a little about them," he said. "From a letter."

"Really? I'm not sure what to think about that." She moved slightly to get a better position on the bed. "They've contacted me and have kept me in the loop of a few things."

"What? That's totally unlike you."

"I've been talking with a man. He says he helped you in Switzerland."

"You know about that?"

"I do."

"Are you mad that I skipped school?"

"Normally, yes. But under these circumstances, of course not."

"How much do you know?"

"I am in contact with Geb. He was the man that helped you. He also gave me a letter to give to you. Some of my biggest fears have come true. I tried to protect you from this. I should've known that I couldn't." She pulled out an envelope and handed it to him.

Jet pulled out the letter and read.

Attn Joshua and friends:

To be honest, I'm not sure if I should congratulate you or wish you my condolence. You've come further along than anyone thought possible. But what's ahead of you is unimaginable. Jet, you have been marked as a Sorcerer, that much is clear. The Brotherhood never intended to contact you directly, but my hand has been forced by what you are doing. We have been watching you from a distance.

My mentor instructed me to follow you from Munich to Bern. Once we realized that you were looking for something in the museum, it didn't take long for us to understand that something inside was undoubtedly significant. It took too long to realize the box you found was the chest we've been searching for. My small part in helping you accomplish that task was quite rewarding.

I am a member of an elite but forgotten Brotherhood who swore secrecy to protect the tablet, the chest, and their rich history. You can call me Geb. Our association approached your family after they tried to open the stone doorway many years ago, and we provided a measure of understanding into this war. You and your friends are at the center of the ripple, and the Brotherhood is being watched. We cannot help you openly. We cannot hide the chest. It would be too likely that we would lose it. If it turns out to be what we think it is, you'll need to keep it well hidden. Keep your own talents, knowledge, and our involvement a secret. Those of the Azurites are searching false leads and misdirection. But there is a group of young prodigies on the same track as you are.

Your task is to locate and find all the tablet pieces. Learn and excel in the abilities that you and your friends have. I'll contact you when I can ... if I can. Your family would be pleased to how much you've unearthed and discovered. The chest's power is far less influential without the tablet pieces. But it's more than just a mindless suitcase. Its secrets will be hard to find, but you must try. May you be blessed justly, judged honorably, and protected fully.

Geb

Jet asked, "Does this all make sense to you?"

"Most of it. I don't know the specifics. I've read the letter a few times. I know about stories from your father and my brother."

"Did you know that I completely forgot what happened the day of the disaster?"

"It became clear to me at the hospital. I didn't know if it was from an injury or something else. Did you get your memory back?"

"Yes. I remembered most everything, now."

"What is your plan?"

"Back to Silverton. We think there is one of these tablet pieces." He slipped past Nana and stood. "We'll leave the day after Thanksgiving."

"I made food for today, so you can do what you need to do tomorrow."

"You knew?" he asked.

"Not specifics. After the letter, I knew you had something you wanted to accomplish."

Twenty minutes later, they all sat down for a Thanksgiving meal that was a mixture of excellent food, laughter, spills, and humor. Jet had never been a big fan of turkey, but this year, it was fantastic. Nana encouraged each of them to recount what had happened thus far. They started with the Washington D.C. disaster, some of the items they knew about, and even the cloak. Jet demonstrated its ability, and Nana was stunned. When they spoke in detail about Switzerland and Shane and the box, Nana listened intently. She soaked everything in. It was comforting to talk with someone outside of themselves about the adventure.

Nana said, "I've heard that Silverton has changed significantly. This Shane character seems to be on the same path you are. I bet he's trying to find where to go. How much does he know about Silverton?"

Jet said, "No clue. But he knew more about Switzerland than we could've guessed."

Nana asked, "Do you know where you're going to start?"

"I think so. When we were younger, Mckenzey and I found a rock that was a meteorite. It has something to do with all of this, but I'm just not certain how. That's where we'll start."

Mckenzey cleared her throat. She appeared anxious. She asked cautiously, "Nana, how come you didn't tell Jet about this stuff sooner. I mean—"

This direct question surprised Jet. But Nana looked unperturbed.

"I'm not sure ..." Her voice trailed off. "Maybe I hoped that if I kept things hidden, this would pass Joshua by and not be his burden to carry. People have died over this for years, maybe centuries. My son, Jet's dad, kept most of this hidden from me. I learned it through secondhand conversations and other letters."

It was a sobering discussion that affected them, or they were still tired. All-in-all, it was the best Thanksgiving dinner Jet had ever had.

CHAPTER 35

After they cleared the food and put away the leftovers, plates, and other items, Nana asked, "Can I see the book?"

Jet rushed upstairs and returned with *The Sorcerer's Guide.* "We've been told to call it a tome."

"Told?" she questioned.

"There's like a master teacher inside. It gives me a lot of information. I think Uncle Joshua even wrote in it."

"Show me."

He handed the tome to her, and she tried everything imaginable to open it. She gave it back, and he turned the pages with ease. She added, bewildered, "Unbelievable."

Jet showed her everything he could. He avoided describing the specifics of magic. When he reached the last page that would turn, his hand became warm, and he knew that the next page was going to turn for the first time. He said, "Perfect timing."

"What do you mean?"

"This page hasn't been accessible before."

Jayco said, "I've never seen a new page open."

"Really?" Nana moved closer and asked, "Will it still be blank?"

Jet leaned in and said, "For you."

"What does it say?" Seyanna asked.

Two dozen words appeared all at the same time. The letters were in block form as if cut from a magazine.

It is time to reconnect with a hidden ally. Say the words *Pyramis of Aurum* followed by the word *Iris* near the golden pyramid. It will obey its master.

Jet remembered similar words, but he didn't think the word 'Iris' had been mentioned before.

Grantham tore up the stairs and retrieved the pyramid. Together, they exited the house into the backyard, surrounded by trees. No nosy neighbors could see what they were doing. Placing the pyramid in the center of the grass, he backed away. No one knew what to expect.

"Any bets on what happens?" Grantham asked.

Seyanna said, "A weapon—like a sword."

"Another book," Latisha whispered, hovering near the back.

"It opens up and is hiding something," Mckenzey answered.

"Nothing," Jayco said. "It's gold, and we're supposed to use it to buy weapons, vehicles, and travel the world. I'm the master, and all of you will obey me."

"Dream on," Grantham said as he took a step closer. "I think it'll be a tool, not a weapon, but something to help us find the tablet piece."

Nana exclaimed, "I'm not good at guessing, but I can't think of anything but a weapon."

All eyes turned to Jet. He'd changed his mind ten times over the last few minutes. Finally, he said, "I'm going with a tool. Something unexpected."

Mckenzey teased, "Everything's been unexpected."

"Let's find out," Jayco said, his eyes narrowed with excitement.

"Pyramis of Aurum," Jet shouted, and a flash of golden light burst from the pyramid, blinding him. Rubbing his eyes, he was still staring at a golden pyramid. Remembering the next word, he added, "Iris."

A small golden bubble developed on the outer surface of the pyramid. It grew, absorbing more of the gold. What was once solid began to transform. The bubble popped, and a wave crossed the pyramid's surface, now mostly liquid. It started to expand and take shape.

"It's a cat," Seyanna screamed as she and Latisha took a few steps backward.

"No, it's a coyote," Jayco countered.

The animal continued changing shapes. Soon there were legs, a tail, and a head. It stopped moving.

"You're both wrong," Mckenzey said coolly. "It's a panther, and it's alive."

The animal was entirely golden, but its chest expanded as if breathing as it walked. It had golden fur and golden eyes, but there was a subtle difference, like the shading of artwork. The underbelly appeared slightly darker than the coat on the back. The panther swiveled its head to stare at Jet expectantly. Jet shifted, and the panther's eyes followed him.

"Tell it to do something," Mckenzey suggested.

Jayco shouted, "Climb a tree." But the animal remained perfectly still, unfazed, staring at Jet.

"Lie down," Grantham said.

Latisha rubbed her hands together and whispered, "Roll over."

"It's not a dog," Jayco said. Looking at Jet, he said, "Bro, you're up."

"Climb the tree."

The panther dashed like lightning, turned, and tore across the backyard, leaping high into the air. Its four legs snapped against the tree, and it climbed gracefully upward. Within seconds, it was nearly twenty-five feet off the ground.

Jet let out a small laugh. "Okay, you can come back."

The panther quickly tore down the tree, landing on all four feet. It advanced playfully over to Jet. Its head went to his right hand and waited. Jet reached out. The golden fur felt as real as anything he'd ever touched. Instinctively he said, "Good girl." The animal rolled over, exposing her stomach, and waited until he rubbed it playfully.

Taking a step forward, Grantham said, "Can I touch her?"

"Be my guest."

Grantham moved in slowly, but Iris paid him no attention. His arm gradually extended, and he touched her stomach. She eagerly soaked up the attention as the entire group mauled her, wanting their own turn. Even Nana was playful with the animal.

"She's the prettiest thing I've ever seen," Mckenzey whispered to him as the others played with Iris.

Nana motioned to Jet several minutes later and said, "Can we talk downstairs?"

He nodded, and they hurried inside.

As they walked downstairs, Nana said, "I'm sorry that I held onto so many secrets. I didn't know how to tell you what your future might be."

"I didn't realize my parents were so involved."

"Neither did I, really—until after their deaths."

Jet remembered the question Shane had inquired of him. "Where did my parents die?"

"Truthfully, I don't know. It was a bus crash. I thought they had left for their anniversary. But it was outside of the country. Maybe in Germany."

Jet was stunned. "I always thought it happened near Silverton."

"Someone did put that in the newspaper," Nana said. "I remember calling the newspaper, and they told me that the source was anonymous. They refused the truth."

Jet said, "That boy, Shane I was talking to you about, he knew it was outside the country."

"You need to be careful of him."

Nana opened the door to a storage room. Jet found it ironic that he had never been allowed in this room since they moved in. "Come in," she said. "Can any of your friends do magic?"

"Not so far. They haven't had anything weird happen to them outside of Mckenzey."

"I'm pretty sure they will, at least some of them."

"How do you know?"

"The Brotherhood hinted that more magic was necessary. They described the magic as being dormant and that you and your friends might change that."

"I want to know more."

"You will. But for now, I need to give you something. When you put on your cloak earlier, you disappeared. That means your cloak is wind or air."

"Okay."

"The other cloaks won't all go invisible, like yours."

"Other cloaks?" he asked.

Removing a blanket covering an old wooden box, Nana reached down and opened the latch. She pulled several smelly and weather-worn coats. Two of the moth-eaten coats were far worse than his had been.

Nana added, "I don't know how each cloak will work. Geb gave them to me and insisted that they were for your friends. No one was sure if the first cloak would work. Glad it did."

"What do the cloaks do?"

"The brethren believe that they will help control the elements with some hidden abilities."

"How many are there?"

"I've heard talk of thirteen. Geb said that he is aware of two that were destroyed beyond repair. There is the one you have, and I have six others. That means four are lost."

"I can't believe all this is happening. Am I doing the right thing?"

"That question needs pondering. An excuse can be made for even the most atrocious actions. All you can do is try your best with the understanding that you have. Keep the course and remember there's always a line you might think incapable of crossing. But you may find yourself feeling justified enough to cross it. Be careful."

"That's not a happy thought."

"It's time for bed. Tomorrow is going to be here sooner than you can imagine."

CHAPTER 36

Jet tossed the cloaks on the couch and glanced out the window. Iris was jumping up and down as his friends were gathered around her. She was leaping nearly ten feet into the air. She had outstanding balance and power. Not in a million years could he have envisioned such an ally. From here, it appeared that his friends could encourage her to perform some tricks, but he knew that he was the only one who could command her. Walking outside, he yelled, "Iris, come."

She turned and sprinted in his direction. Jet added, "Got something to show you guys."

The group hurried from the backyard while Iris navigated directly to Jet's leg. She moved step-per-step as he went inside. He nodded to the end of the couch without a word, and she sat directly where he wanted. Her eyes watched him intently.

He said, "Pyramis of Aurum."

In an instant, Iris transformed back into a pyramid and lay unperturbed on the couch.

His friends stepped into the room, and Mckenzey said, "Iris is unbelievable. I'm so glad she is on our side."

Grantham added, "Jayco suggested that she run after a rabbit in the backyard. She moved so quickly and caught up with the rabbit."

"Did she kill it?" Jet asked.

Jayco sat on the couch. "No. Just pawed it a little."

Seyanna asked, "What is that pile of smelly towels?"

"Your new cloaks."

Jayco sat up quickly. "Wait. What?"

"Like yours?" Seyanna asked, bewildered.

"I think so."

"Finally," Grantham said. "Some good news."

"What do we do?" Seyanna asked.

Latisha moved back an inch or two. "I'm not sure I want anything to happen."

Jet bent down and picked up the first coat; it was in far worse shape than his had been. It was black and barely hung together, with a large hole center mass where a cannon ball-sized object had torn through the fabric. Everyone groaned at its sight. Tossing the coat into the air, the group was mesmerized as the coat floated momentarily, then changed directions and landed near Seyanna's feet. The next coat shot toward Latisha but twisted at the last moment and fell near Jayco. Grantham was next, followed by Latisha.

As the last cloak lay on the floor, Mckenzey threw up her hands and said, "Why not just throw it and see what happens."

"It's got to be yours," Latisha said, clearly annoyed.

Mckenzey insisted, "It has to choose me."

For the first time, it flew directly into the hands of its new owner.

"No confusion there," Jet said.

"Let's see what happens when we put these puppies on," Grantham shouted, and he reached down and plucked his coat from the floor.

The cacophony of shouts was pure excitement. Jet watched as each cloak slipped onto a set of shoulders. Mckenzey's began changing instantly. It changed from brown to pink with a flurry of rapidly changing colors, then blue to black. All the holes disappeared, and the cloak material became light, thin, and far different than his cloak. It was a knee-length, high-end glossy black jacket that bordered on sophistication. The hood lay flat.

Peering around in anticipation, he cringed as none of the others' coats changed. Each of his friends looked pitiful and dejected. Jet said quickly, "I promise, magic is coming your way. Just be ready for it."

"It's stupid. That's what it is," Jayco huffed.

The group glanced at Mckenzey as she slid the hood onto her head. She didn't disappear but instead dimmed. He expected to see fire burning or a block of mud but was surprised to find that he felt little snow or ice crystals lightly hitting his face. A mini storm moved in a linear direction at him. He took three steps back. The ice storm seemed to dissipate as he felt coldness on his lips.

Grantham doubled over laughing, and Jayco asked, "Did you just kiss him?"

Seyanna said, "Didn't need to see that, did I?"

Mckenzey unflipped her hood, returning to view, standing a few feet in front of Jet, her cheeks slightly pink. "It felt like I could control water in a frozen state."

"Pretty amazing," Latisha said excitedly. "But your cloak acted differently than Jet's. You didn't disappear completely."

Jet cleared his voice. "I was talking with Nana downstairs. She told me that the cloaks aren't intended to be invisible. But rather, the cloak brings out a primary element of the earth. Mckenzey's element must be ice or water. I'm not sure which. Remember what Shane said. He knew I was there. This is why I wasn't invisible."

"Who cares? I just want something to work for me for once," Grantham lamented. "I mean, I was flying high. This totally sucks!"

"Amen," Jayco growled, and for the next half hour, he threw a sizable tantrum while the rest of the Echoes discussed the next day's plans. Moving up their schedule was indeed a good plan.

"The traffic might be heavier," Grantham said.

"We'll either beat Shane and his friends to the town or miss them by a few days." Jet said.

"That fool can't beat us to Silverton." Jayco hissed. "It's our hometown."

Latisha said, "We need to get some sleep."

Jayco stood, slightly less angry. "I'm looking forward to tomorrow, but we've got no idea what we're walking into. This could turn into a disaster. We need everyone to be as prepared as possible."

"Let's giddy up."

Grantham and Jayco hugged and kissed Latisha and Seyanna. The girls were sleeping together on the bottom level near Nana. Latisha pulled Seyanna from the room, who appeared slightly nervous.

"Ready for tomorrow?" Mckenzey asked as she sat on the couch across from Jet.

"I'm not sure. Jayco's right, though. We were more prepared for Switzerland."

Mckenzey stood and bent her wrist. A spray of ice shot out of the cloak's sleeve, narrowly missing Jet and onto the couch.

Jet jumped sideways to avoid the spray. After he stood, he tentatively touched the couch. "Good thing the ice didn't permanently freeze the cushions." He and Mckenzey began laughing uncontrollably.

Mckenzey said, "I didn't expect that."

"Me neither. It was sweet, though. That could come in handy."

"Tell me about it."

They sat on the couch cuddling. Mckenzey asked, "Any clue on why our cloaks were the only ones that changed?"

"No idea, but we've experienced many things the others haven't. Nana believes that we'll all have magic."

"Really? That seems hard to imagine." After a moment, Mckenzey confided, "I feel guilty."

"Try not feeling guilty about something you've no control over. It's not like we wanted the cloaks to fail for them."

"No, I guess not," she agreed. She was silent for a few minutes.

"All of this is still hard to wrap my mind around."

"Something tells me that if we survive tomorrow, we'll understand more."

Fatigue overwhelmed them, and Mckenzey rested her head on his shoulder. This was the longest time they'd spent alone since Switzerland. He hadn't realized how much he'd enjoyed being close to her.

"Your house feels great. And I love Nana."

He didn't get a chance to respond as Latisha's voice resonated from the office. "Mckenzey, are you coming?"

"Coming," she shouted. "I did kiss you before, under the cloak, and it felt weird and wonderful."

* * *

Breakfast was sizzling downstairs the following day when Jet stirred from his sleep. The aroma was intoxicating, and his stomach growled. He wasn't sure how he could be hungry after everything they'd eaten yesterday. However, it wasn't the food that pushed Jet out of his bed; an angry conversation was taking place just outside his window, near the front door. Crawling to the foot of his bed, he silently slid open his window. He didn't dare move the curtain while he listened to the voices on the porch.

"You're going to wake the rest of the house."

Jet knew instantly that Mckenzey was speaking.

Seyanna answered, "I just think he should know."

"Why?" Mckenzey protested.

"Are you dating Eric or not?" Seyanna asked.

"It doesn't matter," Latisha interrupted.

Seyanna continued, clearly upset, "Eric called this morning, and you snuck outside."

"It doesn't mean that I'm leaving school after Christmas. I told Eric that I needed more time to decide. Things have been going great between all of us."

"So, where's Eric right now?" Jayco asked.

"He's in Colorado." Mckenzey's voice took on a tone of regret. "I guess he's spending Thanksgiving with my parents."

"That sounds pretty serious," Seyanna said coldly.

Jet was surprised at Seyanna's tone. He thought that he and Mckenzey had already talked this out. However, hearing that Eric was currently with Mckenzey's parents was disconcerting.

Latisha's following words changed everything. "I thought you guys were talking about moving in together after high school."

Jet felt like he'd been punched in the stomach. Turning to leave, he hit his elbow on the window. He froze. Silence reentered the early morning, and a minute later, he heard the front door close. Jet showered, and thirty minutes later, he walked downstairs with his bags packed. Nana brought him some breakfast, and he hugged her. Mckenzey avoided his eyes. Jet ate quickly, and soon the group began moving the artifacts back into the SUV.

As they finished their preparations to leave, no one said anything. Nana seemed to feel the tension after just a few questions about how everyone was doing. She quickly became silent.

Jet opened the driver's side door of the SUV and slipped inside. They decided to leave Jet's new car here at the house for now. Nana came to him and smiled reassuringly. "It'll be all right. Don't be nervous. Call me if you run into any problems. Be careful, Joshua, and don't take anything for granted."

"What do you mean?" he asked.

"Don't assume that your strength alone will save you. Yet don't be afraid to try something impossible. If I've learned anything, it's that there is a power greater than us all. Maybe it's a higher power or it's mother earth, but you've been given something no one else has. Be careful, and trust your wonderful friends." She nodded at the others.

As they drove away, Jet's mind replayed Nana's words. She stood by the front door as they swerved out of the driveway. Right now, his biggest fear was returning to Nana's house, having failed.

For the next four hours, they spoke very little. Jet felt the tension but also the fears and jitters. He hoped it wouldn't elevate to panic. It was early afternoon, but he wasn't hungry and didn't have anything but a knotted stomach as they turned off the interstate toward Silverton. The next twenty minutes were torture.

Mckenzey leaned over from behind and asked softly, "Is everything all right?"

Forcing a smile, he said, "I think so, just a little nervous."

Mckenzey tilted her head and whispered, "That's not what I mean."

"That's all I'm willing to say." He didn't care one lick about Eric right now and couldn't afford any distractions.

"I want to explain."

"Look, I knew the risks. Let's not make this into more of a deal than it is. We need to trust each other during this—no room for anything else. We need to be focused on what we're about to do. I trust you. The rest we can figure out when we get back."

Mckenzey sat back into her seat quickly. He couldn't control her or anyone else right now, and he didn't want to. He purposely drove on a different road into Silverton than where his house had been located. He wasn't that ready yet. He promised himself that he would stop by his old house if they made it. As the outskirts of Silverton came into view, a feeling of regret and despair overwhelmed him. This had been his home. Everything he'd done up to this point was preparing him for this moment.

The town of Silverton was a horror film in reality. The awareness of knowing it so well contradicted what they saw. The most glaring difference was that the town used to be surrounded by four hills. The most eastern hill was demolished by a volcano when it destroyed half the town. The most northern slope was now a small mountain as if it had swallowed the eastern half.

Grantham said, his voice tight, "It feels as if the streets are in all the wrong places."

"It's eerie to be here," Seyanna added as they stopped at the first stoplight.

Jet noticed that the town was modernized, and several new buildings sat closer to the ocean. They were still a mile or so away from the shore. He heard Latisha gasp, then cough, and finally, Latisha's head went down on her seat. She wasn't the only one. Coming into town had been a mistake.

"Look," Jayco said a few minutes later. He pointed to a banner. *The Best Unknown Town in America.* He shuddered and added, "That has to be the dumbest thing ever."

"Who are they kidding?" Seyanna scoffed as she wiped tears from her eyes.

Grantham pointed. "Look at where the bank was?"

They were heading north, but a rocky field was where the ground had sunk several feet to their left. Jet tried to imagine where the bank had been, and his mind flashed to a small half-circle road and a historic red-brick building. Nana visited it every week. The boulders in the field were gigantic. On the far-right side of the field, large dump trucks were shipping in the dirt to cover the area; they'd barely made a dent. The town they had called home was far different than any of them could have imagined.

"Let's pass by the high school," Mckenzey moaned. "I just have to see it."

"It was torn down two years ago," Jayco said. "The new high school was built south of Brandon Highway, outside town, closer to the ocean."

Seyanna squirmed in her seat. "Mom and Dad told me that the closer you go to the ocean, the less damage there is. An influx of population has been built in that direction. First, it was emergency workers and builders. Now, Silverton is one of the most studied areas for two hundred miles or more. My parents considered returning here a few times."

"What about that tasty donut shop?" Grantham asked. "It was just down the street from us."

"Shadow's Pastry?" Jayco asked.

"Dee-lish."

Jet said, "Gone. But it was rebuilt near Jamison Park."

"I can't stand it," Latisha cried out. "Can we just get out of here?"

"I agree," Mckenzey said. "This is way too depressing."

They drove north. Fifteen minutes later, Jet piloted them onto a half-hidden dirt road with hordes of thick trees on each side. The sun had vanished entirely behind some dark clouds that had suddenly materialized. Driving for three-quarters of a mile, the road opened into a large parking lot, marking the trailhead. It felt as if they'd left civilization behind.

The temperature hovered around fifty degrees, and when Jet cracked the window, a mixture of the ocean breeze and pine needles invigorated him. This northern hill was significantly larger than he'd remembered it.

Mckenzey breathed and added, "This is the spot. It's a few miles to the base before we start climbing."

Grantham added, barely containing his excitement, "This is going to be the bomb."

After opening the back latch, Jet pulled out his backpack and filled it with several items, including water and food. He put the golden pyramid into his bag; the added weight was immense. The others did the same with their bags. As they prepared to leave the trailhead, he wasn't surprised that everyone wore their cloaks despite their poor quality.

Mckenzey could be picked out in a crowd with her glossy black cloak, but it also fit perfectly among the trees. Jet had collected some of the items from the glass jars and placed them in his bag. These were handed out. Without another word, the group set off up the trail. It was a slight but steady incline, and the temperature dropped quickly. Soon they were surrounded by even more trees if possible. A cool wind and the promise of adventure swirled in the air.

CHAPTER 37

Jayco, Seyanna, and Latisha each slipped within the first thirty minutes of hiking. The trail was well-worn for the first mile and a half. The cool air, forest of trees, and ocean breeze were surreal and familiar. A creek bubbling to their right made Jet smile. He couldn't believe they were back on their own stomping grounds. Just a few years ago, they had spent hours and days in this wilderness.

Mckenzey stopped suddenly and pointed to the base of a mountain that was much larger than he had remembered. "It'll be quicker if we go in a direct line."

"We're following you," Jayco replied.

"This place is the same," Grantham said, "and different."

"It feels weird," added Latisha, and she pulled her coat tighter.

They stepped off the trail and the terrain was slightly more difficult to navigate. Jet lagged behind and finally relented. He stopped, pulled out the golden pyramid, and tossed it. Shouting, "Pyramis of Aurum," Iris transformed and hit the ground running. She clambered up the nearest tree and raced down the path like she'd been a caged animal for a century. She blended in subtly with the forest floor, the trees, and every background imaginable. She was not like a gecko, changing colors, but rather like a mirage. When she stood still, it was nearly impossible to

320

spot her. When she moved, only a trace around her edges was visible.

Latisha guzzled down a bottle of water and a mouth full of granola. She asked, "Has anyone seen a single animal?"

"Now that you mention it ... it's way too quiet," Seyanna said. "That's spooky." She took a step backward and toppled out of view.

The group rushed forward only to find Seyanna sitting in ankle-high water in a ten-foot-wide gully. Jet noted that it was eerily like the one that had crashed into his house. Standing, Seyanna stomped her feet and walked to the edge. Grantham lifted down a branch intending to pull her out.

"Wait," Mckenzey said, "This gully travels in the same direction we need to go. It'll be faster for sure."

"Looks like rain is coming." Jayco pointed skyward at the ominous clouds circling the peak of the mountain. "Faster is good."

Everyone, including Iris, dropped into the gully and quickened their pace.

Mckenzey joined him ten minutes later. "You've been unusually quiet. Is everything okay?"

"I'm just worrying that we might not be ready for this."

"What do you mean? Second thoughts?"

"What weapons do we have? A few knives. I can perform a little magic. But we're going into this blind."

"And Iris," she added. "That thing is a weapon all by itself." The panther was just ahead of them, jumping in and out of the water playfully.

"Not sure what she can do," he said. "Just be careful."

"Always am."

After a few minutes of silence, Mckenzey strode forward to catch up with the girls.

They swiftly closed the gap to the base of the mountain. It felt far more like twilight than early afternoon. Even the trees on each side of the gully appeared shadowed. Trying to peer a few feet past the outer trees was nearly impossible; it was completely dark.

Latisha hissed and halted as if running into an invisible wall. Following her gaze, Jet watched as a large black animal stepped out from the darkness of the trees on the opposite ledge of the gully, not twenty feet away. Its mouth was slightly opened as if growling, but no sound escaped.

"Is it a coyote?" Grantham asked.

Latisha answered quickly, "No. A wolf."

Seyanna added, "It's huge!"

Jet did not know if wolves were native to Oregon. The black wolf bared its white teeth. A crunching sound echoed from the depths of the trees and a second and a third wolf strolled into view. These two were far smaller than the first. One was white, and the other was light brown.

From the corner of his eyes, he watched as Iris sunk low to the ground, obscuring herself near the ledge. She paused cautiously, sniffed the air, and prodded forward, her golden back hairs bristling. This told him all he needed to know.

"This is bad," Latisha hissed.

"What do we do?" Grantham asked, half panicking.

Jet seamlessly pulled his knife from his belt sheath, placed it flush against his pants, and considered their options. They needed to keep moving, but he hated the idea of giving up his back. Adrenaline coursed through his veins, and he willed his vision to magnify. It obeyed instantaneously. Jet's vision improved, and the darkness retreated slightly. A deep growl, almost like a command, resonated from the black wolf. The other two wolves widened their stances and lowered their heads, glaring directly at Jet and his friends. Their lips retracted slightly. Game on.

Mckenzey slipped on a rock, and all three animal heads swiveled in her direction. The brown wolf dove at her, its mouth snarling; it was fast and bore down on Mckenzey. There was no way she would react in time, and neither could he.

Jet screamed, "Protect Mckenzey!"

Iris leaped lightning-fast, crashing into the diving wolf before it reached Mckenzey. The two animals tumbled over each other, and brown and gold became a blur together. Iris was half the size of the grey wolf. There was a howl of displeasure, but this sound was cut off mid shriek, as Iris sunk her teeth and ripped apart the neck of the brown wolf.

Before the blood stopped spraying, the white wolf dove at him; time slowed, and he watched as the razor-like jaws opened, red eyes narrowing, spittle splashing the air, and even the skin on the snout creased. Jet's reaction was faster than even he thought possible. Sidestepping and simultaneously thrusting his arm forward, he drove his knife, to the hilt, into the wolf's side. His aim was true.

Time returned to normal as the wolf sailed past him, crashing headfirst into the opposite wall of the gully. Jet kept his vision alert and gripped the knife with iron strength. Red blood soaked the rocks, the dirt, and Jet's hand. The wolf somehow stammered onto all four legs and attempted to take two steps toward Jayco. It no longer appeared dangerous but was whimpering. Its front legs gave out, and it collapsed.

Jet's primary vision did not waver from the black wolf. It hissed its displeasure before turning and sprinting into the darkness of the forest behind it. Mckenzey hurried to Iris, kneeling and hugging her.

"Good thing Iris is on our side," Grantham said as he cautiously surveyed the forest, pulling out his knife. "That was quite simply the coolest thing I've ever seen."

Seyanna squeezed Jet's shoulder and said, "Good thing Jet has cat-like reflexes. Two dead wolves in seconds."

Jet wiped his blade on his pants and placed it back onto his belt. He said, "We need to keep moving before finding ourselves with bigger problems."

"Should we be worried about that black wolf?" Jayco asked.

"Probably," Jet said.

Latisha added, "I think the black wolf was telling the other wolves what to do."

Lightning slashed across the sky ahead of them, and large raindrops fell like small bombs. A second bolt connected with a gigantic tree less than two hundred yards away.

Jet gulped down a bottle of mud and water. After finishing, he said, "Let's go."

It wasn't long before the gully started to slope significantly upwards. The rain also turned into a deluge, and Jet feared the water level would rise.

Ten minutes later, Grantham grabbed his shoulder and pointed a way out of the ravine. Over the wind, he yelled, "We need to get out of here. There's too much water."

Jet nodded. Even Iris was struggling to find footing. Jet tried climbing out of the gully at the edge but couldn't find the traction. He ran a few steps only to slip back to the bottom. Jayco and Grantham attempted to push him up, but that was fruitless.

Latisha said, "We need to go back and find a better place."

Jet shook his head and said, "I've got an idea." He distanced himself from the others and flipped on his hood. He understood the closeness he felt to the wind for the first time.

Mckenzey shouted through the rain, "I can kind of see you, or at least your outline. You're not completely invisible."

Jet flexed his wrists, similar to what Mckenzey had done last night, and like a rocket, he was propelled forward up the side of the ravine. Partway up, he tore off his hood, continued sailing upward, reached his peak, and landed gracefully on the top bank.

"Stop showing off," Grantham said. "One of these times, I'm going to be able to do something like that."

"I bet you will," Jet said.

"Really. When?"

"Someday, you'll be exceptional." Jet pulled a rope from his backpack and anchored it to a nearby tree. It didn't take long for his friends to pull themselves out of the gully.

The wind continued to howl, and the rain pelted them as they pushed forward. They were nearing halfway up the mountain.

Mckenzey bellowed, "Last time we were here, things were so different. Finding the entrance is going to be difficult. Let's hope it's this way."

Mckenzey ducked her head and moved into the torrential rain. She guided them left and up the north-facing side of the mountain. A ledge appeared, and they cut back and forth up the side of the slope until they could climb onto the top edge.

When all six situated themselves, they stared at a dozen gigantic boulders preventing them from going forward.

Grantham yelled, "We could try to get to higher ground and then come back."

Jayco added, "I don't think that would work. There isn't anything to anchor our rope. We couldn't climb back down."

Taking out one side of his rope, Jet tied it onto one of the walking sticks. He shouted, "Aer," and the shaft shot a dozen feet upwards as if a tornado had picked it up. It landed in the center of the boulders.

Mckenzey said, "I didn't know you could do that."

"I've been practicing, but it's been slow going."

Jayco pulled the end, and the line tightened. "Is this going to hold us? Should I go first?"

"No way," Latisha said. "I'm the lightest. I'll go first." She pointed at Grantham. "Get below me and promise to catch me if I fall."

Latisha climbed impressively up the rope, moving quickly and steadily. The boulder was twelve feet high. Halfway up, the line shifted, and she was forced to stop. She waited for a few seconds and began climbing again. When she reached the top, she looked down and yelled, "Girl power!"

Jayco went next. If he survived, they were all going to make it. Once he was safely at the top, the rest of the group had little problem ascending the rocky cliff. Jet was the last to arrive, with Iris perched on his shoulder as he climbed, walking back and forth. It was quite disconcerting. She leaped off and began exploring. In total, there were twenty-seven large boulders, but they led nowhere. A huge cliff that was nearly impossible to climb was the backdrop of this side of the mountain.

"Over here," Jayco yelled a few minutes later.

Jet hoisted himself onto a huge boulder and began jumping from one to another. Iris led the way. Standing near the backside of the cliff, Jayco pointed to the wall beyond the boulder.

Grantham laid onto his belly and said, "I can see a partly hidden corridor. I think this is what we're looking for."

Latisha pulled out a flashlight, handing it to him.

Grantham added, "We will need to drop to the ground and crawl in."

"Oh. Fun," Seyanna said, and she hit Jet's shoulder playfully.

Grantham slid down the side of the boulder. His voice echoed. "It's dark down here. My flashlight's working, but it can't penetrate that far into the passage. It looks clear, though. Onward, on our bellies."

Pulling out a headlamp, Jet prepared to slide down the boulder. He was the last in the group. Once he hit the ground, he found two snakes and several spiders lurking in corners. Shrieks erupted ahead of him, and he scanned ahead just in time to see the cloaks of Jayco, Grantham, Seyanna, and Latisha change in a flash of colors.

"What's happening?" Latisha screamed.

Grantham roared excitedly, "This is what I'm talking about!"

"What does this mean?" Seyanna wondered.

Jet thought he understood. "This cave has everything to do with why things happened to Mckenzey and me. Now, the same things are happening to you. We were here before. Now that you've encountered this entrance, things might start happening for you too."

"Finally," Jayco shouted.

"That's interesting," Seyanna said as she felt her cloak.

"I should've brought a headlamp," Mckenzey said.

The passage continued back twenty feet or so. It was five feet wide and three feet high. The floor sloped slightly upward and was a mixture of mud and sand. Shining his light on the walls, Jet hoped to find markings or carvings but came up empty. He shuffled and crawled forward.

Grantham yelled, "When you get deeper, there's a place to stand."

Jet was pulled the last six inches and hoisted into the air. Glancing upward, he cringed at the sleeping winged mammals hanging upside down. The walls and floor were thick with bat droppings.

Jayco said, "Lucky that a larger animal didn't call this place home. Can you imagine if a family of skunks lived back here?"

"Nasty," Grantham said.

Jet inventoried the cloaks of his friends. Jayco had a biker's leather jacket with a hood and several circular metal rings embedded in the material. Latisha's cloak was a mysteriously dark red, and when she moved, it shimmered. It was not as long as Seyanna's, but it was tight-fitting and of a material Jet had never seen before. Seyanna's was white but flared out at the waist. It didn't have a single smudge of dirt or mud. Grantham's cloak was a light tan trench coat that ended at his knees. The differences between each cloak seemed more important than their similarities.

Mckenzey groaned, "I hate bats, rats, and skunks."

"Really?" Latisha asked. "I think they're so cute."

"What's this?" Jayco asked.

Jet found Jayco pointing at a large carving in the back wall. Dirt and mud covered most of the wall. They began scraping off the wall. Jet's heart leaped as he recognized a large falcon carved on the upper portion.

Seyanna said, "There's also another image down here."

Tearing his eyes away from the falcon, a second carving sat below the first. It was a coiled snake with its head staring back at them. Both animals were mammoth in size and missing their eyes.

CHAPTER 38

Grantham bent over and wiped the wall, his hand brushing away several layers of cobwebs and dust.

"What are you doing?" Latisha asked.

"There are some words scratched into the wall."

"What does it say?" Jayco asked.

Grantham said, "It says: I've arrived. I've conquered. And I've stolen the eyes. E.T. Forester."

"Who's E.T. Forester?" asked Latisha, perplexed.

"I'm pretty sure he's the guy that sold two meteorites to Professor Blum. He took two, and Mckenzey and I found one. He later died in South America while on another expedition."

"That's so weird," Latisha said. "Is there one missing?"

"No," Grantham said. "The snake is missing two eyes, but the falcon only one because its head is tilted to the side."

"Right," Latisha said. "All this makes perfect sense."

Seyanna examined the wall more closely. She said, "There's a crack dividing both carvings."

Mckenzey asked, "What's our next step?"

"Let's push the rock to see what happens," Grantham suggested.

Latisha said, "It can't hurt."

They spent the next thirty seconds pushing on an immovable object. Reality still took longer to settle in than wishful thinking. Soon they were each panting, having accomplished nothing. Jet felt a tug on his leg and found Iris pawing at his shoe. She slunk to the far-right side of the stone wall and brushed against it. Near the floor, carved into the wall, was a single-bladed knife. The realness of the image was surprising. Reaching out, he touched it. The image suddenly withered, blackened, and turned to sand. A yellow spark ignited from the spot and shot into the crack dividing the two animals.

"What the ..." Jet said as he stumbled away.

The spark moved slowly, but its bright light was enthralling. It traveled the length of the wall, and once the entire crack was aglow, two sparks jumped to each animal, and the outlines of each animal were quickly illuminated. A blue fog began filling the small cave. The outlines of the animals became hazy. As if a glass wall were being splintered, a loud crack reverberated around them. A gush of air sucked the fog away, and they found themselves standing on the precipice of a gigantic cavern. The wall before them had disintegrated away, and as if physical animals had been preserved in glass, two huge living creatures hovered in the air, not ten feet away.

The two animals started thrashing to escape their hidden bonds. Suddenly, one of the falcon's wings broke through the invisible barrier. It did not take long for the creature to free itself. The snake, however, was trapped.

The falcon's size was astonishing; it was more than ten feet tall. The snake remained suspended in the air. What happened next was unbelievable. The falcon moved forward to the edge of the hidden barrier as its beak opened. The snake, seeing its option for an escape, and without hesitation, vaulted into the falcon's mouth.

The falcon's head lifted skyward and swallowed. A flash of golden light consumed the bird, illuminating the cavern's size behind the animal. The brightness of the light forced Jet and the others to cover their eyes.

When the brightness dissipated, Jet stared at a fifteen-foot-tall creature. The body was that of a falcon, but with a snake's head and a tail that came out somewhere in the hind feathers. It surveyed them as if they were prey. The beast let loose an ear-piercing screech, and Jet's hands clamped over his ears.

Jet and his friends were lifted into the air and dragged farther into the cavern without warning.

Mckenzey screamed, "What's happening?"

Jet, his arms flailing through the air, tried to break the hold on him. It was fruitless, like a fly escaping a spider's nest. He noticed that he was being separated from his friends. After another five feet, he was tossed to the ground unceremoniously. His friends were trapped against the sidewall more than twenty feet away. He turned and sprinted in their direction. Five feet before reaching them, he smacked face-first into an unseen barrier. Jet was knocked off his feet.

Words echoed into the darkness. "So, youngling, you can move despite my cry of silence. You must be the Mikado. Barely old enough to fight, but plenty old to die. You're far from prepared for this fight. I'll give you one chance to leave now, and you and your friends can depart alive. Drop the tome, your cloaks, and the other gifts. Withdraw now, and live."

Jet stood and faced the creature hovering in the air. "I think we'll stay and see what happens."

The creature's head lifted skyward, and smoke curled out of its nostrils.

"Are you laughing at me?" Jet asked.

Without answering, the creature bellowed, "Choice must be chosen, even when that decision is your death. Welcome to Thrantos Grotto. I am Lucretius the Avad. I am Arisol's work servant, and I protect this domain. To gather entrance, you must be victorious in a duel. Do you accept it? And please say that you do; I've been so bored these past decades."

Trying to buy some time to figure out a way to free his friends, Jet yelled, "Too many big words. Not sure what you just asked. Slow it down for me, big guy." He inched back and felt the barrier. It was solid and unbreakable. Moving left, the barrier went all the way to the wall. His friends were stuck in a nook.

"You are not strong enough to break that barrier," the creature hissed.

Under his breath, he said, "Ignisnaeth," hoping to see a fireball or flame attacking the creature. Instead, there was only silence.

More smoke escaped the creature's nostrils, and Jet was sure it was laughing at him.

Lucretius said, "I see you know the old magic. The inferior magic. It doesn't matter; it will have little effect in the grotto. Leave and forfeit your powers or fight me. Those are your only choices. Do you accept it?"

After how far they'd come, leaving was not an option. Jet said, "I accept."

The instant the words escaped his lips, a fiery hot sensation sizzled onto his forearms, and he was forced to his knees. It was as if an artist was carving something onto his skin. Jet watched as two small daggers became imprinted on each arm, like tattoos.

A high-pitched primeval voice bellowed, "And so it begins. You will not continue any further on the Path of the

Phoenix. I have waited centuries for this day. I was born for this. Your demise will be my greatest honor."

Jet's arms moved without his intent; his hands opened and touched the inner portion of his forearm. He peeled authentic daggers from his arm as though they were stickers. The blades were majestic sea-blue with black obsidian handles that felt perfect in his hands. They looked about twelve inches in length.

He stood, regained control of his arms, and glared at the creature. Lucretius flapped his wings and flew backward into the darkness. However, the creature was the source of light in the room. It appeared that the grotto was immense. As the creature flew, three large pillars came into view. The left and right pillars went from ceiling to floor, while the center pillar rose just halfway to the top. Lucretius alighted on the middle pillar.

It raised its snake's head and sprayed orange flames at two gigantic jewels inlaid into the two side columns. They were ignited with light and began to glow. The heat from the flames reached Jet, and his confidence took a hit. The grotto exploded with color.

His head swiveling toward Jet, Lucretius said, "You are a Mikado, a dust breather, and a sworn enemy of my master. Your presence continues the Rivalry. What you seek lies farther through this labyrinth. But I warn you, death is at the edge."

Jet demanded, "What is the Rivalry?"

"My master was the single most powerful magician in the world. He was trapped in the earthly prison by luck alone. Upon his entrapment, his energy was divided, and Runic magic became dormant. The four kings used Elemental magic, and when two of them, along with Mother Earth, gave up their lives, their magic also became dormant. The Rivalry opens the door, ever so small, for magic to be rediscovered. That's why you have this magic. The Rivalry continues a battle to reclaim the ancient magic. It cannot be stopped. Joy flows through my veins because you do not have the endowment to prevent Arisol from reclaiming what is his. The Rivalry will prove that my master is King of the world beyond any measure. So, take up your arms. Death is a whisper away."

"Wait," Jet shouted. "Are you one of the four kings?"

"No." It laughed derisively. "I am the Avad. The kings were just pawns. When the Czaric and other mages arrive, you will be dead, and I will guide them to the depths below to claim what is ours. Runic magic is of the gods. I need them as much as they need me. I cannot pass without their help. But I will make sure that you never take a step out of this den."

Jet asked, "Who are you really?"

"I am the Deceiver. I deluded two of the kings into rebellion. I was rewarded beyond measure."

Doubt crept into Jet's mind. How could he do this on his own? Flipping on his hood, he hoped to find a way to release his friends. He did not disappear, and there was not even the slightest gust of wind.

The creature howled with pleasure as if reading his mind. "Your friends cannot be a part of this. Your magic does nothing here. All you have is your ability, ingenuity, and those two blades in your hands."

Jet swung the blades, trying to gauge their weight and fluidity. He was shocked to find that they felt like extensions of his arms. He had heard of this before, but he'd never felt such force and control. He bellowed, "Let's dance."

Jet willed his vision to magnify in the same instant that Lucretius flapped his wings, rising into the air. Three razor-sharp talons were on each foot, ratcheted out, beginning to glow a fiery red. They were nearly the size of his head. Unlike before, time did not slow.

The creature circled the pillars to gain elevation. When it was sufficiently high enough, it attacked, diving directly at Jet. Both legs were positioned in front as if intending to pin him to the ground. The wind whistled as Lucretius bore down on him. Jet faked right, switched directions, and darted toward the sidewall, opposite from his friends. After covering half the distance, he changed directions again.

"Not working," he yelled to himself.

Lucretius followed, toying with him all the while. Instead of making a power move and cutting off Jet's escape, the creature baited him to make a mistake. Jet panicked and changed directions again, trying to sprint for the left pillar. The creature bore down on him, the beating of its wings becoming louder and louder. Jet scrambled, fear coursing through him.

Ten feet from the column, claws scraped against his back, and he was lifted into the air and launched forward. He rolled in mid-air, attempting to protect his daggers, and landed hard on his left side. A stabbing pain shot through his left hip. He slid for several feet until he crashed into the center pillar. He was protected, at least momentarily.

The creature soared to his left around the three columns and banked. It attacked again. This time, the creature unleashed a spray of fire, and Jet was forced to dive back as a shower of flames connected with the column. The heat was beyond imaginable. As the creature passed by, Jet reached his arm around to his back and was relieved to find the cloak had protected him.

The creature flew upwards, blustering, "You are no match for me."

Standing quickly, Jet aimed and shouted, "Abzu!" Two large ice rods shot into the air. His magic wasn't aimed at the creature but at the ceiling. Lucretius was too distracted by his celebration to notice. One of the falling pieces collided with the beast's neck, while the other hit the stone ceiling above it. The ice crystal that hit the beast crumbled on contact while the second knocked rock particles that slammed into Lucretius.

The beast recovered quickly and said, "I am indestructible by everything except those two daggers. And you'll never get close enough to hurt me." The creature attacked again.

Jet darted toward the back of the cavern, opposite the entrance, searching for a place to hide. There was nowhere to go. Placing his back against the wall, he searched for a distraction. Nothing. The beast was upon him in a matter of seconds. Both wings shot out, and Lucretius slowed its attack, trying to avoid the grotto's walls. It was mere feet away. The creature's fanged mouth began to open.

Jet screamed, "Ventusnaeth!" Again, he directed his magic not at the creature but the ground, and he was lifted into the air, propelled six or eight feet upward while tucking his legs. Using the wall as a springboard, he pushed hard, trying to finagle a way through the defenses of the hovering Lucretius. More than anything else, he'd caught the creature off guard. Imploring his body, he twisted as he held both knives flush against his chest.

Having realized that he was slightly vulnerable, Lucretius pulled together its wings and created a cocoon. Jet's shoulder crashed into the closest wing. He slashed out with his dagger, cutting a small gash into the wing.

The falcon cried out in pain.

Jet spiraled toward the ground, bellowing, "Ventusnaeth!" This slowed his descent, but he still crashed to the ground, smacking the side of his head on the stone floor. His vision flickered out for a moment, and he tried getting to his feet as something wet ran down his neck. Regaining his footing, he sprinted toward the center columns. Bright lights flashed across his vision, but somehow, he kept hold of both daggers.

The creature had ascended several feet, and it dove after Jet.

"Noooo!" Mckenzey's scream reverberated around the cave.

Jayco's voice boomed, "Move!"

Lucretius opened his mouth to deluge Jet with a scorching flame.

He was still a dozen feet away from the closest pillar. He wasn't going to make it. Jet pushed down the bile rising in his stomach. He half-turned and screamed, "Aer," and an explosion of wind battered the head of the creature just enough that the blast of flame careened into the cavern, missing him by inches.

As Jet dove toward the column, he heard Lucretius say, "Your magic shouldn't be strong enough to affect me directly. Killing you is going to be my greatest pleasure." The creature again banked around the column. Jet tried frantically to catch his breath.

The hairs on the back of his neck rose, and he became aware of something he'd never felt before. He felt the movement of air all around him. Without understanding it, he knew exactly where the creature was. Jet reacted more than he planned. He dove toward the center column a millisecond before the creature's snake tail slammed into it and just inches from where he had been. The column cracked in several places, and large rock pieces fell to the floor.

"I am going to destroy you," Lucretius promised. The creature lifted off again and tried attacking from the opposite side. "Stop hiding like an ant. Come out and fight me."

Again, Jet could feel the air and knew exactly where the creature was. This allowed him to move behind the third column.

The creature hissed its displeasure. "You can't hide from me forever." The level of heat directed at his column was unbelievable. The column protected Jet for now.

There was a large crash, and the column shook again; rocks fell from above.

Yelling, Grantham implored, "His wing hit the column. Do something now."

Several rocks crashed around him. The torrent of heat had stopped. Jet peeked around his column and found Lucretius retreating two dozen feet away. It was bending its wing repeatedly as if assessing the damage. Lucretius scanned the area and caught sight of Jet attacking. It shot into the air unsteadily and tried hovering in the air.

Lucretius blustered, "This is pointless. Your magic is like a fly; it's annoying, but it cannot harm me. Don't scurry away like a mouse. Don't make your death a total disgrace."

Jet tightened his cloak and took two deep breaths. There was a movement in the shadow near the base of a column. A crazy plan settled in his mind. He exploded from behind the column and raced directly at the flying creature.

"What are you doing?" Mckenzey screamed.

Jayco answered, "Stupid move."

Lucretius hadn't expected this bold move either. Jet covered the first ten steps before the creature could react, but he needed to cover more ground. Lucretius expanded its wings to gain elevation. Jet gripped one dagger tightly in his hand, and as hard as he could, he threw it end over end at the exposed belly. The beast lifted a leg intending to deflect the flying object, but it missed the hilt, and the blade sunk deep into the flesh of the beast's abdomen, tearing open a large cut. A bellow of pain echoed around the room.

"Beautiful," Grantham hollered.

Jet was forced to retreat to the back wall. Lucretius sprayed the air with its flames, followed by the ground at the base of the columns. He was unable to return to the safety of the columns. When he reached the back wall, he leaned forward and tried to catch his breath. A foul stench filled Jet's nostrils, and drops of green liquid spilled to the floor. The creature flew toward the center pillar and landed.

Jet had to decide if he was going to attack now or try to evaluate the damage done. The creature flashed him a clear look—this wasn't over yet.

Lucretius never saw the next attack. Iris leaped from the right column, having climbed halfway up. Landing on the left wing, she clawed and bit with immense ferocity. Lucretius roared in pain and rolled in the air, sending Iris sprawling. Somehow, the panther landed softly on her feet, closer to the front wall, and dashed across the floor unharmed.

Jet removed his knife and, like before, rushed forward and threw it at the creature, this time at its neck. With surprising speed and minimal effort, Lucretius knocked away the knife, and it clattered to the stone floor harmlessly in the direction of his friends, the part of the grotto farthest from him.

The creature clamored, "You've accomplished nothing. I will be feasting on your bodies soon enough. And now, you have no weapon." Lucretius plucked the first dagger from its belly, and by using a combination of its talon and a snake's fang, he bit the blade, breaking it in half.

Another burning sensation spread across Jet's forearm. A small dagger tattoo imprinted itself on his skin. It was a perfect replica of the dagger that had just been broken, but it was entirely black.

Fluid still cascaded from the creature's abdomen. Lucretius bellowed, "Time for this to end and you to enter the great void."

From the middle pillar, the creature dove at him. It was far from steady in its flight. Jet veered to the left, running first forward and then switching directions toward the cave's opening, close to his friends, pretending to search for the second dagger. He sprinted faster than he'd ever gone before. Jet screamed and cried as if hopeless, and Lucretius hooted its pleasure. Jet's vision magnified, allowing him to see the creature bearing down on him with both feet again extended.

The beast closed the gap relentlessly. Jet couldn't reach his destination, and he felt the claws inches from snatching him off the ground. A claw nudged his back, and Jet dove forward, twisting his body and positioning himself perpendicular to the ground. The claw moved toward his face, and Jet thrust his hand upward, breaking through the skin, and reaching into the abdomen. Immediate pain sliced through his hands, and gravity pulled him away from Lucretius. He landed hard as the creature's momentum pushed it forward until it crashed hard into the stone.

The beast tried to put its legs under its body to stand, but it had lost most of its power and coordination. The snake's head swiveled to face Jet, but it wobbled back and forth. "What have you done?"

"I cut through your belly with my dagger." Jet stood, clutching his hand, which burned.

"That's not possible. I knocked away your last dagger."

Lifting his arm, he held tightly to the remaining dagger. "That was my knife, not my dagger." Jet shook his head as he walked forward cautiously. "You've lost. We're moving on."

The beast let out a long sigh. When it spoke again, it had lost most of its voice. "You may have defeated me, but your demise has already begun. If the Path of the Phoenix doesn't kill you, The Rivalry will—it is inevitable."

Lucretius's eyes rolled out of focus, and he stopped breathing. Jet feigned taking another step, and the snake's head sped at him, fangs craving a bite of flesh. In one clean move, Jet sidestepped the attack, swung his dagger, and sliced off the snake's head. Death was instantaneous. There was an audible pop. The barrier imprisoning his friends was broken, and they were set free.

CHAPTER 39

The collective group hug was well worth it. Jet winced when someone grabbed his shoulder as someone else tousled his hair. He had pain in places he didn't know possible. Blood had crusted on the top of his head and down his neck. His leg had a large gash as well. A bandage was quickly wrapped around his leg, and the wound on his head was cleaned. He was sitting on the floor, trying to catch his breath.

"It's getting pretty dark in here," Mckenzey said.

Indeed, the grotto's light was diminishing significantly, and the glow from the jewels was losing its luster.

Jet felt a tingling in his arm. He said, "What the ...?"

Suddenly, the dagger in his hands shimmered, like an illusion, then disappeared. An outline of the dagger implanted itself on his arm next to the first. The contrast between the two was remarkable. The first image was dark, while the second still had the sea-blue color but noticeably faded.

Jayco said, "It's a reminder of what you did."

"That was unbelievable," Seyanna said. "I thought you were going to die like ten different times."

Latisha added, "Jet. I hate to admit this, but that was the coolest and scariest thing I've ever seen."

"Um, thanks," Jet said. "I think."

Iris sauntered over and wiggled between his legs. To his astonishment, she began purring and looking pleased with herself. She pushed her face against his legs, demanding attention.

"Yes, Iris, you helped too." He reached over, scratching her back.

"Jayco, make sure that nasty thing is dead," Grantham said.

Jayco nodded. As he approached the dead creature, the body erupted into flames. It took thirty seconds for the entire flesh to become emblazoned. When it was finally finished, the whole body was nothing more than dust.

Jayco hurried closer, yelling, "There's still something here."

"Like what?" Grantham demanded.

"A jewel, I think. It's sparkling."

Jayco returned, holding something. Mckenzey turned on her flashlight and illuminated the baseball-sized milky-pink crystal.

"Did that come from where I think it did?" Seyanna asked.

Jayco shook his head. "I think it must've been the creature's heart."

Mckenzey reached out her hands. "But a crystal. I wonder why?"

Jayco laughed. "The spoils to the victor."

"Epic," Grantham added.

Jet said, "I need a drink."

"Not the time or place," Jayco said.

"Really?" Jet questioned. "A jokester now."

"Where's your backpack?" Seyanna asked.

He groaned and said, "It's at the far end of the grotto," indicating into the darkness where he hoped it would be."

"Oh, I see it," Latisha said, pointing across the room. "It's closer to the opening. I'll get it." She hurried off, disappearing after only a dozen steps.

"Can anyone else see the backpack?" asked Jayco.

"Nope," Grantham said. "I think she was joking."

It took Latisha two minutes, and when she came back into view, everyone was staring at her expectantly.

"What?" she asked. "Do I have dirt on my face or something?"

"Or something," Jayco said.

"Whatever." Using her sleeve, she wiped her mouth.

Grantham said, "Don't listen to him. What he means is that none of the rest of us can see the back wall. Are you playing with us? It's so dark in here I can barely see you."

"Whatever, it's as light as day."

"You can see in the dark," Jayco said.

"No, I can't."

Grantham took a step closer. "It's almost pitch-black in here, ever since the light went out of those jewels."

"It looks just normal to me."

"That's what we're saying," Seyanna muttered.

Grantham celebrated. "Our cloaks have changed, Latisha has a gift, and I bet magic isn't too far behind."

"I like that sound of that," Jayco said. "I wonder what I'll be able to do?"

Peering around the cavern, Mckenzey asked, "Latisha, what do you see?"

She said, "There's a doorway on the opposite side. It opened after that creature died."

"Is it a way out?" Jayco asked.

"Nope. It goes deeper into the mountain," Latisha said. "I'll tell you if I see anything running at us."

Seyanna shivered. "What is with everyone? Who knew you had these jokes in your personality?"

Jet retrieved two bottles of dirt water from his backpack, gulping both down. The surge in energy was appreciated. He found some granola bars and a bandage. He wrapped his arm, which had several cuts and burns. Soon they were making their way toward the open doorway.

Latisha asked, "Can I see the crystal?" After it was handed to her, she turned it over and over again. "This thing is sweet."

After covering more than half the distance, Mckenzey asked, "Can you tell us more about this magic?"

Jayco interrupted, "Why did that creature call you a Mikado?"

Jet said, "The magic that is taught in our tome is Elemental magic. The Mikado can learn all the spells. There are five categories of spells: Earth, Fire, Wind, Water, and Spirit. But most people can only do a spell from one element."

Seyanna asked, "Does that mean we can do spells?"

"Eventually. When we're out of here, I'll teach you a few."

"Wait," Jayco said. "You were told?"

Jet nodded. "*The Sorcerer's Guide* can communicate with me. It's more like a programmed response by someone named Wier. The other tome teaches about Runic magic. They also have categories. If I remember them correctly, they are Motion, Life, Darkness, Matter, and Mixture. I've no clue what that means."

"Show us," Jayco said.

Jet spoke. "Chango," and the air temperature around them rose significantly. After it had dissipated, he added, "I've practiced only a few, and even less of those have been successful. I know that one works."

Everyone in the group muttered, "Chango," but nothing happened.

Jet continued, "I don't know everything. But there are magic levels, and I've only been given the basic ones. Chango might do something completely different for you if you have an aptitude for fire. There's still a lot to learn."

"Simply honey badger," Grantham said smoothly.

"I hope that means something good," Mckenzey said, rolling her eyes.

"Oh, it does."

Once they reached the back wall, Latisha said, "This passageway seems to have been cut into a corridor. It's noticeably darker inside, but I can still see pretty good."

"It's even darker than the cave," Jayco said.

Latisha continued, "There's a tunnel taller than Jayco by around six inches and three feet wide. It turns in about twenty feet. Otherwise, it looks empty."

"Good enough for me," Jet said. "But everyone, get your weapons ready."

Latisha placed the crystal in Jet's backpack. Several items, including rings, fell to the floor as she did. She asked, "Why did we bring these?"

"Not sure," Jet admitted. "I'm not sure what they do, but we might need them."

Mckenzey bent down and picked one up. "Can I put it on?"

"I guess."

The ring was gold, but it lacked the typical luster. It was tiny, and Mckenzey only managed to push it onto her pinkie finger. Her facial expression changed immediately. "I think it's giving me energy."

"What?" he asked.

"Put one on," she said.

Jet's ring was golden, matching Mckenzey's eyes. It held no jewel, just a golden band, but it was old and scratched. It wasn't even the largest ring, but he had to put it onto his pointer finger. Jet said, "I see what you mean." He felt the intensity of riding a roller coaster combined with feeling invincible.

"I know."

The rest of the rings were passed out. Most were energy, but Grantham's ring helped him become quicker in his movements. "Pretty useful," Grantham said.

The corridor became frigid after only a few steps. The intensity of the chill caught Jet off guard. An unnatural sound assaulted his ears. It was a mixture of a cat being tortured and a high-pitched motorcycle engine. The sound sent shivers through his body. As he glanced around, he thought it was affecting everyone differently. Grantham and Latisha threw their hands over their ears. Jayco's back became stiff, and he was unable to move forward. Mckenzey clutched Jet's arm to avoid falling. But Seyanna was the most affected, and she fell to the floor, almost spasming. Iris sank low, crawling forward and out of view. A moment later, the sound stopped.

The silence in the absence of the wailing was eerie and unsettling.

"See anything, Latisha?" Jayco asked, his voice shaking as he helped Seyanna to her feet.

"Iris is acting strange," Latisha answered. "It still looks clear in both directions."

"What was that?" Grantham asked.

Jayco wrapped an arm around Seyanna, and together they walked forward tentatively.

"Wait!" Latisha shouted. "Up ahead, the ground drops a few inches, and it's darker than the stone. I can't see into it."

Jayco said, "I think it's water."

Concentrating on the ground, Jet could see subtle changes. There were small ripples in the darkness. Iris was perched at the edge, peering into the water, her tail flicking back and forth as if waiting to pounce on a fish.

Grantham asked, "Do we go forward or back?"

"We don't have much of a choice," Jet said, but he couldn't see a way around the water. They would have to take a dip.

"Could anything be in there," Seyanna mumbled.

"With what we just saw and heard, I wouldn't be surprised," Mckenzey answered.

"Who's going in first?" Jayco asked.

"Let's drop in Iris and see how far down she goes?" Grantham suggested.

"Not a chance," Jet muttered.

"I've got an idea," Latisha interjected. "I could drop my flashlight."

Mckenzey agreed, "Go for it."

Pulling out her flashlight, Latisha tossed it in, and the light glistened off the surface as it advanced toward the water.

Kerplunk.

The instant the flashlight passed under the surface, the light disappeared entirely.

"What just happened?" Seyanna asked.

"About three feet," Jayco noted.

Mckenzey shook her head. "What are you talking about? I can't see anything. It's just gone."

"Really?" Jayco answered with a crooked smile.

Jet said, "The light vanished the instant it went into the water."

"Nope." Jayco pointed into the water. "The light is still as bright as ever. Can anyone else see it?"

No one answered.

Jayco added with loftiness, "I'm not sure how this talent will help, but it's sweet."

"Am I the only one with zip, nada, nothing?" Grantham asked.

Seyanna punched his arm. "You're not the only one, brain dead."

"Me neither," Mckenzey said. "Are we getting in this water or what?"

"Okay, that's freaky," Seyanna screamed. "I can only see half of your arm."

Jayco was leaning over. His arm, up to the elbow, was underwater. "Freakier than that creature we just watched try to kill Jet?"

"Good point," Seyanna laughed nervously.

"Well, the water feels normal." Jayco lifted his backpack over his head and slipped in. He disappeared from the waist down.

"You okay?" Seyanna asked, clearly unsettled.

"I'm better than okay. Have I ever told you how much I love the water? Come on in."

Latisha said, "The water goes for about forty feet. There's solid ground on the other side."

Jet tentatively reached down and watched his hand disappear. It was unnatural, yet the water felt cool and moist. The feeling of coolness lasted longer than he would've expected, even after wiping his hand off on his cloak.

"Iris, let's go." Jet eased himself in as Iris dove into the water and swam quickly.

"Good enough for me," Grantham said.

Jayco motioned for the group to hurry. He was nearly halfway across the water, facing them.

Iris didn't take long to pass Jayco and get to the other side. Somehow, she pushed herself out of the water using the side and the ledge.

Mckenzey, Latisha, and Seyanna all moved into the water. The three of them followed Grantham. The water settled just above Jet's waist. A chill grew in his legs as he caught up with Jayco, and it had nothing to do with the water level.

"This can't be as easy as it seems," Jet said.

Jayco said, "You're right. We need to hurry."

Suddenly, something brushed up against Jet's leg, and it took everything for him not to cry out.

"Sorry about whoever's foot I just kicked," Mckenzey hollered, just a few paces behind Jet.

"No problem," Jet said calmly, unable to relax.

"I don't like this," Seyanna hissed, several steps behind the others.

Jet was close enough to see the look on Jayco's face, who appeared dumbfounded. Suddenly Jayco dove underwater, vanishing.

"Did something just touch my leg?" Mckenzey called out.

Jet pushed forward. "Just keep going. Don't stop."

A moment later, Jayco resurfaced, wiped his face, and met Jet's eyes. He gripped Jet's shoulder and whispered, "We're not alone. The water doesn't end at the walls of the corridor."

"What do you mean?" Jet asked.

"The water extends outward, under the surface." Jayco used his hands to show the wall to his right. Using one hand, he pointed under his other, fixed hand. "It goes for several feet. There are these chambers. I caught sight of an animal with three tails, a long slender body, two hind legs, and two forelegs. It has scales like an amphibian, and it's completely white."

"That doesn't sound too bad," Jet said humorlessly as a wave of uncontrollable shivering crashed through him.

Jayco continued, "The head resembles an alligator with several rows of teeth. Get everyone out and fast."

Jet swam toward the far ledge. A moment later, Jayco pushed at his back, helping him out of the water. Jayco turned and set off toward the middle of the corridor.

"Keep coming," Jayco said in an awkwardly pleasant voice.

Grantham and Latisha were stuck eight feet from the edge. Seyanna had passed them and was closer to Mckenzey. Latisha's arms were wrapped around Grantham's neck as she hissed, "It happened again. I'm not moving another step."

Jayco waved them forward. "Over here! Just keep going."

Latisha nodded repeatedly, but it took Grantham pushing her forward for her to move. Mckenzey approached the ledge, and Seyanna was only a few feet behind her.

Grantham screamed.

"Get away, get away," Latisha shouted. "Don't leave me."

Jet watched in awe as Grantham launched himself clean out of the water, rotated, and continued to the ceiling. Somehow, he grasped the stone ceiling, hanging upside down.

Latisha tilted her head upwards and hissed, "You ditched me."

Jet grabbed Mckenzey's arm and frantically pulled her from the water while Jayco tried getting Seyanna near the edge.

Grantham said defensively, "I reacted. I didn't know it would send me up here."

Through gritted teeth, she said, "Then get back down here."

Once Mckenzey was pulled from the water, they started dragging out Seyanna. Latisha was still frozen.

Jayco yelled, "Latisha, just come forward. I'll help you."

Large ripples of water cascaded away from something just under the surface. It was a dozen feet from Latisha and heading in her direction. Although most of the creature was invisible, there appeared to be at least two tails propelling it forward. Jet's energy surged with fear, and they pulled Seyanna from the water.

Grantham yelled as he hung upside down, "Latisha, behind you!"

All eyes focused on a six-foot-long critter, like an alligator, as it surfaced. Four milky white eyes came into view just as two tails coiled as if preparing to attack. An elongated mouth opened, showing the upper half of two dozen razor-sharp black teeth.

Latisha screamed a blood-curdling shriek.

A blur fell from the ceiling as Grantham landed on the back of the critter. It slashed and spun and tried to rid itself of the weight on its back. Jayco reached out and latched onto Latisha's waist, dragging her toward the ledge. Grantham held on tightly, trying to wrestle and control it. He was losing badly.

Latisha screamed in terror.

The critter rolled, and Grantham lost control of its back. It disappeared, and Grantham began swimming forward frantically. Jet sighed as Latisha reached the ledge and was effortlessly pulled from the water. They turned their attention to Jayco, who was caught in the middle. Jayco needed to leave the water, but he also wanted to help his best friend.

The critter exploded from the water, almost completely exiting the surface, and its teeth sunk into Grantham's shoulder, pulling him partly under. Grantham's left elbow swung back and connected with the side of the critter's head.

This gave him enough time to leap from the water again, latching onto the ceiling.

Jet shouted, "Kali!" An arrow of molten lava formed instantly. The arrow was shot at the critter with a flick of his wrist. It connected with the animal's side causing an explosion of fire, and the critter sank from view.

Seyanna yelled, "Hurry," and she and Latisha pulled at Jayco relentlessly but could not pull him from the water.

A second critter surfaced and flexed its back, opening several holes. A white energy wave catapulted outward. Reaching for Jayco, Jet pulled. When the wave hit Jayco, he still had one leg in the water. He stiffened into a full-body contraction and began sliding backward.

Mckenzey and Seyanna seized Jayco's arm, and together they agonizingly pulled him from the water. His body remained stiff as they laid him on his back. It was as if he was hit with an electrical charge.

Grantham scurried, upside down, along the ceiling, yelling, "How's Jayco?"

Seyanna said, "Breathing, but he's in shock. He won't respond."

Jet stared down at Jayco's pale face. It took a full minute before his muscles began working, and his eyes fluttered open.

Grantham vaulted from the ceiling, twisting in the air, landing on both feet.

"I guess you found your ability," Latisha said. "How does it feel?"

"Pretty good." He quickly added, "But I didn't leave you. I had no idea what was going to happen."

"Uh, huh." Latisha's look revealed she was far from convinced.

Jayco asked weakly, "Did we all get out of the water?"

"Thanks to you," Seyanna said. "What the heck was that thing?"

"A frickin monster," Jet roared.

CHAPTER 40

It took the better part of twenty minutes for Jayco to regain control of his muscle movements enough to stand independently. In the meantime, they began checking their gear and pulling out food.

Jet wasn't sure he would ever get in the water again. "Well, that sucked worse than cafeteria burritos."

"True that," Jayco said as he leaned against the wall.

They set off again, and the first few minutes were slow going. They walked in silence.

Jayco asked, "What happened to me?"

Seyanna described the electrical wave that incapacitated Jayco and everything that followed.

"I'm slowing the group down. Don't wait for me."

Jet said, "We're not in a huge hurry, and we're not leaving you behind."

The group fell into silence again. Latisha guided them all along the dark, cold, and wet hallway. They were weary and on guard for just about anything. It felt like they'd traveled miles and miles inside the mountain.

When they turned the next corner, Jayco slumped against the wall, and Mckenzey hurried forward. "Jayco, will you let me heal you? I feel weird about this and all. But I think I can help."

"What do you mean?" Latisha asked skeptically.

"It's hard to explain, and it certainly can't be done with every wound." Stopping next to Jayco, she asked, "Can I touch you?"

Jayco shrugged. "I guess."

Placing her hands on the sides of his head, Mckenzey concentrated. There was no chanting or words spoken.

"Whatever you're doing," Jayco said, "it feels weird. Like ants crawling over my entire body, but that area goes numb where they touch my skin."

"There," Mckenzey said, her hands falling limply to her side some minutes later. "I'm not even sure what I just did. It was all I could do."

"Thanks. I think."

Mckenzey accepted a bottle of mud water from Jet, which she guzzled down without hesitation. "I can see the appeal now. Fascinating."

Seyanna asked, "How did you know you could do that?"

Mckenzey leaned against the wall. "Coming out of the water, I felt a change in my body. Healing was the first thing that came to my mind. It just felt part of me suddenly."

"My talent needs to get here in a hurry," Seyanna added.

With more energy, Jayco said, "Let's get moving while I still can."

As they progressed, the darkness began to recede. It was as if they'd passed the heart of the mountain. They continued walking for another five minutes.

Latisha stopped suddenly. "Oh, crap."

"What is it?" Jet asked, his voice uneasy.

"There's another large cavern up ahead, like the first one. It's much brighter."

"Please tell me there's not another monster to fight. I can't take much more of this," Seyanna said.

"The cavern is full of water," Latisha said. "I think there's an island in the middle. Those nasty critters are swimming in the water. There are at least six of them."

"Not good news," Jet said.

Stepping from the corridor, Jet felt a sense of wonder despite the chill in the air. Pure beauty, like nothing he'd ever imagined, lined the walls. It was as if every color he knew and some that he didn't were splashed symmetrically on the walls. It reminded Jet of the nighttime sky in Silverton. It was a masterpiece.

"I'm in heaven," Mckenzey said. "This is astonishing."

"It smells hideous in here," Jayco said, but his face changed as he glanced at the ceiling.

"It's mesmerizing," Latisha gushed.

Jet stargazed for several long seconds, trying to imagine the beginning of the heavens and the earth. A moment later, a slight sense of panic brushed up against his consciousness. He tore his eyes away from the ceiling with considerable effort and stared at the ground. Somehow, he'd traveled a dozen feet and stood on the precipice of a ten-foot fall into the water. Iris was tugging at his pant leg, tearing it, but he hadn't felt anything.

Jet screamed, "Agni!" and followed this by saying, "Ea." Two spells that instantly fell into his mind. They were from his tome, but he wasn't exactly sure what they did. The bright light that illuminated the cavern darkness was dazzling, but the confusion of his friends was just as startling.

"I'm blind," Jayco screamed. "Where are we?"

Similar screams ricocheted around the cavern.

Over the entire commotion, Jet bellowed, "Stop moving and stop talking!"

Silence emerged, but the brightness of the spell continued.

Jet, also blind, said, in precise words, "Take two steps backward, and I mean backward."

Both spells began to drain his energy slowly, and he released the second spell. It would take a few seconds for the sense of confusion to disappear. He didn't yet understand the relationship between the Elemental power and the decrease in his energy, but it was noticeable.

He added, "Stare at the ground or close your eyes. When I release the brightness spell, don't look up. Got it?"

Mckenzey asked, "What's going on?"

"I'll explain in a second." Then he spoke. "Ea," and his vision returned to normal.

"What the crap was that?" Jayco asked.

Jet reacted quickly. All but Latisha had followed his commands. She stared up at the ceiling, mesmerized. Jet lunged and caught her arm just as she walked directly off the cliff. She continued staring at the ceiling as she dangled above the water. Iris clamped down on his hood. Anchoring his feet, he soon pulled Latisha to safety.

"How can we help?" Grantham asked.

Breathing hard, he said, "Don't look down. I'll be there in a second." He pulled Latisha, against her will, to her feet and back several steps until they met up with the others.

Seyanna asked, her eyes closed shut, "What's going on?"

Touching Seyanna's shoulder, Jet said, "The ceiling is beautiful but also deadly. We just about walked over the cliff into the water." To Grantham, he said, "Hold onto Latisha's shoulders. Don't let go."

Grantham asked, "What's up with her?"

"I believe she's in a trance caused by this cavern. I'll blindfold her and get a rope, and we'll attach each of us like they do in rock climbing."

It took ten minutes to get Latisha settled and a rope fastened to each of their waists. Jet went first, followed by Mckenzey, Seyanna, Grantham, Latisha, and Jayco.

"Where to now?" Seyanna asked.

Jet willed his vision to magnify. It did. He searched the entire room but avoided the ceiling. "On the far wall to our right, where the rocks meet, there's a staircase built into the back wall. That's our exit."

"How will we make it all the way back there?"

"A path to the right. We'll need to boulder jump a few times."

Jayco said, "If someone falls into the water, we're all going in, so be careful."

The next thirty minutes were spent in misery. It was difficult, and they progressed slowly. If you went too fast, you were pulling the person behind you. Iris led the group, choosing the best boulders. They reached the back wall and found the staircase heading upward. Jet unlatched himself from the group.

Mckenzey asked, "What are you doing?"

"Making sure no one goes over the edge. Everyone, keep looking at the ground."

Mckenzey nodded and started to climb. Jet placed his back toward the edge of the staircase while the group remained up against the wall. There wasn't a handle near this side, and his friends hugged the wall as they climbed.

Mckenzey reached the top and yelled down, "There's another corridor up here."

"Go inside."

Halfway up, Latisha changed course and practically sprinted toward the water. Jet slid down a few feet and blocked her way. She scratched and clawed and tried knocking him aside.

Grantham said, "Sorry about this, Latisha." Taking a water bottle, he smacked the back of her head. She went limp, and Grantham caught her before she hit the ground. Grunting, he said, "Don't anyone tell her that I did that."

It didn't take long to gather everyone in the upper corridor. The constant impulse to stare at the ceiling vanished the instant they stepped from the room.

Seyanna, bending over at the hips, said, "That was the best and worst experience I've ever had.

"Unbelievable," Grantham hissed, still carrying the unconscious Latisha.

A muffled scream pierced the darkness and echoed from the cavern behind them. Jet ran back to the opening and stared in shock. He could see several people on the same cliff's edge they'd been at. But this time, someone had fallen over the edge. The only thing Jet could see was a head above the water. From here, he had no idea who it was, but three of the critter creatures were swimming fast.

"What do you see?" Jayco asked.

"We're not alone. And whoever is behind us, one of them just fell into the water and is getting devoured."

"You're joking," Seyanna said.

"No, I'm not." Jet tore his eyes away from the tragedy. "We've got to keep going."

As they hurried away, a second scream erupted that was far deeper and filled with pain. It echoed around the entire cavern, sending chills through the group.

CHAPTER 41

Jet, feeling anxious, hurried forward. The corridor continued for another ten feet and abruptly opened into another room, but he couldn't get a good look into it from here. The light from his flashlight illuminated almost everything for only a few feet. A scraping sound caught his attention, and Jet jerked his headlamp toward the sound. It turned out to be nothing more than a breeze. He could barely control his emotions; none of them could. There were half sobs from his friends as they shuffled their feet. Iris walked purposefully next to him, steading him.

"Turn off your flashlight," Mckenzey said. "I think there's a light ahead."

There was a faint glow against the wall on their right. He hoped it was sunlight peeking through, but they were too far underground. He slowed as they came to a large doorway and gazed around thunderstruck.

"I might need to take a break," Grantham said, still carrying the unconscious Latisha.

Jayco said, "That's probably Shane and his friends. If we stop, they'll catch up."

"Fine," Grantham said, clearly straining, as he stepped next to Jet. His mouth opened in surprise, and he dropped Latisha, who landed hard but remained unconscious.

The room was the same size as his classroom in the science building, but it was sparkling, bright, and dynamic. Iris jumped into the room without a second thought, and this was good enough for Jet. He followed.

Mckenzey gushed, "Come check out all these crystals."

"How's this possible?" Seyanna asked as she stepped into the room.

There was a wealth of large and small crystals going in every direction. It reminded Jet of a geode broken in half. Some hung from the ceiling, and others darted upwards from the floor. Most of the crystals were long, smooth, and varied in colors, thickness, and clarity. Some spanned the entire length of the room. Each was positioned at a sporadic angle. This room was equally as beautiful as the cavern they'd just left, yet entirely different.

After a few steps, Jet felt a unique sense of peace and accomplishment. It was a feeling that he wanted to last forever.

Grantham bent down and picked up Latisha again and carried her forward.

The room's broadest crystal had a diameter as thick as Jayco's waist, and it was at least his same height. The skinniest crystal, not much wider than a pencil, was the most impressive because it looked breakable. After circling the room several times, Jet noticed a cluster of eight crystals near the center of the room. These were of different heights and colors, but they sprung up from the floor and pointed at the ceiling.

"I think this is where we need to be," he shouted.

"Thank goodness," Mckenzey said. "This room feels incredible. I don't want to ever leave."

His friends gathered around him, including Grantham. A small amount of water condensed on the ceiling and sprinkled directly into the center of the room, inside the eight crystals. He slid closer to get a better look. The center was a four-foot circular area void of crystals or anything but the floor. There was a slightly damp area on the stone ground. He heard a dripping sound somewhere out of sight below them as he bent lower.

Latisha, still held by Grantham, spoke for the first time, "Hey. Did you know that the crystal you're standing next to is the same color of crystal we got from that creature?"

Grantham let out a gasp, and the entire group turned and stared at Latisha as Grantham set her down. She gripped his arm unsteadily.

"I have a serious headache," Latisha said as she touched the top of her head. "What happened? Why was Grantham holding me? And why do I have two lumps on my head?"

Jayco asked, "What's the last thing you remember?"

"Mckenzey healing you?"

Seyanna asked, "Any memory of anything after that moment?"

"Nothing. Why? What happened?"

Seyanna began explaining as Mckenzey pulled out the crystal from Jet's backpack. Seyanna finished by saying, "You hit your head on the rock coming out of the last corridor. Grantham carried you all this way."

"I'm glad I didn't have to go through that trance." She hugged Grantham. "Thanks, babe, for carrying me the entire way."

"My pleasure," Grantham replied. "I did hurt my back a little."

Latisha playfully slapped his arm.

Mckenzey said, "There's a hole at the base of this crystal."

"It's a good thing I woke up when I did," Latisha added.

Jet, passing the crystal to Mckenzey, said, "Let's see if it fits."

She took it and placed it correctly into the crystal with ease. The ground below them began to rumble like a gear, and all eight crystals began migrating outward as the center floor moved, revealing an opening.

"I think there's another room below us," Grantham exclaimed.

"This is getting crazier and crazier," Jayco said.

Seyanna asked, "How are we going to get down there?"

Grantham said, "Tie a rope to one of these crystals, and game on."

"Is it safe?" Mckenzey asked.

"Let's go find out," Grantham added. "Before whoever is behind us catches up."

A cord was soon tied, and the other end dropped into the new room. Jet tossed in his headlamp, illuminating a portion of the space below. He recognized it immediately. "This is the cave I was telling you guys about. The vision I had after touching the meteorite. This room must be why we're here."

Jet descended first, and it didn't take long for everyone else to clamber into the hidden room. The size of this space, the color of the walls, and even the unnatural dial on the far wall were identical.

The differences, however, were far more critical. On a wall near the dial were deep scratch marks from the claw of a gigantic animal. An enormous chunk of one of the standing walls had crumbled to the floor. But by far, the most significant difference was the shelf carved into the back wall, holding treasures beyond belief.

"You failed to mention this loot," Grantham said, stunned. "Were you holding out on us?"

"Fat chance. First time laying my eyes on all of this."

Latisha asked, "Is this all for us?"

"Why not?" Jayco smiled widely. "We got here first. We've earned it."

Seyanna pointed out, "Check out how the cache is situated. All the items on the left side are golden while those on the right side are black."

Jayco said, "What does it matter?"

"Not sure. Just an observation."

Mckenzey said, "In the middle, there is a box with two stone cats on the lid. It divides the golden items from the black. There are three golden pyramids, just like Iris, and three black pyramids. There's also a spot missing for a pyramid of each color. I'd bet that Iris came from this room and that black wolf we ran into coming here did too."

Jayco strolled forward and attempted to pick up a majestic black curved sword. He ran smack into an unseen barrier that stopped him cold. As he stepped away, he wiped his mouth, and there was a small amount of blood. He said bitterly, "Someone else try."

Grantham moved forward carefully and found an unseen barrier. "What does it mean?"

Seyanna hesitantly reached for one of the golden pyramids. Her hands passed quickly through, and she lifted the item and retreated.

Mckenzey asked, "We can touch the golden items, but not the black ones?"

Jet said immediately, "The Path of the Phoenix and the Rivalry."

"What do you mean?" Grantham asked.

"The fable talked about two sides battling it out for the possessions of the kings. I think that we can access the golden items, but the other ones are off-limits."

"We can't let whoever is behind us into this room," Latisha said desperately.

"I'm not sure we have a choice," Seyanna pointed out.

"What next?" Mckenzey asked.

"Let's get our items and find a way out of here," Jet said. "The longer we're here, the more we're at risk."

Several items glittered gold, including a half dozen staffs and shields, vases of jewels and another with dried corn. There was a golden chalice of black powder and several weapons. Jet stepped forward and tried to pick up two large bracelets. They were too heavy for him to carry, and he received a slight shock upon contact with them.

"I think those are mine," a voice said from behind Jet, and Jayco stepped forward. "I can feel it, just like Mckenzey did."

Grantham teased, "If you think you're strong enough, big boy."

"Plenty strong." Jayco flexed as he passed by. "I'm feeling better by the second."

The two bracelets glowed when Jayco touched them and continued glowing bright red until he placed them on his wrists.

"They feel uncomfortable and loose," Jayco said, confused. "Maybe I was wrong."

Seyanna said, "Push them farther up your arms."

Jayco lifted them to his bicep, where they slid into place. "Ah, that's much better."

"You look dashing," Grantham chided.

"Shut it," Jayco huffed. He punched Grantham, who was knocked ten feet across the room. He would've slammed into the wall except for Grantham's cat-like reflexes and his ability to climb walls. Grantham scurried up the wall onto the ceiling.

"I barely laid a finger on you," Jayco snickered.

Grantham lazily fell to his feet, landing noiselessly. "That didn't feel like a touch. My entire arm is numb."

"Strength enhancers. Even better."

Jet and the others quickly searched the remaining objects, trying to find anything that reacted to their touch.

Seyanna found an ornate and beautiful golden bow and two dozen arrows while Latisha touched the chalice of black powder. Grantham picked up the long sheath with a half-circle of metal at one end. The handle was made of smooth dark brown wood. It was skinnier and longer than the other staffs, made from a golden-colored wood.

Seyanna began stroking her bowstring absentmindedly and said, "It feels like I've had this my entire life. So cool. The only thing left is to learn my ability."

Mckenzey touched several items without success until she came across five throwing knives. "Ohhh. These are beautiful."

Jet turned his attention to a shield or two, but nothing happened. This was followed by a javelin, a pyramid, and all the staffs. He was unsure if anything had been meant for him. Maybe his magic was enough. He spotted three small golden orbs against the back of the stone shelf, each just smaller than a golf ball. Reaching out, he touched them, and the now-familiar bright red glow accompanied them. They rolled into his hands on their own, and he felt an immediate connection with them. Tossing them into the air, he caught them as easily as breathing. Slinging one across the room, it returned to him automatically. He stowed them in an inner pocket of his cloak.

"Let's round up the rest of the items," Jet said. "And find a way out of here."

Mckenzey, Jet, and Grantham each stored one pyramid in their backpacks. Jet passed out staffs while Jayco took all five shields in his left hand alone.

"How are you doing that?" Seyanna asked.

"Awesome, huh?"

"Those shields weigh a good thirty pounds each. You're acting as if they weigh nothing."

"They're pretty light," Jayco admitted.

Grantham moved closer. "Give me one." Grantham practically dropped the shield the moment he touched it. "That thing weighs a ton."

Jayco chuckled. "Then, you must weigh nothing. No wonder you flew across the room like a bag of Cheetos."

CHAPTER 42

As Jet's friends finished packing the remaining golden items, he inspected the inventory of the black pieces. He could not know each of their purposes, but he wanted to. There was a black sword, another with a curved blade, three pyramids, several masks, and several Y-shaped items that reminded him of slingshots. He thought he noticed armor-like shoulder pads. A few more particular items were a half dozen small plates or saucers, a hammer with a foot-long handle, a whip with a handle, and an umbrella-looking item. He started snapping a few pictures with his phone.

Latisha's voice cut through his concentration. "We've got bones here."

Jet shifted and found Jayco and Grantham sprinting to an area of the room he'd assumed empty. He quickly followed, and as he got closer, he discovered a small hidden alcove. He found Latisha standing over an old cloth sack, torn and shredded. As he shuffled closer, a pile of bones, yellowish-gray in color, came into view. It was as if the bones had been hidden on purpose.

Latisha said, "When I pulled it back, this skeleton was underneath."

Jayco added, "I can only see one skull; are we assuming this is one person?"

"No idea," Jet stammered.

Mckenzey bent down and, using a stick, pushed around the bones. She asked, "How did someone get in here?"

"Who cares?" Seyanna thundered. "The real question is *how* did they die?"

Grantham slapped his hands together as if realizing something. He added, "Didn't you say that a beast was on the wall? Could that thing have killed this person?"

Jet shivered and said, "I'm not sure."

Latisha groaned. "Not that again. I'm done. I want out of here." She fled from the alcove, and the others followed.

They hadn't taken two steps when Seyanna whispered, "Someone's coming. I can hear them."

Grantham tilted his head, a look of confusion spreading across his face. "I can't."

Jet listened intently but heard nothing. He marched directly to the dial, trying to find a way out. If he was correct, it was their only option. He stayed close to the side wall, and it was exactly as he'd seen it in his vision. There were symbols on the dial itself and animals carved into the rock wall. When his hand touched the dial, he was unsurprised to find it ice cold. He tried twisting it, but the dial refused to move.

Jayco ran forward, yelling, "There's a door here! Everybody, come and help pry this thing open."

Footsteps scuffled against the floor from the room above. Jet howled, "Lights out."

Flashlights clicked off as darkness filled the room. Muffled voices echoed. Jet searched for Iris, and to his surprise, she sat on the stone shelf, directly on top of the box with two cats. He silently ran over to her and noticed that she was perched on a stone lid, as if telling him he'd forgotten something. He pushed hard, and the cover scraped against the rock, but it moved.

"Shhh," Latisha muttered.

As the cover moved, a bright light illuminated the entire room.

"What was that?" a voice demanded from above.

Jet plunged his hand into the box and around a cold, smooth item. Pulling it free, he shoved the diamond-like fragment under his cloak. Every item they touched was designed to help them, but he was confident that this was the ultimate prize.

"I saw something," a voice said.

"Was it your flashlight on the wall?" Shane's voice smirked.

Jet sprinted back to the dial with Iris a step behind.

A voice said, "Over here. There's a hole in the opening of the floor."

Boom!

The sound reverberated around the entire room, and a layer of dust from the ceiling fell into the air. Jayco had slammed both fists into the door in what appeared to be a last-ditch effort to escape. The door didn't move an inch.

"Feel better?" Jet asked as he came to a stop near the dial.

"I do. Thanks for asking."

Jet concentrated on the dial, hoping it hadn't moved because they hadn't seized the most critical piece. The dial remained stubbornly fixed.

"Who's down there?" someone demanded.

Another voice added, "Check this out. Someone slid down using this rope."

Shane's smooth voice said, "Shine a light, and let's meet our competition."

But before they were revealed, an unseen force more potent than anything Jet had ever felt in his life seized control of his movements. The force overran his defenses, and he became frozen in place. The familiar fierceness berated his mind as if trying to find an entry. A shattering detonated from the only corner in the cave he hadn't explored, and an enormous shadow dislodged itself from the wall. Walking on its two hind legs, a gigantic wolf stepped into view.

The creature bellowed, "Breathe in. Breathe out. Die."

This time, the attack was wasteful, and Jet felt the creature's loathing of him. It declared, "I have no idea how you escaped my compulsion or how you are standing here today, but I was so close to killing you four years ago and just as close a few months ago. Now you're the Mikado, the Rivalry has started, and I am forbidden to harm you."

The creature was more than nine feet tall and akin to the Egyptian God Anubis. But instead of a dog's head, it was that of a wolf. It had a long snout, pointed ears, razor-sharp white teeth, a muscular body, and in each of this creature's front claws was a weapon. In the right was a four-foot sword that the creature swung back and forth menacingly. Its left claw held a leather whip where the tip portion was coiled on the floor. The creature was protected by mystical black armor, including a breastplate, arm sleeves, and leg guards extending from ankle to knee, covering the kneecap and up to the groin. It was far more impressive and terrifying in real life.

The wolf half crouched, arched his head, and howled so deeply that Jet's teeth chattered in protest. The wolf was balanced, muscular, and bred to kill everything it came across. It began flexing its forearms and twisting its back unnaturally. Iris's golden hair stood on end, but she cowered behind Jet.

The wolf's deep carnal voice boomed, with words clear, deliberate, and musical. "And so it begins. This isn't history repeating itself. It is the transcendence of the anointed on the path to domination. Who will be the last one standing, I ask?"

The wolf strode forward to the center of the room, just feet from where the hole in the ceiling was. A flashlight still illuminated the area, but Jet couldn't see Shane or anyone else.

The wolf raised its hands and spoke passionately. "The day Silverton was destroyed, the Rivalry began. Upon stepping into this mountain, you followed the Path of the Phoenix to me. I am no friend to the Mikado, but today I act as a sentinel, giving you information and will allow you to escape."

The wolf raised its sword and shouted, "The Mikado and his allies have done all the work, receiving all the spoils." Turning his attention to Jet, the wolf continued, "Only one side will prevail, and either Arisol will be released or killed. Lucretius the Avad was an insignificant pet of Arisol," he said mockingly. "His defeat was because he misjudged you. It won't matter, though; you will not be strong enough in the end. You had the chance to leave before—you declined. One day, I hope we will meet again on the battlefield. Nothing will stop me from tearing you apart."

The wolf shifted purposefully, glaring up at the opening in the ceiling. The condescension was thick in his voice when he spoke. "You've failed and are outmatched. Your sacred book was intended to give you the upper hand, allowing you to arrive first. You should've been better prepared. Maybe my master's trust in you was misplaced. They have the tablet piece. Find a way to make sure that you get it back."

The wolf growled its displeasure. Blue fog began billowing in from the enclosure the wolf had exited. The mist quickly covered the stone floor and inched up along the walls.

Jet was suddenly able to move again. The instant he was free, he worked the dial, and this time, it proceeded without resistance. He mindlessly twisted as he'd seen in his vision. The single line was up first. The circle matched only with the falcon and the snake while the diamond attached to the lion and square with each animal. The triangle was paired with the snake, and the circle ended on the feline. A loud click reverberated.

"It's open," Jet said. The fog almost completely covered the room, and even the wolf was hidden.

The creature continued speaking. "The Rivalry dates to even before the kings. This battle has been foretold."

Shane bellowed, "If we can move, so can they. Get down there. Don't let them escape, or you will pay the consequences."

As his friends ran from the cave, Jet glanced back at the creature. It was less than six inches from him, having moved silently. It hissed, "I hope your death isn't too disappointing."

Jet bolted from the cavern. Ahead of them was another passage, but it was clear this one led directly out of the mountain. It twisted and turned for more than a hundred feet. As they exited the mountain, the nighttime air was fresh and salty. The rain had stopped, but the glow from Silverton hitting the clouds caused an eerie view of their surroundings.

"Where are we?" Latisha asked.

Jayco shouted, "We've gone through the mountain."

Grantham added, "The cars are to our right, about three point three miles away. There are three or four paths we can follow."

Latisha asked, "How do you know that?"

"Not sure, just do." Grantham took off, and the rest followed.

Seyanna yelled, "You have two gifts before I have one. Not fair."

Jet whispered, "Seyanna, your gift is extraordinary hearing."

"That's totally lame," she scoffed.

Jayco passed Jet and was carrying most of the supplies. He hissed, "Like seeing into water isn't."

"Let's go," Jet encouraged, half smiling. "Iris, follow."

Grantham tore down the mountain in the direction of a cluster of trees a quarter mile away. Jayco and Jet, both once injured, felt nothing of their pain from before. Jet was moving better than he had in months.

Mckenzey asked, "What are you smiling about?"

"I think that when we were frozen, we were healed."

"I feel great," Jayco admitted. "I could run forever."

When they reached cover, they quickly assessed their situation. The remaining staffs were passed out. Jayco kept four shields while Grantham and Jet tied one to their backpacks.

Grantham refused his staff and said, "My weapon is much more effective."

Jet spent the next few moments planning their escape.

Mckenzey said, "What kind of weapons will they have?"

"Not sure. I didn't get a clean look at everything. A sword, some knives, some weird Y-shaped items, and masks. They'll also have their animals. Let's stay together if we can. But if we get divided, let's meet back at the SUV."

Latisha said, "Can we release our golden animals?

The three golden pyramids were placed on the ground. Nothing happened. Iris gazed up expectantly at Jet. He had no idea what to do. He finally commanded Iris by saying, "Release your friends."

Jet could've sworn he watched Iris smile and nod. She gently touched her nose to each pyramid. Suddenly, a life-sized lion, a beautiful barn owl, and a gigantic grizzly bear materialized before them, all perfectly golden.

"Oh, we've got this," Grantham said. "Except for the owl, we have the top predators."

Jet pointed northward. "There's another set of trees close to this elevation. Don't go much higher or lower. Let's move."

Along with four animals, all six of them moved swiftly across the open field that sloped slightly. Jet willed his vision to change, and it did. He could see the cave opening behind them. Five figures exited the passage when they were thirty feet from the trees. A short time later, one of them pointed in their direction.

"We've been seen," Jet said. "Keep going."

The five individuals were dressed entirely in black. Their heads were now covered in masks with two eye slits. If it were still Halloween, they could've passed for ninjas. One of them began shouting orders, and weapons and other items were passed out. Even from here, Jet watched in astonishment as the black wolf slunk into view. Like Iris had done, it touched each of the black pyramids. Before he could see what animals had taken shape, they reached the trees and went crashing in.

A wolf howled from behind them.

Grantham shouted, "Was that the black wolf or that freaky creature that tried to enter my mind?"

An elk bugled from farther up the mountain. This was followed by some hissing and barking from below them.

"I'm guessing the black wolf," Seyanna said.

Jayco asked, "What's happening?"

"Be ready for an attack by any animal, black or normal." Latisha added, "Remember those other wolves. I think the wolf is trying to recruit any other animal around."

"Onward," Jet said, and they weaved around tree trunks and jumped over small rocks. This grouping of trees was large and hid them for several minutes.

"We should split up, spread out, and make ourselves tougher targets," Jayco suggested.

"Not yet," Jet said hesitantly. "No idea what they can do. Splitting up may make it easier for them."

Ten minutes later, they exited the clump of trees. It was far darker on this mountainside, no longer exposed to Silverton's radiant lights.

Latisha pointed downward and said, "Look."

Five wolves were scampering over rocks to their left and down the hill, angling at them. Farther back, Jet watched as six elk, two bears, and several coyotes joined the chase.

"Keep running," Jet yelled. "They're going to try to slow us down." He pulled out his orbs and threw them at the closest animal. It tore through the neck of one elk and returned to his hand. Jet caught it and continued running. "Iris and friends, protect us!"

CHAPTER 43

Things became intense and complicated over the next several minutes. The number of animals chasing them doubled, a small explosion took place behind them, and bright lights flashed in all directions. Iris hissed as if communicating, and the other three golden animals broke off and charged at the oncoming attacks from above. This left Jet and the others to concentrate on the wolves and any other dangers that might spring up. It didn't take long to disrupt the wolves, killing two. The new weapons gave his friends new skills and fighting capabilities.

After the remaining wolves disappeared into the undergrowth, Jayco grabbed Jet's shoulder and said, "Bro, it's time to split up. Tracking all of us will be easier if we're together."

Jet shrugged and glanced at Mckenzey. She nodded back.

Pointing to a clearing below them, Grantham said, "Let's head this way." He shuffled down the slope of the hill. As Grantham passed Jayco, he was punched in the arm and was launched into a tree ten feet away.

Jayco howled, "This is going to be so much fun."

The four golden animals reappeared, and Jet commanded, "Iris follow us. The rest can follow Jayco and the others."

Mckenzey pulled Jet's arm. Before he had taken a step, he noticed Seyanna glancing back and forth between Jet and Jayco, as if unsure which she should follow.

"Stay safe," said Jet. "Follow the others and we'll see you at the SUV." Her smile was tight as Jet let Mckenzey pull him slightly up the hill; Iris was a step behind.

Jayco sprinted after Grantham, followed by Latisha, Seyanna, and the other three golden animals. Several seconds later, Seyanna screamed unexpectantly with satisfaction.

Jet and Mckenzey stopped and looked back in surprise. Mckenzey said, "Take a look at Seyanna. Look how fast she's going!"

Jet was awestruck. Seyanna ran faster than anyone he'd ever seen. She was like a blur. Jet added, "That's a terrific second talent."

As they started working their way up the hill, Mckenzey asked, "Are you going to get a talent?"

"I think I already have mine."

"What do you mean?"

"My abilities saved my life back in Silverton and while rock climbing."

"That makes total sense."

They traveled up the mountain for another fifty yards until they reached a rocky cliffside. Iris had no problems keeping up with them. They moved northward through scrub oak. Several minutes later, they crouched to search for the others and catch their breaths. It was hard to tell if they were being followed. Jet's gut tightened as he saw the large black wolf, a giant elk, and two coyotes catch up with their friends and encircle them.

Seyanna was outside the circle, unsure what to do. The black wolf howled orders to the other animals.

"What should we do?" Mckenzey asked. "They're in trouble."

Before moving an inch, two golden creatures bull-rushed into the clearing and instantly knocked aside the elk. The two coyotes dove at Jayco, who swung one arm holding two staffs, and connected like a bat, crushing both animals twenty feet away. Grantham kept the black wolf at bay with his long pole, and Latisha threw rocks at lightning speed. Grantham slashed the air expertly as if he'd trained with his weapon his entire life.

The bear and lion turned their attention to the black wolf, allowing their friends to retreat and disappear.

"I guess they can handle themselves," Jet muttered, and relief enveloped him.

Jet's arm gripped Mckenzey's shoulder, and he helped her forward. Through gritted teeth, he said, "We've got our own problems."

He'd spotted three black animals thirty feet back; a jackal, a snake, and a falcon coming on fast. A golden blur entered the fray, soaring into view from above the rock cliff. The barn owl maneuvered into a controlled dive and impacted with the black falcon just above the tallest tree. A fowl fight ensued.

Iris remained a step behind as Jet and Mckenzey sprinted forward. The rock cliff ended, and they tore into an open field that tilted downward. The jackal and even the snake were gaining on them. They reached the next set of trees and dashed through them, branches scraping their faces. Once clear, they vaulted over a small ravine and landed smoothly.

Jayco came into view from his side vision, swinging his staff at the black wolf who had caught back up. Simultaneously, Jet watched as five dark figures entered a clearing overlooking the valley directly behind them. They were much closer than Jet thought possible, gaining tremendous ground. The jackal bellowed loudly, just twenty steps behind. One of the figures pointed in their direction, and two of the figures took off. The other three ran after Jayco and the others.

"Keep running," Jet yelled. "We're being hunted."

Up ahead, on their left, was a wide gully, like the one they'd entered earlier, just farther up the hill.

Jet yelled, "Let's cross!"

They ran adjacent to the gully until they found a fallen tree spanning across the entire width. They crossed quickly, with Iris slipping ahead of them. Jet yelled, "Ignisnaeth," and a flame burst onto the fallen tree. Despite the rain, it still burned with ease.

The jackal hissed from just feet behind them. It would need to find a different crossing. Overhead, the barn owl flew by fast, closely followed by the black falcon.

Mckenzey was ten feet ahead, but she stopped immediately.

Jet caught up, asking, "What's wrong?"

"Look." She pointed down the hill.

A few hundred feet away, a figure emerged out of a group of trees, taking something from their pocket; a Y-shaped weapon. As they twirled it, sort of like a lasso, the upper two branches moved apart, and a rope-like projection was shot forward. It was incredible to watch.

The blue rope flew end over end at Seyanna. She must've seen it because, at the last moment, she sprinted out of its way, and it wrapped itself around a tree just inches from where she'd been. A second figure shot his lasso rope in Latisha's direction, but she didn't react soon enough. The line hit her squarely in the chest, slamming her against the closest tree, pinning her. She struggled to free herself but couldn't.

Latisha began screaming. The rope appeared to be burning her.

Seyanna was distracted, and the black wolf used this moment to attack. He leaped at her, a claw slashing at her back, and she was knocked forward. Grantham soared from a twenty-foot tree with his weapon slicing down; the black wolf was forced to retreat. Seyanna sprinted to Latisha, and using an edge from one of her arrows, she cut Latisha free. The instant the rope broke, the blue tinge to it vanished. Jayco tossed a car-sized boulder down the hill, scattering the two figures and several animals. Their friends, now injured, slipped out of view once again.

Mckenzey said, "I thought they were in some serious trouble."

"Me too," Jet agreed.

They ran for the next five minutes on a heavily used trail. After the rain, it was more mud than dirt. They each slid and fell twice. It wasn't long before they scampered on the terrain next to the path. Cresting a hill, the decline dropped fast, and they were forced to bend down to avoid falling face first.

A blue rope sailed just over their heads, missing them by inches. It crashed into a tree a dozen feet away. Mckenzey lost her balance, tilted sideways, and slipped, landing hard on her hip and tumbling down the remaining few feet. Jet reached the bottom of the incline and rushed to help her up.

Trees snapped to their right as if something was running parallel to them. Before Jet had time to pull his orbs from his pocket, a bighorn sheep with massive horns burst through the underbrush.

Mckenzey recoiled slightly and added, "Its eyes are glowing blue."

Jet barely had time to push Mckenzey away from him. The sheep missed by inches, running between them. The animal slammed its front two feet into the ground, and it turned one hundred and eighty degrees to face them.

"That sheep is not acting normal," Mckenzey insisted.

"Yeah. It's acting like something else is controlling it."

Iris sprang into the path of the animal. She was a third of the size of the sheep but kept it from attacking.

"It's trying to prevent us from going forward," Mckenzey noted.

"Iris, attack," Jet screamed, and she dove forward, her claw landing partially on the sheep's left shoulder. The sheep countered by flicking its head and knocking Iris several feet away, but she landed gracefully on her feet. Jet and Mckenzey didn't wait to see what happened next. Finding the path, they weaved back and forth until they had covered some serious ground and hid behind some trees to catch their breaths.

"Don't lose their scent," shouted a voice in the darkness, only a dozen feet from where Jet and Mckenzey were hiding. Jet swore silently, motioning Mckenzey, and they crawled behind a large rock just as two figures swept past some trees to their right.

"We can't lose them," one of the figures said.

"Except for that girl, we're faster than they are. I'm confident they came this way."

The two figures were less than five feet away. Jet felt around his feet, found a baseball-sized rock, and launched it away from them. It bounced ten feet away and crashed down the hill.

"Go! Go! Go!" shouted one of the figures, and they both left the pathway, bursting through the forest.

"The oldest trick in the book," Jet whispered. "Stupid idiots."

At that moment, a flash of lightning illuminated the night. A blue fog was spilling from the mountain and settling in the valley. But the bolt had illuminated something else; a creature was coiled into an attacking position, just ten feet away. Iris was too far away to help.

Jet's mind focused, and he yelled, "Aer," just as the snake struck.

Despite his power, the snake's body seemed to withstand the air. The spell only slowed its approach like it was caught up in a gust of wind. Mckenzey spun, pulled a throwing knife, and threw it for the first time in her life. The knife was superbly on target. The eyes of the snake focused on the golden blade. The head moved just slightly, and in that instant, the snake was propelled backward as if Jet's spell finally had a kick to it. Mckenzey's knife whirled back and stuck into the ground at her feet a moment later.

Shrugging, she asked, "Did I hit it?"

"I don't think so."

Pulling the knife from the ground, she pointed to the tip. A small black fluid marked the end.

"I stand corrected."

Iris bolted back into view, and the three of them took off, moving slightly upward along a different path, away from the direction the two figures had gone. This time, stealth was ideal.

The trees around the parking lot came into view for the first time. But before a jolt of excitement had time to materialize, Jet's energy took a sizable dip, and he slowed his run to a walk. Mckenzey must've felt a similar change. Soon they were each hunched over, breathing hard.

"What just happened?" she asked.

Jet removed the ring from his hand and felt a sizable drop in his energy. "The ring is still working. I'm not sure what to think." He quickly replaced the ring, and some of his energy returned. He searched through his backpack and found the last of his mud water.

Mckenzey also pulled out a bottle, and they drank greedily. Jet fished out some beef jerky and granola and inhaled his food.

"Should we find the others?" Mckenzey asked as she scanned the area.

"No, we—"

Something collided with his back, and he was flung forward abruptly. Every ounce of oxygen was forcefully expressed from his body. Ahead of them, the black jackal sprung out of a bush, colliding with Iris, knocking her to the side.

Jet sailed through the air, but time didn't slow. He could not stop his momentum as he realized a blue rope had wrapped around his chest. It was eerie watching a disaster approach yet unable to stop it. He landed hard, his face smashing into the ground.

One figure rushed at him, pulling a black hatchet from his belt. Mckenzey, still crouching, aimed and threw her knife. It embedded itself into the back shoulder of the figure, almost toppling them off their feet. The figure's momentum carried them into Jet's legs, and they tripped and fell to the ground, the hatchet sailing into the bushes.

Jet struggled to free himself from the cord around his arms and chest. He couldn't stand and rolled over a few times. He unleashed a kick to the head of his attacker. After a second and a third blow, the person slumped, unconscious.

Mckenzey rushed forward and tugged at the rope.

Jet bellowed, "Nice shot. That was a perfect aim."

Before she could answer, Mckenzey was flung several feet away as a second rope caught her around the waist. The cord had entangled one of her arms to her chest. She landed awkwardly on the ground, face down. She had very little room to free herself.

A second figure stepped out from behind a tree, only a dozen feet from Mckenzey. His triumphant laugh was frightening. He held a black scythe loosely in his right hand and strode forward as he put away the Y-shaped weapon.

Jet screamed, "Abzu!" A dozen ice crystals formed and launched themselves forward.

The figure reacted quickly, drawing something in the air. A barrier of some sort formed, and the crystals exploded as if running into an invisible wall. The figure came to a complete stop just a few feet from Mckenzey. He glared at Jet. "We prepared for you. You're not powerful enough for that to work on me."

Ten feet behind the figure, the jackal and Iris were in a full attack, with the jackal leaping onto Iris's back only to be flipped over. The figure he'd kicked was starting to stir on the opposite side of him.

"Hello, Jet Black. I'd know your voice anywhere, but I can't exactly see you, other than your figure. It's sort of weird. But in the end, it doesn't matter. I'm truly shocked that you're the one. To be honest, a little bit of a letdown. You know, the Mikado was supposed to be challenging." The voice was so familiar; Jet should know who this was. "I assume this is Mckenzey or Latisha. Last year, Shane was confident that the sorcerer was Jayco. You're not big enough to be him. Shane will ensure that none of your friends make it out of here alive."

Silently, Mckenzey rolled over and over until she came to rest against a tree.

"I know you," Jet said.

The figure continued talking. "Even Grantham was a more likely choice than you. We always thought that you were holding the second book for him, and that's why we broke into your dorm. We were stupid to dismiss you so quickly. Falling off the cliff after Shane used a rune to cut your rope convinced us that you were a nobody. You tricked us and wasted our time for months. If that was you in Switzerland, I'm not sure how you escaped?"

The recognition of the voice clicked in his mind. "You're Jake Hurley, friends with Vinny and Jocelyn. Not sure why Shane even picked you to come along for this adventure. You would've been my last choice."

"Good enough to knock you down."

Jet snickered. "We got here first, fought a huge creature, navigated the maze, and were the first to escape the mountain. It wouldn't have been hard to catch up with us. Please, don't give yourself too much credit."

Glancing at Mckenzey, Jake hissed, "It's not surprising that you surround yourself with those stronger than you. That's why I attacked her first. I've got nothing to worry about with you."

Ignoring this, Jet asked, "Why didn't my spell work on you?"

Jake grinned as he raised his hand into the air and drew a circle with a line to each side. Then he pushed. An unseen wave of pressure rammed Jet back several inches across the dirt. "We know enough about the Sorcerers to have safeguarded ourselves. You can't hurt me."

"What did you just do?" Jet asked.

"It's called a shield rune, a staple of Matter conjury. After I'm done with the two of you, I'll go help the others. Every treasure you've found will be ours."

Throughout their exchange, Mckenzey had been cutting frantically at her rope, but she needed more time. Jet was almost finished untangling his own. It was too late though.

Jake took a few steps forward and lifted his scythe to strike Mckenzey.

Jet tucked his knee and shifted his weight, allowing him to stand. This movement caused Jake to glance over his shoulder. Jet reacted without delay and screamed, "Pan!" A deep and wide crack appeared in the ground, forcing Jake to take a few steps back, dividing him from Mckenzey.

"You've accomplished noth—"

Jet pulled the last of his arm free. Seeing this, Jake bolted toward the fissure and vaulted into the air, intending to reach Mckenzey before Jet could. Jake lifted his weapon to strike. In an instant, Jet had his three orbs in his hand, and he hurled them forward. Jake's feet barely touched the dirt before the objects battered his body with such force that Jake was pitched sideways, landing a few feet past where Mckenzey lay. He shook for a few more moments, then stopped breathing.

By the time Jet reached her, she had cut away the cord trapping her. She was sobbing uncontrollably. Helping her to her feet, Jet wrapped an arm around her and walked her back to their supplies.

The jackal, realizing what had happened, swiped one last time at Iris. The attack was meaningless and Iris dodge it easily. The beast kicked a spray of dust and vanished into a clump of trees.

Jet held onto Mckenzey until she calmed down. Iris moved closer, standing guard. When Mckenzey was ready, he gave her some room and bent down to begin repacking everything, including both cords.

"Well, that sucked," Jet said.

Mckenzey, sucking in a deep breath, ran her hand repeatedly over her face to wipe away the tears. Her body shivered, but she nodded. Jet busied himself with the last few items. When she found her voice, she added, "Worst ever." Her golden-brown eyes sparkled as tears slid down her face. She walked over to him, and he stood.

She mouthed, "Thank you," but couldn't say anything more.

He hugged her quickly. "We need to keep moving. This isn't over. Are you ready?" Iris stalked into view and rubbed against Mckenzey's legs. This seemed to steady her. As they made to leave, Jet picked up a piece of wood and smacked the still-unconscious remaining figure on the back of the head. He tried pulling the scythe from the ground but could not grasp the handle.

As they began running, the first few steps were agonizingly painful. But soon enough, they each became more comfortable with their movement. Speed was again essential. They were still more than half a mile from the parking lot, but they could barely make out their vehicle. It appeared that they were entering the darkest part of the night.

A scream cut through the air from their left, but it was hard to understand precisely where it was coming from. A red glow soared into the air a few hundred feet away, followed by a plume of smoke. They were tempted to change course, but wisdom told them to keep moving. Over the next few minutes, they heard more screams and the breaking of several large tree branches.

Ten minutes later, they were again on flat ground. The trees were slightly less sparse, but the path was clearly marked, and it wound back and forth. A cacophony of sounds told them that they were being chased from behind them. Grunts, claws hitting the ground, heavy breathing, and the smashing of trees pointed to a large group of animals.

Despite the darkness of the night, Jet's vision allowed him to see what was stalking them. He urged, "Must. Go. Faster." Several steps later, he added, "A dozen animals ... closing in fast ... Get to the car!"

Mckenzey shook her head. "I'm not leaving you."

Jet pleaded, "Get the car started. Be ready for me." He added to the panther running next to him, "Iris, protect Mckenzey."

Mckenzey fumed as she tore ahead. He couldn't keep pace with her. His legs were starting to burn, and along with all his other items, he just didn't have the energy. He felt relief when Iris ran off with her.

The parking lot came into view between openings in the trees. The trail wasn't straight, and it veered back and forth. The jackal and snake had located the black wolf, and those three black animals were leading a group of other animals. Jet spotted a few moose, several elk, wolves, a coyote, more bighorn sheep, and several smaller creatures. He was dismayed to realize that the animals were gaining on him.

Ten steps later, though, something changed, and the animals left the main path, away from him, and headed on a direct route to the trailhead. Without a doubt, Jet would've gotten caught. It was like they had a different plan. He started glancing around for the next attack. He wasn't surprised as he rounded the next corner, and was forced to slow down as a masked figure stepped out in front of him.

CHAPTER 44

Jet stared, his hood still covering his head, captivated at the figure standing less than twenty feet away. The flawless bronze skin and handsome features were easy to observe, as was his charismatic smile. Only his hazel eyes voiced his seething anger. Shane Fallon wasn't going to let him pass without a fight. Jet hoped he still had a few options up his sleeve. If he turned to run to his right, farther north, this would force Shane to follow him. He would find a way to escape. Before taking a single step, Shane slammed a five-foot shaft with a black crystal on its top into the ground. The instant it collided with the dirt, an orange barrier, like a dome, sprang outward from the shaft, encompassing the surrounding area, including Jet.

"I knew this would come in handy," Shane said, his voice slightly muffled.

Equally remarkable as the bubble itself, the landscape outside the dome was shocking. Jet mumbled, "How in the—"

"Everything is frozen."

The animals who just moments ago had changed direction to follow Mckenzey were now caught in a snapshot as they collided with a grouping of trees and shrubs, the force of the stampede splintering the wood.

Behind Shane, only a dozen feet from the parking lot, Mckenzey was still on the path and she and Iris were also frozen. Up on a small rise to his left were two masked figures in the middle of picking themselves off the ground.

Jet faced Shane and a weak puff of wind cascaded away from him.

"Are you Black?" Shane asked. "Or could you be Ralph or Dexter? You're not big enough to be Jayco. It's doubtful that you're Grantham. Regardless, you're from Chadwick's. I can't understand why your face is hidden from me."

Jet remained silent.

Shane continued, "Just like back in Switzerland, you're protected, but I can still see you." After a pause, he said, "No matter, I'll find out who you are at last when I kill you. I sure hope it's Jet. That *would* be magical. You also carry the tablet piece; after all, that's why we are here."

"We know exactly who you are. No surprises there." Jet was shocked to find that his voice was different than usual. What made things more surprising was that just a few minutes ago, Jake Hurley had recognized his voice. He didn't even have a theory.

Shane had evidently been listening for him to speak. Anger swelled, and his face contorted as he took two steps forward, lifting both hands. Jet knew all too well that Shane was about to try to kill him. No longer was an innocent and misguided sixteen-year-old boy standing before him. Shane had seen and done things that Jet could only imagine. The intensity and determination on Shane's face made Jet take a step back.

"You're dead," Shane hissed.

Jet said, as calmly as possible, "Good luck with that. We've beaten the beasts in the mountain, got to the tablet piece first, and escaped your goons. I think we're good."

Shane's arms flexed as he said, "But you've never fought me. I know you go to Chadwick's. I've been becoming more powerful all year. I nearly killed Jet Black in the first week of school. While he was rock climbing, I broke apart his rope, and it was only luck that he survived. Now months later, I'm even more dominant."

Jet couldn't afford to lose focus. He leaned forward and threw his orbs as hard as possible at Shane, simultaneously yelling, "Ea," intending to blind Shane and search for an escape.

Shane lazily raised his right hand and drew three circles inside each other. He was far faster than Jake. The orbs crashed into an unseen barrier; the sound was akin to a car crashing full force into a wall. The orbs fell to the ground harmlessly.

"That was pointless," Shane said. "Though I could feel your weak spell, it just missed me. Let me take a moment to explain." Lifting his arms to elaborately demonstrate where they were, he added, "This is a magical realm. Only magic works here. My magic, however, will be far from weak. Inside this bubble is what they call a *Duelist Berth*, and magic has been reawakened."

Jet flicked his hands, and the three orbs slowly crawled back to his feet. Jet bent over and pocketed the items then placed his backpack on the ground.

Shane continued, "I let that happen. I apparently can't touch them anyway. Rules of the Rivalry. You heard the great Faunal."

"That's his name? Faunal? It's so unimpressive."

"You know nothing about him!" Shane shouted, barely controlling his anger. "And pray you never do. He was the captain of the armies of Arisol. I imagine you know who he is."

"How'd Faunal get trapped in Silverton?"

Shane explained, "When the travelers placed the tablet pieces around the world, they didn't understand that some creatures had been captured within the pieces. Faunal is forced by the bonds of his subjection to initiate the Rivalry. But his invisible shackles will soon be gone. He'll be a nice addition to my army."

"You have an army?"

Shane scoffed. "You've no idea what I'm capable of. We're similar. I'll grant you that. Magic chose you, but I'm so much further along than you are."

Jet noticed that Shane wasn't wearing a cloak. He did have a breastplate, and Jet felt the power emanating from it.

As if following his eyes, Shane said, "This armor is bathed in conjury. But this armor is more than just good looks. It'll block knives, swords, and basic Elemental spells." Shane pulled out two long swords from his back with a slight curve to each blade, very similar to a Katana. He swung them back and forth and, like Grantham, appeared that he had spent years training. "Speaking of swords, these are two of the best in the world. I hope you live long enough to appreciate all that I am."

"Bravo," Jet said. "You must be so proud."

"Your bravado is on full display, and it's pitiful."

"If this is a magic realm, those Katanas are nothing better than twigs. I have a question for you: When were you going to notice that crate in Switzerland is a fake?"

"No, it's not," Shane protested. "It never left my sight."

"Except when you were getting knocked over by an older man. We switched that little tracking device to our replica. You keep referring to someone from Chadwick's. I can tell you that I've never set foot on that campus. You're so narrow-minded."

For the first time, Shane appeared unsettled. "What do you mean? You're certainly not from Dillon Lake. That's becoming our stronghold. I don't think that the other three campuses have any real power. Chadwick's is the only option."

"Even at Dillon Lake, logic wasn't your best skill."

"Do I know you?"

"When you kill me."—Jet laughed—"you can find out." An edge crept into his voice when he said, "I stole that crate in Switzerland from right under your nose. What have you truly acquired? Nothing."

"You'll regret you ever taunted me." Shane's face tightened, and he returned his Katanas to the sheath on his back.

"So predictable," Jet said. Not wanting to overstep his luck but wanting more information, Jet decided to take one last chance. "Have you ever actually been to any of the other campuses? Do you have a clue about what's really going on?"

"We have spies everywhere."

"So pathetic. Just a pawn, no power."

Shane reacted violently, drawing a triangle, two sets of shapes resembling diamonds, and a line connecting each. Shane punched the air, and an enchanted rope with a ball on each end hurled in Jet's direction.

Jet yelled, "Aer!" and a small tornado shot forward, which did nothing to slow the rope. They bore down on him. He screamed, "Ventusnaeth," while pointing to the left wall and catapulted to the right, evading the rope. He crashed into the barrier with such force that he was flattened against it. He sagged to the ground. There was a stab of pain in his leg. He'd erroneously assumed that the barrier would be more accommodating to his weight, but it was more like an immovable wall.

Shane laughed. "Didn't I mention that this dome will allow my powers to be stronger than yours? Essentially, you have no chance to win. So, as lame as it sounds, pass over the tablet piece and live."

Jet quickly got to his feet and yelled, "Kali." He stepped to his left and said, "Pan." Next, he ran sideways, and after a few feet, he kneeled and said, "Abzu." He thought he some small firebolts, a rumbling with the ground, followed by ice—but without real focus, they were largely ineffective. Jet sprinted toward his backpack. Jet's entire body was gripped three steps from his bag as an invisible hand lifted him ten feet in the air and tossed him like trash. He went end over end, directly at Shane.

Shoving both hands ahead of him, he yelled, "Aer." A wind tornado slowed his dissent. His mind focused, and he realized that in this moment the spells Aer and Ventusnaeth did similar things. One was the parent spell of sorts, and one was the basic category. This should have clicked in his mind sooner, and he wondered if this meant something. As he hovered, he recognized that the tornado holding him aloft in the air was green in color. He felt a sense of warmth that told him this was the proper use of this spell at the right time. For the first time, he felt harmonized with the magic. He yelled, "Ventusnaeth," and was heaved away from Shane. The spell had no green aura and was far less effective this time.

He thought he might understand another rule of Elemental magic.

Shane said, more conversational than before, "That was impressive. Not the feeble fireball, land shaking, or even the ice crystals from before. They did almost nothing. But whatever you did right there was far more effective. I don't pretend to fathom your magic, just as you have little understanding of mine. Time slows for me when I'm creating a rune. It's the best feeling in the world."

"How do I get out of here?"

"I think that's obvious." Shane glanced at the staff. "Either you die, or you give me the tablet piece."

"Best of luck to you." This time, he whispered the word "Agni" at the exact moment he closed his eyes. An explosion of light brightened the space, but it didn't have quite the intensity he wanted.

Shane bellowed, "Feeble once again." Shane's hands moved rapidly, a smile spreading across his face. His hand movement appeared more complex this time, but Shane moved in a blur.

What Jet beheld was hard to grasp at first. Initially, six metal discs, no larger than a few inches, were thrust at him. As they approached, the discs grew in size. They were rotating saw blades. None of them were overwhelmingly fast, yet each closed at different speeds and patterns, but there would not be one area inside the bubble that was not affected. One switched back and forth, another up and down, and another directly at him.

Jet dove for his backpack, fumbled for the staff, and untied a shield. He threw his backpack on and sprinted to the edge. Using the staff, he swung at the bubble. Nothing happened except a sharp pain spiraled through his hand. He yelled, "Aer," again, but the tornado did not change to the right color this time, and the blades approaching were unaffected. He cried out more spells, but they were equally ineffective.

The first blade reached him; he swung at it as hard as he could using his staff. The force of the edge cut entirely through the golden staff as if it were nothing. Jet felt the vibrations in his hands. But it worked well enough to knock it off track sufficiently enough to miss him altogether. The blade sunk into the barrier behind him, as did the next two, with the same results. The remaining staff was now nothing more than broken golden wood. He tossed the pieces on the ground as the last three converged at once. This time, he used his shield to partially block the first. He missed the second, and it sliced into his left shoulder. He bellowed with agony and fell back onto the ground.

With one remaining, and barely enough strength to get out of the way, he screamed, "Aquaenaeth," and a green aura appeared. A water deluge sprang upward from the ground, connecting with the final disc. It became embedded in the facade above his head. Jet dropped the broken shield and stumbled to his feet. All the pieces of the two damaged items transformed into golden dust and blew away.

Shane howled excitedly, "That was a powerful rune. Wow. I'm even impressed with my talents. Broken and beaten, the grand reveal is just moments away. Friends and foes, we have"—Shane raised his hand—"my final rune."

Jet felt a prickling in his forearm, and his first thought was that he'd been cut there. But it was the dagger from earlier, bright as before. In one movement, he pulled it and sprinted forward.

Shane was caught off guard.

Jet yelled, "Vesta," having no idea what it did, relying on instinct. There was a faint green tinge to his vision as he saw the spell reach Shane. His reaction was immediate as he jerked rearward, clearly in pain, trying to keep his balance. Jet still had some ground to cover, and he did so quickly. He swung his dagger, but somehow it collided with Shane's Katana, and it was Jet's turn to try to keep his balance. Shane's Katana took the brunt of the blow, and it shattered into fine particles, spraying Shane, who was forced to turn away.

That was the opening he needed. Jet's next swing was at the jewel at the top of the shaft. It didn't shatter, but the entire handle was pulled from the ground, and it flew end over end to the far corner of the wall. Except, the bubble and orange glow vanished. Time and movement were restored as if they had never stopped. Jet darted down the path, pressing the dagger back into his arm and, like before, it imprinted on his forearm like a tattoo.

Shane's voice roared into the early morning. "KILL HIM! KILL THEM ALL!"

CHAPTER 45

Jet wasn't quite sure what kept him upright and running. He was thoroughly exhausted, and he wasn't sure his left shoulder was working. Inside the bubble, he hadn't felt any diminishment of his energy when using a spell, but now, he was barely conscious while standing. Skirting the last corner, he stepped into the gravel parking lot. He was momentarily relieved to see that the SUV was idling in the middle and facing the road. He still had too far to travel before he would feel safe. Mckenzey was just about to reach the open hatch of the SUV. Iris had arrived sooner than Mckenzey. She'd already touched two of the other animals, and they were transforming back into pyramids. The owl was the last one to change.

Behind him, the animals crashed through the underbrush and were closing the distance. Jayco and Seyanna stepped out from the SUV. As Mckenzey began tossing the pyramids in the back of the car, Jayco picked up some small boulders like they were marbles and tossed them at the animals like he was playing dodgeball. Seyanna pulled out her bow and expertly shot arrows that never injured a single animal but instead were used as a distraction. The arrows would return and embed themselves near her feet.

The black wolf refused to be stopped and avoided everything thrown or shot at it. Jet could feel the feral breath on his back. Jayco and Seyanna began screaming for Jet to run faster. There was no way he would make it, and he had no energy for a final spell. Jayco and Seyanna retreated inside the SUV, and it began driving slowly forward. This was not what he wanted, as it meant that he had farther to travel.

Jet tried removing the dagger from his arm, but it remained stubbornly indisposed. He felt his front pockets, and they were empty as well. Reaching back around to his backpack, he hoped to find one of the ropes he'd grabbed. Reaching inside he only found some arrowheads, eagle talons, and shark teeth. He didn't know what these did, but he thought this might be a good time to find out. Instead, three kernels of corn, tumbled out the back pocket.

He was shocked when a perfect replica of himself sprung up in the same spot the kernels hit the dirt. They were also doing the same thing he was doing. In the next instant, all three images converged and separated again. He found himself on the far left with three duplicates on his right. He was now less than ten feet from the SUV.

The black wolf hesitated, then lunged at the center image and missed entirely. The animal was not wholly deterred, swiping a paw at the image to its right but missing to connect with anything solid. Jet used both hands and shoved the wolf, using its momentum to get closer to the SUV. He dove inside. The instant his feet left contact with the ground, the single remaining duplicate began running in circles. Mckenzey grasped Jet, pulled him into the back area, and closed the hatch.

"Floor it," Seyanna screamed.

Through the window, Jet watched as the black wolf stalked over to the duplicate, but before anything happened, the last replica vanished.

"You're bleeding," Mckenzey said, pulling Jet from his trance. "How in the world did that happen? I didn't see you get attacked."

"I'll explain everything, but I need to stop the bleeding."

Mckenzey helped Jet remove his backpack, and together they crawled into the back seat.

Jet asked, "Where's Grantham?"

"He's unconscious," Latisha said, poking her head over the seat ahead. "We had to carry him back."

"You mean, I did," Jayco said from the driver's seat.

"Are you guys all right?" Latisha asked, hugging Mckenzey from over the seat.

"I think so," Mckenzey said, still trying to catch her breath. "We barely made it."

Seyanna said, "Everything fell apart. It was so chaotic. But, honestly, without these weapons and abilities, we wouldn't have escaped."

Mckenzey exclaimed, "Same." For the next several minutes, Mckenzey worked on stopping the bleeding from Jet's arm. She used some of her ability but didn't have the strength to finish. She sat back, breathing harder than when she had sprinted to the SUV.

Jet sat up and asked, "What happened to you guys?"

Seyanna shook her head. "When we broke apart from you, it was a fiasco. We were way too confident because of our new abilities. Those black animals are crazy. They somehow forced some of the other creatures in the forest into this trance. It causes their eye colors to change."

"We saw that too," Mckenzey said between bites of granola.

Jayco spoke. "We ran and dodged, but they had these weapons that shoot a rope with an electrical force trapping you."

Jet fished out the rope from the backpack. "We also had that experience."

Jayco continued, "After we fought the black wolf and Shane's friends, we got trapped along this ravine. It was bigger and deeper than the gully. We had nowhere to go. The idiots came at us fast. Grantham used his ability and his sheath and created a bridge of sorts. He had to hold onto it as the rest of us crossed, and then he ran over. He was about to catch up when one of their goons jumped across the entire ravine. Using a black club, he smacked Grantham in the head. Before he could kill Grantham, I caught the second swing and threw the kid into the ravine. He landed hard."

"So, they have abilities too," Mckenzey said.

Latisha took up the story. "Looks like it. It got much worse; Shane almost caught us with a spell. It wrapped around all of us, binding us. Jayco managed to flip on his leather biker hood, and a gust of fire shot into the air. It burned a second figure, a girl. She got hit pretty good. The fire unlatched the spell somehow, and we took off."

Seyanna added, "The creep from the ravine caught up with us. He doesn't run but leaps like a frog. I shot an arrow into his knee, and he wasn't jumping after that."

Latisha finished by saying, "Jayco carried Grantham back to the SUV."

"How about you?" Jayco asked as they turned another corner and started to pick up speed.

Mckenzey said solemnly, "We were beyond fortunate." She began explaining their movements. However, she became quiet when talking about when they both had been trapped.

Jet said, in a hollow voice, "I think I killed Jake Hurley from school. He was about to do the same to Mckenzey. My orbs ripped right through him."

"Oh my," Latisha said. "Are you sure?"

"He wasn't moving," Jet said. "There was a lot of blood." A pause followed, and Jet continued, "After that, we ran back to the SUV. Mckenzey sprinted ahead of me. That's when Shane stepped onto the path."

"What?" Mckenzey exclaimed. "You saw Shane?"

"More than that. He had this staff that created a barrier that stopped time. We fought each other using our magic. He's so strong."

"Did he know it was you?"

"Not exactly. He named a few people as if trying to guess who I was. But I tried to trick him into thinking it could be someone from another school. That set him off." Jet explained the fight, the escape, and the extreme luck in getting back to the SUV.

Jayco asked, "Did we get the tablet piece?"

Jet pulled it out from his backpack and handed it to Mckenzey. "We certainly did."

His best friends, his battle companions, each hollered and cheered so loud that Grantham stirred.

The tablet piece was almost like a clear diamond fragment. It was a few inches thick, with four flat sides, including the top and bottom, and two jagged sides. It reminded him of a giant puzzle piece. Mckenzey touched it, and it soon went into the hands of all his friends except Grantham.

They drove north of town for many minutes until they reached another road heading to the freeway. Ten minutes later, Jayco asked, "Back to Nana's?"

Jet nodded. "I should call her and tell her we're on our way. I know it's early, but I doubt she slept all that much." He fished his cell phone from the bottom of his backpack and dialed his home number, but the line was dead. He tried her cell phone.

The phone picked up before the first ring ended. "Joshua, is that you?" There was fear in her voice.

"Yes. It's me. I was—"

"Where are you?" she interrupted.

"A few hours away," he said quickly. "Just left Silverton."

"Go to Los Angeles, Colorado, or back to school," she demanded.

"Why?"

"I've had some visitors." Before Jet could ask, she added, "I'm fine. They knocked on the door around midnight, asking if you'd been around. I said that I hadn't seen you but that you'd gone to Colorado for Thanksgiving."

Jet said quickly, "If someone came to your door, we need to get you out of there. You can't be alone."

"I'm not. Geb stopped by. He's helping me."

"How do you know you can trust him?"

"Trust me," Nana said. "We're fine and heading north. I won't tell you where exactly. I'll contact you when I can."

"This sounds like a bad idea."

"We are fine." After a brief pause, she asked, "Did you succeed?"

"I think so."

"Then go back to school. Don't worry about me. I think Geb has some things for me to do."

"What do you mean?"

"I'll explain when I can. But I'm safe for now. Drive safely. Talk to you soon."

The line went dead.

Mckenzey asked, "Is Nana okay?"

"She's had some visitors. She sounds fine. But we can't go back there."

"Back to school?" Jayco asked as the SUV veered toward the median and slowed down.

Jet said, "Colorado is way too far. We could go to Grantham's for a few days or back to school."

Seyanna pointed out, "They're both in the same direction. We can decide in the next few hours. We'll need to stop, use the bathroom and get some breakfast."

Jayco flipped around and drove for the next four hours. They stopped in northern California to get food and gas. Jet and the others crashed hard and got some sleep. Grantham finally awoke, feeling refreshed, and as they ate, they filled him in on their escape.

Once back in the SUV, Grantham swooned over the tablet piece. He found some lettering on the tablet that no one else had seen. It was in a language no one knew. When he handed it back to Jet, he asked, "How did I manage to get knocked out and miss the best part?"

Latisha hugged him tightly. "You saved us; we would've been caught without you."

"I know, right. But still ..." He smiled brightly. "Just wanted some more action."

Jet patted him on the back. "Without a doubt, there will be more of that."

Seyanna drove for the next few hours. Along the way, they decided to head to Grantham's for the weekend. It was now the day after Thanksgiving, and they still had a few days. They would get there tomorrow and rest for most of Sunday before heading back to school.

"What are you thinking about?" Mckenzey asked, interrupting his thoughts.

"How lucky we were to have gotten out."

"Yes. But still. I am impressed with what we can do."

"Me too. Just glad we got to the tablet piece first."

She placed her hand in his and snuggled closer. She whispered, "I would've died without you." Her cheeks reddened, but she didn't glance away.

"That was a tough spot," he agreed.

"That sound when your weapon tore through him."

His hand reached up and touched her face. "We didn't have a choice."

"I know that. I'm glad it happened, but it still makes me feel sick."

"What do you mean?"

"It was satisfying to know that he died. He was going to kill me. I would've never thought I could be like that."

"It's not necessarily bad." He searched her eyes.

"I know," she said softly. "I know." After a few minutes, she asked, "What do we do now?"

"Great question. Shane will guess that we were involved, but he won't know for certain."

"But what about it being another school?"

"Doubtful. After he gets all the information, he'll realize it was us. He'll never let this go. We'll need to find a better hiding place for the objects, weapons, and items. He mentioned that there was some magic disguising us. We need to be prepared."

Her next question was equally sobering. "What about you and me?"

"I guess that depends on if you're leaving school in a month. Dillon Lake is not where you should go for what it is worth. The way Shane was talking about it."

"Our group has been through so much. And you really seem to understand me. I know you overheard something about Eric. But you and I already talked about him. I've been accepted to Dillon Lake, but I told the school that I wouldn't accept, even before we went to Switzerland. Eric and I aren't together. I want to see what happens between you and me. How does that sound?"

"I like that. A lot."

"Good." She leaned in and kissed him. Her warm lips felt energizing. Thirty minutes later, she fell asleep.

As he had grown accustomed to, he felt a sudden urge to pull out *The Sorcerer's Guide.* He silently retrieved the tome. So much had spilled out from its pages and turned his life completely upside down. He didn't regret a single thing. Well, maybe a few things.

He forced himself to read from the beginning, pushing down the nagging feeling. This tome had taught him who he was, and maybe it had shown him a fraction of what was ahead. Somehow, everything they'd done tonight had been because of his dad, his great uncle, Lady Gaea, and the Kings. But more importantly, this meant Arisol would someday break out of his prison. If Lucretius and Faunal were this powerful, he couldn't imagine what Arisol would be like. When he finished reading the last page, he freely turned to the next page.

A feeling of hatred overwhelmed him. This page was different from any page he'd seen thus far. It was black and half burnt. It wasn't exactly part of the tome but instead forcefully shoved in. Letters emerged in handwriting, clear and perfect, yet a feeling of foreboding stunned him. The writing was dark red and resembled blood.

Sorcerer, or I should say, Mikado. Your death has been foretold by generations. You've accomplished nothing. Your success only delays my return. Misfortune will be your shadow. Failure will be your companion. Death serenades with laughter as it glistens your approach. The War continues, and soon enough, I will be free at last.

The page ignited, burning an ember red until it was nothing more than ash.

Acknowledgments

I want to thank:

My wife Lauren and my children Kayla and Landon, for their continued support and willingness to give me feedback and be my first readers along the way.

My parents Larry and Susan, for teaching me hard work and dedication in everything that I do. They bought me books and books and ignited a love for first being a reader and then becoming an author.

My sister Jenni, for being my lifelong support. We read so many books when we were younger. We created fantastical worlds and believed we could do anything.

My friend Paul who first spoke with me about the concept of publishing my book on my own. He pushed me to research and learn about things that have become very important over time.

Any teacher, friend, or mentor who pushed me to do difficult things or gave a positive word to a struggling kid. Over the years, I have grown and changed, and none of that would've been possible without many of you.

My beta readers: Heather, Matt, Louisa, Robert, and anyone else who gave any input.

I want to thank God for the blessings he gives me each and every day and the desire and motivation to succeed after I have failed so many times before.

ABOUT THE AUTHOR

L. Scott Clark is intrigued by the magical world surrounding each of us. He writes young adult novels influenced by the incredible beauty of nature, the vastness of our world, and the psychological complexities between each of us.

Born and raised in Colorado, L. Scott has a deep love of nature, mountains, oceans, and the sense of adventure that awaits us each time we step outside.

He is the author of **The Sorcerer's Guide** YA Fantasy series and hopes to expand his writing capabilities. He has written one book in the series – *Path of the Phoenix*. He plans on having seven books in the series. He has written stories in YA, mystery, Short Stories, and more.

His path to becoming an author started in high school with his love for reading and writing. Initially, he pursued a degree in Physician Assistant Studies and has worked for many years in the medical field, correctional medicine.

L. Scott Clark began writing shortly after graduation and it has been his own adventure to become a published author.

You can visit him online at www.LScottClark.com or on Twitter (@LScottClark) or Instagram (@lscottclarkauthor)

If you enjoyed reading this book, please leave a review on Amazon or Goodreads (or both). This is an incredible way to support authors and we appreciate each and every review. I read the reviews with an open mind and equally important, they help new readers discover my books.

Additionally, you can sign up for my Newsletter at my Author Website https://lscottclark.com/. This will give you the chance to stay up to date on the latest book news, promos, and other awesome opportunities that might come down the line. It will also give me the opportunity to get to know you better. I try to update my readers at least once a month.

THE SORCERER'S GUIDE
TO THE

SOUL OF
ANESIDORA

CHAPTER 1

Walking down this street at this time of night revealed how desperate and stupid Jet really was. Searching for a missing student made the entire risk close to being worth it. However, if Jayco was right, this might turn out to be nothing more than a trap. An alley ahead on his left seemed like it could be the right spot. Glancing up and down the sidewalk, he found himself alone. Long shadows hung on to the ground as if afraid for the night to completely take over from the day.

His footsteps came to a halt on the brink of the narrow passage. The passageway was far darker and more unsettling than he wanted. He wished he had brought Iris with him, but she was off protecting Mckenzey. The golden panther was sensational at keeping out of sight.

A movement caught his attention from the doorway, across the alley, about ten feet away. This was the type of movement that made you question if it really happened. Jet pushed his vision to magnify, but only slightly, and his eyes found a figure sitting on the ground, with a hood over her head. She was likely homeless. The girl's face was partially hidden, but she was pale, with dark smudges of dirt around her eyes. She couldn't have been much older than he was. After everything he and his friends had been through, he wasn't convinced that she was just sleeping.

Instinct told him that this was a distraction, intentional or not. He had to find Kevin tonight, no matter who or what got in his way. The homeless girl's eyes flew open, and a small shriek escaped Jet's lips. Her eyes glowed a scarlet red, which somehow enhanced her beauty. A sound from down the alley pulled Jet's concentration from the girl. He prepared for an attack. Nothing came. He allowed a slight glance to the doorway, only to find the space empty. He was confident that there had not been any movement from the homeless girl. Scanning the street, he discovered that he was still alone. Taking a deep breath, he strolled into the darkened alley.

Jet choked back bile as he was assailed with the smell of rotten food, urine, and wet dog. The darkness swallowed him, and suddenly it felt like he stood on the streets of London. Nothing about this alley spoke of anything inviting, but it had to be searched. This was the fourth street along North Broadway in Chinatown he had investigated. The night air appeared to mock him in his futility. The first part of the alley was narrow, with brick buildings on both sides. After a dozen feet or so, he thought that it might open up to a small parking lot.

He listened intently as he cautiously moved forward. He had less than a quarter of an hour to rendezvous with Mckenzey, the only other member of the Echoes willing to drive to Los Angeles from Chadwicks on this pursuit. To his right, instead of the alley opening up like he thought, it was a parking lot with a few covered stalls. Cars were already parked in two of the three stalls; the third was full of furniture and other trash. Locals used this area to sleep at night. As he continued forward, the darkness seemingly was getting darker.

Like a metal hook cutting into a plastic bottle, a grating sound resonated from behind him, and Jet flew into a shadow, remaining hidden for a full two minutes. When he thought it was clear, he poked his head from the archway of a back door. A stray cat scurried from under the back fender of one of the cars and darted under a metal door.

Further down the alley, the foul smell of food decay was replaced by a more pungent odor. The width of the passage doubled, and as the back wall came into view, the smell intensified. He was cautious with each step, understanding that this was likely a trap. Pulling three golden orbs from his pocket, his anxiety dismissed significantly. These beauties were the size of small rocks, and lethal. Rotating them around his hand felt natural. They'd saved his life a few times before now. He kicked out at a half-broken cardboard box, expecting to see rotten food staring up at him from underneath. Instead, a smeared red substance covered the ground, heading in the direction of the farthest trash bin in the corner.

Peering over his shoulder, a cat watched him from under a dumpster, unconcerned. Pushing forward, he strolled to the edge of the bin next to the wall. This bin had been shoved into a tiny area adjacent to a second, larger black trash bin.

"Do I even want to take a look?" Jet asked himself, his voice strained.

Gripping one side, he tugged the smaller green bin, and it moved several inches. He shuddered as the grinding sound. Jet swore silently as he recognized a blue sheet hanging partially out. It was a match for one of the sheets used by Chadwicks boarding school.

As he stared at the blue sheet, he feared what he was about to find. After placing the orbs into his pocket, he shoved open the lid. The sheet was wrapped around an object, but he couldn't tell what it was. There was dried blood spattered everywhere. Reaching inside, he pulled hard at the sheet, but it was stuck. Stepping onto a wooden crate, he placed one hand on the fabric, intending to pull. He recoiled as he felt a leg below the sheet.

His next yank was like swiftly removing a Band-Aid from a cut. The sheet peeled back, and another wave of stench stunned him. He glimpsed hair, pale skin, and a sunken face. He vomited into an empty cardboard box against the back wall.

Is this really happening? Jet peered closer at the dead body and easily recognized the face staring up at him, unblinking, but it wasn't Kevin McCormick.

"You're the last person I expected to see here." A voice echoed from behind him.

Bounding off the cardboard box, Jet reacted as if he was going to be attacked. As a dark figure stepped into view, Jet asked, "What are you talking about?"

"We checked you out months ago, and nothing. Since Silverton, we've been watching you more closely. Zip. I told Shane that you were a waste of time. We tested you with red powder, and you didn't change colors like the others. I guess you proved me wrong."

"No clue what you're talking about." A slight smile spread across Jet's face. "My car broke down, and I'm lost."

"I watched you pull back that trash bin, find the body, and puke. I thought you were stronger than that. Wrong again."

"Good to see you Vinny Estes, but you've got me confused with someone else. I was walking by, looking for a gas station, when I smelled something foul down here."

Jet cringed at the stupidity of his own excuse. He continued, "I'm traumatized at what I found." For the first time, Jet noticed the sword blade in Vinny's right hand.

He willed for his vision to change and was relieved when his eyesight magnified. This had happened before. His peripheral ability to see expanded to include almost everything in front of him, on both sides and most of the area directly behind him. The sword was an exact match to one he'd seen inside a cave near Silverton a month ago.

Using the sword Vinny pointed at the trash bin. He asked angrily, "Do you know who that is?"

"Why would I?"

"Because I'm certain that you or one of your friends was there when he died."

Jet took a step to the side and challenged him. "Vinny. What on earth are you talking about?"

"Shane said that if we put out the word that Kevin had been spotted in Los Angeles that the right people would come running." Vinny sneered and spat on the ground. "And boy, was he right."

Jet stared closely at Vinny; something was off, and he was about to lose it. His eyes had a yellowish glow, and dried froth was caked to the corners of his mouth. "What's going on here, Vinny? You're talking crazy." Jet took another step away from the trash bin.

Vinny stopped him with a shout. "I don't know if you're the Mikado or an Occultist, but my Runic magic and my protection are stronger than anything that you can throw at me. Shane also announced that he fought one of you and you cheated to escape. Not sure if that was you. The weapon of choice for that coward was three small orbs. Is that you, Black?"

"Have you lost your freaking mind? What's this about fighting Shane? Now you have a sword and are screaming at me."

"Thy mouth doth protest, and I conclude that you are guilty. Tell me where the fragment is, and we won't kill the others. You guys killed my roommate and best friend."

"Who's the dead guy, Vinny?"

"Didn't you recognize him?" His voice rose to a tortured scream.

Jet said nothing but shook his head.

"That's Jake Hurley." Vinny shook, tears running down his face. "You do remember him, don't you?"

Jet knew that Jake and Vinny were more than just friends. They were goons of Shane Fallon, who had been searching for an ancient artifact. It had been a race to find the first missing piece, and Jet and his friends had reached it first. Jake, Vinny, Shane, and several others had chased them, trying to recapture the artifact. Jake and Vinny had caught up, and Jake had pinned Mckenzey to the ground, a few seconds away from killing her. Jet had been fortunate and unlucky enough to stop him. He had killed Jake, dreaming about it every night for the last three and a half weeks.

Jet reacted, his voice far calmer than he felt. "I remember Jake. I mean, we weren't friends, but who could forget all the bullying and name-calling you guys did. Sorry to hear that he died."

Vinny seethed, shaking his sword at Jet. Spittle flew everywhere. "I'll kill you, Black. I don't really care about this war, releasing Arisol, or finding all the hidden pieces. You took my best friend, and I'm going to end you."

Jet's shoulders sagged. "Okay. Fine. I'll tell you the truth. I heard about what happened, but I wasn't there. You guys have this all wrong. The Mikado doesn't even go to Chadwicks, I think he or she attends San Mateo. I was brought in to help look for Kevin. I've no idea how Vinny died."

"What? San Mateo? That doesn't make any sense. Shane is convinced that it's someone from Silverton who is going to school at Chadwicks, right now."

"Sorry to disappoint. I have known Kevin since elementary. That's the only reason why I'm here."

Vinny didn't appear to be buying what Jet was selling, and he didn't know how he was going to escape. Jayco had warned him not to go looking for Kevin, but Jet couldn't allow someone else to suffer.

"That means that you know what the Mikado is. You are involved." Vinny swung the black blade expertly. "There are ways I can get the truth from you."

This time Jet was curious. "What are you talking about?"

"We can control your thoughts and emotions. We can't force you to do anything against your will, but we can cause a nuisance. I'm proficient enough to get you to tell me the truth."

"Why do you have a sword?"

"Stop playing stupid." Vinny rolled his neck as if fixing to attack. "We also found some weapons that night in the cave. You think you were the only one. I can smell the fear from here."

Jet scoffed. "The smell isn't coming from me; it's coming from that stray cat. But what you smell is pheromones. She's in heat, and she has her eyes set on you."

"You're a dead man walking."

"We'll see." Jet reached up and pulled the hood of his cloak onto his head and disappeared. A gust of air swirled around the alley.

Vinny had been prepared for this action, and using the pointer fingers on both hands, he touched an invisible spot near each temple. Jet watched as a purple film slid over Vinny's entire eyes. Once it was in place, it was unnoticeable. "That's interesting. You disappeared, but I can see your vague shape. I can't tell who you are. Shane will be very interested in this little fact."

With both hands, Jet arched his wrist, and a small jet of air propelled him into the air, a few feet off the ground.

"So your cloak helps you control your primary element, which is air. You can't be the Mikado, but you'll have enough answers to make this ruse worth it." Vinny held the dagger in his right hand. From behind his back, he pulled out a device that Jet knew all too well. It was a Y-shaped item, similar to a slingshot. It shot a powerful blue rope that could bind him.

Jet pulled out his own sword, but it wasn't magical or impressive, and he held it for only one purpose. When Jet and his friends had escaped Silverton, they had managed to capture a rope from this Y-shaped device. Only two things worked, cutting the rope with a magical item or an immense amount of heat. Silently Jet whispered a spell that poured energy into the sword. He hoped that Vinny wouldn't notice.

"That sword isn't going to protect you."

"As I told you, I'm not in the inner circle. This is all that I have."

"How did you get involved?"

"After Shane attacked several students on campus at the memorial, San Mateo sent recruiters to Chadwicks. They started with Jayco and Grantham, who ended up not having a lick of magical talent. I had very little, with air. I was supposed to keep tabs on Shane, but none of the heavy lifting."

"Why would you freely give me this information?"

"I've heard about that sword and those things you have. You must be someone important. I can't beat you. But I can give you enough information for you to leave me alone. It's the Mikado and his followers that you need to worry about."

"Who is it?"

"Don't be an idiot. You think they would give me that information. I'm nothing more than an errand boy."

"You've kept up that air spell for a long time."

"I can do one thing; that's it. That's how it works for our Elemental magic."

"Let's let Shane decide what to do." Vinny aimed the Y-shaped device, and Jet recoiled.

As the rope was launched, time slowed, and instead of allowing the rope to snare him, Jet flew at the rope, lifting his sword, and cutting cleanly through the cable. It sailed past him harmlessly.

Vinny raised his black sword and prepared for an attack.

Jet yelled, "Aquaenaeth," and a green aura appeared, and he knew that he'd chosen the correct spell. A water deluge sprang upward and smashed into Vinny's body. However, a protective shield, like an unseen helmet, prevented the water from hitting his face. He was still knocked off balance.

Somehow Vinny swung his black sword, and it connected with Jet's simple sword. Despite the heat the sword shattered into a dozen pieces. Jet released the handle as it disintegrated. He plucked a golden staff from his back and swung it forcefully at Vinny's head. Jet knew that Vinny couldn't react in time. Then the unexpected happened, and Jet learned of Vinny's talent. The boy side-shifted three feet to his left and reappeared. Jet's staff only connected with foul-smelling air. A cruel smile crept across Vinny's lips.

Jet yelled, "Aer," and a green tornado of air with a green aura sped toward Vinny's face and connected hard. Vinny's head snapped back, and he hit the wall. The purple contacts vanished, and Vinny slumped to the ground, dazed. He was no longer visible and could escape easily.

There had been a slow and steady decrease in his energy, and Jet knew that he couldn't remain hovering forever. He planned to go two blocks and drop onto the ground and meet up with Mckenzey.

As he soared out of the alley, the movement behind him was so fast that even Jet's enhanced vision barely caught it. Turning, he watched as something sprinted into the alley and went directly at Vinny. Jet could have never reacted in time. What he beheld was unimaginable. The creature was over eight feet tall, with long legs and dangling arms. It was covered from head to toe in black fur and ran on four legs, but as it approached Vinny, it stood on its hind two legs. There were three antlers in total. The first two were large and typical, but the third was smaller and on the top of its head. The creature had fanged teeth and a deer's head and body. The animal's arms reached for Vinny, who was still dazed as its jaws opened. The boy was pulled close, and the creature clamped down on the back of the boy's neck. Vinny was suddenly lifted into the air as if he weighed nothing, and an unnatural sound reverberated through the air as the creature's head shook back and forth. Vinny's neck was broken, and his body was severely beaten. An orange glow transferred from Vinny's neck to the creature's mouth, and the animal gained bulk before his eyes.

Jet reversed direction and advanced closer to the creature, removing the orbs from his pocket, intending to attack. He hovered twenty feet in the air, remaining silent and invisible.

The antlered deer tossed Vinny's body aside like it was a dead dog, and his milky white eyes stared up directly at the spot where Jet was hidden. Almost as fast as it could run, the creature removed a bow from its back and unleashed an arrow at Jet. There was barely enough time to react. He twisted, and the arrow slammed into his back. The golden shield linked to his back took the brunt of the blow. Just like his simple sword, the shield shattered, and Jet was propelled through the air at an alarming speed. Most of his energy vanished, and he had no control of where he was going.

When Jet finally hit the ground, he was a mile from the alley. He landed hard on his left side. Pain shot through his entire body, including his back; his face was gashed, and he had failed at almost everything tonight. None of that mattered right now. He needed to find Mckenzey so they could escape. Pulling himself off the ground, he ran as fast as he could in the direction of Union Station.

With every turn he was convinced that the antlered deer was closing the distance. He hated the idea of being chased by animals. He was about to set up a red flare when intuition told him to avoid any magic. He was already low on energy, and if he overexerted himself, the consequences could be severe. Without slowing, Jet crossed a busy intersection. Cars swerved and honked, but he kept running. A grouping trees came into view off to his left, and he changed course. As he ran he fished out his cell phone to call Mckenzey, only to find that it had shattered. He entered the far side of a parking lot and found Jayco's jeep at the far end. It appeared empty.

He ducked behind the far side of the jeep and searched the area. Every movement caught his attention, but there were no signs of an attacking deer, Iris, or Mckenzey. Unlocking the jeep, he reached inside and pulled his backpack closer. They'd prepared some homemade energy drinks. Magic drained Jet's energy, but he had realized early on mud and water could give back some of it. After returning from Silverton, Grantham began experimenting with the best possible mixtures. Turned out that lemongrass herbal tea and gray clay offered the best bang. Jet guzzled two full bottles and felt a measured return of his stamina.

From back across the parking lot, Mckenzey appeared, and she was sprinting fast. Off to the side, closer to the buildings, Iris, the golden panther, was mimicking her. Jet jumped to the front seat and started the engine. Thirty seconds later Mckenzey fumbled at the door, finally opened it, and let Iris leap inside first. She followed closely behind. Jet hit the accelerator, and they shot off.

"Well, that sucked worse than cafeteria food." Mckenzey rested back in the seat, sweat dripping off her forehead.

"Ain't that the truth," said Jet.

"Remember a few months ago when Shane cornered us, and you tried to punch him.

"How could I forget?"

"There was this stocky guy with Shane; I think his name is Clyde. And the girl I knocked over, Jessiva."

"Great memories."

"They're here."

"Did they see you?"

"Maybe. Hard to say. They might've been following me. If so, I'm not even sure that they recognized me. They got a phone call and headed in another direction. That was when I sprinted back to the jeep."

"Kevin was never here." Jet's voice was distraught. "This entire thing was a trap. I found Jake's body in a bin of trash. Vinny Estes, Jake's friend, cornered me in the alley.

He recognized me, but I found a way to escape. Something came into the alley and killed Vinny."

"What are you talking about?"

"Sorry. I'm all over the place. There was this antlered deer, moving faster than anything I'd ever seen. It shot into the alley and attacked Vinny. I was up in the air, and the thing tried to shoot me with an arrow. I'm not sure what to even think. How many creatures do we have to fight?"

"It attacked both of you?"

"Him first, then me."

They lapsed into silence as they both caught their breath. Twenty minutes later, on the freeway heading north, Mckenzey asked, "Are we heading back to campus?"

"I think that's the best idea. We need to tell the others what happened."

"Are you sure this is the best plan?"

Jet watched Mckenzey closely. He thought she was struggling with something, even before tonight. He didn't want to pry, but she hadn't been herself the last few weeks. She had been distant and secluded. They hadn't kissed or snuggled once since Silverton. It felt like she didn't want to be alone with him. He was surprised when she volunteered to come along with him. He said, softening his voice, "We only have four days before Christmas vacation."

Mckenzey glanced over and asked, "Are you still considering traveling to Argentina the day after Christmas?"

"I don't know that we have a choice."

"We're not ready," Mckenzey said, slightly frustrated. "Besides you, none of us can do any magic to speak of. We need more time."

"Maybe you need to be pushed into it." Jet wiped his forehead.

Mckenzey answered quickly, "Jayco's right. This has turned into a vendetta with you."

"No way," Jet said. "That's not the case. I'm just trying to do what's right. If we wait too long, Shane will get the next piece of the Phoenix first. Is that what you want?"

Mckenzey practically screamed, "Of course I don't. But we've been watching him, and he hasn't made a single move."

"Not until tonight."

"Fine." Mckenzey relented. "You refuse to listen to anyone else's ideas. I guess we have to do it *your* way."